STATE of NATURE

Book Three of The Park Service Trilogy

By Ryan Winfield

State of Nature
Book Three of The Park Service Trilogy
By Ryan Winfield

ISBN-13: 978-0-9883482-5-7
ISBN-10: 0-9883482-5-X

Cover art by Adam Mager
Cover art and design Copyright © 2013 Ryan Winfield
Cover image: kaipic.com / Flickr Open / Getty Images
The Licensed Material is being used for illustrative purposes only; and any
person depicted in the Licensed Material, if any, is a model.
Author photo: Sarah T. Skinner

Summary: After leaving the Isle of Man, Aubrey and Jimmy return to
the Foundation to confront Hannah about her betrayal and to free the
people of Holocene II only to find themselves facing new and more difficult
challenges in a world where nothing is as it seems.

Printed in the United States of America.

BIRCH PAPER PRESS
Post Office Box 4252
Seattle, Washington 98194

Also by **Ryan Winfield**

The Park Service
Book One of The Park Service Trilogy

Isle of Man
Book Two of The Park Service Trilogy

South of Bixby Bridge

Jane's Melody: A Novel

For Great Big Little Panther
Because even the best of boys must someday grow up

STATE OF NATURE

Book Three of The Park Service Trilogy

Part One

CHAPTER 1
The Return

My father said there's no revenge as sweet as forgiveness.

Even so, part of me would like to watch Hannah die for what she did. But in the end, my father's wisdom wins.

Jimmy's not feeling as forgiving, however, and if we didn't need the professor to pilot the submarine, I'm afraid he might have tossed him overboard days ago.

Our time on the Isle of Man seems like a dream already; or perhaps a waking nightmare. We talk little and eat even less. The professor's mouth is a swollen mess, most of his teeth having been knocked loose by Jimmy's heel, and despite Jimmy's suggestion to let him starve, I heat him algae broth on the stove and watch him wince with pain as he sips it. He's fallen into one of his moods now, wavering between mumbling obscure obscenities and staring cross-eyed at the controls. But he seems to be guiding us in the right direction as we retrace our journey, re-crossing the Panama Canal, then turning north to follow the coastline toward the Foundation.

I'd say toward home, but it feels like anything but.

I keep having conversations with Hannah in my head, rehearsing the things I want to say to her and trying to guess her responses. It's crazy-making, really, but the silence of the submarine is deafening, and I can't help myself. I know she'll rationalize having faked giving Jimmy the longevity serum by saying that she wanted to reproduce it in her lab and then give it to him. But I can't imagine how she'll explain sending us out blind and then slaughtering all those people with the antimatter bomb. I suppose it doesn't matter what she says anyway, because when we return, she's done—Jimmy and I are in charge now. She's going to extract that encryption key from the DNA in Finn's severed hand, and we're going to take control of the drones and free my people from Holocene II.

No compromises, no discussion.

End of story.

And Jimmy's getting that serum, too.

A hand on my shoulder snaps me away from my thoughts. It's Jimmy come to relieve me from guarding the professor.

"Did you get any rest?" I ask.

"A little," he says, taking the knife from my hand.

"One more sleep and we should be back."

"Good," he says, sitting down. "It'll be nice when we ain't gotta stare at the back of this creep's ugly head all the time."

The professor sighs but doesn't respond.

I head for the bunkroom and strip out of my clothes and take a hot shower. The Park Service crest that Finn carved into my chest is healing, but I know there will be scars beneath the scabs. I think about how close I came to dying, and how much I regretted having never told Jimmy what he really means to me. But now that the crisis is over, the timing doesn't seem right. Plus, Jimmy's understandably depressed about losing Junior and Bree. Junior meant a lot to both of us, but Jimmy had a special bond with him. And with Bree too.

After my shower, I wash Finn's pants and shirt that I've been wearing since we left. Then I wrap a towel around my waist and carry the wet clothes with me out onto the submarine deck to dry them. I wrap them around the open hatch handle and let them flap in the breeze while I sit with my back against the sail and watch the scenery slide by. It's full on winter now, and the air has a bite to it, but the cold feels good against my naked skin. Something about the cold air makes everything seem clear and close, and I can see the rocky cliffs and white bursts of spray from waves crashing against the distant shore. Behind that, hills of green and gold, and even farther, snow-covered mountains. It's wild and wonderful and somehow more majestic without any people to spoil the view. I wonder what it will look like in another thousand years, after we free the people of Holocene II. I hope we've learned our lesson.

The cold finally raises bird bumps on my skin and starts me shivering, so I stand and grab my clothes to head in. I freeze when I see the ship—tall and gray, a warship just like the one that slaughtered Jimmy's family in the cove—so close behind us that it's throwing a shadow onto the submarine deck. I dive inside and seal the hatch, rushing into the control room with my towel still tied around my waist.

"Take us down!"

"Why should I?" the professor mumbles.

"Jimmy, grab him, will you?"

Jimmy gladly grabs the professor, jerks him from the pilot chair, and forces him against the wall, holding his knife blade just inches from the professor's throat. I take the controls and flood the ballasts, dropping us beneath the waves. Then I steer us hard to port, planning to come around in a long arc behind the warship.

"How do I launch a torpedo?"

"We're not launching anything," the professor replies.

"Jimmy, if he doesn't answer my questions, cut him."

"I'll be more'n happy to," Jimmy says.

"Now, where are the torpedo switches?"

"The red button there on your left," the professor says.

I hit the button and an LCD screen slides up with an aerial rendering of the submarine and its surroundings. The ship is outlined on our rear starboard side, its shape unmistakable.

"What's that?" Jimmy asks.

"A drone warship."

"Like the one that killed my family?"

"Just like that one."

"What are you planning to do?" the professor asks.

"Sink it."

"But why? It's no threat to us as long as you're not up top. It's programmed to hunt humans, you fool, not submarines."

"Well, it's about to see what's it's like to be hunted itself," I say. "How do I launch a torpedo?"

The professor doesn't answer.

"Jimmy . . ."

Jimmy pushes his knife against the professor's throat, the blade sinking into his saggy, whiskered flesh.

"Fine, fine. Just touch on the target." Then he adds under his breath to Jimmy, "Ficklefrick! Easy with the knife."

I tap my finger on the outline of the ship, pulling up a full screen rendering.

"Tap it again," he says.

Red crosshairs show up on the midpoint of its lower hull.

"What now?"

"Hit the blue button to flood the tube. When it's flooded the red button will illuminate and you can press it to fire."

"But I want to see it on the screen."

"You want to see it sink?" he asks.

"Yes."

"You're so sentimental. Press the periscope switch."

The periscope rises, and the camera zeros in on the ship, showing the live video image on the main screen. I notice Jimmy shudder slightly at the sight.

"You come and do it, Jimmy."

When Jimmy releases the professor, the old man sinks to the floor and sits staring at us with a defeated look on his bruised face. Jimmy steps over and peers at the ship on the screen, its side coming more into view every second as we turn. He rests his palm on the fire switch. His eyes narrow, and I'm reminded of his laser-like focus when I watched him poised with a harpoon and ready to leap onto the back of that whale. That was the day that this ship, or at least some other ship just like it, showed up and gunned his family down.

Jimmy slaps the switch.

For several seconds nothing happens.

We watch and wait.

Then there's a burst of white water, and the ship buckles in the center and jumps beneath a fiery explosion. Just as it's dropping again, a secondary explosion tears it fully in two and the ship slams down, the twisted and torn halves turning in on themselves and sinking in a boil of white water. Jimmy stands entranced, a look of satisfaction on his face, as the last of the ship's upturned bow descends beneath the waves and the water closes over it and settles, as if the ship had never even been there at all. I grab him and hug him, watching over his shoulder as the professor scowls at us from the floor. Despite what my dad said, revenge feels good. Even if it is just against a brainless drone carrying out the commands of evil humans.

The next morning we arrive at the tunnel that leads to the locks and the Foundation. We make the professor drop anchor and then, using wire from the engine room, we bind his hands and feet and leave him lying stretched out on a bunk while we climb out onto the submarine deck to make a plan in private. We're anchored several hundred meters from the entrance, the tunnel beyond cast in pitch black shadow, and I don't think either of us is ready to leave behind the open air view for the claustrophobic darkness that waits beyond.

"You promise you won't hurt Hannah?" I ask.

"I'm leavin' her to you," Jimmy says. "All I wanna do is get this over with so's we can stop the rest of them damn drones and get back above ground."

"What about the professor?"

"I dun' care nothin' 'bout him either."

"Well, let's leave him tied up anyway, just in case. Besides, I'm sure he could use some rest."

We turn and look back at the shimmering ocean meeting blue, cloudless skies. It's a hard view to part with. I look at Jimmy standing next to me, tall and proud, his hair tousled in the breeze, his jaw set and his eyes focused on some distant hope only he can see. Perhaps a wish to someday be reunited with his family. Perhaps just a wish to someday live free. I hope he gets it—whatever it is he desires—and I hope maybe, just maybe, his wish somehow includes me.

Jimmy stays on deck to drink in the last of the view while I return to the control room to start our ascent. From the pilot chair, I can see the pool of sunlight from the open hatch slowly disappear from the passageway floor as we pass beneath the overhang and enter the tunnel. I set our speed for ten knots and recline in the seat, preparing for the sixteen hour trip.

I guess I should spend the time planning how I want to confront Hannah with her betrayal. And revenge or not, maybe what her punishment should be.

CHAPTER 2
Hannah, How Could You?

I can hardly keep my eyes open, but I don't dare sleep.

Eventually, Jimmy relieves me from the controls.

I skip the bunkroom where the professor lies bound, going out instead to sit on the deck. The submarine's shadow is cast by green light onto the tunnel walls, where it passes like some half-submerged monster from the depths returning to its cave. The journey up the escalator locks is seamless, with one stretch of water rising to meet the next, and I rest my head on the cool metal deck and watch the green light dapple the distant cavern ceiling. It reminds me of my days spent down in Holocene II, looking up at our own sparkling ceiling and imagining a world of adventure waiting above. I sure found it. I just never could have imagined it being so beautiful and cruel at the same time.

I close my eyes and try to think of something good. Junior comes to mind. I see him as a pup, trotting along behind us as we walked that river toward the lake house. I see him growing bigger and following Jimmy everywhere he went, always on his heel. I see him saving us from the pig people. I see him running with deer hounds while Jimmy and I follow on horseback. He'll forever be in those high, heather-covered hills for me.

Some netherworld nightmare wakes me.

By the pain in my back and the cold metal deck, I assume I must have been sleeping awhile. I sit up and notice that we're in the last stretch of locks, cruising toward the Foundation cavern bay, and that the familiar red glow is once again illuminating the opening, as if the Foundation were on fire. I get up and walk to the forward deck and watch. The entrance grows and the red light slowly envelops the tunnel and then the submarine. We cruise into the cavern, awash in the red glow of Eden's dome.

Eden? I don't understand—Eden was destroyed.

"What's that thing doing all lit up again?"

I jump at Jimmy's voice. Then I feel panicked, wondering who's navigating the submarine.

"You didn't free the professor, did you?"

"No," Jimmy says, "but I gave him some tea."

"Well, who's piloting the submarine?"

"It's steerin' itself," he says. "Some kinda computer voice came on and said autopilot was takin' over."

A clamor echoes across the cavern to us—the clang of metal being hammered, the whine of a drill. I smell iron oxides and some kind of gas. Shadows move on Eden's roof. We watch from the deck as the submarine approaches the docks.

"What's goin' on?" Jimmy asks.

"I have no idea."

"Well, that ain't Hannah and Red raisin' all that ruckus."

"No," I say, shaking my head, "it sure isn't."

The submarine guides itself deftly into the open slip from which we departed and eases to a stop by reversing the screw. We open the deck hatches that hide the ropes, reel them out, jump onto the dock, and tie them to cleats. And that's it— we're back, once again standing on the same dock where we said goodbye to Hannah and Red all those weeks ago.

"Not quite the homecoming I was expecting," I say.

"Whaddya want?" Jimmy asks. "A hug? She killed Junior."

"I know, I know. I just thought somebody would be here to greet us. Let's go see what all this noise is about."

We walk up the dock, past the sintering plant we broke into to get the chemicals to burn Eden. It seems so long ago already, and I know a lot has changed since then, but I'm not at all prepared for what I see when we round the living quarters and step out onto the walkway that leads to Eden.

Strange men scale Eden's roof, lurching along the dome's perimeter, or hunched over halfway up, working. They look like medieval roofers retiling some building down in hell, their odd features appearing in the pulse of red light and then retreating again into shadow. And that's not all. On the train platform is parked an enormous machine that looks as if it would hardly fit in the tunnel from which the tracks arrive: a long, cylindrical land-borne submarine with a missile-shaped nose made of some fantastic alloy that seems to glow.

"What's that?" Jimmy asks.

"I think it's a subterrene."

"A what?"

"A nuclear boring machine. I've only read about them, but it's what they use to make the train tunnels and how we mine for minerals in the deep south."

"And what are them there, then?"

He points to a group of strange albino men who emerge from the rear subterrene hatch and go grunting down the path, snorting and snickering and slapping one another on their hunched and hairless backs. They have an air about them of workers taking a break.

"Those must be tunnelrats," I say.

"Tunnelrats?"

12

"Yeah. I've never seen them in person either, but they work the mines."

"Well, what are they doin' here?"

"I have no idea. I wonder if Hannah and Red are alright. Let's go see if we can find them and get some answers."

"Where should we look?"

"Let's start with the control room."

We thread our way along the path, staying as close to the buildings and as far out of sight as possible. When we reach the control room, the Park Service mission statement engraved above its door reminds me of this place and its evil purpose.

MISSION STATEMENT
THE PARK SERVICE THUS ESTABLISHED SHALL PROTECT AND CONSERVE THE NATURAL BEAUTY OF THE EARTH BY EMPLOYING ALL AVAILABLE MEANS TO ERADICATE FROM THE PLANET THE VIRAL SPECIES KNOWN AS HUMANKIND.

I punch in the code, but I either misremember it or it's been changed. I'm about to turn to Jimmy and suggest that we return to the submarine and force the professor to retell us the code, when the door opens and a tunnelrat walks right into me. The force of the blow nearly knocks me over, but Jimmy grabs me and stands me back up. My eyes rake up the tunnelrat's nearly naked body, landing on its albino chest. Its skin is near translucent, and I can see the spidery web of blue veins pulsing with every heartbeat across its flesh. Then I lift my gaze to its face. Reptilian eyes, red and milky, flickering as a membrane closes and opens like a horizontal shutter.

I take this all in in the blink of an eye, and before either of us knows what to make of the other, I hear a female voice moan from inside the room. Without thinking, I shove the tunnelrat hard to the side and force my way past. It takes a moment for my eyes to adjust to the bright LED lights, and then I see Hannah's red hair draped over the back of a control chair and the outline of another tunnelrat kneeling at her feet. I rush toward her, ready to pull her attacker away, but then I stop myself when she comes fully into view. She's leaned back in the chair with her eyes closed, enjoying its massage feature while the tunnelrat kneeling at her feet files her toenails.

"Get your hands off me!" Jimmy shouts, appearing beside me, wresting to free himself from the grip of the tunnelrat.

Hannah's eyes snap open at the sound of his voice, and she slowly turns her head. The tunnelrat kneeling at her feet stops filing and watches us too.

"Look who's here," Hannah says.

"Are you surprised?" I ask.

"Of course not," she says, waving the tunnelrat away from her feet and sitting up. She looks behind me, probably to see if anyone else is with us.

"Are you looking for the professor?" I ask.

"Isn't he with you?"

"He's catching up on his rest in the submarine."

"And is anyone else with you?"

"Who else would be with us?" I ask.

"I don't know," she says.

The tunnelrat beside me screeches, and I turn just in time to see Jimmy break free of its grip with his knife clenched in his free hand. The tunnelrat looks at the blood running from the cut in its forearm, and the veins in its neck begin to expand. Its red eyes flare and its huge hands ball into fists.

"Stand down," Hannah says, before it can hit Jimmy.

The tunnelrat reluctantly relaxes its hands.

"Looks like you've made yourself right at home while we were away," I say.

"Made yerself some new friends too," Jimmy adds.

Hannah rises from her chair and looks us over.

She appears older to me somehow, more devious, even though she's shorter than I remember her being.

"Are you sure no one else is with you?" she asks.

"I'm sure," I reply. "What's going on around here?"

"Nothing much," she says. "I've just been sitting here, worried sick and watching the screens, hoping to catch some glimpse of you all out there. Just to know that you were okay."

She waves absently to the wall of screens where various scenes from around the world are being broadcast from drones. It makes me sick to think that she's been sitting here getting massaged and groomed while watching drones look for humans to slaughter. It makes me even sicker to think that she wants the encryption code so that she can keep them on the job.

"I've been so worried I've hardly slept a wink," she says. "Didn't you miss me?"

All the things I had planned to say to her flee from my mind—which is probably best since I hadn't counted on confronting her with two tunnelrats standing by her side. Think, think, think—I'm lost for anything to say.

"Where's Red?" I finally ask.

"Oh, he's around somewhere," she says. Then she turns to Jimmy and changes the subject. "How are you, Jimmy?"

Jimmy can't hide his contempt for her. It's written all over his face. He's still holding his knife, and I notice that when she addresses him, his hand grips it tighter until his knuckles turn white. For a moment, I'm worried that he might just stab her.

"I'm 'bout as happy to see you as you is to see me."

Hannah grins at him, appearing to admire for once his witty choice of words.

"Fair enough then," she says, clapping her hands together. "Shall we get down to it and see about this encryption code? I'm assuming you have it, of course."

An uncomfortable silence falls between us. I look at the tunnelrats and notice that they're not looking at Jimmy and me. They're looking at Hannah, waiting on instructions. The hair on my neck stands up, and my heart rate quickens. A silent threat hangs heavy in the bright room.

"We couldn't find it," I say.

"I don't believe you," she replies.

"And I don't believe you either."

She places her hands on her chest and feigns being hurt.

"You don't believe me?" she asks. "Now, what would I lie to you about?"

"I don't believe that you've been sitting here doing nothing and waiting on us, for one thing. Why are the lights back on in Eden? And why are all these tunnelrats here?"

"Geez, you just arrived and you can't even hardly say hello before you start hammering me with questions."

"Apparently, I didn't ask enough questions before we left."

"And what's that mean?"

"It means you're a traitor and a liar."

It feels good to say it, but Hannah sucks any pleasure from my accusation by smiling at me as if she were proud of it.

"So, I guess you know then," she says.

"Hannah, how could you? You killed them."

"I think I'd like to talk with the professor now."

"I'm not done—"

I grab her shoulder to stop her from passing me, but she casts a glance at one of the tunnelrats, and it yanks me away with such force that I'm thrown halfway across the room. Jimmy looks at me, a question on his face: *Should I fight?* I shake my head. We're no match for these two. Jimmy stands down, and the other tunnelrat pries the knife from his hand. The opportunity is gone. It grunts something to its fellow, and they push us after Hannah and then follow us out the door. She leads us down to the docks. I feel stupid for having walked in like this without a plan. But how was I supposed to know?

When we reach the submarine, she turns to us and says, "You four keep each other company out here while I go and wake the professor." Then she stops halfway up the ladder and turns back, catching me eyeing the small boat on its lift. "You know what? Just the four of you might get a little lonely." She puts her fingers in her mouth and whistles. The sound carries over the din of the work being done around the Foundation, and soon everything falls quiet. A few moments later other tunnelrats begin to appear on the path, heading for the dock. Hannah smiles down on us and then continues her climb toward the hatch.

By the time Hannah reappears a few minutes later, carrying Finn's plaster-encased hand cradled in her palms, a mass of tunnelrats stands between us and the shore, cutting off any hope of escape. The professor follows her onto the submarine deck, rubbing his unbound hands. Jimmy casts me a look that says: *Don't you wish we'd thrown him overboard now?*

The professor descends the ladder to the dock and then reaches up and takes Finn's hand from Hannah so she can climb down. I assume she'll confront us about having tied the professor up, but instead she takes her brother's amputated hand back from the professor and marches off the dock with it.

I start after her, but strong hands grip my shoulder and pull me back. I smell the tunnelrat's musty mouth breathing on my neck as I watch Hannah disappear toward her lab. I look at Jimmy with an apology in my eyes, but he only sighs.

"Take these two and stick them in a hole somewhere."

Having given the order, the professor walks off too. But as the tunnelrats seize us, he seems to have second thoughts and turns and walks back to stand in front of me.

"I never was a fan of Dr. Radcliffe, but I did respect his mind. And you, young man, are a disgrace to his legacy." Then he turns to face Jimmy and says, "And I want you to know that I'm glad I killed that stupid fox of yours."

Jimmy struggles against the tunnelrat's grip on him, a new look of murder burning in his eyes. The professor smiles at him with a coward's courage.

"Let me see your teeth, you little savage."

Jimmy spits on him. "Go to hell, old man."

The professor balls his hand into a fist and smashes it into Jimmy's mouth. Jimmy takes the blow without flinching, but the professor leaps back and yelps in pain, cradling his hurt hand and whimpering. Jimmy spits blood at him, then laughs after him as the professor storms off up the dock mumbling profanities.

The victory is short lived, however, as the tunnelrats drag

us off the dock. Now that they're alone, they speak to one another in a kind of pidgin language that is nearly impossible for me to decipher. It sounds like English mixed with squeals and grunts and accented with clicks of their tongues.

My heart begins to race when I see that they're dragging us toward Eden. There's no way Hannah would let them do that. Would she? Is she that far gone? They take us inside, using the same door Jimmy and I did when we broke in and burned it, and they lead us down the hall to a flight of stairs. I remember the killing chair, and fearing that they're taking us there, I begin to struggle and kick. But a second tunnelrat grabs my legs and lifts them off the ground, and they carry me down. I hear Jimmy yelling and fighting as they drag him down after me.

At the bottom of the stairs, they open a steel door and drop me on the floor. I hit my elbow, and pain shoots up my arm. A few seconds later, Jimmy lands hard next to me, his head thudding on the concrete. Then the door slams shut and the room goes dark.

CHAPTER 3
Laughing in the Dark

The last thing I expect to hear is Jimmy laughing in the dark.

"Jimmy? You alright, Jimmy?"

"Yeah," he finally says, "I'm okay."

"Well, what's so funny?"

"Ever-thin' is."

"Everything's funny?"

"I jus' keep seein' the professor's face after he hit me. I ain't never seen someone so afraid. It was like I bit him or somethin', but he's the one hit me. Ain't this jus' a kick?"

"Did you hit your head? You sound a little delirious."

"I'm fine," he says. "I'm jus' gonna lie down and rest."

"Jimmy, you know where we are, right?"

"I'm jus' tired is all," he says. "I'll feel better after I get some sleep. Dun' wake me up unless this has all been a dream."

I listen as he curls up on the floor next to me.

After a while, I hear his breathing change its rhythm and I know he's fallen asleep. I'm pretty sure I heard his head hit when they threw him in after me, and I'm worried that he might have a concussion, or worse. I reach out and find him in the dark and run my fingers over his head. I feel a few lumps on his scalp but no blood. Maybe he is just tired. I scoot closer to him and caress his hair, humming the song his mother used to hum to me. It's a reassuring sound in the uncertain dark. I had an uneasy feeling returning to the Foundation, but I had no idea we'd end up like this. I can only assume that they'll eventually come and either test the new and improved Eden with our brains, or, if we're lucky, just drop us down the meat grinder and wash our remains out to sea. Oh, well. The truth is, I'm tired: tired of searching for answers; tired of struggling to do the right thing; tired of worrying that Jimmy, or me, or both of us will be killed. Maybe Jimmy has the right idea going to sleep. I stretch out beside him on the cold concrete and close my eyes. I open them again when I hear my name.

I sit upright and stare into the blackness, as if I might somehow see the ghost that called to me. Just when I'm sure that my mind is playing tricks in the dark, it comes again— feeble and frail and impossible to pinpoint in the black room.

"Aubrey?—"

"Hello . . .," I call, my own voice echoing back to me.

"Help me."

"Who's there? Hello . . ."

I sit and listen, but the voice does not speak again. I crawl in the direction from which it had come, moving cautiously in the darkness. I can't see a thing, but I begin to smell the reek of urine and human waste. Then my hand lands on something cold and clammy and I recoil from it in fear.

"Help me," the voice says. I reach out again and feel the skin of a hand. An arm. A shoulder. When I feel the coarse hair and the size of the head, I know I've found Red.

"Red? Are you okay, Red? What's happened to you?"

He's lying on the floor in the fetal position. I grab his clammy hand and check his pulse. It's weak and slow. I wonder how long he's been here like this.

"Thirsty," he moans.

"Is there anything in here to drink?"

He doesn't reply.

It takes me a while to locate the door, and when I pound on it with my fist, the sound echoes loudly in the pitch-black room. I pound and pound, but nothing happens and nobody comes. My knuckles ache, and sweat rises on my brow.

"Open up!" I shout. "Open up, you cowards!"

I feel a hand on my shoulder and stop to catch my breath.

"They ain't comin', Aubrey," Jimmy says.

"Red's in bad shape."

"Red?"

"Yeah, he's over there."

"Is he hurt?"

"I couldn't tell, but he said he's thirsty."

"Well, how long's it been since he's had any water?"

"How the hell should I know, Jimmy?" Realizing how rude that sounds, I add, "I'm sorry. I'm just so tired of all this."

But Jimmy's already gone, and when he speaks next, his voice comes from across the room.

"Aubrey, give me a hand over here."

Together, we drag Red to the far wall and lean him up against it. He's much lighter than he should be, given his build.

Jimmy has me hold him up while he feels him for any wounds or broken bones.

"He's in one piece," he says. "But he needs liquids."

"Let's search the room," I suggest. "You follow the wall that way, I'll follow it this way, and we'll meet in the middle."

I inch along the wall, feeling for any pipes or a sink, but there's nothing but concrete. When I hit the corner, I turn and walk the other wall. Still nothing. Another corner. Nothing. I run into Jimmy midway around the room, near the door.

"I got zilch," he says.

"Me either. It's just a bare room. You got any ideas?"

"One," he says, "but it ain't pretty."

"Well, what is it?"

"I gotta go."

"Gotta go where? We're trapped in here."

"No, I gotta *go* go."

"Ah, man. No way. I'd rather die of dehydration."

"But you ain't him. And he might die if we do nothin'."

The idea turns my stomach, but I'm sure it wouldn't hurt.

"Do what you think's best," I say. "I'm going to try and get someone's attention again."

By the time I finish pounding on the metal door, my hand is numb, my voice is hoarse, and the effort has yielded nothing. I might as well be banging on the ceiling of my own coffin.

"Save your energy," Jimmy calls. "You might need it."

I walk to the far wall with my hands in front of me, like some sleepwalking zombie in the night. I find Jimmy sitting next to Red, propping him up, and I slide down the wall and sit on Red's other side.

"Is he doing any better?"

"Some," Jimmy says. "He was talkin' a bit more. He said he thought we was a dream."

"How long's he been in here?"

"He didn't say."

I reach over and shake Red's shoulder. "Red? Can you hear me, Red?"

He moans. I feel his head lift and then drop again.

We sit lined up against the wall for hours—three lonely felons waiting on our fate. The only thing worse than the darkness is the silence. I play a game with myself to pass the time, trying to guess what Jimmy's thinking. Of course, I never know if I'm right or not because I don't ask him. I'm not sure why I don't. Maybe because I'm worried that he's thinking all of this is somehow my fault. Then again, maybe he's playing the same game and trying to guess what I'm thinking, and neither of us is really having any thoughts of his own.

Red stirs next to me. "Aubrey? Are you still here?"

I reach over and rest my hand on his arm. "I'm still here, Red. You okay?"

"I've seen you before but you always disappear."

"I'm really here, buddy. So's Jimmy. He's right there on your other side."

"He is?"

"Hey, Red," Jimmy says. "I'm right here."

"Are you both stuck in here too?"

"Let's not worry about that right now," I say.

"Well, I was wishing you'd show up, so if I wished you here and it's my fault you're stuck, I'm sorry."

"It's not your fault. Red. None of this is."

"Yes, it is."

"Why would you think that?"

"Because I caused the strike."

"The strike? What strike?"

Red lets out a prolonged sigh. A long time passes in silence, and I assume he's gone back to sleep. Then he sighs again. "I shouldn't have done it," he says.

"What'd he say?" Jimmy asks.

"He says he shouldn't have done it."

"Done what?"

"I don't know. Shouldn't have done what, Red?"

"I sent a note down on the train to my girl. I wanted to let her know I was okay. And then . . . and then . . . well, I guess word got around, and they decided they weren't gonna send up any more supplies until their retirement started again."

"Is that why Hannah threw you in here?"

"She said I was stupid."

"You're not stupid."

"She said I was responsible."

"Responsible for what, Red?"

"For killing everybody down in Holocene II."

He says it softly, but the words hit me like a hammer. Did

Hannah flood Holocene II? Is that why all the tunnelrats are up here? An image of all those people waking up to water gushing in to fill the caverns sends a shiver up my spine.

"Red, did you see her do it? Did she flood Holocene II?"

When Red doesn't answer, I shake him, but he only moans and falls over to lean on Jimmy. There's no way I heard him right. It can't be. She wouldn't.

"Jimmy, did he say Hannah flooded Holocene II?"

"He dun' know what he's sayin'," Jimmy replies. "He said we was ghosts too. Let's let him rest."

"Well, we can't just sit here," I say.

"What else are we s'posed to do?" he asks. "All we can do is wait. Wait and save our energy until somebody comes."

"And what if nobody comes?"

"Then we wait some more."

"And dehydrate like Red here and maybe die?"

"There ain't nothin' else to be done."

"Fine," I say, "but I'm not drinking your piss."

"Damn straight you ain't," he says. "You drink your own."

CHAPTER 4
The Ultimatum

Blinding light in my eyes.

Am I dreaming? No, the door is open.

Strong hands grab my arms and jerk me up. My legs are asleep and give out beneath me, and my feet slide along the floor as I'm dragged toward the light, out from the room, and up the stairs. I struggle to turn and at least say goodbye to Jimmy, but I hear the door slam shut behind me before I can.

So this must be it, I think.

But they don't take me into the killing room, at least not right away. Instead, they drag me into Eden's control room, now remarkably restored from the fire Jimmy and I set, and slump me into a chair. As my eyes adjust to the light, I look about at sour-faced tunnelrats and at the new equipment in the room. It's amazing that they've restored it so quickly. I lean forward and look through the window into the pool of red-glowing liquid where my mother and father's brains had been enslaved before Jimmy and I blew it up. It has been refreshed, and countless new hoses turn and coil in the soft, gelatinous current, like serpents just waiting for new brains to latch onto. I can't believe Eden's back in business.

The door opens and Hannah walks in, followed by the professor. She's wearing a pressed white zipsuit, with her red hair pulled back and tied in a ponytail. She looks professional and competent, like some futuristic executioner, especially next to the professor, who looks more frazzled than ever with his wild hair and his missing teeth.

"You need to get water down to Red right now," I say.

Hannah smiles, pulls out a chair from the control panel, and sits facing me. She says, "We've got to work on your manners, Aubrey. Once again, you don't even say hello before you start barking at me."

"He's dying down there. You need to bring him food and water. Please."

"Well, since you asked nicely." She nods to the professor. "Get them some algaecrisps and something to drink."

"Have the rats do it," he says.

Hannah shakes her head. "I'm telling you to do it. Now get on it. And do the other thing too. Just in case."

The professor reluctantly marches to the door and leaves the room. I can only hope he goes down there alone and that Jimmy can have his way with him. I doubt he'd be that stupid though, especially after what happened on the dock.

Hannah looks me over and then sighs. "Aubrey, Aubrey, Aubrey. What's going on with you right now?"

"What's going on with me? How about what in the hell's going on with you? You send Jimmy and me out there with that crazy fool, filled with misinformation. You lie about wanting to free my people. You damn near kill us. You did kill Junior. And you killed all those people . . . even your own brother, Hannah.

You killed your own brother."

"I didn't intend for him to die," she says, as if that were her only crime. "I thought maybe you'd get him to come back with you. I was actually hoping to meet him."

"Well, he cut off his hand to do the right thing, Hannah. And then he died for it. You know what? I'm almost glad he didn't get to meet you, because you'd be a disappointment to a good man like him. You didn't deserve to meet him."

Hannah leaps up from her chair and points her finger at me, as if she'd like to stab me with it. "You have no right to say that to me, Aubrey! No right."

"I have all the right in the world, Hannah. I don't even know who you are. And I don't think I ever really did."

When I finish speaking, I realize that I'm standing too. A tunnelrat steps over and pushes me back down into my chair.

"You and I are no different," she finally says.

"Oh, yes, we are. I'm nothing like you."

"We do what we have to do," she says. "Just like the wave. You killed my father and Tom and all the scientists down here because you thought you had no choice."

"No, I didn't."

"Well, why did you do it then?"

"No,"—I shake my head—"I didn't do it. I didn't set off that wave, Hannah. I couldn't do it. I couldn't kill one life, even to save many."

"Well, then, who did, if it wasn't you?"

"Your mother did."

"You're lying."

"No, I'm not. She came down and set off the wave, and she gave me those vials of longevity serum, and she said we needed to do the right thing this time, Hannah. The right thing. That's what she said. And none of what you're doing here is the right thing, and I know you know it too."

For a moment, Hannah looks sad. Maybe even remorseful. Ten years seem to erase from her face, and she looks once again like the girl I first saw hitting tennis balls. She paces the room, her hands clasped behind her back and her eyes focused on the floor. The tunnelrats' heads swivel to follow her, as if entranced by her movements. But when she stops and looks up at me again, her expression has transformed back to its practiced passivity, her chin slightly raised and a half smile on her mouth. Wherever she's gone, there's no coming back.

She says, "My mother was sick, and sick people do irrational things."

"Yeah, right," I reply. "Because your father killing Gloria and then trying to flood Holocene II was completely rational."

As soon as I mention Holocene II, I remember what Red said to me about being responsible for killing everyone.

"Did you flood Holocene II, Hannah?"

Hannah leans on the edge of the control panel, her hands resting on her thighs and her green eyes drilling into mine.

"I'm glad you asked that," she says, "because that's actually why I have you here. I'm going to give you a chance to save them, Aubrey. I'm going to give you a chance to be the hero."

"I don't want to be a hero," I say.

"Oh, yes, you do," she replies. "Don't be silly."

"What are you up to, Hannah?"

"Up to? I've been hard at work getting things back in order here. It's amazing, really, what you can do when you have the plans for everything and 3-D printers. It's like machines giving birth to more machines. But we still need products from Holocene II where they have much larger sintering equipment than we do here. And things were moving along smoothly when your little friend Red couldn't help himself—he just had to brag about being at the Foundation. Well, now he's set them to worrying down there, and they won't send up the supply train until they're reassured."

"Just set them free, Hannah. It's the right thing to do."

"You're not very bright, are you, Aubrey? I thought you were once, but I'm not so sure now. I'm not letting humankind destroy things again. I'm fulfilling my parents' mission."

"You mean your father's mission."

She waves my comment off, saying, "Whatever. But what I am willing to do is fulfill the original promise of Eden. I think we can make it a pleasurable experience for the occupants."

"Occupants?" I ask, doing my best to sound sarcastic.

"Yes," she says, "occupants. I'm convinced that there's no reason to run any further tests on them, so now I'm willing to provide them with pleasure."

I look again into the red pool of coiling hoses.

"No way, Hannah. This is insane. Even if you won't set

them free, why not just let them live out their full lives below? Why put them in that soup and torture them?"

"Because we have to, Aubrey," she says. "It's resource management. If we let people get old, there will be too many of them down below. There's only so much space, you know."

"Why not just let them have fewer babies?"

"That won't work either. We'll have an aging population that will be less productive and drain precious resources. Plus, you know as well as I do that if people don't have something to look forward to, they start to want to change the conditions they're currently living in. We can't allow that."

I look at her and think how surreal this is. It's as if I'm sitting in this chair listening to Dr. Radcliffe speak through his daughter. I can't understand her. I just can't.

"So what do you want from me, Hannah?"

"I want you to go down and reassure them that everything is fine. Let them know Eden is just undergoing improvements and will be up and running and better than ever in no time. Let them know they have no reason to question anything. They'll listen to you, Aubrey. You're from there. They know who you are. I can't send the professor; he's too old. I couldn't possibly risk going myself. And Red's too stupid. You have to go."

"Are you insane?" I ask. "Why would I help you?"

"No, I'm perfectly rational. And you'll help me because if you don't, I'll have no choice but to flood Holocene II."

"I don't believe you."

"You don't?"

"Oh, I'm sure you're heartless enough to do it, but you couldn't get by without them. Who would build your drones? Who would produce your supplies? Who would mine your chemicals for weapons? You can't carry out the Park Service mission on your own, Hannah, and you know it."

"Maybe you're smarter than I thought," she says, raising an eyebrow. "But you're still going to help me."

"Why would I help you murder all those people, Hannah?"

"To stop me from murdering one," she replies.

She steps over to an LCD monitor and switches it on. An image pops on the screen. My heart pops from my chest . . .

Jimmy is strapped into the killing chair, just as my father was when I watched them take out his brain. He's stripped naked, and his head has been shaved. I feel suddenly hot. My vision blurs. The next thing I know, I'm being restrained in my chair by several tunnelrats.

"No! No! No! No!"

"You can stop this, Aubrey."

I catch glimpses of the monitor as the robotic saw drops from the ceiling and descends toward Jimmy's head. I thrash in my chair, my heart racing, my teeth clenched to near cracking. Drool dribbles from the corners of my mouth, and I hear myself screaming like a pig being slaughtered.

"Just say you'll do it, and you can stop this, Aubrey."

It isn't until the saw stops and Hannah turns the monitor off that I hear myself chanting, "I'll do it, I'll do it, I'll do it."

Hannah smiles at me as if this were all some big game.

"I thought for a moment there I was going to get to test the new Eden," she says. "But you made the right choice."

I settle back down in my chair, but the tunnelrats on either side of me keep a firm grip on my shoulders.

"I have two conditions," I say, when I've recovered a little.

"Oh, you do, do you? And what are they?"

"Well, three, actually. First, you give Jimmy the longevity serum that you lied about. And I'll inject it myself this time."

"You caught me again," she says. "I guess you are smart. I've managed to reproduce it, so I'm fine with that. What else?"

"After I do this, we get to go free. Red, Jimmy, and me."

"Go free? Go free where?"

"Up there. Outside."

"What about the drones?"

"We'll take our chances, unless you want to let us stay in a safe zone, like the lake was before all this happened."

She pauses to consider this. Then she says, "Fine, but only if I can give you each vasectomies."

"Vasectomies?"

"Yes. I can't have you reproducing with others up there, for reasons you well understand. It won't hurt. I promise."

"Okay," I say. "Deal. The idea of possibly having had a kid with you has turned me off to it entirely anyway."

"No need to be nasty," she retorts. "What's the last one?"

"The last one what?"

"Your last condition. You said you had three."

"Jimmy and Red get to go down to Holocene II with me."

She shakes her head. "Absolutely not."

"Then no deal."

"Then I'll put your brain in Eden right next to Jimmy's. He's still in the chair, if you'd like me to give the order."

I shake my head, trying my best to look unafraid. "Jimmy goes with me or no deal. I don't trust you, Hannah."

"Well, why should I trust you if I let him go?"

"Because if we go down, we have to come up. Plus, you could drown us and everyone else too if we pull anything."

"They'll know he's not from the Foundation," she says.

"No they won't. We'll put him in a zipsuit and they won't know a thing. He can be my assistant."

She stares at me for a moment, the wheels turning in that gray matter behind her green eyes. Then she seems to settle on a thought, and a smile teases the edges of her lips.

"Fine," she says. "But Red stays here."

I think about Red lying in that dungeon dying without water or food, and I want to tell her no way. But then I think of Jimmy strapped into that chair, inches away from having his brain sliced out, and I can't risk losing the deal I've made.

"Fine," I say. "Jimmy goes, Red stays."

Hannah nods, signaling that we have an agreement. The tunnelrats release their grip on my shoulders.

"You have to promise to treat Red well," I say. "No more locking him away down there."

"Hmph," she says, apathetically. "He can have the run of the place as long as he stays out of my way."

CHAPTER 5
Take Care, Alex

Jimmy winces as the needle goes in.

I pause with my thumb on the plunger and look at him.

"You sure, buddy? I won't do this unless you're sure."

Jimmy glances over at Red, passed out on the bed in the sleeping quarters we've temporarily taken residence in.

"So Red there'll just age like anyone else, but I won't?"

"That's right."

"And when will I die?"

"Well, it looks to be about nine-hundred years or more before the brain begins to give out. At least that's how it was for Mr. and Mrs. Radcliffe and the other scientists up here."

Jimmy looks down at the needle in his arm and asks, "And you've got this in your body already?" When I nod that I do, he continues, "Well, I dun' wanna leave ya hangin', so let's do it."

I press the plunger and empty the syringe into his vein.

"Well, that's that then," I say. "Now we can be best friends for a thousand years."

Jimmy smiles at me as I cap the empty syringe, and for some reason I feel suddenly shy. Maybe he doesn't consider us best friends. I don't know; I've never asked. But then he stands and hugs me—a surprisingly uncomfortable gesture for us still, especially considering all we've been through. When he pulls away, I notice how different he looks with his head shaved. Different but good. I remember seeing him for the first time, crouched on that coral rock with his long hair hanging to his shoulders. I reach up and run my fingers through my own hair, more aware than ever of how long it is.

"Jimmy, if I go get the clippers from Hannah, will you help me shave my head?"

"Look at you," he says, "copyin' my new look already."

"No, I'm not. I just know that they'll never believe we wear our hair this long up here when we get to Holocene II."

"Whatever you say," he concedes.

"I did grow it out for that reason though," I admit.

"What reason?" he asks.

"To try and look like you."

Jimmy laughs. "And here I've been workin' so hard on the way I speak, tryin' to sound more like you, and you's tryin' to look more like me. We better be careful or we'll each end up as somethin' in the middle, and neither of us will be able to stand the other a minute. And that would be bad if we've got to be best buddies for a thousand years."

"Shoot," I say, "that serum must be doing something already. You've up and got wise on me all of a sudden."

"Wise? Me? Never."

"Well, wise for a hairless savage anyway."

The tunnelrat assigned to guard our door brings us to Hannah. She's standing near the train platform, handing out bottles one at a time to tunnelrats lined up in front of her with expectant looks of desire on their odd faces. They each take their bottle with a jubilant squeal and hustle off with it to the nearest place where they can flop down and begin sucking on it like overgrown piglets. Their eyes close and their heads loll, the milky meal dribbling down their strange albino chins.

37

"What is that they're drinking?" I ask.

Hannah turns to look at us, a desperate tunnelrat frozen before her with its hands outstretched for its milk.

"This is their meal," she says. "And their medicine."

"Why do they need medicine?" I ask.

Hannah hands the tunnelrat its bottle, and another moves up the line.

"You may have noticed that they're all boys," she says. "Silly, silly, boys. That's because the few females are kept below for breeding and for milking. They're sedated with a drug that makes them happy. We used to use it in Eden too. Anyway, it has the lucky side effect of making these fellas here born addicted. So every afternoon they get their medicine. They're a nightmare to control if they don't have it."

"Well, you sure seem to have caught up quickly on how to run things around here," I say. "Makes me wonder how much of what you told me before about never having left the lake house was even true."

She turns to me. "Why aren't you two ready to go?"

"I think I need a haircut before I go down."

"Yes," she says, looking me over, "you most certainly do. And you both need to put on zipsuits too. The professor's sleeping off a shock, but you can use one of his from the submarine for Jimmy. When you're all set, meet me back here."

As the tunnelrat leads us down to the prep room for Eden, I have to keep reassuring myself that I'm only going for a haircut. There's a mirrored window in front of the chair and I watch in it as our tunnelrat chaperone stands behind us with its arms crossed, and Jimmy passes the clippers over my head. In just a few minutes, my hair is piled on the floor. I run my hand over my scalp and feel the bristly stubble.

"How come I don't look as good as you do without hair?"

"Shit," Jimmy says, "prob'ly 'cause you didn't look as good as I did with it."

"Oh, shut up," I say, trying to contain a laugh. "I think it's because my head isn't shaped as well as yours."

"Well, that makes sense," he says. "You've got to have all kinds of nooks and crevices to keep all them crazy ideas in."

I take one last look at my pile of hair on the floor.

"Let's go get changed into our suits, I guess."

The tunnelrat shadows Jimmy and me to the submarine, but when it tries to follow us up the ladder, I block its ascent.

"Where are we going to run to inside a submarine, stupid?"

It grunts and points a white finger at its red eye, saying, "See see. You you."

"Yeah, yeah," I say. "We see you too. Wait out here."

It feels strange being back inside the cramped submarine, as if we'd returned from our journey to the Isle of Man a decade ago rather than a day. I remember Jimmy running up and down the passageway, exercising Junior with some rabbit fur on a string. I remember making meals on the stove. I remember crashing the submarine and swimming out to the island of pig people.

I open my bunkroom drawer to collect my reading slate, but quickly remember that I had given it to Bree when we left the island. When I think of her being evaporated with all those other people, an awesome anger rises inside me, an anger that could drive me to murder. But murder who? Murder Hannah, murder the professor, murder them all, maybe.

Breathe, Aubrey, breathe. You're not like them.

I slide open the other drawer and pull out my Holocene II zipsuit. I remember wearing it when we went down to get the mastercode, and again when we started our journey for the Isle of Man, because my shirt was wet from drying Junior. I strip off Finn's clothes, fold them neatly, and place them in the drawer. But I can't seem to put the zipsuit on. I look at myself in the mirror. My head is shaved, my eyes tired. Just go down and get this over with, I tell myself. Go sell the people of Holocene II and buy Jimmy and Red and yourself your freedom. But what if Hannah doesn't keep her end of the deal? I ask myself. What if she betrays us again?

"Aubrey," Jimmy says. "You okay, buddy?"

I snap out of my thoughts and realize I'm standing naked in front of the tiny mirror, with my hands touching my chest and the Park Service symbol that Finn carved there. The scabs are mostly gone now, leaving wide, red scars.

"Does it hurt?" Jimmy asks.

"Only when I see it," I say.

He nods, a look of painful understanding on his face. And if anyone could understand, I guess it would be him. My need to cover up the enemy's emblem on my chest overcomes my trepidation over donning a zipsuit again, and I step into the legs, slip into the sleeves, and zip it up to my neck. Then I look in the mirror. Jimmy stands beside me. He's already changed into one of the professor's zipsuits, and with our shaved heads and matching outfits, we look like a couple of brothers heading off to war. Then again, maybe we are.

"I guess now you get to see where I grew up," I say.

"Guess so," he says. "I still ain't sure what we're doin'."

"We're bartering for our freedom."

"Yeah, but how?"

"I just have to convince the people to get back to business as usual. That everything's fine. Then we get to go free."

"But is it?" Jimmy asks.

"Is it what?"

"Is ever-thin' fine?"

"I don't know about fine. But business as usual is better than being flooded."

"Whatever you say, then."

"You think what I'm doing is wrong?"

Jimmy doesn't answer; he only sighs. He sits on one of the bunks and pulls the game ball that Finn gave him from his pocket and bounces it off the curved submarine wall.

"Jimmy, I asked you something."

"I know ya did."

"Well, do you think what I'm doing is wrong?"

"I dunno, Aubrey," he says. "I dunno what's right and what's wrong no more."

I reach and intercept the ball, forcing him to look at me.

"Listen, Jimmy. This is our only shot. We tried to do the right thing. We really did. But who knew that this is what we'd find when we got back? Hannah was going to kill you, Jimmy. Worse. Enslave you in Eden. And me and Red too. Not to mention kill everybody in Holocene II as well. She's got control of the drones; she's got these stupid tunnelrats eating out of her hand. We've got to do this. It's our only chance."

"I guess so," he says. "I jus' get a feelin' if we go down there, we won't be comin' back up. Maybe I'm jus' nervous."

"Don't be nervous," I say, doing my very best to sound

reassuring, "because I can handle this."

Jimmy looks at me and smiles, but it's not very convincing.

Before heading to meet Hannah at the train platform, we bring some broth back to the room and sit Red up in bed and help him drink it. He's getting better by the hour, but he's still sleeping round the clock. He lost a lot of weight locked in that room, and the thin blanket wrapped around his wasted frame gives him the appearance of some unearthed mummy with a shock of perfectly preserved red hair.

As I'm tucking him back in, I notice cuts on his forearm.

"What happened there, Red?"

He stretches his arm out for me to see. The cuts form a crude message, undoubtedly gouged in his skin with unclipped fingernails in the dark. The message reads: I'M SORRY BETH.

"Is Beth your girl down below on Level 3?" I ask.

"Yeah," he says. "It's actually BethAnn, but I ran out of arm. I was sure I was going to die in there, Aubrey. Just sure. But now it seems silly because I can't recall why I thought she'd see the note if I did. Maybe I am dumb, like Hannah says."

"You're not dumb, Red. And I'll get BethAnn the message and let her know you're fine and thinking about her."

"You'd do that?"

"Of course, I will."

"You're the best, Aubrey. Thank you."

"If you say so, Red, but you had better thank Jimmy there too. He's the one that saved your life."

"How'd you do that, Jimmy?"

"You might not want to know," Jimmy says.

"Well, thanks anyway," Red replies. "I owe you both."

Seeing him lying there in bed, with his lips swollen and his eyes sunken into his head, I feel guilty for not having pressed Hannah harder to let him come down with us. But then again, she's probably right about the risk.

As if reading my mind, Red asks, "Will you be gone long?"

"Nah," I say, trying to convince myself. "Couple days, maybe. We'll be back before you know it. Just relax and stay away from Hannah. She assured us that you can have anything you need and that no one will lock you away again."

Red nods that he understands.

I stand from the edge of the bed where I had been sitting and lead Jimmy toward the door so we can start our journey.

"Aubrey . . ." Red calls from his bed.

I stop at the door and turn. "Yes, Red."

"I did what I promised. I kept an eye on Hannah for you while you were gone."

"I know you did, Red. I know."

"And I'm sorry how things turned out," he adds.

"You're a good man, Red."

A smile rises on his gaunt face, and he almost looks once again like the boy I said goodbye to all those months ago at the elevator platform in Holocene II.

"You really think I'm a man now?"

"I know you are, Red."

"It's Alex," he says.

"Alex?"

"Yeah. I know everybody always called me Red, but Alex is my real name."

I smile to think how far he's come from the boy bully who always buried me in sand.

"Take care, Alex."

CHAPTER 6
Home, Home Again

Hannah awaits us on the train platform—impatiently tapping her foot, of course.

Several tunnelrats inspect the subterrene. They look a little tipsy yet from their afternoon milk; I hope they're not driving.

"You're holding things up," Hannah says.

"Yeah, yeah," I say. "What's the rush about anyway?"

"They're expecting you below."

"That's great, but I have a few questions before we go."

"Of course, you do," she says.

"How do I know that you'll let us go when we get back?"

"You'll just have to trust me," she replies, with a smile.

Jimmy laughs so loud it echoes in the cavern.

"But that's just it," I say, "I don't trust you. Not one bit."

Hannah steps closer to me and lowers her voice.

"Listen, Aubrey. I know things have gotten all mixed up. But I'm not a cold-blooded killer. You know that."

Jimmy laughs again.

Hannah turns to him. "You better knock it off, Jimmy, or you can stay here, and I'll give you something to laugh about."

Jimmy turns away and spits on the ground.

Hannah turns back to me. "Now when you get back, we'll get you three all snipped up, and I'll happily have you dropped off up above. The drones still steer clear of the lake, and you can make a home somewhere near its shores. Sound fair?"

"And what should I tell the people of Holocene II again?"

"Just what we rehearsed together: that Eden is undergoing improvements and will be up and running in no time. Tell them that their loved ones are still here safe and waiting for them. Tell them that they'll have even more bliss to enjoy when the new and improved Eden comes back online."

"And what if they ask about Red?"

"They know he snuck around to see his girl, right? Isn't that why we bumped into him in the first place?"

"Yeah."

"Well, just tell them that he snuck into a train car headed for the Foundation and that he was somehow exposed to an unsterilized location. Tell them he's contagious."

"Contagious with what?"

"They don't care, Aubrey. All they know is that the closer to the surface you go, the more dangerous it is. Don't you get it yet? They've been down there all this time, and they don't want to ask questions. The answers might scare them. They just want to work their twenty years and then enjoy their retirement. And all you have to do is assure them that they will. That's it."

"And you think they'll believe me?"

"Of course, they'll believe you," she says. "You're their favorite son. The boy who was called up to Level 1. You might as well even take some credit while you're down there for these new *improvements* we're making to Eden."

The entire time we're talking, Jimmy stares at the ground and I can tell that he wants to cut in and tell Hannah off. And I can't blame him, because I do too. But I have to do this. For Red, for him, for all of the people down in Holocene II.

"Okay, I'll convince them."

"Great!" she says, patting me on the back. "I knew you were a smart kid, Aubrey."

She reminds me so much of her father that I can't believe I didn't see the similarities before.

"They have a supply train ready to come up that they're holding," she continues. "You can return on it as soon as you convince them to send it. Here's a keycard to allow you to pass between the levels, but you shouldn't need it. I've arranged for you to give a talk on Level 3 tomorrow that will be streamed to the other levels. Just seeing you back there should be all the reassurance they need."

Jimmy throws me a look. "You two done talkin' yet?" he asks. "I'd like to get on with it already."

Hannah turns to face him.

"And no funny business from you, Jimmy. Just keep your mouth shut and let Aubrey do the talking. You're only going because he bargained for it, and if anything goes wrong down there, you'll all be flooded before you can fart. You got that? And drowning isn't a fun way to die, as you well know from rounding up the floaters when we came here after the wave." Then she turns back to me and grins. "Good luck."

She twirls her finger in the air and a tunnelrat opens the subterrene hatch and calls something to another inside. The machine fires to life and winds up with a screech and whine that climbs in pitch until it's almost deafening. Then it either passes beyond the frequency audible to the human ear or ceases entirely as the cavern falls silent again. The metallic cone glows, pointing into the dark tunnel through the open cavern doors, as if it were some manned missile preparing to dive into the earth.

Jimmy and I are about to drop down onto the tracks and

head for the hatch when I hear the professor shout.

"Wait! Hold them there!"

He comes bumbling up the path, juggling something in his hands as he mumbles profanities to himself. He's breathless by the time he joins us on the platform.

"Hold them," he says. "I've got the bracelets ready."

"I told you we don't need them," Hannah replies.

"Oh, yes, we do," he insists. "I've been out there with these two weasels. We need the insurance."

Hannah takes one of the bracelets from him and looks it over. "Couldn't you make them smaller?" she asks. "This will never do. It's much too large and obvious. We don't need to give these people anything new to wonder about."

"What about him?" the professor asks, pointing at Jimmy. "They won't be looking at him. He's just along for the ride, isn't that what you said? These two might as well be Siamese twins, so shackling him is as good as shackling both of them."

"Fine," Hannah says, handing him back the bracelet. "Put one on Jimmy, then. But only on him."

"You want *me* to put it on him?" the professor asks.

"It's your idea," Hannah says.

The professor inches toward Jimmy, his head held back as if to keep from being hit.

"Let me see your ankle," he says.

"What's that thing do?" I ask, stepping between them.

"It's an incentive," the professor says.

"An incentive for what?"

"To come home, of course," he answers. "If this isn't back here to be deprogrammed in a week, it will detonate."

"Detonate?"

"It's just a precaution, Aubrey," Hannah interjects.

"No way," I say, shaking my head.

"I'm not giving you an option," she replies.

"So? I said no."

"Then no deal," she says, hooking her hands on her hips. "It shouldn't be a problem if you don't plan on escaping."

"You're crazy. There's no way you're putting that on him."

"Fine," she says, turning her back and calling down to the tunnelrats. "Trip's off. Come and take them back to the hole."

"I dun' care," Jimmy says. "Let 'em put it on me."

"Are you sure, Jimmy?"

He nods and sticks out his foot.

The professor steps closer, kneels, and clamps the bracelet around Jimmy's ankle, locking it. When he goes to stand again, Jimmy feigns kicking him, and the professor throws his hands up and screams, lurching backward and falling on his ass.

Jimmy and I laugh.

"I wouldn't be so brave if I were you," the professor says, picking himself up off the ground. "I've got a remote way to detonate that thing."

Jimmy takes a step toward him, and he runs and cowers behind Hannah for protection. She just shakes her head.

"Don't worry," she says, as if she were somehow on our side. "Just make sure you're back here in less than a week, and I'll take that stupid thing off myself."

We turn for the subterrene.

As Jimmy steps inside, I pause and look back.

Hannah stands on the platform with her red hair pulled back, and the professor stands next to her with his gray hair more frizzed than ever. They're an odd pair, that's for sure, but a pair nonetheless. I wish we were leaving for good and that this were the last image I'd ever see of them. I just hope I can trust her to keep her word when we return. I know I shouldn't, but I have no other choice.

Hannah smiles and raises a hand.

I duck inside the subterrene without waving back.

As the hatch closes and seals behind me, I look about and take in the cramped space. Several tunnelrats line the walls, sitting in foldout seats. A cluster of others stand at the forward part of the machine, manning the controls. They move in perfect synchronicity, communicating with gestures, and I get the feeling they've done this trip many times before.

I take a seat next to Jimmy and buckle in. I'm glad I do, because as soon as the belt clips into the latch, the subterrene launches forward at an amazing speed, pulling Jimmy and me to lean together in tandem, as if being blown by a strong wind before settling and coming to sit upright again. I watch as the tunnelrats across from us drift in and out of napping, their milky second eyelids slowly coming to a close over their red eyes and then snapping open again, as if remembering that they're supposed to be watching us. But even so, I get the feeling that we're just another bit of cargo being hauled through the tunnels they inhabit. By the look of their skin, they certainly don't get a UV light where they hang out.

I look down at Jimmy's legs and see the slight bulge of the ankle bracelet. The very idea of it causes me panic. He seems to have none of my worry, however, because when I look up at his face, he's napping too, or at least his eyes are closed. I'm reminded of my first train ride up to the Foundation and the surprise accident that started all of this. I'm sure if we crashed at the speed this thing is going, there'd be nothing left to clean up. I don't know where I heard to do it or why I even think it will bring good luck, but I cross my fingers and lean back into the headrest, determined to only grab a little sip of sleep.

The next thing I know, I lean hard the other way, and the subterrene comes to a halt. Before we can even unlatch our belts, a crew member opens the hatch and waves us off with a grunt. We duck out into the dim loading level of Holocene II and step away from the tracks. The hatch closes, and the subterrene rockets away on silent magnetic rails, the backwind raised by its departure tickling my naked scalp. Jimmy and I watch it disappear down the track and into another tunnel.

It looks to be rest hours on the deserted transfer platform. I'm sure that's how Hannah planned it.

"So this is where you grew up?" Jimmy asks, taking in the dreary view. "Seems kinda dark. Like it ain't too much different than where we jus' come from."

"This is only the transfer station where they move supplies between the levels."

"Oh," is all he says.

"There's the loaded train that they're refusing to send up. We'll hitch a ride back on that, if all goes well."

I point to the train hovering at the platform. Most of the cars are fully enclosed, but a few open cars carry cargo too large to fit inside, including several drone wings and a drone fuselage. I know Hannah needs the parts they're sending, to keep killing people; not just outside people either, but the very people who are building and sending up parts for the new Eden.

"Come on," I say, pushing the thought away. "Let's go see if this keycard works the elevators."

The bank of elevators are open and empty, and as we walk past them their shiny metal interiors display our bloated and silly reflections, like some funhouse carnival mirror I've only read about in stories. All those years growing up, I never had access to any other levels besides ours, and I'm tempted to use the keycard Hannah gave me to go explore them now. But then I remember the bracelet clamped onto Jimmy's ankle, and a sense of urgency pushes me toward the elevator for Level 3.

As the elevator descends, I debate whether or not to warn Jimmy about the decontaminant, but before I can decide what to say, we come to a stop. I cast him an apologetic look.

"Just breathe it in," I say.

"Breathe what—"

The gas cuts him short. When the elevator opens, we both spill out, clinging to one another and coughing.

"Just as late as ever, I see," a familiar voice says.

I look up at Mrs. Hightower, just as tall as ever, despite how much I've grown. She still looks mean, too. Her eyes dart from me to Jimmy and then to the slate clutched in her hand.

"I don't see anything about anyone accompanying you."

"This is Jimmy," I tell her. "He's my assistant."

"Assistant? Well, well, aren't you important. Fifteen years teaching here on Level 3, and I still have to grade essays myself. Now, if you don't mind, it's late and I'd like to get a little sleep before productive hours start again. I've been standing at this elevator longer than I care to mention."

She turns on her heel and leads us off through the cavern valley. It's a strange feeling, being back—as if I walked here in some prior life, or maybe in a dream. The whir of cooling fans is impossible to ignore now, although I hardly heard it before.

That, and the air smells odd to me—conditioned, not fresh.

Jimmy walks along beside me, silently taking in the sights. He looks different here too—shyer, less self-assured, as if his confidence were left on the surface, above. I point him up to the sparkling benitoite high in the cavern ceiling, and we gaze at it as we walk. We are so consumed that I run right into Mrs. Hightower when she stops. She shrugs it off with an annoyed grunt, digs through her pocket, and pulls forth a key. I can't believe we're standing in front of my old living quarters door.

Mrs. Hightower pulls the door open and steps aside for me to enter, but my feet are suddenly bolted to the ground. They won't budge. Our yellow nightlight is on in the kitchen, and it washes the small apartment in sepia shadows. I can just make out the kitchen table and chairs beyond the small living room. I would have thought it would be occupied already, but then the horror of my father's retirement—no, my father's slaughter—and how recent it was hits me like a cold wave. He must have left this apartment for the last time just a few months ago.

"Aubrey? You look pale. Is everything okay?"

Her question seems to be coming from far away.

"Is everything okay?" Mrs. Hightower repeats.

"He's just tired from our journey," Jimmy says, speaking very clearly and without his usual accent.

"Well, then," Mrs. Hightower says, handing the key to Jimmy. "See that he gets some rest and have him in the square by the mid-production break." Then she turns again on her heel and struts off into the silent valley, the squeak and squish of her shoes fading with her silhouette into the shadows.

"You okay?" Jimmy asks, quietly.

I reach out and steady myself against his shoulder.

"I will be, I think. Just give me a minute."

Jimmy stands as still as a statue beside me, and it's only because of his patient strength that I can bring myself to step across the threshold. My eyes are already adjusted to the dim light of the cavern, and I glance around at the shadowy time capsule that was my only childhood home. Everything is as it was. Well, everything except that my father is gone and dead. I walk over to the kitchen where the yellow light washes across our tiny table and chairs. I can still see our elbow indentations on the table's surface, his across from mine. How many quiet breakfasts together? How many evening stories after dinner?

Then I see it, sitting on the counter, as if he'd just stepped out and might be back at any moment. My father's tobacco tin. I pick it up and open the lid and hold it to my nose. The sweet smell of his tobacco conjures his image from the shadows and for one heavenly moment, it isn't Jimmy standing in front of me; it's my dad. Maybe it's the professor's zipsuit he's wearing and the new buzz cut, or maybe it's just the power of the smell mixed with the place, but my father is standing right in front of me in the flesh.

"I love you."

The words come out almost in a panic, as if there's no time. As if he's about to walk into Eden again, and I've got to say it before he disappears behind the door.

"I love you too."

Jimmy' response startles me back to the room, the tobacco tin forgotten in my hand. I close it and set it on the counter, afraid of whatever drug it is inside that has me hallucinating.

"I must be losing my mind," I say, shaking my head. "I thought I just heard you say that you loved me."

"I did," Jimmy replies.

"You did?"

"Of course. You said it to me first. It woulda been rude to leave ya hangin' there, wouldn't it?"

"But did you mean it? Do you love me?"

"My pa used to say that when you love someone, you do stuff for 'em. And after all you done for me, there ain't nothin' I wouldn't do for you. So, yes, I love you."

I take a deep breath to clear my mind.

"What was in that container?" Jimmy asks.

"My father's pipe tobacco."

As soon as I say it, I realize what I've done and I slam my palm into my forehead—"Stupid, stupid, stupid."

"What's stupid?" Jimmy asks.

"I've gone and lost my father's pipe."

Jimmy smiles and sinks his hand into his zipsuit pocket, pulls out the pipe, and hands it to me.

"You brought it!"

"Of course, I did," he says. "You gave it to me for safe keepin', remember?"

"No," I say, correcting him, "I gave it to you to keep. I just thought we'd lost it on the Isle of Man, or maybe left it up there with the professor and Hannah."

"I'd never lose somethin' so important," he says. "And it's yours. I was jus' holdin' it."

I look at the pipe in my hand and tears come into my eyes. I remember my father sitting at this little kitchen table and telling me all about the butterflies and what they meant. And I remember him handing it to me to smoke for the first time, and how I coughed and embarrassed myself. I'm tempted to fill it now and have a puff in his honor, but I think I've had enough remembering for one day.

"Come on, Jimmy. We had better get some rest before I start sobbing like a sissy and telling you that I love you again."

I lead Jimmy upstairs to my old room. It seems half the size I remember it. Jimmy goes to look out the window, and I open my closet and look through my drawers. There's my old gray hoody, right where I left it all those months ago now. I remember leaving it behind because I wanted to make a good impression at the Foundation. Wasn't I silly? I know that the boy who left here then is somehow connected to me now, but he's not me. He's a past version of me, an innocent pedestrian that I look back on now with a kind of painful longing to help, a strong desire to warn him of what lies ahead.

When I turn around, Jimmy's lying on the bed.

"So this is where you slept?"

"Every night of my life before I met you."

"Must have been nice to have a place all your own. I mean somethin' that didn't change. We was movin' all the time."

"I hadn't thought of it like that. I know I didn't think it was nice back then. I felt trapped here, and I would have given anything to get out."

Jimmy props himself up on an elbow and looks at me.

"Anything?" he asks.

"Yes," I answer. "Anything."

"Even as much as you did give up to get out?"

His question leaves me stumped for an answer. Would I go back? Would I undo everything if I could? Would I give up knowing the truth to have had those extra months with my father? Would I give up this new life that promises to last a thousand years for the belief that I might join my mother and my father someday in Eden, even if it was just a lie? Would I give up wisdom for innocence?

"Yes, yes, yes,"—the words are half-truth, half apology to my father—"I'm sorry, but I would do it all again."

As I fall asleep in my father's bed with his pillow beneath my head and his blanket pulled up to my nose, I try to imagine what it must have been like to be him, lying here going to sleep on his last night before heading up to Eden. I imagine the excitement he must have felt about seeing my mother again; his sense of accomplishment for having made it to retirement. I know he would have celebrated with a pint or two of algae ethanol at the pub in the square. I know he would have had one last smoke. I know he would have lain in this very bed, with his head on this very pillow, and I know he would have thought about me just as sure as I'm here now thinking about him.

I wonder who will think about me when I'm gone.

It's an interesting thought to fall asleep to.

CHAPTER 7
The Speech

Pounding on the downstairs door wakes me.

My initial panic is quickly replaced with dread.

I know what I have to do today, and the idea of it sickens me. I couldn't set off that wave at the lake house and kill Dr. Radcliffe and a few heartless scientists to save everyone in Holocene II, but now I'm going to send everyone in Holocene II to their early deaths in Eden just to save Jimmy and myself.

My door cracks open, and Jimmy pops his shaved head into the room.

"Hey, that giant lady is downstairs, and she's less friendly than she was last night. She says we're late."

"Tell her we'll be in the square in a few minutes."

There's no time to shower, so I brush my teeth and splash cold water on my face before joining Jimmy downstairs.

"I found some of 'em crisper things," he mumbles, crumbs tumbling from his mouth. "But they taste pretty stale."

I chew a handful of ancient algaecrisps and wash them down with some tap water, which for some reason tastes of chemicals to me now. Then we head for the door together. I stop before we leave the apartment and address Jimmy.

"You still think I'm doing the wrong thing?"

"Hey," he says, "I'm just along for the ride, remember?"

"Come on, Jimmy. I need to know what you think."

He sighs and looks away, gazing toward the kitchen. When he looks back at me, I see pain deep in his gray eyes.

"I dun' know what we're doin' here, Aubrey," he says. "All I know is I'm sick and tired of Hannah and these people and their lies. All lies. I just wanna get back to livin' in the world, ya know? Like outside again. Like we was in the cove. Like we was on the island before they blew it up."

"Me too, Jimmy. And if I do this thing today, then we can do just that. We can have a life away from all this."

He bends and reaches to pull the leg of his zipsuit over his ankle bracelet. Then he stands again and says, "You keep on trustin' Hannah, but you shouldn't."

"I'm not trusting her to keep her word this time, Jimmy. I'm trusting her to be logical. There's no value in keeping us around once I do this, and there's no reason to kill us if we're out somewhere minding our own business."

"But I thought they was tryin' to kill all humans."

"And they are. But not all right away."

"Ain't they worried we'll make more?"

"More people?"

"Yeah."

"Well, I kind of agreed that we'd all get vasectomies."

"Vasecto-whats?"

"Just a little operation so we can't have kids. No big deal. Don't look at me like that. I saw you get circumcised with an old knife and no pain killers. You'll be fine with it."

"But what if I want kids?" he asks. "My pa always said I'd have a son to carry on the name, remember? I brought you to the cave and showed you the head."

I remember his cave and their fearless leader who was really just the bust of an old movie star they'd dug up.

"Jimmy, who would you even have kids with?"

"Whatever," he says, pulling open the door. "That big lady wasn't very happy, so we better hurry on."

The valley is strangely quiet as we weave our way along the path toward the square. We pass the gray education annex and it seems somehow smaller and less impressive to me now, so much so that it's difficult to even imagine the anxiety I felt that day I tested with all the other 15s. Back then my biggest fears were moving to a different level and getting punched by Red.

A steadily growing buzz of conversation foretells what we'll see when we turn onto the public square—everyone, and I mean everyone, is there. I've never seen so many people gathered in one place before. I guess we never had occasion for it, growing up. Mrs. Hightower's head floats above the others where she stands at a makeshift stage, scanning the edges of the crowd for our arrival. She sees us and waves us over.

"It's about time," she huffs. "They were about to come and drag you out here themselves in another few minutes."

She points to a platform where a microphone waits for me. I look to Jimmy for reassurance, but all I get is a sad mixture of anxiety and disappointment written on his face. I climb the step to the platform and pull the microphone toward my mouth.

"Hello."

I jolt away from the mic when my voice echoes back from every corner of the cavern. The crowd ceases its murmuring and focusses on me. It's a sea of blank faces, although a few of them form into loose approximations of people that I used to know. Is that Mrs. Kelly from the infirmary where I went once with a fever? I was lucky it hadn't gotten worse, she'd said, because otherwise they would have sent me up to Eden. Then I see Chad, my father's old friend from work. He must be due to retire any day. There are kids I know from class too, standing in groups, whispering and pointing. One girl who was a few years ahead of me is in the front row, and I see that she's pregnant. Her husband is holding her hand. There are others I know I should know but can hardly remember. They're all looking at me and waiting for me to speak—waiting for me to tell them that everything is okay, that their lives can go on just as they always have. And they'll trust me because I'm one of them.

"Hello, friends."

Just saying the word "friends" makes me feel like a fraud. What is a friend anyway? Someone you feel affection for? Someone who will do you no harm? I push my self-doubt away, take a deep breath, and speak to the crowd.

"As many of you know, retirement has been on hold for the last few months or so. I'm here to explain why. Eden is undergoing some simple improvements to make the experience even better than it already was. But I can assure you that no one is going to be forced to work beyond age thirty-five and that the promise of Eden is alive and better than ever."

"What's better about it?" someone shouts from the crowd.

"Well . . ." I stammer, not having thought of any particular improvements to pitch to them. "For one thing we had to expand it to make more room. But that's just the start. As many of you know, you can be anywhere you want while you're in Eden. Any paradise you can imagine. Well, imagine being able to be in multiple paradises at once."

"How would you do that?" someone asks.

"The software behind it is quite complicated, of course," I say, lying through my gritted teeth, "but basically you can be in more than one place at a time in the new Eden."

After it comes out, I realize that I'm just mixing in the professor's crazy submarine speech about particles existing in more than one place at any given time, and I'm not really even sure how you could enjoy being in two places at once. I look at Jimmy for his reaction, but I can't tell if he looks impressed by my speaking skills or my ability to lie.

"What else?" another asks.

I close my eyes for a moment, trying to think, trying to not lie too much. Then I open them and go on:

"New places to go and explore without even having to imagine them. Like gorgeous coastlines of blue water, and pine forests, and snowcapped mountains, and beautiful lakes with homey houses on their edge for you to relax in. Tennis courts. Beds made of feathers. Planes that fly you over the landscape and show you deserts and prairies and grazing beasts that had long ago gone extinct. And whole islands across the sea where castles rise up out of the water, and where majestic hills roll on forever, and you can ride horses and hunt deer and eat feasts prepared for kings."

When I finish, the crowd oohs and aahs. But I notice that Jimmy just looks sad. I'm guessing that's because he knows that I'm not talking some imagined reality in Eden, but our life.

"Now," I say, feeling the time is right to go for the close, "if we can just get back to business as usual and get the supplies sent up, we'll be able to restart retirements in almost no time."

The crowd parts, and a young girl about my own age steps to the front and looks up at me.

"But what about Red?"

This must be BethAnn, Red's girlfriend.

"He's fine," I tell her. "But he can't come back."

"Why not?" she asks.

"Well, because he sneaked around and was exposed to some unsterilized areas. I'm afraid he's contagious."

I see the crowd collectively cringe at the word contagious, many shaking their heads and others waving the word away as if waving Red away with it. We've lived long enough in these close quarters to know the danger of a foreign agent infecting us; even if that foreign agent is the truth.

But BethAnn doesn't wave Red away.

Instead, she looks up at me with dewy eyes and says, "Maybe Red and I could go to Eden early then. That way we could be together forever."

Her willingness to go render her brain into Eden early just to be with Red rips my heart out. There she is, true as they come. I look over at Jimmy, and he's shaking his head. I look out at the crowd, the trusting faces colored with hope that they too will someday be reunited with their loved ones in Eden. Then I see Mrs. Hightower and her unforgiving face and I'm reminded of the video of Dr. Radcliffe that she showed us on the big test day, the one where he lied to us all about Eden and about him being the first one to enter it.

Suddenly, I'm back in that classroom, taking my test. I'm looking again at the question: would I kill an entire level to save humankind? I answered blindly then. But I'm not blind now. I'm standing here with my eyes wide open, lying to these people and sending them to be slaughtered when they turn 35. I'm no better than Radcliffe was. But I can be. I can still change the course of my destiny. I can still redeem myself. I can still make my father proud, wherever he is.

I turn back to the microphone.

"I owe you all an apology because I've been standing up here lying to you this whole time. Eden is a sham . . ."

Just as I realize that the microphone has been killed and that none of my last statement was broadcast, a strong hand grabs my arm and yanks me off the platform. Then I'm being pulled through the crowd by Mrs. Hightower. Hands reach to pat me on the back, faces smile at me, voices cheer my name, and all of it slides by so fast, I can't get a word out to anyone.

When the noise of the crowd fades away behind us, I look back and see Jimmy following along with his hands stuffed in his pockets and his head down.

"Where are you taking me?"

"Home," Mrs. Hightower says, without turning back.

We arrive at the door and she throws it open and pushes me inside. Then she lets Jimmy enter before stepping inside herself and pulling the door closed.

"What was that about?" she asks.

"What was what about?"

"You know damn well what I mean," she insists. "What were you thinking, saying what you said?"

"You heard me?"

"Of course, I did."

"Then why aren't you shocked?"

She sighs. "There's a lot you don't yet understand."

"Well, why don't you fill me in?"

"I can't," she says. "Not here."

"Where then? When?"

She glances at Jimmy. "How does he fit in?"

"He's with me," I say. "He's my best friend."

"So, he knows?"

"Yes, he knows everything."

"Fine," she replies. "You two stay here. Keep low profiles. Don't talk to anyone. We'll come and collect you at midnight."

"Who's we?"

"You'll see," she says. "You'll see."

Then she steps to the door, pulls it open, and looks back.

"Not a word to anyone. Got it?"

I nod that I do.

"You too," she says, glancing at Jimmy.

"Yes, ma'am," he replies.

She looks at us one last time, as if to be sure, and then she stoops through the door and pulls it shut behind her.

CHAPTER 8
BethAnn, the Beach, and the Vote

"What the hell?" Jimmy asks.

"I don't know," I say, shaking my head. "I tried to tell the truth at the last minute, but the microphone cut off, and then Mrs. Hightower dragged me from the stage."

"I dun' trust her."

"Neither do I. But what can we do except wait for her or whoever to come back?"

Jimmy flops on the couch and pulls the ball that Finn gave him from his pocket, tosses it into the air, and catches it.

"What do you think woulda happened?"

"What do you mean?"

"I mean," he says, "If you'd got off the truth."

"I don't know," I admit, taking the only other chair in the small living room. "Maybe Hannah was tuned in somehow and would have flooded us on the spot. Maybe we'd be drowned by now. Or maybe the people would have been angry enough to do something for once. The only thing I know for sure is that I was wrong to lie to them. Eden is a slaughterhouse."

"But why does this high-legged lady seem to know?"

"Mrs. Hightower? That I don't understand. It's a mystery. And what else has me curious is why is she down here if she knows? Do you think she's working for Hannah?"

"I wouldn't put nothin' past her," he says.

We each fall quiet with our own thoughts. I sit and watch the ball rise and fall as Jimmy lies on his back playing catch with himself. It's hypnotic to watch, and I begin to sort through all these mysterious pieces of information. Hannah betrayed us, blowing up the Isle of Man. Red accidentally betrayed Hannah to Holocene II with a note to his girlfriend. Hannah sent us down here to fix it. I try to tell them the truth and am stopped from doing it by Mrs. Hightower, who already knows. It's puzzle enough to make me dizzy.

"That was sad about Red's girl," Jimmy says.

"I know," I reply, happy to free my mind from the maze of questions there. "And I promised Red that I'd tell her he was okay. That he was thinking about her. And I kind of did, but not really. I should go find her and reassure her that he'll be fine. You want to come with me?"

"But that lady said to stay here."

"Yeah, but midnight's a long time from now. And besides, maybe they're just coming to kill us anyway, whoever they are."

Jimmy tosses me the ball and I catch it.

"I'm in for whatever," he says. "Jus' lead the way."

We stick to the edges of the valley and the mostly empty living quarters, since everyone would have gone back to work after my speech. But the problem is, I only have a general idea where BethAnn lives from having seen Red sneak out his window and head to her block of buildings in the middle of the night. Turns out, we don't need to know much more than that, though, because as we approach a row of apartments, I can hear weeping coming from an open window.

"BethAnn," I call up.

When she doesn't respond, Jimmy whistles. The sobbing ceases and a pale face appears in the window.

"What do you want?" she calls down.

"Let us up. I need to talk with you."

"You can talk with me from there," she says.

I look around, but there doesn't seem to be anyone about.

"Fine," I half whisper, half shout. "I have a message from Red. He said to tell you that he's thinking about you, and that he misses you, and that everything will work out just fine."

"What's that mean?" she asks.

"What's what mean?"

"That everything will work out?"

"I don't know. That's just what he said. So don't cry."

She leans out the window a little farther and looks around. Then she looks back down at me with a question on her face.

"How come you can talk to him?"

"What do you mean?" I ask.

"If he's contagious like you say, why can you talk to him?"

It's a good question, and I should have considered it before coming to find her. Maybe this was a mistake. I stumble to find an answer, but Jimmy jumps in and saves me.

"He wrote the message and Aubrey read it," he says, which is brilliant because it's kind of the truth.

"Is that it?" she asks.

"What do you mean is that it?"

"Is that all he wrote?"

"He said he was sorry."

"Well," she says, "you told me. Now go away."

Then she pulls the window closed. We turn to walk away, but we don't get far when I hear the window slide open again.

She calls after us, "Will you give him a message for me?" When I turn and nod yes, she says, "Tell him that I love him. Just tell him that for me, will you?"

Before I can promise her that I will, she pulls the window closed again and disappears into the shadows of the room.

"That could have gone better," Jimmy says.

"Tell me about it. And it didn't kill much time either."

"How much longer till midnight?"

"Too long," I say. "But, hey, I know what might help pass the time. How about a trip to the beach?"

"The beach?" he asks. "Here? Underground?"

"Come on, I'll show you."

We take the lift up to the recreation tunnels and walk the corridor to the locker room door. Inside, we grab clean shorts from the rack and change into them, leaving our zipsuits and our belongings in lockers. I'm disappointed to see that the sign on the beach access door reads: LIFEGUARD NOT ON DUTY

I was hoping Bill would be here so I could show him how much taller and heavier I am. I think he'd be surprised.

But at least Jimmy is surprised, because when we step through the door, his jaw drops and he stands transfixed by the scene in front of him. It's as if the cavern has disappeared and been replaced by blue skies and sandy beaches. The gulls call, the waves tumble up the sand, the perfect clouds float in their windless skies, and although the illusion is not as convincing as it was to me before, it's still a remarkable likeness.

"I dunno whether to trust my eyes," Jimmy says.

"Why not?"

"Because it looks like a beach, but it ain't."

"How do you know it isn't?"

"Well, the air smells funny for starters. And those gulls in the sky is flappin' but they ain't goin' nowhere. And there ain't no shells or no rocks in the sand. It's too perfect. Look at those clouds. They seem to be at the same height, but they's goin' in different directions. That jus' ain't possible. Plus, you can look right at the sun there without your eyes burnin' up."

"Well, we can at least enjoy the UV lights awhile," I say, just a little bummed that he wasn't more convinced.

We walk toward the water's edge and sit on the sand.

"Are we goin' swimmin'?" he asks.

"I guess we could," I say, "but the water's only about a meter deep."

"How deep's a meter?" he asks.

"About up to your waist."

"No wonder I had to teach ya to swim," he says, laughing as he flops onto his back in the sand and closes his eyes.

I lie down next to him and close my eyes too. I remember coming here to get away from the gray depression of the cavern and to dream about one day discovering a world without walls. Now I've found it, and hiked it, and swum in its oceans, and climbed its mountains, and sailed its seas, and here I am back again, right where it all began. Only this time, I have real worries and fears, not the silly boyhood problems I had then.

I feel a cold sprinkle of water hit my naked chest, and I'm momentarily frozen, with my eyes glued shut. I have to remind myself that Red is no longer a bully and that I'm no longer a victim. I open my eyes and sit up and see Bill, the lifeguard, crouched in front of me, scooping another handful of water from a retreating wave. He sees me and grins, letting the water drip between his open fingers.

"Thought I was going to have to chase for my bucket to wake you up," he says. "You always did sleep like a stone."

"I wasn't sleeping," I reply.

"Well, that'd be a first," he says. "Didn't they used to bury you to your neck in sand while you slept? Who's your friend?"

"This is Jimmy."

Bill reaches out and shakes Jimmy's hand. "Nice to meet you, Jimmy. What's that thing on your ankle there?"

"Oh, that?" Jimmy asks. "It's jus' a thing, you know."

"It's something people wear up at the foundation," I say. "Like a monitor that warns you when the air is too thin."

"Oh," Bill says, nodding, "I see. And why do you have the Foundation's emblem carved onto your chest? Is that just something they do up there too?"

I look down and realize that my scars are bright red in the UV lights. There's a perfect upside down valknut there, carved in my flesh halfway around the globe by a five-hundred-year-old descendant of Dr. Radcliffe. This descendant had since been vaporized, along with the entire island and our fox. Maybe I should just tell Bill the truth—but he'd never believe it.

"That's just . . . well; it's from an accident with a thing I was doing. A misunderstanding, really. It's still healing."

Bill shakes his head. "Looks painful, whatever it is. Listen, I heard your speech today in the square."

"You did? What did you think?"

He scoops up a handful of sand and lets it fall between his fingers, thinking over his answer. The pause makes me nervous.

"I thought it was convincing," he finally says.

Convincing? What does that mean? I want to ask him, but before I can say anything, he stands and says:

"Anyway, I came over to let you know that we're shutting down rec time so that everyone can meet back in the square."

"What meeting?" I ask, standing up and brushing the sand

off my shorts. "Are we invited?"

"I don't see why not," he says. Then he looks me over and adds, "Man, they must have you lifting the drones off the trains by hand up there. You sure are bigger than when you left."

I feel my chest swell a little with pride.

Then he says, "Nice to meet you, Jimmy," nods goodbye, and jogs off to shut down the illusionary beach.

As Jimmy and I walk toward the locker rooms, the sun clicks off, the waves disappear, and the blue sky goes gray. We enter the shower together and shut the door. Jimmy follows my lead and strips off his shorts and stuffs them with mine in the hamper. Then we raise our arms and wait for the blast of hot water, looking like a couple of naked and surrendering refugees being washed down before being admitted into civilization.

Dry and clean, we don our zipsuits again and head for the lift to the valley. There's a crowd gathering again in the square, so we duck behind buildings and work our way up to where we can watch from the safety of a breezeway. After several minutes waiting, Mrs. Hightower steps to the microphone.

"Welcome, Level 3 residents and those watching below."

I nudge Jimmy and whisper, "They must be streaming this to the other levels as well."

"After Aubrey's speech today," Mrs. Hightower continues, "I confirmed with the Foundation everything he said. Eden will be back online within the week if we begin sending up supplies again. You've been called here to vote, since it was a vote that put us all on strike in the first place. I'd encourage you to think about your fellows who are already overdue for retirement, and of yourselves, and the implications more delays might have on your own retirement plans."

"Why is she lying?" I ask.

"I dunno," Jimmy says. "I told you I dun' trust her."

"You can bet I'm going to ask her tonight," I reply.

"So," Mrs. Hightower says, "all those in favor of ending this silly strike and returning to business as usual, please raise your hands now."

She steps back from the microphone and is the first to raise her hand high. Another hand goes up in the crowd. Then another. And another. Then, almost all at once, every hand in the place rises until the crowd assembled there in the square looks like some underground army returning the salute of their giant queen standing tall before them.

"I'll be damned," I mumble. "They bought my lies."

CHAPTER 9
A Midnight Meeting

The knock comes softly on the door at exactly midnight.

I toss the ball to Jimmy one final time, concluding our long game of catch, and rise to answer it.

When I open the door, a hooded stranger stands with his or her back to the door, looking nervously left and right. When this visitor turns to face me, I'm shocked to see that it's Bill.

"What are you doing here, Bill?"

"There's no time for that now," he says. "You have to follow me. Fast and quiet. No talking, no questions. Got that?"

I nod that I do.

"Do you have something to cover your face with?"

"I have an old hoody upstairs."

"Grab it," he says.

"What about Jimmy?"

"He's fine; nobody will recognize him."

Leaving him at the open door, I race upstairs and grab my gray hoody and pull it on. Then I check to make sure I have my father's pipe in my pocket before heading back down.

"You ready for this, Jimmy?" I ask.

"As ready as I'm gonna get," he says.

"Okay, let's do it."

We leave the apartment and follow Bill across the dark valley. I have a strange feeling that this may be it for me, that I may never be coming back here again. I pull my hood lower over my face and walk beside Jimmy, my steps rhyming his.

Wherever we're going, at least we're going there together.

Bill leads us to the elevator platform and swipes his card to open the door. We step inside and ascend to the transfer station on Level 2. When the elevator stops we all three suck in the disinfectant gas like pros and wait for the door to open.

The transfer station is empty, the dim lights casting the waiting train in shadow, but Bill doesn't lead us to the train like I expect him to. Instead, he steps into the waiting elevator right next to the one we just got off.

"Doesn't this elevator go to Level 4?" I ask.

Bill glares at me and draws his hand across his neck, telling me to be quiet. I look at Jimmy, but he just shrugs.

The ride down to Level 4 takes longer than the ride up from Level 3 did, and by the time the elevator finally stops, I've almost forgotten about the gas. It eventually clears and the door opens. Bill pops his head out, looks left and right, and then motions for us to follow as he exits the elevator.

Nothing I thought I knew about Level 4 prepared me for what it actually looks like. The platform is elevated enough to provide me with a sweeping view of the enormous cavern, although not quite as large as Level 3, illuminated by countless LED light strips hanging from the high, curved ceiling. There are so many lights that even though they're turned down for rest hours, it's almost as bright as being in the daylight, above. Every inch of polished floor is organized into manufacturing assembly lines, and enormous 3-D printers are unattended and working on their own. I see the nose cone for a flying drone taking shape in one, giant fan blades for our cooling systems being printed in another, and other various indistinguishable parts and pieces being honed and polished and packaged. But what strikes me as the most strange about the setup are the living quarters. They are all windowless and entered by porthole doors off of catwalks that circle the entire perimeter and rise to the ceiling. They are built into the walls, I'm assuming, in order to maximize available workspace below.

I lag behind Jimmy and Bill and take all of this in as we descend an open flight of stairs to the production floor. It's an eerie feeling, being surrounded by autonomous machines as we hurry across the facility in the strange, shadowless light that seems to come from nowhere and everywhere at once.

At the far side of the cavern, Bill leads us up steel stairs to a wall of duct vents where giant turbine fans blast cool air into the level. Bill stops in front of one of the fans. The circular opening is twice as tall as he is, and the spinning fan is protected by a cage. I momentarily forget that I'm not supposed to talk, but it doesn't matter because the blast of cool wind is so strong here that when I open my mouth, it fills with air and my cheeks flutter and flap. I feel like some kind of flatulent idiot.

Bill presses his palm to a glass plate in the wall next to the fan, and a door in the steel grate slides open. The fan blades whirl just on the other side, spinning so fast that I can clearly glimpse the dim tunnel beyond. Bill turns and gathers Jimmy and me into his arms in a kind of huddle.

"Listen up," he says, his voice just barely audible above the wind. "When the fan stops, you've got to pass through quickly. No hesitating, understand?"

We nod that we do.

With no further instruction, he steps inside the steel cage and we follow. The door closes behind us, and we stand in a narrow breezeway, being blasted with cold air. The fan blades are spinning so close that if I reached out my hand, it would surely be hacked off instantly and blown back into my face.

The fan comes to an immediate halt. Bill ducks between the blades without a word and disappears on the other side. Jimmy follows. I don't know why, but I'm gripped with fear. I inch toward the crack between the two blades where the others passed, leaning down to look, but hesitating. Strong hands reach up, wrap around my throat, and jerk me through. The blades take off again full speed, catching my foot and sending my amputated shoe hurling back the way we came. I hear it thud against the steel cage. Jimmy releases his hands from my neck, and we both look back with horror to see if my foot is gone with my shoe. But it's still there, thankfully. Bill just shakes his head. I kick off my other shoe and carry it in my hand as I follow them barefoot down the windy tunnel.

The tunnel terminates at a large, vertical shaft into which Bill seems to disappear without a trace. Jimmy and I lean out over the edge and see him clinging to a ladder. There is no light in the shaft itself, but other intersecting ducts cut descending beams of light across its never-ending void. It seems to plunge to the center of the Earth itself.

"No way am I getting on that ladder," I shout.

"You had better," Bill shouts back, "because there isn't any going back, unless you want to join what's left of your shoe by being sucked through the fan."

That said he starts climbing down.

"We've climbed tougher stuff," Jimmy says, swinging out into the void and grabbing onto the ladder.

I stuff my remaining shoe as far as it will fit in my zipsuit pocket and follow after him. We climb down, one rung at a time, into almost absolute blackness, with only the distant wands of light crossing from ducts above. My hands grow tired; my legs grow shaky. I'm certain that only the cool air rushing past us keeps my fingers from sweating and sliding off the rungs. We climb in silence, the wind whistling through the ducts all around us, only my wild thoughts of falling to mark the passage of time.

"Hey! Where you going?"

Bill calls to us from a ledge that we were about to pass. Jimmy takes Bill's offered hand and steps off the ladder onto the ledge. Then Jimmy turns and offers me his hand, and I do the same. Bill leads us deeper into the dark recesses of the ledge, my bare feet stepping in something wet. I smell some kind of metallic element, maybe iron, maybe rust, and then I hear the screech of metal on metal, and a door opens. We're washed in yellow light.

A small gathering of people greets us with nervous stares as we enter the room. They're sitting at a worktable surrounded by tools. There's an old, vinyl, blueprint map of ducts and tunnels plastered to the wall behind them, its corners worn and peeling past the concrete nails that hold it in place. The only face I recognize is Mrs. Hightower, so I'm guessing the three others are from different levels.

Bill motions Jimmy and me to overturned metal drums that wait unoccupied, and we join the others at the table.

"No problems at all getting down here, I'm assuming," Mrs. Hightower says.

Bill glances at the shoe sticking out of my pocket and chuckles. "No, not really," he says. Then he turns his attention to a man sitting next to Mrs. Hightower and asks, "Are our friends ready for us, just in case?"

The man nods. He must work in Agriculture on Level 5, or maybe Sewage Treatment on Level 6, because his calloused hands are resting on the table, and he's wearing a trimmed beard. All the men on Level 3 are clean shaven. A small man sits next to him, twirling his thumbs nervously. On the other side of Mrs. Hightower sits a woman wearing glasses, which is also strange because everyone on Level 3 has perfect eyesight— at least until 35 when we retire.

"What are the odds they'll make it?" Mrs. Hightower asks the bearded man.

He shrugs. "Fifty, fifty. Maybe more. Who knows? Better than the odds of letting them go back up, I think."

"I disagree," the little man says, twirling his thumbs faster, as if it were some kind of nervous tic. "It's all too risky."

"What about you, Jillian?" Mrs. Hightower asks.

Jillian removes her glasses, closes her eyes, and pinches the bridge of her nose, as if puzzling over an impossible problem. Then she opens her eyes and addresses the table. "I think we have to go for it while we have the chance. It's just too risky to let Aubrey go back up now."

"What do you say, Bill?" Mrs. Hightower asks.

"Hey, now!" I jump in before Bill can respond. "Wait just a minute. What are we voting on here? And why are you talking about me as if I weren't sitting right in front of you?"

Mrs. Hightower looks from me to Bill. "You want to tell him, Bill, or should I?"

"You go ahead," Bill replies.

Mrs. Hightower sighs loudly, as if what she's about to say

is a chore. "Aubrey, when you go back up to the Foundation, Hannah intends to kill you."

Jimmy looks at me and raises an eyebrow, his expression mixed with worry and I-told-you-so.

"How do you know about Hannah?" I ask.

"We know all kinds of things," Mrs. Hightower says.

"So you know about the . . ." I stop myself, not sure yet that I can really trust them.

"The serum?" Mrs. Hightower asks.

"Yes, the serum. You know about it?"

"Of course, we do. And no. None of us has it. Do you?"

I look at Jimmy, but he doesn't move to answer or give me any clue what he's thinking.

"No, we don't have it," I say, lying.

"But Hannah has taken it, hasn't she?" Jillian asks, leaning forward and looking suddenly interested.

"Yes," I reply, "she has."

"Does she have any serum left?"

"I don't know. Why?"

"Let's keep this on topic," Mrs. Hightower says, casting a glance at Jillian. "If you want to talk about the serum, you'll have to talk to the Chief."

"Fine," Jillian says, crossing her arms unhappily.

"Let's assume you're right," I say, "and Hannah intends to kill me. What I want to know is how you know about Hannah and about Eden being a sham and why it is that you pulled me off that stage before I could tell the people the truth."

"You were going to tell them what you think is the truth," Mrs. Hightower says, "but thinking it doesn't make it so."

"If that's the case," I say, "then you tell me the truth."

"That's not always so easy," she replies. "I'm not so sure how much of it you're ready for. Sometimes the truth has to be fed to people in small doses."

"Ain't that jus' the same as lyin'?" Jimmy chimes in.

"He makes a good point," Bill says.

"Who's he. anyway?" the nervous man asks. "I wasn't told anyone was coming besides Aubrey."

"Relax, Roger," Mrs. Hightower tells him. "They're both in this together."

"Please!" I shout, slamming my fist on the table. "For the love of Eden, tell me what it is you're all talking about."

"Just tell him already," Bill says.

"Fine," Mrs. Hightower replies. "I'll tell you what I can. First, Hannah isn't exactly who you think she is."

"Well, who is she then?" I ask, when she pauses.

"She's twice your age, for starters."

"Twice my age?"

"Almost, yes. She's my age. She's thirty."

What she says doesn't make any sense. Hannah, twice my age? No way. I'm beginning to believe that maybe these people aren't altogether with it; that perhaps they've been infected with something themselves and are going a bit batty. In fact, the way the nervous man keeps twiddling his thumbs I'm sure of it.

"What do you mean she's thirty?" I ask, once I'm over the shock. "That's impossible."

"No it isn't," Mrs. Hightower says. "I'm sure she told you she was sixteen, but she's thirty."

"She doesn't look thirty."

"Neither would any of us if Dr. Radcliffe had slowed our development with hormone blockers."

"Okay, fine," I say, "but I met Gloria, the surrogate who gave birth to her. So did Jimmy here. Didn't you, Jimmy?"

Jimmy nods.

"And how old is she?" Mrs. Hightower asks.

"She's dead now," I say.

"Well, how old was she?"

"I don't know," I reply. "I hadn't seen anyone older than thirty-five before I went up top. I know she was older than any of you. Maybe she was fifty."

Mrs. Hightower raises her eyebrows. "And she would have given birth to Hannah when she was nineteen, so add Hannah's thirty years and you've got Gloria's age, don't you see?"

What she's saying is crazy. She has to be wrong.

"Why would they lie?" I ask. "Tell me that. Why would Hannah say she was sixteen if she's thirty?"

"Because Radcliffe kept her young and waiting for you, and she had no choice but to go along with it. At least she didn't have a choice until now."

"Jimmy, does this make any sense to you?"

Jimmy shakes his head. "Ain't none of this ever made no sense to me, though."

"She's telling you the truth," Bill says. "The Radcliffes had Hannah thirty years ago, but Dr. Radcliffe wanted a boy to turn the Park Service over to."

As soon as he says it, I remember Dr. Radcliffe telling me that he couldn't trust a mother to make the logical choice when it came to his doomsday mass suicide. Maybe they're not lying.

"Radcliffe was a male chauvinist and a murderer," Jillian says. "Makes me sick just to hear his name."

"What's a chauvinist?" Jimmy asks.

"I don't know," I say.

"It doesn't matter," Mrs. Hightower says. "What matters is that he made her wait for you, and she resented it. Then, when you came and overthrew him instead of going along, Hannah saw her chance to take control, and now she's taken it."

"Even if you're telling us the truth," I say, deciding to at least play along, "where do all of you fit in?"

"We've dedicated our lives to the cause."

"Okay, great. But what cause?"

"Protecting you first," she says. "Overthrowing the Park Service second."

"But why? How? I just don't understand any of this. If you all are against the Park Service, if you know what the hell's happening up there, then why did you stop me from telling the people in the square today the truth about Eden? And why are you telling them to go back to business as usual? Why are you sending retirees up to be slaughtered?"

"Because it isn't time to tell them otherwise just yet," Mrs. Hightower says. "They're not ready. We're not ready."

"No, it's much too soon," Roger adds, nervously.

"Why aren't you ready?" I ask.

"Because things aren't yet in place," Bill offers. "Hannah could flood us all out with the flip of a switch. And she would if she thought we were attempting to break free."

"So what's your plan then?"

I look from face to face, waiting for an answer, but they all avoid my eyes and look to Mrs. Hightower.

"Our plan is to tunnel out," she says. "And we've been working on it for years. We knew Radcliffe and the others were getting sick, and we knew he was putting his hope in you. So our primary mission was to help the Chief rescue you, to keep you from Radcliffe, but that didn't work quite the way we had planned, as you well know."

"No," I say, "I don't know. Rescue me when?"

"The train crash," Mrs. Hightower says, as if it should be obvious. "We planned that derailment. The Chief set explosives to drop the boulders and block the train from going through. You were supposed to be rescued and taken away that day. But not everything went as planned." She pauses to look at the bearded man and he bows his head. "Anyway," she continues, "after the crash the Chief assumed you must have been killed."

"Who is this Chief?"

"It doesn't matter right now," she says.

"You just told me he planned the train crash that almost killed me," I say. "It matters to me."

"We didn't have any better option."

I look at Jimmy and shake my head. "I'm so confused."

"Me too," he says.

"So you have tunnelrats on your side?" I ask.

"A few, yes," she replies.

"So they spy for you then? Is that how you know what Hannah's up to at the Foundation?"

"Yes. We had another scientist on the inside, but we lost all communication with him. We found out later that that was because of the flood you triggered that killed Radcliffe."

"I didn't trigger it," I say.

"Then who did?"

"Mrs. Radcliffe."

"Well, why am I not surprised?" Jillian says, as if I've just validated some belief she had long held.

"Whoever triggered it," Mrs. Hightower goes on, "we were in the dark after until Hannah called the tunnelrats up to help her repair Eden. Then we got word from our spies. That's why we used Red's mistaken message to his girlfriend and the delayed retirements to orchestrate the strike."

"Wait. You orchestrated the strike?"

"Of course, we did."

"Then why did you lie to the people to stop it?"

"Because it had served its purpose," Mrs. Hightower says.

"Okay, call me stupid," I say, "but exactly what purpose would that be?"

"To get Hannah to send you down to us."

"To get me here? In Holocene II? This was your plan?"

"That's right," Mrs. Hightower says.

"But why then?" I ask. "Please. Someone. Anyone. Tell me why. Why me? Why all of this over me? The train crash—the botched escape—Dr. Radcliffe—Hannah—this fake strike—this sneaking away in the night—why? All because I scored well on some stupid test?"

Mrs. Hightower shakes her head.

"Why are you shaking your head no?" I ask.

"Because none of this has anything to do with that test."

"But you said it yourself when the results were announced, before I left Level 3 for the Foundation. And Radcliffe said the same thing when I finally arrived. A perfect score. Isn't that what everyone said? I was the first perfect score."

Mrs. Hightower laughs a little.

"It's not funny," I say. "Tell me."

"That test was rigged," she says. "I'm not even sure how well you really did, and it doesn't matter."

"It doesn't matter?" I ask.

"No. You were going up no matter what."

"I was?"

"Yes," she says, "you were."

"But why then? Why me?"

"Because you aren't who you think you are either."

"I'm not?"

"No."

"I suppose now you're going to tell me I'm thirty too."

"Don't be ridiculous," she says.

"Then how am I not who I think I am?"

"You're just not."

I look around the room at the six pairs of eyes staring back at me. They seem strange and aloof and oddly at home here in this hidden room, tucked away in the walls of some stupid shaft, kilometers underground. Well, all except Jimmy.

"I know who I am," I say. "You're all crazy."

"We're not crazy," Mrs. Hightower says. "You'll eventually understand yourself."

"I know who I am," I repeat. "Bill, tell them. You watched me grow up. Go ahead. Tell them."

"It's not how you think," Bill says. "Not really."

"Yes, it is. I know exactly who I am."

"I told you that you weren't ready yet for the whole truth," Mrs. Hightower says. "Maybe you will be by the time you get there. Assuming you make it, that is."

"By the time I get where?"

"To see the Chief."

"And where's that?" I ask.

She smiles. "China."

CHAPTER 10
The Other Side

"China? As in all the way to East Asia?"

"Yes, that's right," Mrs. Hightower says. "I remember that you always were interested in pre-War geography. The Chief is waiting for you there, and you've got to leave right now."

The bearded man stands from the table and steps over to the map on the wall. He points to a series of tunnels stretching south from Holocene II and speaks to us over his shoulder.

"You can hitch a ride with friendly rats here in the south tunnels. They'll take you as far as the Yucatan mines. It's risky, but I think they can breach you to the surface there. We had hoped to get closer to the landing site, but we haven't had time, so you'll have to hike it."

"I don't understand something," I say. "If we want to get to the surface, why don't we just follow these shafts up? I mean, the cool air has to come from somewhere, right?"

Roger stops twiddling his thumbs long enough to laugh at me. Mrs. Hightower reaches over and slaps his hand.

Bill says, "Give him a break, Roger. He doesn't know."

The man with the beard answers my question: "The shafts don't' actually go to the surface, son. They only go as far as deep aquifers, where exchangers dissipate the heat into bedrock and liquid, pumping down cool air. You have to remember that this whole place was designed to be autonomous from the exterior atmosphere, even producing its own oxygen."

"Okay, then," I say, "but why not ride the train up to the

Foundation and just physically take over from Hannah?"

"Another good question," Bill says. "He is a smart kid."

"Maybe," Roger replies, "but we don't have time to sit here and humor him."

"Quit being so rude, Roger," Jillian says. "And remember who it is you're talking to."

Mrs. Hightower shuts them up with a glance.

"As you can see, boys, we're a little like a dysfunctional family here." Then she turns to me and says, "We can't go up and overpower Hannah because she has to approve every train and its cargo. That, and even if we did sneak up on her, don't think there aren't safeguards to flood everyone down here. You saw yourself what Radcliffe had with the wave."

"Why can't you just bore a way out?" I ask. "I mean, if you have tunnelrats on your side?"

"We've been working with our tunnelrats for years to do just exactly that," she says. "But we're just near to penetrating the surface now. The Foundation keeps a leash on subterrenes, and we've had to pretend to be going after precious silver—which we use for all sorts of things, including the electronics and optics in drones—to even get permission from them to get as close to the surface as we have."

"That's right," Bill adds. "And now that your flood left fewer scientists up there to monitor things, the time is right to make an opening."

"So you're going to sneak us three thousand kilometers south in tunnels and then somehow get us from there to East Asia? And what will Hannah do when we don't return?"

"We already thought of that," Mrs. Hightower says. "We plan to tell Hannah and company that you died trying to escape in one of these air shafts."

"Now I get it," I say. "And she can't even investigate. And, of course, the professor can't come down either. He's too old. Everyone would wonder why he isn't in Eden."

Mrs. Hightower smiles. "Maybe you did score well on that test after all, young man. You're very smart.

"But you don't think she'll be suspicious and retaliate?"

"Why would she? You gave your speech, we're happy and sending up supplies for her so she can go on killing humans, and the retirees are lining up, begging to be rendered into Eden. There's no logical reason to harm Holocene II, and Hannah's nothing if she isn't logical."

"Okay, but then what do we do? When we get to China?"

"You'll have to discuss that with the Chief when you get there," Mrs. Hightower says. Then she stands from the table and adds, "Now we had better get going."

I stand with the others, but Jimmy stays seated.

"I can't go," he says, shaking his head.

"Why not?" Mrs. Hightower asks.

Jimmy hikes up his pant leg and lifts his foot up onto the table, the ankle bracelet clanking loudly on its metal surface.

"Oh, no," I say, just now remembering.

"What's that?" Bill asks.

"Some sick trick of the professor's," I say. "He said if we weren't back in seven days, it will detonate."

"Like a bomb?" Roger asks, edging himself behind Mrs. Hightower as if to use her as a shield against a possible blast.

Jillian steps up and inspects the bracelet, feeling all the way around it, as if her delicate fingers themselves were eyes.

"He didn't design this himself," she says. "We had made

similar devices to keep tunnelrats from straying too far. Radio-frequency identification deprograms it at the Foundation."

"The professor said he could detonate it remotely," I say.

"Well, he lied about that," she replies. "We're much too deep and far away for any signal to reach it. I could remove it fairly easily, but it has a pulse regulator, which means as soon as it registers a few missed heartbeats, it will detonate."

"Could we take it off and toss it really quickly?" I ask. "Maybe down the shaft?"

"This thing could easily destroy any one of these shafts. You'd need some kind of quick containment system and we don't have any time to build that."

Mrs. Hightower sighs. "It looks like you'll have to go on alone, Aubrey. Jimmy can buy you some time and return to the Foundation just before his seven days are up."

I cross my arms. "No way. Jimmy doesn't go, I don't go."

"I'm fine with stayin'," Jimmy says. "Really, Aubrey. This is your chance to get away."

"I'm not leaving without you, Jimmy. Period."

The man with the beard steps over and takes a look at it. "What if you take it off of him and put it on me?"

Jillian pauses, considering his idea. "That might just work," she says. "If we do it really fast."

"How would it be deprogrammed once it's on you?" I ask.

"Hell," he says, "I'm a week past due for retirement. Now that the strike's over, I guess I'll just go up with the train and say I woke up with it on me. Make like you did it."

"Wait a minute," I say, "you're going up to retire?"

He nods. "I'm five years older than these other youngsters here," he says. "My time's up."

"But you know that Eden's a sham, right?"

"I know it," he says. "But we all die sometime."

"And it's an honorable thing to do," Mrs. Hightower says. Then she turns to Jillian. "Now let's get this bracelet off of Jimmy so they can get started on their journey."

Jillian moves into action and has Jimmy and the bearded man lie next to one another atop the table, shoulder to shoulder, leg to leg. Then she hunts around the room and brings back a collection of tools to meticulously work the lock on the bracelet.

Jimmy turns to look at the man lying next to him and asks, "What's your name?"

The man looks back at Jimmy. "What's that?"

"You's the only one whose name I ain't heard yet, and I jus' feel like I should know it, since you's takin' my fate."

"Oh," the man says. "I'm Seth."

I expect Jimmy might thank him, or say something else, but he only nods and looks back up at the ceiling.

When Jillian frees the lock, we all stand back and hold our breath while she makes the switch. She presses a finger to Jimmy's thigh and feels his pulse, waiting with her other hand on the unlocked bracelet. Then, with a fluid motion, she slips the bracelet off Jimmy and onto Seth. The bracelet locks with an audible click, and all in the room collectively sigh.

"So that's solved," Mrs. Hightower says. "Now let's get moving. I've covered for Bill on Level 3, so he's going to escort Aubrey and Jimmy out. Seth, you see them all as far as the tunnelrats' den, since you're on your way back to Agri. Jillian and I will head up together through the vents in Engineering."

"What about me?" Roger asks, still twiddling his thumbs.

"Oh, sorry, Roger," Mrs. Hightower says. "I forgot about you. You accompany Bill and the boys."

"Me?" he asks. "Going to the surface?"

"Yes, you," she says. "We can't have Bill going it alone."

"I couldn't possibly," he says, shaking his head.

Mrs. Hightower looks at him like a teacher admonishing a spoiled student. "Don't be silly or selfish, Roger. You know all those horror stories we grow up learning about the surface are just that—stories. Right? It's probably a paradise up there, and nothing to harm you at all. Isn't it, boys?"

I'm tempted to mention bears and parasites and sunburn, maybe even sharks and drones too, but I look at poor Roger, twiddling his thumbs faster than ever, and I just nod.

We say goodbye to Mrs. Hightower and to Jillian at the ladder. Jillian's farewell is formal and aloof, but Mrs. Hightower actually takes my hand and kisses it, wishing me good luck. Then we watch them climb into the windy dark, heading back up to their levels. I turn away from them, ready for our own climb down, but Seth hauls forth a heavy bundle of rope and heaves it into the void. It spirals and snakes down into the darkness. He repeats the exercise with a second rope.

"Why aren't we just taking the ladder?" I ask.

"Way too far," Seth says. "You lose your grip, and you're ground algaeburger when you hit the turbines down below. We rap-jump down. Usually Jillian waits to pull the ropes in before she heads up, but we're running late tonight."

Jimmy grabs one of the ropes and wraps it in loops around his body, stepping up toward the edge, ready to rappel.

"Looks like you've done this before," Bill says.

"My pa and me used to drop down cliffs for bird eggs,"

Jimmy replies, looking proud.

"Well, step out of that there rope, young man," Seth says, handing us each a harness. "We've got better equipment here that will keep you from using your crotch as a friction break."

I follow Seth's lead and slip into the harness, buckling it and pulling it tight. Bill has his secured in seconds, but Roger seems to struggle. When we're all harnessed in, Seth shows us how to attach our harnesses to the rope and use the hand brake to lower ourselves down. Then he disappears into the shaft. Bill goes next on the other rope, and Roger goes after him.

"You sure this will hold?" I ask Jimmy, now that we're alone on the ledge.

"I dunno," he says, "but they dun' seem worried."

Then he's gone too.

I back up to the edge, lean back, and lower myself off into the shaft. The harness bites into my legs some, but otherwise it's a secure and relatively weightless descent. As I drop farther into the windy shaft, the rope disappears above me until it seems as though I'm climbing down the very darkness itself—deeper and deeper, heading in the wrong direction, if you ask me. I drop for a long time before there's a tug on the rope below, and I'm pulled toward the wall of the shaft, and a strong hand yanks me into another intersecting duct, this one with no lights—just a pitch black wormhole in the middle of the Earth. I hear clinking buckles as everyone gets free of their harnesses.

"Make sure you leave them clipped to the rope," Bill's voice says next to me in the dark. "There. Good. Everyone ready? There are a lot of twists and turns down here, so we link up and hold hands. Here, take mine, Aubrey. And grab Jimmy's with your other. Okay, let's go. Steady and slow."

We walk off together into the blackness, hand in hand like a chain of children being led to some secret fort you can only get to by trust. My shaved head is tickled by alternating gusts of wind that tell me we're passing other ducts or fissures into even deeper voids. As we twist and turn and wind our way slowly forward, I'm painfully aware of how vulnerable I am here in this subterranean underworld with no sight and nothing to guide me but the hand pulling me ahead. Jimmy must feel it too, because he squeezes my hand in his as if it were the only thing connecting him to life.

Finally, the heads of the men in front of me are silhouetted against a growing blue light. Eventually, it engulfs the entire tunnel until we're all standing in the wash of its melancholy glow and looking out from a raised vent onto the growing fields below. I've never seen so many lights, mirrors, and plants. The plants are packed together on shelves with the light reflecting through them in some kaleidoscopic trickery that makes the shelves themselves seem illuminated. Beyond the racks of plants are algae tanks, also glowing blue.

"Wow," Jimmy says, eyeing the operation. "It's like an underground garden."

"Where do you all live?" I ask.

"Oh, Level 5 isn't like your cavern," Seth says. "It's comprised of many smaller wings, if you will. That way we can create different conditions for different cycles of plants. Our living quarters are north of here, but we'll be heading south."

"And we had better get hurrying that way, Seth," Bill says. "You've still got to get back in time."

"Maybe I should stay behind with Seth," Roger suggests.

"If I had my way, Roger," Bill says, "I'd have left you

behind up there. But you heard Hightower. Now let's go."

We climb down from the vent and weave our way through the towering racks of plants, walking on elevated metal walks built above some kind of drainage field. We're still among them when a fine mist begins to rain down, soaking the plants and us with them. We walk beneath the arch of a monochrome rainbow until we leave it and the plants behind to descend onto a stone path. As the others walk ahead, Jimmy grabs my elbow and slows me until we're lagging several meters behind.

"Whaddya think of all this?" he asks in a whisper.

"I'm not sure," I say. "It's all happened so fast."

"I know it," he says. "But dun' let all this talk about how you ain't who you are get ya down. I know who you are."

"Thanks, Jimmy. I just wish we knew for sure if we could trust them or not."

"Me too," he says, "but I guess we ain't got no choice."

"No, I guess we don't."

"Hey," he adds, a minute or so later, "I meant to ask you somethin' back there, but I didn't wanna sound stupid."

"Sure, what is it?"

"Where's China?"

"It's a long ways away," I say.

"Like as far as we went to the Isle of Man."

"Even farther."

The path eventually leads us to a long, narrow cavern lined with piles of sand and clay and other minerals for mixing and making soils. We pass several large machines sitting idle against the walls. On the far end of the cavern, giant steel doors stand closed, and as we approach them, they loom above us like the forgotten entrance to some long extinct race of giants.

Seth punches a code into a keypad on the wall, and the doors groan and rumble as they swing slowly inward, revealing an enormous hidden den, its countless openings glowing a dim and hellish kind of red. Piles of waste and junk rise like some subterranean dump, nearly touching the ceiling of the cave. Tunneled paths lead into and out of these piles as if it were a huge hill built for a colony of ants the size of people.

"I'll say goodbye to you all here," Seth says. "Good luck out there. All of you."

Jimmy turns and shakes Seth's hand. He says, "I'll never forget what you done for me, mister."

Seth nods solemnly, not bothering to lie and say that it's no big deal. Then he turns to Bill and they embrace. The look on Bill's face makes it clear that they've been more brothers than friends, and that this will be their last farewell.

"I'll see you on the other side, if there is one," Bill says.

Seth forces a smile. "Just promise me when we win, which we will, that you'll pull the plug on Eden and let me rest."

Bill nods that he will and then steps aside so Roger can say goodbye. Their farewell is less personal, just a quick hug and a promise to take care. Lastly, Seth turns to me and I feel like I should say something, but I don't know what. He smiles as if he understands. Then he looks at my bare feet, strips off his own shoes, and hands them to me.

"I won't be needing these where I'm going," he jokes.

I watch him walk away, trudging past the piles of earth and the idle machines on his way home for the short time he has left there. Then Bill punches a code into the wall, the giant doors swing closed, and we're on the other side.

CHAPTER 11
Subterrenes and Strange Dreams

When we enter the tunnelrat den, I notice the smell first.

Dried urine, or maybe decades of dried sweat.

Bill leads the way, with Roger close on his heels, and the pathway we walk is illuminated by intermittent red lanterns that are set out on stands, as if to be always ready for relocation as the tunnels change shape. The walls are made of earth, old machine parts, and bits of synthetic fabric all laid long ago to waste. I recognize some ancient cracked and broken reading slates amidst the rubble. There is even an earlier generation zipsuit with the original Foundation crest looking cartoonlike on its faded breast. Here we are, walking inside a time capsule of our nine hundred years living underground. Jimmy looks with great interest at these artifacts, and I can't help but think that he's reminded of his own cave of treasures by the cove.

Soon boisterous grunts and bellows echo through the maze, and then the tunnel opens abruptly onto a large den where the strangest sight I've ever seen lies before us like some nightmare painting come to life. Several behemoth tunnelrat mothers, too large to ever exit the tunnel we've just passed through, sprawl on junk-piled beds. They are nursing countless infant tunnelrats, hairless and helpless and squirming blindly against one another to get at their milk. Other young tunnelrats lie slumped drunkenly against the walls, sucking on bottles. One particularly plump mother opens a large, milky eye and watches us cross the den with only the mildest interest.

Another tunnel leads us away from the den. Just as the squealing noise fades completely into the maze behind us, we step out onto a platform where a subterrene idles, its glowing nosecone pointed toward a wall of openings that might lead to any number of deep and dangerous mines. A tunnelrat leans against the contraption, feverishly smoking some kind of tiny cigarette. It sees us, drops the cigarette, and stomps it out with its bare foot.

"Where ye been now, where ye been?" the tunnelrat asks, opening the subterrene hatch and waving us aboard.

"Sorry if we're late," Bill says. "We really appreciate this."

"In ye go now, in ye go."

Once inside the subterrene, we take our seats and buckle in for the ride. Bill opens a cubby and produces lunch rations and passes them around. Jimmy and I swig our water and tear into our food, realizing just how long it's been since we've eaten anything. Roger sits across from us, picking at his, a sour look on his face as if someone had purposely prepared him his least favorite food. Bill consults the tunnelrat at the controls.

"Hey, Roger," I say. "You ever ridden in one of these?" When he shakes his head no, I continue, "Well, we have, and if your stomach comes out of your mouth, be sure not to bite down on it. Just swallow it again and you'll be fine."

Roger sets his ration aside and begins feverishly twiddling his thumbs. Jimmy elbows me in the ribs, but he still laughs.

Eventually, Bill buckles in next to Roger, the tunnelrat winds up the subterrene, and we shoot off into the tunnels like some underground missile launched from a slingshot. As the initial inertia of its acceleration wears off, we settle into a smooth ride, lifting softly up and falling softly down, arcing gently left and gently right, as if winding our way through an underground amusement park like I read about growing up.

The tunnelrat takes its seat next to Jimmy.

"How fast does this thin' go?" Jimmy asks.

"Thousan' kilometers an hour now," the tunnelrat says, "thousan' kilometers an hour." Then it hauls a large bottle of milk from its pouch and begins drinking.

Sometime later, as we're all beginning to drift off to sleep, the tunnelrat gets up to check the controls. Jimmy nudges me and points to the milk bottle sitting in the tunnelrat's vacated seat. I shrug. Jimmy picks it up, wipes the nipple off with his sleeve, and raises it to his lips. He suckles fast and furious, his cheeks pumping as he mimics the baby tunnelrats we saw, and he looks so suddenly ridiculous that I have to fight back the giggles. When he sets it down again, he has milk on his chin.

"Not bad," he mouths silently.

The food in my belly and the motion of the speeding subterrene lulls me to sleep, and as I drift off I dream I'm being swallowed by a snake—

I'm being swallowed by a snake, and it's surprisingly comforting. The unhinged jaw stretches over my head and the throat of the serpent slides over me like a second skin, protecting me from the harsh realities of the world. I come to rest in the warmth of its stomach, our shapes entwined now as one. The digestive juices there begin their work, breaking down my fear and my identity until I know I will be absorbed into this creature that has no need to ponder the existence of stars, or its existence, or anything's existence—just a mindless, legless mouth, roaming the dark places and seeking out other beings to add to itself in a never-ending circle of life; mouth to tail, tail to mouth.

Jimmy is stoned when I wake. I rub the sleep from my

eyes and watch him.

He lurches about the subterrene, bouncing off the walls and laughing hysterically, as if listening to some private joke.

"What's wrong with him?" Bill asks.

"I don't know," I say. "Unless it's that milk he drank."

Bill leaps to his feet, grabs Jimmy, and settles him back into his seat. "Help me hold him, quick. Roger, see if there's any active charcoal in the first aid kit. Now, Roger! Hurry."

"What's the matter?" I ask.

"Fentanyl," Bill says. "That milk is laced with it."

I look at the tunnelrat sleeping soundly in its seat and say, "But the tunnelrat was sucking it down like nobody's business."

"Yeah, and he has been since he was born. Jimmy doesn't have any tolerance. Here, hand me that charcoal."

While Bill mixes the charcoal powder with the water in his ration bottle, Jimmy sways back and forth in his seat.

"Hold him upright," Bill says. "See if he can talk."

"He couldn't hardly talk before," Roger says.

"If you're not going to help," Bill snaps at him, "then sit down and shut up, Roger."

I try to get Jimmy to focus on me.

"Jimmy? Can you hear me, Jimmy?" His eyes open slightly and he smiles. "Well, he's not coherent," I say, "but he's in there somewhere."

Bill hands me the bottle of liquid charcoal. "You've got to get him to drink it himself. We can't risk him aspirating it."

I crouch down and look Jimmy in the eyes. His pupils are constricted to just tiny dots in his beautiful blue-gray irises.

"You need to drink this for me, Jimmy. Can you do that?"

"I dun' need no water," he slurs, pushing it away. "I need

some more milk."

"The milk is what got you into trouble in the first place."

"Milk, milk, milk," he mumbles. "Good for the tummy."

Then I get an idea. I step over and lift the milk bottle from the sleeping tunnelrat's hand. It stirs but doesn't wake. I twist off the top and pour the last of the milk onto the floor, rinsing the empty bottle with my water ration and dumping that out too. Then I pour the liquid charcoal into the bottle, screw the top back on, and hand it to Jimmy.

"Here, Jimmy. Drink this."

He clutches the bottle in both hands, tips his head back, and sucks it down. When he finishes, he smiles at us and drops the bottle on the floor. Then he closes his eyes and falls asleep.

"Will he be alright?" I ask.

"He should be," Bill says. "Just let him sleep it off now. The charcoal will help."

Four hours later we arrive at the Yucatan mines.

The tunnelrat wakes, as if responding to some internal alarm, and reaches for its bottle. When it finds that the bottle is empty, it seems momentarily puzzled before appearing to decide that it must have drank it itself. It slips the empty bottle into its pouch. Then it steps up to the controls and brings us in and slows the subterrene to a stop.

I reach over and shake Jimmy awake.

"What's the score?" he asks.

"The score?"

"Guess I was dreamin'," he replies. "We's playin' handball against Bree and Finn. Junior was yelpin' for us to win."

"That sounds like a good dream," I say.

He's a little wobbly yet when he stands, and the crooked

smile on his face tells me that he might be slightly stoned still, but he manages to walk without aid. We follow the tunnelrat out the open hatch with the rest of them.

The subterrene is stopped in an enormous cavern lit with the same red lights that were in the tunnelrats' den. The light doesn't reach the upper limits of the cavern, and the pillars of stone left to support the ceiling seem to rise up and disappear into the void above. The cavern wall in front of the subterrene is streaked with thick veins of silver that reflect the red light.

Jimmy seems not to notice how peculiar our surroundings are as he reaches into his pocket, pulls out the game ball that Finn gave him, and starts playing catch with himself.

"I don't like it here," Roger says.

"You think I do?" Bill replies. "We're here to do a job."

The tunnelrat grabs a chunk of silver off the ground, steps over to Jimmy, and thrusts it at him.

"Trade, now," it says. "Trade."

"What's that?" Jimmy asks.

"He wants to trade with you," Bill says. "For your ball."

"But I dun' wanna trade," Jimmy says.

The tunnelrat presses the silver against Jimmy's chest.

Jimmy pushes it away. "Forceful, ain't he?"

"Just trade with him for now," Bill says. "Something else will catch his eye and he'll drop it. Or else he'll forget why he even wanted it, and you can trade him back."

Jimmy shrugs and hands him the ball, taking the silver.

Bill walks us up to the wall and lays his open palm against the thick vein of silver there, bowing his head and closing his eyes for a moment, as if in prayer.

"So this is it," he says, turning to address the tunnelrat.

"This is really the way out?"

The tunnelrat nods. Then it notices another, larger hunk of silver on the ground and drops Jimmy's ball to pick it up. When I nudge Jimmy and point, he scurries over and snatches his abandoned ball off the ground.

"How far to the other side?" Bill asks.

"No more than three hundred meters now," the tunnelrat says. "Three hundred meters and no more."

"I think it's too risky," Roger says, twiddling his thumbs again. "Maybe we should go back."

Bill ignores Roger and turns to Jimmy and me and says, "You two have been out there. What should we expect?"

"It's nothing like they told us it was," I say. "It's clear skies and no ice, and the sun in the sky and everything. You'll be fine. You really will. Won't they, Jimmy?"

Jimmy's busy tossing his ball again. The tunnel rat notices, walks over, and thrusts the larger piece of silver at Jimmy.

"Shoot," Jimmy says. "This again?"

After the exchange, Jimmy has two hunks of silver and the tunnel rat has the ball again.

"Will you be able to keep it open?" Bill asks the tunnelrat.

The tunnelrat shrugs. "Not sure, now. Not sure."

As we return to the subterrene, Bill takes the silver hunks from Jimmy's hand and tosses them in the path in front of the tunnelrat. When the tunnelrat drops the ball and picks up the silver, Bill snatches the ball and hands it back to Jimmy.

"Now keep it in your pocket this time."

We pile back into the subterrene and close the hatch. The tunnelrat fires up the machine. It hits a switch and we rise on some kind of landing gear, or maybe traction belts, since we're leaving the tracks behind here. Then the machine whines loudly and begins to crawl forward. When we hit the wall, there's a brief jolt. Then we ease into the rock as if cutting through algaebutter, the resistance melting away against the advancing point of superheated metal. The tunnelrat is deeply focused on its work, reading gauges and moving levers, nosing us up at a gentle angle as we melt through the rock. I realize that despite their odd manners and lack of communication skills, these tunnelrats are very good at what they do.

The closer we get to breaking out, the better I feel. My relief does not appear to be shared by Roger, however, because he's sweating and twiddling his thumbs as if trying to start a fire with them. Bill has his head bowed and his eyes closed in meditation, the moment obviously a personal one for him. Jimmy is grinning beside me, still in his fentanyl stupor.

And then it happens—the resistance gives, the subterrene lurches forward, brakes, and comes to a stop. We look at one another, silently acknowledging the importance of the moment.

Bill pats Roger's knee. "You ready, Rogg? I know you're nervous, but it's been a long time dreaming about this for us."

"Yes, it has been"—Roger nods—"a long, long time."

Bill stands and talks quietly with the tunnelrat. I hear him mention not wanting to be trapped outside, and I wonder why he would ever want to get back in. Then Bill opens a cubby and hands us each a backpack filled with water and food rations.

"Okay," he says, "as soon as we open that hatch, we've got to get out of this thing fast. Gridboy here isn't too fond of the open air, as you can imagine, and he's got to get back to his post before he's missed. We all owe him a huge thank you."

I step up and shake Gridboy's huge hand, thanking him.

Now that I know his name, he seems less like a thing and more like a friend. He smiles and bobs his head as if it were nothing. Jimmy steps up next and hands Gridboy his game ball.

"I want you to have it," he says, as Gridboy looks around for something to trade. "Jus' dun' drop it somewhere."

Gridboy nods, making a show of placing the ball carefully in his pouch. Then he pats Jimmy on the shoulder and nearly knocks him over. Our goodbyes said, he returns to the controls and prepares to reverse the subterrene back the way we came. Bill grabs the lever for the hatch and takes a deep breath.

"You know what, Aubrey?" he says, pausing with his hand on the open lever. "After all those years lifeguarding on that fake beach, this will be the first real sky I've seen. I can't wait."

He smiles and opens the hatch.

As soon as he releases the lever, the hatch is yanked open and slammed against the exterior of the subterrene with a metal boom that sounds like an explosion. Bill's face goes blank as something dark tries to force its way into the opening.

Then Roger begins to scream.

Part Two

CHAPTER 12
The Jungle

Hurricane winds, driving rain, and lashing leaves.

That's what greets all four of our faces as we cram them into the hatch opening and look out of the subterrene.

It appears as if we've broken ground halfway up a lush hill. Once we clear the windblown foliage from the open hatch, we're looking down into the nearly pitch black night. Then a streak of lightning illuminates the scene, and I see a vast jungle spreading out beneath us, its thrashing canopy swaying back and forth in the wild wind, as if warning us to go away before it retreats back into darkness again.

Bill pulls us back inside the subterrene for a huddle.

"We have to go now," he says. "We can't stay here and hold up Gridboy any longer, or they'll find us out for sure."

The brief exposure to cold wind and rain must have sobered Jimmy, because he takes charge and lays out a plan.

"I saw a way down the hill to our left," he says. "We can go single file, usin' the lightnin' for sight. Once we hit the tree cover, we can make a shelter and ride out the storm."

"Sounds good to me," I say.

Roger tries to shake his head no, but Bill shoulders his pack and shoves him ahead, out into the wind. I'm the last one out. I turn to close the hatch, but Gridboy has already shut it. I watch as the subterrene's shadow reverses out of sight, swallowed by the lush hill. By the time the next lightning flash comes, not only is the subterrene gone, but the windblown hill has already covered up the tunnel from which it had come.

The wind is too wicked to talk at all, so we follow Jimmy down the hill in stops and starts, navigating by lightning. A flash lights the jungle ahead, and Jimmy leads us ten or twenty meters. Then we stop and wait for another. I'm soaked in seconds. We lurch on in the dark like this for a long time, and when we reach the bottom of the hill and find cover in the trees, Roger is crying. I couldn't hear him out in the wind, but protected now by the trees, his sobbing carries above the sound of the crashing canopy above. When lightning flashes again, I see him sitting on the ground with his face buried in his hands. Bill attempts to comfort him while Jimmy and I hunt up blown down branches and fronds and begin to fashion a makeshift shelter for the night.

It takes us an hour of steady work, but we weave a lean-to shelter against the gnarled base of a large tree. The four of us huddle inside it to wait out the storm. Roger's sobbing has turned to just a whimper, and I hear Bill's voice occasionally soothing him. Jimmy and I lean into one another for warmth, our shoulders touching, our heads resting on our knees.

Eventually, the wind above lulls us all to sleep.

When Jimmy nudges me awake, the first thing I notice is the steam. I can see beyond the branches of our shelter that the green jungle lies dappled in golden sunlight, and a shimmering veil of steam rises off the jungle floor. I rise from the shelter and find Bill already up and sitting with his back against a tree, eating a meal ration and looking around as if gladdened by the endless hues of green surrounding us. Roger is standing several meters away, turning slow circles with his head leaned back and his mouth open, as if in some kind of trance, or perhaps angling to catch one of the droplets of water dripping from the canopy of leaves. I remember how it was for me the first time I saw the forest. Watching them reminds me how beautiful everything is.

"I told you it wasn't all a wasteland up here," I say.

"It's beautiful," Roger mumbles, still turning his circles.

"Like nothing I've ever imagined," Bill says.

"I can't see the sky through all the trees," Roger adds.

"Well, there aren't this many trees everywhere," I tell him. "You'll see. But right now you both sound like you might have been sipping Gridboy's milk. Could you tell us what's next?"

"We hike it east to the coast," Bill says. "Your ride will be waiting there."

"Jimmy might be able to sight us east by the sun."

Bill smiles and reaches into his zipsuit pocket, producing a compass, which seems somewhat odd since we have no need for directions down in Holocene II.

"We might be rushed and unprepared," he says. "But I've been waiting for years to use my compass. My dad made this."

Then Roger drops his gaze from the canopy, looks past me, and screams. I spin around and see Jimmy holding a meter-long snake, the head pinched in his strong fingers. The snake writhes as it hangs from his hand.

"I caught us breakfast," he says.

"Ugh," Bill says, shaking his head and chewing the last of his ration bar. "No way am I eating that thing."

"I remember that feeling too," I say. "But you'll change your tune about what you will and will not eat if we run out of rations. Hunger is a powerful thing."

"I think I'd rather starve," Roger replies.

"Maybe we should skip the snake roast, Jimmy," I suggest. "We should probably get moving."

Jimmy shrugs and tosses the lucky snake on the ground. Roger watches as its tail disappears into a bush.

"Is that where you found that thing?" Roger asks. "I'm not getting anywhere near a bush if you did."

"Oh, they's ever-where," Jimmy answers. "I got that one out of the tree jus' above our shelter."

Roger looks like he might cry again he's so frightened, but Bill tosses him a ration bar, closes up his pack, and stands.

"Time to get moving," he says.

We make slow progress through the thick jungle, using Bill's compass and doing our best to keep moving east. The problem is that we can't sight a straight line because we have to constantly go around thick trees, or gnarly bushes, or tangles of hanging vines. And it's uncomfortably hot too. Sweat drips down and stings my eyes; sweat soaks my zipsuit through. The others are all drenched as well. Jimmy and I try not to drink much, knowing that our water rations will run low. I'm worried that Roger and Bill will get sick if they drink unsterilized water. In fact, I worry that Roger may already be sick, because he keeps swatting at bugs the rest of us can't see and mumbling to himself about snakes and how he wishes he were back underground.

The day wears on, with most of us too weary to even talk, and by late afternoon the trees thin, and the jungle opens into a parkland of palms dotted everywhere with strange puddles of blue water. As we get closer to them, I notice that they're deep pools and not puddles at all.

"What do you think caused them?" I ask.

"Maybe meteors," Bill suggests.

"Or maybe they're old dinosaur footprints," Roger says.

"Dinosaurs?" Bill laughs. "That's ridiculous."

Roger huffs. "Not any more ridiculous than meteors."

Jimmy gets on his knees, leans down, and scoops up a handful of water and smells it. It must smell okay, because then he drinks it. I notice that the pool edges are limestone, and I wonder if we're not walking over some ancient aquifer exposed by countless sinkholes. The thought makes me nervous.

"Maybe we should move to higher ground over there on the left," I suggest.

Come late afternoon, we make camp on a small rise that overlooks the pools, resting with our backs against a limestone outcropping and sipping our water rations.

"We better make a shelter," Jimmy says.

"Why?" Bill asks, obviously tired. "There's no rain."

"There will be tonight."

"How do you know?" Roger asks.

"Because it rained last night," Jimmy says.

"That's just silly," Roger replies. "I might have spent my entire life underground, but I know just because it rains one night doesn't mean it'll rain on another."

"Is that so?" Jimmy asks. "I s'pose you could say the same thin' about the sun. But it came up this mornin', and I'm bettin' it will rise tomorrow too."

Roger and Bill begrudgingly agree to collect firewood while Jimmy and I construct the shelter in the lee of the limestone overhang, weaving branches and fronds into the vines that cover the rock. I don't think Roger wanders far or does much searching, though, because he returns an hour later with two pathetic branches and a lone piece of bark. Fortunately, Bill has a better haul, and within minutes we have a small fire going. Exhausted, we sit down to enjoy it.

Turns out Jimmy has been filling his pockets with small lizards that he's snatched and brained along the way, and he spears them on sticks and roasts them in the fire. They sizzle and pop, shrinking until they're not much more than gnarled kabobs of skin and soft bone. They have a nice crunch. They actually taste pretty good. Roger and Bill elect to pass on the protein, eating algaecrisps instead. I remember my first time eating meat too. They'll get over it.

After we've all eaten and drunk our fill, we sit with our

backs against the warm limestone and watch as the setting sun casts the sky shades of orange, the likes of which I've never seen. The high clouds collect the light, and the countless pools below reflect them back. This creates the illusion of another sky beneath us, seen through windows bored into the slab of earth on which we sit, so that up is down and down is up. It gives me an unsettling feeling of hurling through space, which, of course, we are. For some reason the idea of it makes me think of the professor and his lecture on the submarine about subatomic particles and shooting stars.

The fire burns down, the orange sky fades, and some kind of animal begins to call out in the darkening jungle.

"So," Bill says, breaking our long silence, "is it always this unfriendly and this beautiful up here all in the same day?"

"I had the same feeling when I first came out," I reply. "I remember how gorgeous and wild everything felt. Like it had been painted from my dreams or something. I would have been okay if I could have just sat and looked at it. But I was in it, you know? And it nearly killed me. Jimmy here saved my life. That's the only reason I'm here. Isn't it, Jimmy?"

Jimmy turns over a coal with one of his lizard sticks.

"You saved my life too," he says. "Couple times now."

"I don't like a place where people have to be saved all the time," Roger says. "It isn't civilized."

"And you think Eden's civilized?" I ask.

"No," he answers, "I didn't say that. I just think there are advantages to living underground, and I'm not sure we should be throwing all that away."

"What about you, Bill?" I ask. "Do you feel the same?"

"No way," Bill says. "I'm all for us getting out and living free. Look at all this. It's paradise. We're lucky we all haven't turned into tunnelrats, we've been underground so long."

"I've been meaning to ask you where tunnelrats came from in the first place," I say, thinking of it now that he's brought them up. "And why does Hannah have control of them?"

"I think they were bred in the basements even before the Foundation," Bill says. "Some kind of experiment in the deep labs. I heard they have to drug the babies or else they kill one another in the womb. At least that's what Beth says."

"Who's Beth?"

"Mrs. Hightower. Her first name's Beth. She says that the babies are born addicted. The Foundation controls them by doling out fentanyl in their milk."

"That stuff's no joke," Jimmy says. "My hands are still a little numb."

Something woos and barks from nearby trees.

"What was that?" Roger asks, his voice quaking with fear.

"Probably one of your dinosaurs whose footprints we saw earlier today," Bill jokes.

"Very funny," Roger says. "Should we build the fire up?"

"Why?" Jimmy asks. "You hungry? I might have another lizard here somewhere, if you want it."

Roger just leans back and twiddles his thumbs. I know it's his nervous habit, but I don't see how it could help, because it causes me anxiety just to watch him do it.

"Bill, you know what I always wanted to ask you?"

"What's that, Aubrey?"

"How come you never married? I mean almost everyone on our level had a family, but you didn't."

"Most of us thought it would be too difficult to try and keep our secret from a spouse," Bill says. "It was just easier to stay single. Beth was married, though, until her husband had cancer and went to Eden. That was rough, because she knew and couldn't tell him. And Seth had a wife once too."

"So you don't have anyone either, Roger?"

Bill laughs. "Who would have him?"

"I actually quite like being alone," Roger says. "I find that it's comforting. But no, I don't have anyone special. I'm a plant engineer on 6 and I enjoy my job."

"You're on 6?" I ask. "You don't seem stupid."

"Gee," he says, "thanks. Not everyone down there is low IQ. Someone needs to run things you know. And besides, I was educated on Level 3 just like you. I volunteered for 6 when I was fifteen because the Chief needed someone down there to access the basement."

"You've been to the basement?" I ask.

"Of course," he says.

"I've been down there too," I say. "It's creepy."

I expect them to ask me when I was in the basements, but they don't. Perhaps they already know. The sky has grown dark and so has the jungle surrounding us, but the pools still glow against the blackness, somehow holding onto the last of the reflected light a little longer than everything else. A log pops and a coal rolls out of the fire. I kick it back, thankful for Seth's shoes. For some reason my hand moves to my pocket to make sure I still have my father's pipe. I pull it out and run my fingers over the butterflies engraved on the stone pipe bowl.

"So are you all the only ones who know? The truth, I mean. About the surface and about Eden?"

"We're the only ones," Bill replies.

"So my father didn't know any of this?"

Bill shakes his head. "No, he was kept in the dark. That's the way the Chief wanted it."

"So what all do you get out of the deal?"

"What deal?" Bill asks.

"Well, you're staying single, keeping secrets, and now you're out here risking your life, all for this Chief."

"Yeah," Bill says, "so what?"

"So what do you get out of it?"

"Isn't our freedom enough?" he asks.

"Maybe," I say. "Is that all he promised you?"

Neither of them answers me and we sit in silence, listening to wild jungle calls echo in the blackness. Even the pools have now disappeared into the night.

"There's the rain," Jimmy says.

"What rain?" Bill asks.

"I don't hear it either," Roger says.

They hardly get the words out when a downpour drops all

at once, the last of the coals hissing and going out. We scamper into the shelter, and the sound of the rain hammering the roof and pounding the ground outside makes any further discussion nearly impossible. One by one, we find comfortable positions in which to hope for sleep as we pass the night.

I have questions running through my mind like so many veins of silver in the tunnelrat mines. I want to know who this Chief is and what his interest is in me. And why China? I mean, it's practically the other side of the world. And maybe I'm just jaded, but I don't believe that these people would sacrifice so much for me and for Holocene II, just because it's the right thing to do. So what's in it for them?

Space is tight in the shelter, and Jimmy lies next to me on his back with his arms clasped on his chest. The sound of the rain outside soothes me into a welcome rest. My thoughts drift to the Foundation and to Hannah and the professor. I wonder how they're getting on and what they're doing. I know they're the enemy now, but a small part of me still misses that companionship we all had when we shared the goal of setting out to get the encryption code from the Isle of Man. Where did everything go so terribly wrong? And what kind of monsters must they be to have destroyed everyone on that island? And to have locked Red away like that with no food and no water?

I bolt upright in the dark, my breath caught in my chest. Red! I forgot about Red. I lean over and shake Jimmy.

"Jimmy, we forgot about Red. We have to go back."

Jimmy groans and knocks my hand away. "Can we talk

about it in the mornin'?" he asks. "I jus' got to sleep."

I reach past him and poke Bill. "Bill, we have to go back. We left Red at the Foundation with Hannah. Wake up, Bill."

There's a great rustling from the other end of the shelter as Roger thrashes around wildly, nearly taking off the shelter roof.

"What is it?" he calls. "Another snake?"

"Relax, Roger," Bill says. "It's just Aubrey."

"We need to go back and rescue Red," I say. "I shouldn't have ever left him."

"There's nothing you can do now, Aubrey," Bill replies. "Maybe the Chief can help."

"I'm sick of hearing about this Chief already. It's Chief this and Chief that. Who the hell is he anyway?"

"Let's talk about it over breakfast," Bill says. "Now go back to sleep. Please."

Frustrated, I storm out of the shelter and into the pouring rain. As I stand there getting soaked in the dark, my anger subsides. I realize how silly it was to come outside in the middle of the night. Still, I'm too proud to go back in now, so I plop down against the limestone where I'll at least have a little cover, cross my arms, and grit my teeth to wait for sunrise.

There's no wind tonight, and the rain falls down steady and straight. The jungle in front of me is nothing but shades of darkness out of which my mind makes a mural of monsters, all set upon tormenting me. My eyes droop and close. When they open again, the rain has stopped, and a sliver of moon hangs low above the treetops beyond the pools. I'm not sure why, but

I stand and walk several feet to the edge of our camp and take in the quiet view.

A black jaguar crouches at the base of the hill. Its shiny coat glistens in the moonlight. The monochrome spots are just barely visible on its powerful hindquarters, and its sharp shoulders support its reach as it laps up water from the pool. It raises its head to look at me. In that moment I know what it means to be at the mercy of another creature's whim.

It licks its dripping chops, turns slowly, and trots away into the jungle without looking back.

CHAPTER 13
Monkeys, Skulls, and Blue Holes

"I've never seen so many shades of green."

That's what Bill says when he steps from the shelter into the golden glow of a glorious sunrise.

I must have fallen asleep, because I'm lying on the rocky ground. My back is sore. I notice the fire burning with fresh wood, which tells me Jimmy's already up too. Sure enough, he appears from the jungle just a few minutes later, stopping to rinse something in one of the pools before carrying it up to us.

"A fella could get fat livin' 'round here," he says.

He displays two pink rodents that may have been squirrels when they still had their skins. The moment he holds them up, Roger appears from the shelter rubbing his eyes and runs into them. He veers, leans over, and begins to retch.

"Man," Jimmy says, spearing the rodents on his lizard sticks, "these two are bigger wimps than you was, Aubrey."

After everyone has done their morning business, we sit around the fire and eat while watching the shadows disappear back into the jungle as the sun climbs above the trees.

"What was all this barking last night about Red?" Bill asks.

"We left him up there," I say. "With Hannah."

"Didn't he used to bully you all the time?"

"Yeah, but we made up. He's actually a pretty good guy.

We can't just leave him behind."

"I think Aubrey's right for once," Roger says. "We need to go back right away."

"Oh, be quiet, Roger," Bill says. Then he turns to me. "We can't go back. Hannah will kill you, Jimmy, and Red."

Jimmy cracks a bone and sucks the marrow. Roger winces.

"I'm up for whatever you decide, Aubrey," Jimmy says. "My loyalty is with you, not this Chief they keep talkin' about."

"Thanks, Jimmy. But now that I've slept on it, I know Bill is right. Even if we got back to Holocene II, and even if we made it to the Foundation, Hannah would surely kill us anyway. Our only hope is to hurry and get to this Chief and see if he can help us somehow. Can you promise me he'll help, Bill?"

"If anyone will know what to do," he says, "it's the Chief."

I lick the last of the squirrel fat off my fingers and wipe my hands on my zipsuit. "Well, let's get moving then."

Before we leave, Jimmy crushes up charcoal from our fire in a limestone hollow and mixes it with water from one of the pools. Then he calls Roger and Bill over and smears it with his fingers on their faces, covering almost all of their exposed skin. Sometimes I wish I were as smart as he is.

We trudge east all morning and all afternoon. The jungle thickens then thins; the pools disappear then reappear again. When it gets hot, I unzip my suit and peel the upper half off and let it hang, walking bareback. Roger cringes when he sees the valknut scar on my chest, but he doesn't ask anything about it. He does do plenty of complaining, however. He looks like some mad mud person spit out of the Earth and trying to find his way back—the whites of his eyes are staring wildly out from his dark, charcoal-smeared face, and his lips are quivering as he mutters endlessly about how happy he'd been underground.

When we enter a dense portion of jungle, I notice the trees rustling as we pass, as if something concealed there in the branches is following us. Soon, we're all looking up to the canopy to try and spy what it might be. I hear a bark, followed by a high-pitched holler, and then more barking all around us. Then, all at once, the trees come alive, branches shaking violently, leaves dropping. Something wild has us surrounded.

Jimmy bends and picks up a stone.

The trees shake harder; the barking gets louder.

Then, as if this weren't enough, Roger screams bloody murder and jumps around like some berserker embattled with ghosts. What in all of Eden is happening here, I wonder. He hops and shimmies and jiggers as if he's doing some lunatic dance, all the time surrounded by the shaking trees. It's as if some maniac convention has convened right here in the jungle. Then Roger sheds his pack as if it was on fire, unzips his zipsuit, peels it off, and emerges from his discarded clothing naked and still dancing. No sooner is he free and away when a black monkey drops from a tree, races over and snatches Roger's zipsuit, and carries it off. Two others drop and fight over his pack. Jimmy rushes them with his stone upraised, but they settle on sharing and scamper back up into the trees with the pack between them. I spy the other there, already picking the ants from the zipsuit fabric and eating them.

Roger sits on the ground, crying. Fire ants crawl in his hair. Bill flicks the ants away one by one and then helps Roger to his feet. We all hurry past the swath of trees, away from the crazy monkeys and the ant nest Roger had been standing on.

Roger plods along in silence, either unashamed or unaware of his nakedness. I want to ask him if he's okay, but the answer is so obvious, the question seems silly. Bill tries to speak with him, but he won't respond. He just walks with his head hung, as if marching to his own funeral.

Sometime later, when the sun is high in the sky, we come to a small clearing in the center of which lies a perfectly round, perfectly blue, pool. We stop to collect ourselves and inventory our rations. I tear the top of my zipsuit free and pass it to Bill, who ties it around Roger's waist like a kind of toga. Roger lets him do it but lifts no hand to help, almost like an infant being dressed. Then Roger flops down on the ground, lays his open palms in his lap and stares at them. Why, I can't guess. Perhaps he's reading his fortune.

As we're bending over the pool, refilling our water bottles, Jimmy points down into the blue water.

"What's that down there?" he asks.

The water is so clear that it could be two meters or twenty meters deep. It's impossible to tell, but several round objects are plainly visible lying on the bottom. They look like a dozen rusty cannon balls to me. Or maybe turtles. When I turn to ask Bill to come and take a look, I hear a splash and turn back. The ripples clear away from the water's surface, and I see Jimmy swimming down into the depths of the pool. Bill joins me, and we watch as some trickery of liquid magnification causes Jimmy to shrink as he descends into the pool, and then grow again as he dives even deeper, returning to nearly his normal size as he reaches the bottom.

"How deep do you think it is?" Bill asks.

"I don't know," I say. "But it must be deep, as long as it took him to dive it."

Jimmy picks up one of the balls and turns it over in his hands, examining it. He looks up to us on the edge of the pool, his face as plain as day down there on the other side of all that water. He seems to be deciding something. Then he swims back up, repeating the process of shrinking and then growing again. He breaks the surface, gasping for air, climbs dripping from the pool, and hands me a human skull.

The skull is brown and ancient. It is a calcified and misshapen head, born from some alien species spawned from a human dream. The mandible is missing, and the row of upper teeth seem to silently snicker at us, suggesting that there might be some grand joke in death we can't yet understand.

"I wasn't gonna disturb it," Jimmy says, "but I thought you might wanna see it. I ain't never seen no head like that one."

"How old do you think it is?" Bill asks.

"I dunno," Jimmy says. "But there was some slabs down there like the roof had fallen in on this hole not too long ago. I bet it was covered up for ages."

"Maybe we should put it back," I suggest.

"I agree," Bill says.

Jimmy reaches for the skull to return it, but before he can take it, Roger appears at my side and snatches it from my hand, scurrying off and cradling it to his breast.

"Is he alright?" I ask.

"I don't think so," Bill says.

We pack up and move on.

Bill checks his compass every half hour to confirm we're traveling east, but I begin to wonder if maybe the thing doesn't work. I bring this up to Jimmy on the sly, but he observes the sun moving across the sky for a while and puts my mind at ease by confirming our direction. We all cast worried glances back at Roger as he follows along behind us in his nearly naked rags, the charcoal dripping with his sweat and streaking his pale chest, the bared skin already turning red in the sun. He won't let go of his skull for anything and keeps it cradled in his arm like a child, occasionally whispering to it as he lurches along.

We camp beneath a sprawling tree with branches so thick we don't even need to construct a shelter to stay dry. Before I fall asleep I notice Roger's shadow crouched out in the pouring rain with his skull. When I wake at sunrise he hasn't moved.

After breakfast we cross through a lush valley of vines hanging heavy with chilies. The waxy skin of the fruit seems to capture and magnify the sun, and these hanging bulbs of living light are so plentiful along the path that their glow casts us all in hues of orange as we pass. Jimmy reaches out and plucks one to eat, but before he gets it to his mouth, he casts it away from him as if it were a coal. And it might as well have been for the way his hand is burned.

We walk all day until finally, with our feet dragging and our patience running thin, we arrive at the lip of a wide escarpment that rings a much lower, much flatter piece of land. Far in the distance we can see the trees give way to two horizons—the dark blue ocean and the lighter blue sky above. But what draws my eye is a distant clearing in the middle of that lowland jungle, with a stone pyramid rising up above the trees.

"That's our rendezvous point," Bill says, stepping beside me and stuffing his compass in his pocket. "We should make it there by mid-morning tomorrow."

"How old do you think it is?" Jimmy asks.

"I'll bet it's pretty old," I say. "From way before the War."

"Older than my bust?"

"Oh, much older than that," I reply. "Much, much older."

"Why do you think it survived all this time?"

"Probably because they used stone and gravity to make it," I answer. "All of our fancy skyscrapers rusted away. At least the ones that weren't bombed. Concrete reinforced with steel rusts. That thing down there is made of the Earth itself."

"I hate to admit how little I read growing up," Bill says. "Guess I liked the beach more than my lesson slate. Were these the Aztecs here, Aubrey?"

"No, I think the Aztecs came later," I say. "If I remember correctly, these were Mayans."

"Whoever they was," Jimmy says, "they sure knew how to build somethin' that would last."

Jimmy and I get busy making a shelter by weaving a foliage roof above a round depression in the ground. Bill sees about nursing to Roger. He coaxes him to drink a little water, but Roger refuses to eat any algaecrisps or even a meal bar, fighting Bill away and claiming that Bill is trying to steal his skull.

"I don't know what to do with him," Bill says when he joins us again. "He's always been nervous, but not like this."

"Could be heat stroke," Jimmy says. "I seen people get it worse. He needs shade and water and rest."

I nod, agreeing with Jimmy. "Why don't you have him lie down here awhile, Bill? In the shelter. Let him get some rest without worrying that one of us is going to snatch his skull."

It takes some convincing, but Roger eventually agrees to stretch out in the shelter. Bill stays with him to monitor his condition. Jimmy and I move far enough away to not disturb them and search up wood to build a fire. It's plenty warm without it, and we have nothing to cook on its coals, but we build one anyway—maybe out of habit, or maybe because of some instinct imprinted in our DNA. We sit and toss twigs into the flames and look out over the darkening landscape as the top of the stone temple catches the last of the day's light. It's a patient place, and I get the feeling a person could sit here for a day or for a thousand years and never know the difference.

I think about how strange it is that Jimmy and I have Dr. Radcliffe's longevity serum inside of us, rewiring our cells right now so that we'll live for almost a thousand years. Well, maybe we'll live that long, if we somehow manage to survive this crazy adventure. What will it feel like? I wonder. A millennium. Ten, maybe twelve, lifetimes stretched together into one. It hardly seems right that Bill and Roger and the others will have grown old and passed away while we're still in our prime years. I wish there were enough serum for everyone.

"You know what this view reminds me of?" Jimmy asks, breaking the silence. "It reminds me of when we was sittin' on the bluff above the lake after that wave. You, me, and Hannah. You was smokin' your dad's pipe and she was gripin' about it, you remember?"

"Yeah, I remember. You said she was a spoiled brat."

"Because she called me a savage first," he says, defensively. Then he adds, "But I was right about her, wasn't I?"

"You're always right, Jimmy. You always were."

"Not always," he says.

We watch as several columns of bats pour out of hidden caves on the jungle floor beneath us, twisting into the dusky sky and heading out for the night to hunt.

"You ever think about runnin'?"

"Running where?" I ask.

"Jus' gettin' away from these two and all this talk about China and some Chief nobody knows nothin' about. I mean, we could make out pretty good by ourselves here, Aubrey."

"We have to stop Hannah, Jimmy. We have to. And if this Chief—whoever he is—has some kind of plan, then we need to hear it. Plus, we need to save Red. We promised we wouldn't abandon him there."

Jimmy sighs. "You're right. I'm sorry I was bein' selfish, same as when you woke me about goin' back for Red. I shoulda got up with you that night. Truth is, goin' back scares me."

"It scares me too," I say. "But so do drones."

"Yeah," Jimmy sighs, "so do drones."

"Scary thing about them is you go so long without seeing one you forget. But it only takes one encounter and snap," I say, snapping my fingers. "Just like that and you're dead."

"I know it," Jimmy replies. "We'd go years without a sightin'. Then you wake up one night to screams and half the group is gone. Well, you know. You was there in the cove."

Bill comes over and joins us, sitting down, crossing his arms around his knees, and looking into the fire. What is it that makes every man stare into a fire, I wonder. Does each see the same thing? Bill seems reflective, maybe worried. It's funny, because when I was growing up, he was always tan and strong and ten feet tall to me. He was as unreal and as untouchable as the blue sky at that electric beach. But here now, above ground and sitting next to Jimmy, he appears small and fragile and tired. Maybe our adventures have aged us; I don't know.

"How's Roger?" I ask him.

"He's finally sleeping, but I can't pry that death head away from him. It's falling apart already in the open air. All the teeth have come out, and Roger's fingers broke through the crown. I just hope maybe it'll wear down to some small token he can keep in his pocket by the time we get back."

"Get back where?" I ask.

"To Holocene II."

"You mean you're not coming to China with us?"

Bill shakes his head. "We're just taking you as far as that temple down there. Once your ride shows up, we go home."

"You'll never make it," Jimmy says.

"Why not?" Bill asks. "We made it here."

"We did," he says, "but we got lucky and come out here on this high spot and seen the pyramid down there. And findin' the coast is a whole lot easier'n findin' a hole in the jungle."

Bill turns and looks back over his shoulder at the dark and endless jungle, silhouetted against the last bit of visible sunset. He appears to be considering what Jimmy just said. I expect him to try and refute it, but he just turns back and stares into the fire again without another word.

There's no rain yet, and none of us wants to disturb Roger now that he's finally resting, so we eventually find comfortable positions on the ground and watch the fire burn down to just glowing coals. It illuminates little ashen worlds for each of us to populate as he pleases. I see tunnelrats and sometimes dragons.

A scream wakes me in the night, or so I think. I sit up in the absolute blackness and listen for a long time, but the only sound I hear is a distant rumbling that echoes faraway and deep in the belly of the night. Maybe thunder, maybe wind. But there is no lightning, and there are no stars. I can't see my hand when I hold it in front of my face. My temptation to investigate is trumped by fear of tumbling off the face of the escarpment where we lie, or worse, stepping on a snake. I close my eyes and drift back into a world that's even darker.

In the morning, Roger is gone and so is the shelter.

Swallowed in the night by the earth.

We all three stand around the sinkhole in silent disbelief. A perfectly round tunnel bored into the center of the world, so bottomless in appearance that I can imagine him falling all the way to China and meeting us there when we arrive.

I expect Bill to cry, or even scream Roger's name.

What I don't expect is for him to jump in after him.

CHAPTER 14
Yet Another Goodbye

Jimmy is faster than I am.

And I'm thankful for it, because I would have missed him.

Jimmy has ahold of Bill's forearm, and he's lying on his belly at the edge of the sinkhole as Bill dangles over the terrible void, calling out, "Roooooooggggggggggggg!"

Bill's desperate lament comes whirling back up from the depths, as if perhaps Roger were down there yelling his own name up just to mock us. I dive for the dirt, reach in, and get ahold of Bill's other arm. Jimmy and I haul him back onto solid ground. He sits there in a trance, shaking his head. I want to console him, but I don't know what to say. Instead, I just sit with my arm over his shoulder, both to comfort him and to keep him from jumping into the hole again.

After several minutes sitting like this, Bill pushes himself up, dusts himself off, and looks around as if just waking.

"Well," he says, matter-of-factly, "all of our supplies were lost with the shelter, so we had better not waste any time."

As we pick our way along the edge of the ridge, looking for a way down, I see just how stupid we were to have camped there. The sun-bleached and shell-encrusted limestone is dotted everywhere with dark, foreboding sinkholes. I have the uneasy feeling we're treading on a fragile and hollow geologic crust deposited here by some upheaval of a prehistoric ocean. Wherever Roger is, I doubt if he's alone down there.

We reach the jungle floor again and walk into the sparsely treed landscape, a sad and silent procession heading toward a crumbling pyramid and the end of an adventure. I'm sullen over leaving one of our own behind. Several hours into our walking, Bill begins to cry quietly. He picks up a stick and hacks at bushes as we pass as if they might somehow be responsible. Jimmy and I just keep to ourselves and let him work it out.

When we pass a shallow sinkhole filled with rainwater, we hold onto vines and lean down in and each drink our fill. Eventually, we begin to glimpse the top of the pyramid above the trees, but never in the same place. It plays some strange trick, constantly appearing in one direction and then in another, as if to taunt us now that we've reached the final stretch. Then, without warning, we push through a dense patch of jungle and emerge into a clearing, all three of us looking up at the pyramid, wild-eyed with wonder.

"How did they build that?" Jimmy asks.

"I don't know," I say. "But I'll bet it wasn't easy. Look at those stones."

Despite crumbling blocks of limestone at its base, and the weather-worn edges nearer the top, the temple is in remarkable shape. As we approach it, a sort of silent reverence settles over our ragged group. We take slow and solemn steps. We climb the giant stairs, past the tumbled stones, weeds, and abandoned birds' nests. Jimmy kicks an old brittle paper wasp hive, and it tumbles down and explodes in a puff of gray dust. Then we all three climb the last steps and turn to look down over the ruined kingdom. It's not quite midday, and the sun and the sea are at our backs. Below us, the jungle stretches away in shades of green and gold that go on forever and then just keep on going after that.

"What do we do now?" I ask.

"We have to clear a runway," Bill says.

"A runway?"

"For the drone."

"Well, how are we supposed to do that?"

Bill points down to the wide courtyard in front of the pyramid, where two thousand years' worth of weeds and small trees have made little progress against the heavy blocks of stone that lay as pavers there.

"You want us to clear that?" I ask.

"Just a strip of it," Bill says. "At least thirty meters long."

"We better get on clearin' then," Jimmy says.

It takes us the rest of the afternoon to root out the gnarly weeds and haul away the loose stones, especially since we have to keep taking breaks and hiking back to the watering hole to slake our thirst. But by sundown we've finished, and we climb up the pyramid in the twilight and look down upon our work.

"How'd you know this would make for a landing strip?"

"I didn't," Bill says. "The Chief had been here before."

"And just who is this Chief you all keep talking about?"

"We're not supposed to say," he replies. "Besides, you'll

see for yourself soon enough."

There's a long silence where I hear my stomach grumble.

Jimmy must hear it too, because he says, "I'm so hungry, my stomach is thinkin' my mouth's sewed shut."

"What should we do for food?" I ask.

"I dunno," Jimmy says. "Might have to wait 'til mornin'."

The last of the golden sunset climbs the temple's flanks, leaving behind only darkness. When it finally comes to rest on us where we sit on its summit, it makes me feel as if we're spotlighted on some ancient stage, perhaps preparing to put on a show for an audience in the jungle below. Then the last light leaves us too, and we climb down into shadows. The big stones at the base of the temple retain some of the sun's heat, and we try our best to make ourselves comfortable amongst them. It's less than ideal, but we're all exhausted from the day's work, and I don't think any of us trusts sleeping on the ground tonight.

"When do you think the drone will show?" I ask.

"Could be any time," Bill says. "Maybe it'll be here when we wake up."

"I hope it has some food on board," Jimmy says.

We lie quietly for a long time, listening to the sounds of the jungle—insects chattering, a bird call, a bark.

"Hey, Aubrey," Bill says, after a while. "You awake?"

"Yeah, it's not very comfortable here."

"You don't think it was my fault, do you?"

"Do I think what was your fault?"

"Roger."

I fight my immediate impulse to tell him no, and instead consider what it is he's asking. It's an honest question, and it deserves an honest answer.

"No," I finally say. "Roger wasn't anyone's fault."

"I just wish I'd treated him better, you know? I razzed him a lot, but I think he knew that I cared about him. Don't you?"

His question reminds me of something Jimmy said when he told me he loved me back in Holocene II. He said when you love someone you do things for them.

"Yeah," I say, "I think he knew."

We wake in the early quiet before dawn, the stone having long gone cold underneath us. It rained sometime in the night, because our clothes are all damp. We scramble up the steps high enough to see the entire runway, but the drone isn't there.

"I was hopin' for a breakfast delivery," Jimmy says.

"It'll be here," Bill replies. "The Chief said so."

We hike into the jungle to refresh ourselves. And we're not the only ones. As we approach the watering hole, several long bushy tails stick up over the edge.

Jimmy reaches out both arms and holds Bill and me back. Then he signals for us to be quiet as he creeps closer. When only a few steps remain between him and his prey, he rushes up and seizes one of the wavering tails. There's a wild scream, a flash of gray, and Jimmy staggers backwards, swinging a crazed mammal by its tail. As the other creatures leap out of the hole and bound off into the jungle, Jimmy wrestles with his catch. It looks like a raccoon to me, only bigger. And it isn't happy. Its teeth are bared, and it's hissing and clawing at the air as Jimmy swings it left and right to keep it away from his body. But it arches its back, swipes a blow, and bloody claw marks appear instantly on Jimmy's forearm. As it twists and turns and snaps at the air with clicking teeth, Bill and I jump out of the way just in time to miss being clawed ourselves. Then Jimmy begins to spin in circles, still gripping the tail with both hands. The centrifugal force stretches the animal out to its full length, arms and legs spread, until it looks like some giant flying squirrel, its confused little face and white nose whipping past us as it whirls by again and again. There's a loud crack when Jimmy smashes its skull against the tree, and the animal falls to the ground in a limp pile of flesh and fur.

Jimmy leans over the dead animal to catch his breath.

Bill stands, mouth agape, with a look of horror on his face.

It only takes Jimmy about twenty minutes to skin and clean his kill, using a sharpened flint. We gather wood on our way back to the temple and build a fire near its base. Jimmy fashions a kind of rotisserie out of sticks and spears the animal on a pit to roast it over the coals. As horrified as he appears, Bill can't seem to stop looking at it.

"It doesn't seem right," he says, almost as if talking to himself. "It was just sentient and now it's about to be eaten."

"It was hard for me the first time too," I offer up, trying to be supportive. "You'll get used to it."

"I dun' see what the big deal is," Jimmy says, turning his meat over the coals. "Ever-thin' is made of ever-thin' else, and this is jus' goin' back into the system."

"In a theoretical way you might be right," Bill opines. "I mean, we are all just stardust in the end. But still, how would you feel if something just snatched you out of your morning drink and bashed your head into a tree and ate you?"

"You mean like the drones do?" Jimmy asks.

Bill nods. "Except drones don't eat you."

"Well, it would be better if they did. At least it would make sense why they was doin' it. I can understand somethin' wantin' to kill me 'cause it's hungry."

Despite our conversation, Bill turns down eating any of the meat. Still, it was a big animal, and there's plenty left over in case he changes his mind—which he will if he gets hungry enough. When we finish, Jimmy wraps the leftovers in grass and then bark and wedges them in a shaded crack between two stones. Then we hike to the watering hole again to wash up. Fortunately, the wound on Jimmy's forearm is superficial. It looks much better already.

We're heading back when Jimmy dives to the ground.

"Quick," he says, "get down!"

Bill stands with his eyes on the sky, following the drone as it descends toward the temple. It's waiting on the runway when we return, gleaming like a sleek metal wasp. It's smaller than the others I've seen, and much more compact than the drone that Dr. Radcliffe used to fly Hannah and me on tour of the park. Also, the Park Service crest has been scraped off of its nose, and just a hint of the valknut outline is still visible beneath the sanded metal. As we approach, I see there are two cockpits capped with clear glass. I stop in my tracks and look from the drone to Bill and then back to the drone again.

"Bill, there's only room for two of us in that thing."

He nods as if this is fine. "You boys had better go do your business now if you need to," he says. "It's a long flight, and there isn't any bathroom on that little thing."

"No way am I leaving you here, Bill. You'll never survive."

"I'm going back," he says. "That was always the plan. Roger and I would go back."

"But Roger isn't here, Bill. And even if he were, there's no way you'd find that hole again in all that jungle. No way. It's a death sentence staying here."

"I can't go," Bill says. "I'm sorry. I told the Chief I'd get you this far, and I did. Once you climb in, the drone will do the rest. Now I've got to be getting back."

Bill turns and walks away from us. Jimmy shakes his head, making it clear that he also thinks Bill's a goner. I race after Bill, grab his shoulder, and spin him around.

"We have to find a way to all fit," I say.

"Sorry, Aubrey, but this is the end of the road for me."

Then he turns and walks on again.

When I grab him this time, he shakes me off and keeps marching, so I tackle him. I drag him to the ground and sit on his chest. He struggles to get free, but he's pinned.

"I'm not leaving you here to die," I say.

Jimmy appears at my side. "He can have my spot," he says.

"What? No way, Jimmy. Don't be stupid."

"I can hang around here and take care of myself," Jimmy replies. "Maybe you can come back for me."

"No, Jimmy. Just no."

"Listen, you two," Bill says, giving up struggling and lying his head back on the ground. "This is really cute what you're trying to do. But I knew this was the deal when I agreed to come. Now, Gridboy's planning to meet me back at the mine entrance, and I intend to be there. So get off me." He pushes me clear, stands up, and brushes himself off. "I can't believe how incorrigibly persistent you two are."

"You're sure about this?" I ask.

"Yeah," he says, "I'm sure."

Bill follows us back to the drone. He unlatches the cockpit lids, opens them, and then gives us each a boost up: Jimmy first, then me. I slide into the narrow seat behind Jimmy and look for a safety belt. There isn't one. There's hardly even room to breathe. I notice a ration pack at my feet and stretch down to get it. I drag it up by sucking in my gut. I hand it out to Bill. He tries to hand it back.

"But you'll need this," he says.

"It's yours," I say, refusing to take it back.

Jimmy holds his out to him. "Here, take mine too."

Bill relents and accepts the packs, but only after opening them and handing us the water bottles.

"I can drink along the way," he says.

As Bill goes to close Jimmy's hatch, Jimmy smiles at him

and says, "There's some meat left over there in them rocks."

Bill laughs and closes the hatch. Then he turns to close mine, but I put my hand up and stop him.

"I always looked up to you."

"You did?" he asks.

"When I used to come to the beach all the time, I would lie there and watch you. I wanted to be just like you."

Bill smiles and lays a hand on my shoulder. "Well, you're grown up now, and you're even better than me, kid."

I want to say more, but I'm not sure what. Bill seems to understand because he removes his hand from my shoulder, looks at me and nods, and then closes the lid. His face already seems a thousand kilometers away on the other side of the glass, as if he's looking at me from undersea. He steps back and gestures farewell, raising a hand to touch his forehead, almost as if saluting us. Then the drone winds up, its electric engines building momentum, and when the brakes release, we launch down the cobbled runway at a frightening speed, lifting off just in time and nosing up into the blue and cloudless sky.

Jimmy turns in his bubble to look back at me, and I can't tell whether he's thrilled or terrified.

We circle wide above the pyramid and double back. I look down and see Bill standing on the edge of the runway, looking up at us, already a sad and helpless speck on the edge of all that endless wilderness. As we leave him behind and fly west over the sprawling jungle canopy, I know I'll never see Bill again.

CHAPTER 15
China and the Chief

Claustrophobia sets in almost immediately.

I can tell that Jimmy feels it too, because I see him through the glass ahead of me, squirming to get comfortable.

The drone rises, and the jungle disappears beneath us as we cruise west across the peninsula and fly out over the Pacific. The canopy glass ices over and then clears again. The cabin is pressurized, but my ears still ache from the altitude. We're so high I can see the curve of the Earth on the horizon ahead, and I wonder just how far it must be to China—ten, twelve, maybe fifteen thousand kilometers. I hope this thing flies fast.

I wish I could talk to Jimmy, but we're separated by several feet of empty space and two panes of glass, so I pass the time trying to make shapes out of the clouds. The near ones whip by so quickly I have to guess fast. I see an algae ice cream cone, a billowy brontosaurus, an outsized ostrich. I wonder if there are any ostriches left. Probably not in China. A cylindrical cloud shaped like a submarine makes me think of the professor. And he makes me think of Hannah. I wonder if she's been told already that we're dead. I wonder if she believes it. Then I think about Red. I can still see his sad face the day we left him for Holocene II. I hope they treat him all right until we find a way to get him free. I think about Seth, heading up on the train, wearing Jimmy's ankle bracelet and walking willingly into Eden and his death. I think about Mrs. Hightower and Jillian and all the other people still trapped in Holocene II. And I think about poor Roger, tortured on the surface and then swallowed by the ground he so hated to leave. Finally, I think about Bill left there alone. No, I won't think of him. Not now. It's too much.

I come out of my daydream and notice Jimmy waving through the glass, desperate to get my attention. He points to our right where another drone is flying on our wing. I reach instinctively to do something, change our course, whatever, but there are no controls in the tight cockpit. We're trapped and powerless. The other drone has no space for passengers, and the Park Service emblem is painted on its nose. Missiles hang from its wings. I watch helplessly as its belly-mounted camera swivels to take us in, running the image against some database no doubt, or maybe even beaming it back to the Foundation. Then it tips its wing and drops away, shrinking into the distance until it disappears.

My breath fogs the glass as I sigh with relief.

That was too close for comfort for me.

The sun slides slowly down in front of us, and we appear to be flying directly into it, some human torpedo on course for a fiery death, but the entire flight it never does set. I close my eyes to shield them from its glare and try for some much needed rest. I wonder what we'll find in China—I wonder about this Chief—I wonder about a lot of things—but mostly, I wonder what Mrs. Hightower meant when she told me that I had no idea who I really am. But wondering won't solve a thing, so I push the thoughts away and sleep.

I wake when my head hits the glass ceiling.

It's dark inside the thunderstorm.

On all sides of us, including above and below, enormous clouds pulse with lightning, their shapes stitched out in the shadows by the blue electricity flickering within them. Bluish strobes silhouette Jimmy's head in front of me, and I wonder how he's doing up there. I know my feet have gone to sleep and I have to pee. I swallow down the last of my water and size up the empty bottle. I think I'll hold it for now.

The clouds eventually lighten from black to a less ominous gray, and the lightning flashes fade. At last, we pass through the thunderheads and fly into clear skies and the most breathtaking view that I've ever seen. The drone has dropped in altitude, and majestic mountains spread to the horizon, their snow-dusted peaks and ridges bright in the golden light of sunset, the deep valleys between them shrouded in silvery shades of purple. It's windblown and wild and altogether barren, but something about the harsh landscape makes me feel at home, as if perhaps I've been here already in some other life, or maybe just visited in a dream. Jimmy turns around and smiles at me, obviously marveling at the view outside our windows himself.

The drone turns to follow a mountain ridgeline, and I begin to notice something different about this range from the rest. A faintly visible line connects its summits to the saddles between them, a kind of crumbling marker made out of stone.

Some old wall for who knows what purpose, built so high in the hills I could only imagine it served to keep out giants, or perhaps to keep some sure-footed defectors in.

After following the wall for some time, losing it in places where it has worn to nothing then picking it up again, the drone approaches a rocky portion of the mountain intersected by the most intact portion of wall. I feel the wheels drop as the drone lowers for its landing, but something must be terribly wrong—we're heading straight for the mountainside beneath the wall. Jimmy turns around, and his panic mirrors my own. I instinctively pull my knees up in the tight cockpit and cross my arms, bracing for impact. The drone drops, the mountainside looms, and at the last possible moment, a hidden door opens and we pass inside the mountain and come to a stop. The door quickly closes. We're trapped inside in the absolute black.

Then LED lights come on, and I see that we're inside a tunnel at the end of a narrow runway. The drone taxis forward to where the tunnel terminates at a larger, circular hangar, then spins itself around and comes to rest facing out again. The canopies lift open, and my lungs fill with cold, biting air.

Jimmy turns and looks at me. "We made it," he says.

When my feet hit the floor, my sleeping legs give out from beneath me, and I fall on the polished concrete. Jimmy jumps down and reaches to help me up.

"You alright, buddy?" he asks.

"I think so," I say. "But I need to find a restroom."

"You wanna use my water bottle?"

"Nah, I can hold it a little longer. Let's go investigate."

Other than miscellaneous drone parts and chests of tools stacked against the walls, the hangar is empty of furnishings. It has no doors and no windows, but a metal ladder leads up the far wall and into an opening in the ceiling. There isn't any light coming from above, so we cautiously climb the ladder, with me leading. When I poke my head into another pitch black space, I take a deep breath and hoist myself up into the room.

As soon as I stand, LED lights snap on and illuminate what is obviously someone's home. Jimmy joins me and we inspect the cozy space. Stone floor, concrete walls, a bed in the corner behind a curtain. A simple wooden table and chairs. An icebox. An electric stove. On the far end of the room is a desk with a chair, a computer screen, and wires running up the wall. It looks like some forgotten outpost from an earlier era.

I notice a heavy wooden door and step over to see where it leads. The door is locked with a crude mechanism that requires some kind of primitive key. Jimmy squats and eyeballs the lock. Two trips down to the hangar for tools and ten minutes later, the lock is sprung. We swing the door open on its heavy hinges and step out onto the pathway on top of the wall.

The sun has set and it's snowing. Cold wind drives flurries past where we stand, sending them whirling down into the twilight canyons below. It's a wild and windswept scene, and I can't imagine who could scrape by in such an unwelcoming place. Despite the biting cold and the fact that I'm half naked after having given up my upper zipsuit to Roger, I haul out my shriveled manhood and send a golden arc of relief down into the falling snow. Jimmy joins me. We stand on the wall and piss together into the wind until we're both relieved and ready to head back in.

With the wind and snow once again sealed outside the heavy door, we inspect the living quarters more closely, this time in search of food. There's a cupboard built into the stone wall hung with jerked meat, and a shallow cold cellar built into the floor contains root vegetables. We find clay jugs of milk in the icebox. Settling on milk and meat, we sit on the bed and eat as if we've been starved our entire lives. We chew the nearly frozen jerky and chase it with milk, passing the jug back and forth between us until it's empty. When we finish, we pull the rough blanket around our shoulders and prop ourselves up on the bed with our backs against the wall to watch the door.

"Someone has to come eventually," I say.

"Who do you think lives here?" Jimmy asks.

"I'm guessing it's this Chief they keep talking about."

"Whoever they is," Jimmy says, eyeing the small room, "they ain't the Chief of much."

With both our bodies heating the air trapped inside the thick blanket, I actually begin to feel quite cozy sitting here next to Jimmy. My thoughts wander and my eyes droop. Just a sip or two of sleep, and then I wake again and watch my breath blow plumes of smoke into the cold room. At one point the lights click off, leaving us in darkness, but I wave my hands in front of me, and they turn on again.

"Do you think Bill's okay?"

"What's that?" Jimmy asks, waking from a nap.

"Bill. Do you think he'll make it back?"

"I dunno," Jimmy says. "I hope he does." Then he leans his head back against the wall and closes his eyes again. A few moments later, he adds, "I'll bet he makes it."

Eventually, I'm overtaken by a combination of boredom and cold, and I drift off and sleep for a while. I'm not sure if I dream, but I am faintly aware of opening my eyes and the room being dark. I reach over to make sure Jimmy is still next to me beneath the blanket before falling asleep again.

I get the feeling many hours have passed when I'm startled awake by the sound of a key in the lock. I watch from the bed as the door creaks open. A hooded figure is framed in the moonlight there, his shadow cast long and blue on the concrete floor. Then he stomps the snow off his boots, steps into the room, and pulls the door closed. There's a moment of darkness where I'm tempted to announce our presence, but then the light turns on, and the figure is standing over the bed looking down on us, his face obscured in the shadow of his hood. I can smell the outside on his clothes. I nudge Jimmy with my elbow. He lifts his head and looks at me. With a swing of my eyes, I direct him to this stranger standing before us.

A long time seems to pass with him taking us both in, as if perhaps trying to figure out how two boys came to be in his bed. Then he reaches up his gloved hand and pulls back his hood. But he is not a he at all. It's a woman. And not just any woman, but one I know from my dreams.

She smiles and simply says, "Aubrey."

If I wasn't sure before, the sound of her voice so perfectly matches the way I'd imagined it that any doubt is erased from my mind. My voice catches in my throat when I finally speak.

"Mother . . ."

CHAPTER 16
Aubrey and Aubrey

The similarities are impossible not to recognize.

The dark hair, the dark eyes.

It's as if I've died again and gone to Eden, but for real this time. I wonder if perhaps my father won't step in from outside and announce that he's home too.

She sits on the edge of the bed and pulls me into her arms.

"Aubrey," she says, "my sweet, sweet Aubrey."

Her cheek is cold against mine, and her hair smells like snow. Her arms are wrapped around me, and the fur of her coat tickles my neck. Time seems to be moving slowly. I'm numb and confused. I don't know whether to be happy or angry or sad. Maybe I'd be all three if I could wrap my mind around what's happening and allow myself to feel anything. I've dreamt about this moment, about meeting my mother and what it might be like, but in my dreams we always met in Eden, not in the flesh, and certainly not high in some China-mountain hideaway.

Maybe this is a dream.

I pull away and look at her face in the light. Her cheeks are red with cold, and her eyes are wet with tears. Her dark hair is silky and thick. She looks just as my father had described her looking all those years ago when she died.

"Mom? Is it really you?"

"Yes, Son," she says, cupping her hand beneath my chin and turning my face to the light to see it better. "It's really me."

"But I don't understand . . ."

"Of course, you don't," she says. "How could you? We have much talking to do. I'll explain everything, I promise. But first, please introduce me to your friend."

I had forgotten Jimmy. When I look over at him now, his eyes dart back and forth between me and her, obviously noting the similarities in our features despite his disbelief.

"This is my best friend Jimmy," I say.

She peels her glove off and reaches to shake Jimmy's hand. "Nice to meet you, Jimmy. I'm Aubrey, but seeing as how that could get a little confusing, you can call me Miss Bradford."

"Are you the one they call Chief?" he asks.

"You can call me that too, if you'd like," she says.

"Why not Mrs. VanHouten?"

"What's that, Son?" she asks, turning back to me as if she hadn't heard my question.

"Why did you just introduce yourself as Miss Bradford and not Mrs. VanHouten? Dad's name was VanHouten."

"You ask smart questions," she says, "and you're certainly entitled to answers. Why don't we get you both settled and into some warm clothes and then you and I can take a little walk?"

It isn't really a question because she stands from the bed and steps over to one of the corners, opens a chest, and pulls out wool shirts, socks, and a pair of fur coats and hands them over to us. When I stand and let the blanket drop from my shoulders, she sees the valknut symbol scarred onto my naked chest. Her hand jumps to her mouth. I expect her to ask about it, but she doesn't. Instead, she crosses the room and turns on a small electric heater.

"The sun isn't out enough this time of year to keep the batteries fully charged, but this should be good to warm the place up a bit tonight. Jimmy, would you like something to eat while Aubrey and I take a short walk?"

"No, thank you, ma'am," he says. "I'm afraid we already raided your jerky and your milk."

"Good," she says. "That's what it's there for. You'll find a wash basin and fresh water over there. And there's a crude but workable privy behind that curtain."

Then she steps to the door and waits beside it while I finish dressing. When I join her, she hands me her gloves. I pull them on and look back at Jimmy where he's sitting on the bed, swallowed up in the enormous fur coat she gave him. I'm reminded of that silly rabbit fur jacket he wore in Finn's castle, seemingly a hundred lifetimes ago now. We share a knowing look, a silent oath to be there for one another no matter what, and then Jimmy lifts a hand to wave goodbye. I wave back. I don't know where she's taking me, or how long we'll be gone, but I have a feeling I'll be different somehow when I return.

She opens the door, and I follow her out into the darkness and the cold. The snow has ceased, but the wind is still blowing. I pull the jacket tight and follow her along the top of the wall, walking away from the shelter. The wind whistles through the stones at my feet and howls in the canyons below. The clouds have moved on, and a cold, clear gibbous moon reflects off the surrounding snowdrifts, lighting our way. Just as my teeth begin chattering, we arrive at a tower built up in the wall. She unlocks the tower door and leads me inside. The wind abruptly fades when she closes the door. We're alone in a small passage. She takes my hand in hers and leads me through the dark up a narrow, spiral staircase. At the top of the staircase, we enter a square room with windows on two sides and the moon hanging in one of them as if it were painted there, casting us and the room in its silver light. She crosses to a stone bench and sits down, motioning for me to join her.

"Where are we?" I ask.

"This is the watchtower," she says. "I brought you here so we can talk in private. There's a lot you need to know. But first, I must ask you a few questions."

I pull my coat tighter. "Okay, ask me."

"Beth and Jillian sent word about Seth. But how are Bill and Roger?"

"Roger's dead," I say.

She nods her head, accepting the news, but she doesn't say anything or even ask how.

"He fell into a sinkhole. Bill was heading back alone, but I don't think he has much chance."

"Can you tell me how many are left at the Foundation?"

"Just the professor and Hannah. And the tunnelrats, of

course. Oh, and Red. We left him there but I didn't mean to, and we need to get him before Hannah hurts him."

She ignores my comment about Red, changing the subject instead. "And Hannah has control of the drones?"

"Yes, we went to the Isle of Man and got the encryption code. But we didn't know what she was planning to do."

"No," she says, "of course, you didn't."

"And I don't really understand what's going on now either. Are you even my mother? Because she died giving birth to me. Burst appendix. Rushed up to Eden. That's what I was told."

"Yes, you must be very confused."

"You think? So tell me, how come you're alive?"

"I'm sorry to have to tell you this, Aubrey. It isn't easy. But my appendicitis was a lie. It all was. It was just an excuse to get me out of Holocene II and up to the Foundation."

"Okay, but why?"

"Because that's where I came from."

"What do you mean?"

"I didn't come up from Level 4 like everyone believed. That was just a cover. I came down from the Foundation."

"But why?" I ask. "And why did you have to go back up there when I was born?"

"Because I couldn't stay," she says. "I wanted to, Aubrey, believe me. I just couldn't."

Then it hits me. She looks exactly as my father described her, but the last time he saw her was nearly sixteen years ago.

"You have the serum in you, don't you?"

"Yes," she says. "How much do you know about it?"

"I have it in me. So does Jimmy."

She nods. "And Hannah too, I assume."

"And Hannah too."

A moment of silence passes between us. I can hear the wind outside. I notice that the moon has moved. Only half of it is now visible in the window.

"So you've probably guessed then that I'm a little older than I look," she says.

"How old are you?" I ask.

"I'm not exactly sure," she says, "but I think I'll be about three hundred and ten in the spring. My birthday is close to yours. I just can't remember what year anymore."

"Only three hundred? But the Radcliffes were over nine-hundred years old. And the professor. So how do you fit in?"

"I did come up from Level 4," she says, "but all the way to the Foundation and nearly three hundred years before I went back down to have you."

"I don't understand."

"I know," she says. "Let me tell you."

"Okay, tell me."

"They were reworking all their hardware and software systems at the Foundation. Making an upgrade. I was especially gifted with writing computer code. I don't know why, but I loved it. Anyway, Radcliffe called me up when I was fifteen and they trained me there. At first, I couldn't understand why they were so old and why they weren't in Eden. Then he gave me the serum when I was twenty. I didn't know then what it was for. I didn't even know there was a lake over our heads or that the surface was like it is, until maybe fifty years or so after I had come up. They kept a lot of things from me at first, until they thought they could trust me."

"Could they trust you?"

"Do you mean to ask if I was one of them?"

"Yeah. Are you?"

"I was. But not anymore."

Hearing all of this is such a shock to me, I don't know if I can trust her or not. "Well, what changed you?" I ask.

"You did," she says.

"I did?"

"Yes."

I'm suddenly aware of how cold the bench is. I stand and cross to the window and look out at the moon. It's strange to think that it's been up there circling the Earth all this time, shining down on everything since the beginning of humankind but concerned about none of it.

"Did Dad know?" I ask.

"Did he know what?"

"Any of this," I reply. "How old you really are. Where you came from. That you're not really dead."

"Of course not," she says, as if the very idea of it shocks her. "He didn't know anything about that."

"So you just let him think you were dead until he walked right into Eden to have his brain cut out?"

She stands to approach me, but I step away.

"You don't understand," she says.

I peel her glove off my hand, reach into my pocket and pull out my father's pipe and hold it up.

"I don't understand?" I ask. "I understand that he sat me down and gave me this pipe because he wanted to pass it down and because you always hated the smell of his tobacco. Look. Do you remember? I understand that he talked about you as if you were some kind of saint. He couldn't wait to see you, Mom. Or maybe I should call you Chief? Or Miss Bradford?"

"Aubrey, please—"

"Please nothing. I tried to stop him. I tried to tell him the truth about what was going on. But he wouldn't listen. You know why? He wouldn't listen because he couldn't wait to get inside Eden so he could see you. But you weren't even there. And you weren't there because Eden is a sham, and you knew it. You let him get slaughtered, Mom. I saw it. I saw his brain being lifted out of his head. I saw it put into that soup. And I risked my life to free him and to free you. Jimmy did too. And you stand here and tell me I don't understand."

She sits back down on the bench and sighs deeply. "You just don't understand, Aubrey. You don't."

"Then you tell me!" I shout. "What don't I understand?"

"He wasn't your father."

"What?"

"He wasn't your father, Aubrey. He knew he wasn't, too. He'd never tell you that, of course, but he knew. Sure, he had no idea who your real father was. But he knew I was already a month pregnant when I showed up there. He was a good man, Aubrey. A good, good man. But you have to understand, we were only together for eight months. Just long enough for me to have you, and then I was gone. I didn't expect him to fall in love with me like he did. And I sure didn't expect him to spend fifteen years making me out to be something I never could have been. He was a good man, and he was the right man to raise you, but he wasn't your father."

I look at the pipe in my hand, the yellow-stone bowl gray in the moonlight, worn smooth by my father's hands.

"You're lying," I say, backing away. "You're lying."

When I run into the wall, I slide down it and sit on the cold stone floor, cradling the pipe in my shaking hands.

"I know you're lying. He was my father. He was."

"I'm not lying," she whispers. "He wasn't your father."

I look up at her through tear-filled eyes. She's sitting on the bench, leaning forward with her elbows on her knees, her chin resting in her hands, and her long, dark hair framing her face in the soft moonlight.

"Then who is my father?" I ask.

"Your father," she says, "was Dr. Robert Radcliffe."

CHAPTER 17
The Rest of the Story

I'm alone in the shelter when I wake.

Dreams must have had me thrashing in my sleep, because I'm tangled in the bedding and the motion sensor lights are on. As the nightmare fades, however, another one takes its place.

I remember learning the truth last night in that tower room. I remember running out and fleeing across the wall, desperate to get away. I remember falling, catching myself, my knees scraping stone. I remember pushing her away, screaming, "Don't touch me! I hate you!" And I remember Jimmy's strong hands helping me up, his shoulder supporting me, his gentle touch as he tucked me in. I remember sobbing myself to sleep and the sound of concerned voices beyond the curtain.

I get up out of bed and look around. The knees of my zipsuit are torn and blackened with dried blood. My coat and shirt are draped over a chair, my shoes parked on the ground. A pot of porridge steams on the stove. There's an empty bowl and a clay carafe of cream nearby. After eating my fill, I wash my face in the basin, and use the latrine—which turns out to be a hole in the floor that drops away to who knows where and covered with a hinged wooden lid. Then I dress again in my shirt and coat. I'm still trying to force the shoes Seth gave me over the thick wool socks when the door opens and Jimmy and my mother walk in together, laughing.

"Oh, good," she says. "We were hoping you'd be up."

"Look what I shot," Jimmy says.

The creature he holds up looks like some half-aborted monster in the making, and I can only imagine by the thin flaps for arms and the bumpy pink skin that it must be a bird he's plucked of its feathers. Then I notice the bow and arrows slung over his shoulder. He must be right at home here.

"I need to talk to you," I say, addressing my mother.

"Okay, sure," she replies. "You look like you could use a little cleaning up. Here, carry these." She hands me two towels. "Jimmy, would you mind putting things away by yourself while Aubrey and I go out for a bit?"

"I'll be fine," Jimmy says, over his shoulder. "Dun' hurry back. I might need to rest some anyhow."

There's only a slight wind outside, and the sun hangs in perfect blue china skies, reflecting brightly off the stone and the drifts of snow. Despite the ache it causes my lungs, the winter air is invigorating. She leads me down a mountain path, away from the hut and the wall. I want to talk with her, but the path is only wide enough to accommodate us single file, so I follow along behind, carrying the towels, cautious of my steps, and look out over the wild world folding away beneath us.

The path hugs the slope and eventually turns a bend and switchbacks down toward a mountain cove, a hollow cupped between surrounding peaks. In the center of this hollow, an oasis of trees and plants, some still green, stand out brightly against the surrounding gray. A gentle steam rises up. Birds chirp and flit between the spindly and leafless maples.

I see as we approach that the steam comes from a set of pools—springs heated by some geothermal workings deep in the mountains. My mother peels off her coat and her shirt and lays them out on a flat rock beside the pool. Then she steps out of her pants and wades into the water in her underclothes, lifting her thick hair and tying it up on her head.

"Aren't you coming in?" she asks, smiling at me.

I don't know whether I'm more uneasy about seeing my mother half naked or having my mother see me. But the water looks relaxing, and after our hike across the Yucatan and the long flight here, I sure could use a bath. I set the towels down and undress as quickly as possible. When I step down into the pool, the water is silky against my skin, and the heat soothes away pains I didn't even know I had.

My mother leans her head back and sighs. She says, "This is one thing I sure would miss about this place."

I spin slow circles in the pool, enjoying the view of the trees set against the gray cliffs rising sharply behind them.

"How long have you been here?" I ask.

"Oh, about nine or ten months now."

"That's all?"

She nods. "You were supposed to come here with me."

I stop my spinning and look at her. "I was?"

"Yes, you were. At least that was my plan." Then she looks at my bare chest and asks, "How did you get that scar?"

I lower in the water until only my head and neck are exposed. "I think maybe I should be asking the questions."

"Fair enough," she says. "I didn't get to finish telling you everything last night. If it's alright with you, I'd like to now."

"Go ahead then," I say.

"I know this is hard, Aubrey. But you need to understand why things happened the way that they did."

"I'm listening."

"Okay, then. I told you last night how I had arrived at the Foundation. Now let me tell you about how you arrived. When Robert—that's Dr. Radcliffe—and his wife had Hannah with their surrogate, he was disappointed that she wasn't a boy. He had funny ideas about the differences between women and men. Anyway, they had made several attempts, and it was Katherine's last egg, so he immediately began looking at the fifteens below to see if anyone might be a suitable mate for her. If he couldn't have a son, maybe he could at least have a grandson. I see how you're looking at me, and I know how it sounds. It's crazy. But you have to understand that to him it wasn't. And when you're around someone like that all the time, it begins to stop sounding crazy to you anymore too."

"So how do I come in? I mean, if he is my father."

"I think he had just assumed that I was no longer fertile. None of the others had been when they had reached my age on the serum. But then, most of them had taken it when they were already quite old, and I had only been twenty. Anyway, he was cataloging our manufacturing database for sintering machines when he discovered—let's see, how do I say this to a boy?—well, he discovered an applicator system that I had designed for the tampons I was having sent up from Holocene II. I made it for me, but I also thought it might help the girls down below. Anyway, Robert cornered me about it, and once he realized that I truly was fertile, his relentless pursuit began."

"Did you love him?"

"Love him? Of course not."

"So you just slept with him, then?"

"Lord, no, boy," she says. "Wherever do you get your crazy ideas? I didn't sleep with him."

"You didn't?"

"No way. He didn't have anything going on anymore that way anyway. But he did have sperm left in the freezer. And he wanted to be a father more than he wanted anything. He made a convincing case about it too. He said I was a perfect genetic match. It was quite flattering in a way. He told me I could help save the planet with my egg. And I'm ashamed to admit that I was swept up in it. You have to understand, Aubrey, he had shown me videos of the destruction. Of what humankind did to one another before, during, and after the war."

"I know. He showed some of the same images to me."

"It's still no excuse," she says, "but I went along with it. And then as soon as I was pregnant, he sprung this whole thing on me about having to go down to Holocene II to have the baby. I couldn't believe it."

"But why?" I ask. "Why not have me at the Foundation?"

"Because of his wife, Katherine."

"You mean she didn't know?"

"She had no idea. And I think he was scared to death to tell her. You see, Hannah was around fifteen by then and just coming into being a sexually mature young woman herself. But he immediately placed her on hormone blockers and whatever other cocktail he and his buddies cooked up to keep her young. His plan was to wait until you turned fifteen, and then he'd call you up and have her perfect mate. That way he gets his son and his grandson, and his wife and daughter never know."

"Hannah doesn't know?"

"I don't think he ever told her."

I suddenly have a sour taste in my mouth and I turn to spit on the edge of the pool. "Ugh."

"Did you swallow a bug?"

"No," I say. "But I kissed Hannah and she's my sister."

"Half-sister," she corrects.

"Yeah, but still. And what was Radcliffe thinking? I mean, I don't know much about it, but aren't we given genetic tests down in Holocene II, just to make sure we're not too closely related to someone we intend to take as a mate?"

"Yes. And I said the same thing to Robert. But you have to understand what an egoist he was. He thought the risk of defective grandchildren was far outweighed by the chance that they'd be of—let me remember exactly what he called it—oh, yes, 'superior intelligence' he had said." She pauses to stare off into empty space, as if seeing Radcliffe's image there above the pool. Then she says, "You know, for someone who claimed to hate humankind, he sure did love himself."

"So how do we get to where we are now?"

She leans her head back and sighs, then continues:

"Everything changed when I had you. Actually, before I had you. As soon as I was down in Holocene II and away from Robert, I began to question all the things he had taught me. It really was a brainwashing. Then, as you began to grow inside me, it became impossible to maintain the belief that human beings are some kind of virus that needs to be stamped out. I just couldn't accept that you, this perfect person who wasn't even born yet, that you were evil."

"You loved me?"

She smiles. "I love you still."

"So what did you do then?"

"That's when I began recruiting."

"Recruiting?"

"Yes, the others that you've already met—Roger and Bill and Beth and Jillian. You met Seth too, but not his wife, Nicole. They were students of mine. And they were all smart in their own ways. Seth and Nicole were older. They were up from Level 5 temporarily, learning how to teach so they themselves could educate tunnelrats. It began with them. Then I included the others. I'd keep them after for special classes, preparing for a plan that was taking shape already in my mind. You see, I knew then that I had very little time. That the minute I had you, I would be heading back up to the

Foundation. And I knew that Radcliffe would call you up in fifteen years. I knew he'd brainwash you and make you into a monster just like him. And I couldn't allow it. I wouldn't."

"So what did you do?"

"After I went back up, I secretly stayed in touch with the others down below. Beth and Bill stayed on your level, so they gave me frequent reports on how you were doing. I watched you grow up through them. I also befriended a few tunnelrats with Seth and Nicole's help. Then we began to have them bore farther south and closer to the surface, hoping to one day be able to break out. But fifteen years passes fast, and before I knew it you were all grown up, and we weren't ready yet to make an opening. That's when we cooked up the last minute plan to break you out of the train. The tunnelrats helped me get explosives and showed me how to use them. I found a spot I could land in a glade not too far from the trestle where the train comes out of the mountain."

"The place where I wrecked?"

"Yes," she says, suddenly looking sad. "I planted those explosives myself and set them to detonate when the lower tunnel doors opened. It was just supposed to block the tracks and stop the train. I didn't think it would do what it did."

"I nearly died when that rockslide came down."

"I know," she says. "And Nicole did die."

"Nicole?"

"Seth's wife. She had agreed to help me rescue you, and she was in the car of retirees ahead of yours. I had sent her down a key, and when the train derailed, she was supposed to let you out and take you to me. I was waiting to fly you here."

Then I remember boarding that train for the Foundation and the retirees getting into the car in front of me. I remember a woman had looked back and made eye contact with me.

"So what happened?" I ask.

"Nicole and you never arrived where I was waiting, so I eventually left the drone and hiked to the trestle. It was getting dark, and the tunnelrats were already there working. When I saw the train . . . well, I'll just say that it was the worst moment of my life. I thought for sure that I had killed you. I didn't know what to do. I knew Robert would figure out what I had done. I couldn't go back, so I came here alone."

"Why this place, then?"

"I had been here before. It was an old workstation of ours that we had abandoned after the two scientists assigned here committed suicide together. And I have to tell you that I nearly followed in their footsteps that first several months here alone. I thought I had killed you, Aubrey. My own son." She chokes up and looks away. Then she takes a deep breath, appearing determined to keep it together, and continues. "Then I heard that you weren't dead, that you were back. I can't tell you how happy the news made me. I remember I went out on the wall there and looked up at the stars and I cried until there weren't any tears left. I only hoped that Radcliffe wouldn't completely brainwash you before I could get to you. But he hadn't, and, of course, you know the rest, because here you are."

"This is a lot to digest," I say.

"Yes, I know it is. And you should take all the time you need and ask all the questions you want."

I lean back against the edge of the pool and look at her. She's beautiful in an unconventional kind of way, and I can see how my father would have fallen for her. I'm torn between wanting to love her because she's my mother and hating her for what she did to my father. The father who raised me, anyway. The thought of him walking into Eden to be with her when she was here the whole time sends a shiver up my spine, and despite the warm water, I'm suddenly cold. It's horrific what he went through, and I'm not sure if I can forgive her.

A loud screech turns my head skyward. An eagle cruises in wide circles high above our heads. My mother sees it too.

"It's time to go," she says, wading over, stepping out of the pool, and grabbing a towel.

She seems in a hurry to get back, so I get out and dry off as quickly as I can. As I pull my shoes on, I look at her where she stands, already dressed and waiting on me.

"He was my father, just so you know."

She tilts her head and looks down at me. "Radcliffe?"

"No"—I shake my head—"Jonathan VanHouten. He might not have donated his sperm, but he was my father, and I don't ever want to hear anything different."

She nods. "Fair enough."

She leads me quickly up the return path—so quickly that I struggle to keep up, despite my legs being longer than hers.

When we turn the corner, I see the eagle again. I follow its flight with my eyes and see it land on the outstretched arm of a man sitting a horse. There are several of them there on top of a distant ridge, mounted on horseback and watching us. Because they're bundled up in brown furs, they have the appearance of being continuations of the horses themselves, as if they're really strange, star-gazing centaurs from a reading slate fantasy book.

"Who are those strange men?" I ask.

"Just look ahead and keep walking," she says.

CHAPTER 18
Stories and Wild People

"I thought I seen 'em too," Jimmy says.

"You boys keep clear of those people," my mother replies.

Jimmy and I have decided to ditch our zipsuits. We're sewing kilts from alpine deer skins my mother had in her chest.

"If you want us to stay away from them, Mom, you need to tell us who they are. Otherwise, we'll find out for ourselves."

I'm testing this idea I have that if I call her Mom, she can't refuse me anything. She looks over from her computer desk, where she's been diligently typing for hours, and sighs.

"I don't know much about them except that they're wild," she says. "They're wild and they saved my life."

Jimmy and I both stop our sewing and sit with our half-finished kilts in our laps.

"They saved your life?" I ask.

"Now you gotta tell us the story," Jimmy says.

She smiles and turns her chair around to face us.

"Okay, since you enjoy stories, I'll tell you what happened. As soon as I arrived here, I knew that Robert would be sending drones to all of our old places to look for me—maybe to report back, maybe just to bomb them out. So I took the launch tubes off of my drone and converted them to fire by hand."

"You can do that?" I ask.

"Oh, it's quite easy," she says. "You have to understand that down in Holocene II they think they're building them for unmanned exploration. The drones are weaponized later at the Foundation. I had to hack their onboard programming, of course, to make them seek the metallic signature of a drone instead of the heat signature of a human."

"So what did you do with them?" Jimmy asks.

"I sat up in that watchtower and waited. Day and night. I pretty much came in here only to eat and use the privy. It became an obsession of mine to shoot down a drone. I don't know why. I guess I was angry at the way everything had turned out—about having thought that I lost you in that train wreck. But I also had a more practical reason to do it. I knew with resources stretched as thin as they had been at the Foundation, if I was able to shoot down a drone, Robert would think twice before sending another. It wasn't a permanent solution, but it would buy me some time."

"Did you get one?" Jimmy asks.

"It's my story," she says, "you either listen to how I tell it, or I go back to my work and you can go back to your sewing."

I slug Jimmy in the shoulder. "Never mind him. Tell us."

"Okay, then," she says. "But don't hit Jimmy, Son, even if you're only playing. It's bad manners. So, getting back to my story. I was using the radar on my drone to send up an alarm if anything approached, and every day I sat in that tower and waited. And every morning I'd see these riders on horseback, the ones you've seen now. They'd come to the ridge to look at me. And every day they got a little closer. I was sure that they were sizing me up and making plans to kill me. They're wild, I tell you, wild. Once, one of them sent his eagle down to the tower. It perched on the sill, filling the entire window, and looked in on me with eyes so intelligent that I half believed one of the men had turned himself into the bird. Then off it flew, directly back to its owner, as if to report what it had seen. I swear I saw that bird whisper in the man's ear. But then I hadn't slept in a while either by then."

"Do they all have eagles?" Jimmy asks. "And how do they catch them? How do they train them?"

"I don't know," she says, "but let me finish, will you? One morning, a few days later, they dismounted their horses and came down to the wall and stood not a hundred meters away, taking counsel. They all had bows and one had a spear. I knew my time had come, and I made my peace with it. But just then my alarm went off. I grabbed my rocket and rushed to the window. Sure enough, I saw the silhouette of a drone coming in from the east, marked out against the sun like a bird. Of course, I forgot all about the men on the wall. I raised my rocket and waited. And I kept waiting. I wanted to be sure. Then, when the drone was sweeping in low, so close now that I could see the Park Service emblem on its nose, I fired."

She stops talking and looks at us with a smile on her face, as if that were the end of her story. The room is silent. We sit on the edges of our seats, our half-completed kilts forgotten on our laps. Afraid to be chastised again for interrupting her,

Jimmy nudges me to say something.

"Come on, Mom," I say. "Tell us what happened next."

"Well, I really don't know," she says.

"You didn't hit it?"

"Oh, yes, I hit it all right. But I didn't know it until a week later when I found the wreckage. I think the blowback from the rocket slammed me against the stone wall and knocked me out. It really was a bad concussion. I'm lucky I survived. I woke days later in my own bed. My wound had been cleaned and dressed. The blood had even been washed from my hair."

"So the wild people helped you," I say.

"I assumed it was them," she replies. "Although I never did see or talk to them. But from that day on, I began finding gifts left at my door. The bow and arrow I gave to you, Jimmy, that was from them. The milk in the fridge is from them. Most of the furs you're wearing. In fact, I'm certain that I'd never have made it once winter set in if it weren't for their gifts."

"They seen you shoot that drone is why," Jimmy says.

"You think that was it?" she asks, as if considering it for the first time.

"Sure," he says. "I know we never took well to strangers, but if they was against the Park Service and we seen it for our own selves, then they was friends of ours."

"You have a very wise friend there, Son," she says to me.

"Yeah," I say, grinning, "most of the time he's all right."

Jimmy slugs me in the shoulder. "Whaddya mean, most of the time?" he asks.

By the next afternoon, Jimmy and I are roaming the snow-covered hills in our new kilts, looking for the wild people and their camp. He has his bow and arrow over his shoulder, just in case we run across something actually worth hunting, since that's what we told my mother we were heading out to do.

"They gotta have a place around here somewhere," Jimmy says. "If it was me, I wouldn't be too far from that hot spring."

"Let's try over there," I suggest, pointing. "On the other side of those cliffs, where I saw them."

We walk awhile without talking, listening to the sound of our breathing and our shoes crunching in the new snow. It's hard to believe that just a few days ago, we were trudging through a rainforest halfway around the world.

"Your mom sure is somethin'," Jimmy says.

"How so?" I ask.

"The way she shot down that drone. She sure is cool."

"Yeah, I guess so."

"What? You dun' like her?"

"I like her. I'm just not sure about everything. I mean I had her built up in my mind one way, and she's nothing like it."

Jimmy nods that he understands.

A few paces later, I add, "Maybe I'm just not sure yet if I can trust her."

"What makes you think you can't?" Jimmy asks.

"Well, she lied to my father, for one thing."

"That's true," Jimmy says. "But your father isn't you."

"And you know what else is strange?" I ask. "I remember

when Dr. Radcliffe was showing me his control room for the first time, explaining the drones and how they hunt humans and all that. Gosh, what a nut case he was, now that I think about it. But while we were down there, he mentioned to me that they had lost a drone in China. He said they sent another after it and that they lost it too. And here he was talking about my mother and I didn't even know it. And maybe worse, he was my biological father, and I had no idea about that either. I mean, it makes me wonder what else I don't know right now."

"That makes sense," Jimmy says. "But jus' remember how lucky you are."

"Lucky? How am I lucky?"

"I'd give jus' about anythin' to find out my mom was still alive, even if she had lied to me."

I stop in my tracks and look up at the clear blue sky. He's right. I would have traded my left arm and maybe my right too just days ago if I had thought it would bring my mother back. And here she is, and I'm refusing to forgive her for being alive. Maybe I should give her a chance. Movement catches my eye. I spot an eagle soaring on a high breeze.

"Look, Jimmy. An eagle. Think it's one of theirs?"

"I dunno," he says, "let's follow it."

We take off at a jog, losing sight of the eagle when we dip down into a gulch and then picking it up again when we come out the other side. We climb a small peak to get a better view and see that the eagle is circling above a wide valley with a river running along its edge. The snow is trampled on both sides of a shallow ford, the river having recently been crossed by horses.

"That's where I'd build a camp," Jimmy says, pointing to the other side of the valley. "Under those cliffs."

There's a hill between us and the base of the steep granite cliffs, obscuring the view of where any camp might be.

"Should we go check it out?" I ask.

"The universe hates a coward," he says.

We scramble down to the banks of the river and cross it in the tracks of the horses, with our shoes slung around our necks and our new kilts hiked up. The water is only knee deep, but it's cold enough that I can't feel my legs or my feet when we wade out the other side. With our shoes back on, we jog the rest of the way, trying to warm up.

When we crest the hill, we both come skidding to a halt. Several feet away, a fawn stands staring at us with enormous, dewy eyes. The young deer is spotted, not unlike the kilts we're wearing, and it's tethered by a rope to a wooden stake driven into the ground. The snow is trampled in a circle that marks the end of the leash. When neither of us moves to harm it, the fawn drops its head and begins grazing on the frozen ground.

"It must be someone's pet," I say.

"I dunno," Jimmy replies. "Why would you keep one? I ain't never seen anyone milk a deer."

The fawn raises its head to look at us again, as if perhaps it had heard us talking and might speak to clear things up. Then a shadow races across the snow, swelling as it approaches, until it casts a pool of darkness over the fawn. Then a golden eagle slams into the fawn's back, digs its talons into its neck, and bears down on it. The fawn's front legs buckle, and its head drops to the snow beneath the weight of the great raptor. Its helpless hind legs continue to rear and kick, and the eagle's wings continue to beat wildly, so close that they blow wind in our faces. Surprisingly, neither the eagle nor the deer makes a sound. The struggle lasts for several seconds. Then the eagle severs the fawn's spine with its powerful beak. The fawn twitches once and is still. The eagle tucks its wings and perches atop its kill, looking at us as if we were nothing more than a sideline curiosity.

Jimmy slips his bow over his shoulder and strings an arrow. Just as he's pulling back, horses gallop up behind him on the hill, and one of the riders kicks Jimmy and sends him and his bow flying to the ground. I jump over to help him up. We stand together and watch as the riders encircle us.

The horses are small but stout, and so are the men. There are six of them, all bearded except one boy much younger than we are. They're hard-looking and wild, with the exception of the child whose dark eyes seem to take us in with a humorous curiosity, his baby-like face blanketed in his hood of furs. One of the men motions with his gloved arm, and the eagle flies to him and perches there. Then he pulls up a wooden brace where it's tied to his waist and props it under his elbow to help hold the eagle's weight. Another man dismounts and pulls the stake and carries the dead fawn back to his horse, drapes it limply over the withers, and then mounts up again. Then the men all turn to look at the eldest among them, a thick man with a gray beard and a missing eye—no patch, no eyelid, just a pink and empty socket. He and the strange boy next to him look at us, as if considering together our fate. The old man reaches into his fur and pulls out a little jade bottle. He removes the stopper and a small spoon attached to it, holds the spoon to his nose, and sniffs. Then he dips the spoon again and repeats with the other nostril before returning the bottle to the folds of his furs. Then he lifts up his hand, not in greeting but as some kind of command to his men, and says something in a tongue I don't understand. They turn their horses and gallop off the hill. The boy lingers for one moment, smiling at us from his hood. Then he too turns and is gone.

Alone again on the hill, I look at the trampled snow, stained with the fawn's blood. I feel fortunate that we're not draped over their horses ourselves.

"Well," Jimmy says, "I guess your mom was right."

"That we should have stayed away from them?"

"No, that they's wild."

We start back together, retracing our path. The sun drops behind the western peaks, and the temperature drops with it. I'm not looking forward to crossing the river again.

After we walk quietly for a time, me contemplating our brush with death, Jimmy contemplating who knows what, he turns to me and says, "How do you think they get 'em?"

"Get what? I ask.

"The eagles."

Two days later the blizzard comes.

We stand in the doorway and watch it come down.

"Close that door," my mother calls.

Jimmy's more disappointed than I am. He sulks around the shelter for the next three days, constantly going to open the door to see if the snow has stopped.

"Stop letting all the heat out," my mom barks, looking up from her workstation. "The batteries are already low enough with no sun in the sky to recharge them."

Jimmy jerks the door shut, stomps to the table, and flops down on the chair next to me. He runs his fingers through his hair, then pulls his bangs down toward his eyes and looks up to try and see them, with a surprised look on his face, as if he'd forgotten his hair had been shaved before coming here.

"This blows," he says.

"Come on," I say. "It's growing back."

"Not my hair," he replies. "Bein' stuck in here. I've done worked every pelt in the place. I made us some boots too, so we can go out when it clears."

"You want to go down and check out the drone again?"

"No, I'm sick of looking at it. I'll tell you what I'd like to do, is fly it. See if we can find them horsemen's camp maybe."

"Mom says we can't risk it. I already asked."

Jimmy leans in and lowers his voice. "I'll bet if you asked her again nice, she'd let us. Call her Mom like you do."

"Maybe," I say, "but there's no sense in asking if the snow hasn't stopped."

Jimmy looks at the door and sighs. "And now I can't even check anymore or she'll yell at me."

"I heard that," my mother says.

Two days later, Jimmy and I are loaded up in the drone while my mother programs the flight path into its computers. She seals the panel and turns to give us yet another warning.

"If you see anything out of the ordinary, anything at all— another drone, or threatening weather, anything—you press the return button, and the drone will bring you home."

"Yes, Mother."

"I've programmed it to fly for about an hour, which will actually be good for charging its batteries since the sun is finally out. You boys be safe."

Jimmy smiles. "Thank you, Miss Bradford."

"You're welcome, Jimmy."

She pushes his glass canopy down and latches it.

Then she turns to close mine. "You have your water?"

"Mom, stop worrying. We flew here, remember?"

She smiles and closes the canopy, stepping away to watch us go. The door at the end of the runway opens, and the tunnel fills with light. I look at my mom, and then she's gone in a flash of gray as we jet forward and launch out of the mountainside.

Of all the days and places one could go flying, I can't imagine any other as beautiful as this is. After five nonstop days of snow, a blanket of white covers everything except the high and jagged peaks that rise into the blue sky like the backs of enormous prehistoric creatures surfacing in a sea of white. Giant icicles hang frozen where waterfalls once ran, glinting in the sun like diamond stalactites. Shaded valleys lay so deep with snow that only the tips of trees stick out—conifers thick with frozen cones, leafless aspens with their upper branches frozen into intricate frosted sculptures, like ice-carved skeletons. And the quiet of it all is haunting. The drone is propelled by silent electric engines, and the only sound I hear is the beating of my own heart. Jimmy turns in his glass enclosure to grin at me, and his smile is as wide and white as the snow out our windows.

Later, I see a small red fox laboring across a narrow combe surrounded by high cliffs, a trail of trampled snow marking its insignificant progress out of all that untouched beauty. Jimmy sees it too, and the way he leans to follow it with his eyes as we pass tells me that it reminds him of Junior. I know he misses him. I do too. Never has there been a better fox.

The drone glides slow and easy, dropping then rising. The pristine winter views roll by like pages from some incredible brochure Radcliffe might have devised to convince me to join his mad plot to save the planet from people. But then again, no. There must be room in this global wilderness for humankind. Otherwise, who are we saving it for? What other species can have an appreciation so wide? An eagle might be able to soar like this, but can it also dive to the depths of an ocean reef, or tunnel into caves of crystal, or write about these experiences and share them with others? No, no, no. And what creature can look to the stars from where we all came and contemplate the creation of everything from nothing? A woman can. A man. This planet is beautiful only because there are human minds here to discern that beauty from ugliness. Otherwise what is the difference between fragile Earth and the timeless deserts of Mars? What preference would a mindless universe have for one above the other? None, or so it seems to me.

As the drone sweeps low through a wide glade, I notice a small herd of horses prancing through the deep snow. Then I notice that several of the horses have riders dressed similarly to those Jimmy and I already met. As we glide by, stunned faces look up within their upturned hoods. Several mouths open as if to shout something, but I hear no sound. An instant later an arrow clanks pathetically against the underside of the drone. I turn and see another arrow arc in the empty sky behind us before gravity turns it back toward the ground.

My mother waits for us in the hangar as if she'd never left. She smiles once the hatches open and she knows we're okay.

"How was it?" she asks.

"It was beautiful," I say.

"Did you see anything interesting?"

Jimmy glances at me, a silent plea on his face not to tell her about the people or else we'll never be allowed to go out again.

Not wanting to lie, I say, "Nothing we hadn't seen before."

Later that evening, after we've all eaten a supper of cured meat and boiled yams that were left as a gift at our door, we all sit around in our furs to stave off the cold, since we can't risk draining the batteries by running the heater. Jimmy and I spend several hours catching my mother up on our adventures. We tell her about my meeting Jimmy and about the cove. We tell her about our journey over the mountain and about finding Junior and then the lake house. We tell her about blowing up Eden and about the wave that killed Radcliffe. We fill her in on our journey to the Isle of Man too, and we tell her all about the people there. Mostly we talk about Finn.

"So that's how you got that scar then," she says.

Then it hits me—Finn was my half-brother.

"You sure you didn't know about him or about the island, Mom?"

She shakes her head. "I had no idea. But knowing Robert, I'm not surprised."

When we tell her about our return journey, Jimmy gets excited, recounting how we sank that warship with a torpedo.

"I'll bet it was the same ship that killed your family that day in the cove, Jimmy," my mother says. "There was only one that patrolled the west coast of North America that I know of."

The next day we spot the drone.

Jimmy is coming back from hunting alone when he rushes into the shelter and tells us. We race to the tower together, my mother carrying her rocket launcher, and watch as it passes by twice, staying just out of range.

"You think Hannah knows we're here?" I ask.

"I don't know," my mom says. "The professor knew about this place, for sure. And he's smart enough to put me and you two disappearing together, even if he is no good at math."

"Well, I guess we'll know if it comes back."

"I hope I get a chance to shoot one," Jimmy says.

My mother nods. "I hope so too. But remember we only have this one handheld rocket left, so if I'm not around and either of you needs to use it, be sure to do just like I showed you. We can't afford to waste it and we can't afford having you blown back against the wall like I was, either."

"If we shoot one down, can't we jus' use the weapons off of it?" Jimmy asks.

"There sure wasn't much left of the one I shot," she says. "I collected all the useful parts. They're in the hangar, but the munitions were destroyed."

"Maybe we could catch one some other way," Jimmy says.

"Catch one? They're not birds that you can trap."

There's a pause in their conversation while Jimmy works out some wild idea in his head. I take the opportunity to ask my mother something that's been on my mind.

"Mom, what do you do on your computer all the time?"

"Just work mostly," she says. "Nothing fun."

"Yeah, but working on what?"

"I'll tell you about it when the time's right, Son. Right now it's still a long shot. I'd hate to get your hopes up."

"You can communicate with Holocene II, though, right?"

She nods. "I have a back door into their system, and I send and receive short text messages. But it only works when the satellites are lined up with my dish, which is on a nearby peak but hard to get to. That's where I was when you both showed up, adjusting it for a connection so I could get some word from Beth on how long you had been out there."

"Well, have you talked with them since we got here?"

"Yes, I have. What are you driving at, Son?"

"Do you know if Bill ever made it back?"

The second I ask it, her eyes drop to the tower room floor.

She slowly shakes her head and says, "I'm afraid not, Son. And worse, the tunnelrats discovered the opening and filled it in, so even if he had found it again, he would've been trapped above in the jungle alone. I'm sorry."

"Can't you have them reopen it?"

"No, the Foundation is monitoring all subterrenes now."

"So Hannah knows we got away, then?"

"Probably," she says. "I'm guessing that's why this drone was just here. They must be looking for you."

That night, as Jimmy and I lie in the hammocks that we've rigged up for ourselves, I can't seem to fall asleep.

"Jimmy," I whisper. "Are you awake?"

"Yeah," he whispers back. "I's thinkin' on trappin' birds."

"What do you want a bird for?"

"I dunno. Huntin' maybe. What's on your mind?"

"I was thinking about Bill."

"It's sad, ain't it?"

"I keep imagining him out there in the jungle all alone."

My mom groans in her sleep, the bedding rustling as she turns over. We lie quiet for several minutes. Then Jimmy says:

"He was a good man, I know that. He stayed behind so we could go. He sure was a good man."

"You think he's dead, then?"

"I ain't said that."

"No, but you said he *was* a good man."

"Well, however you say it, he was."

I stare up into the blind darkness and try to picture Bill's face. It's already fading away to just a blur, same as my father's image has. My real father. The man who raised me. I only wish I could forget Radcliffe's evil face instead. Why is it that anger sometimes outlasts love? I push my thoughts of Radcliffe away and focus instead on my real father and on Bill. As I drift off, they merge together into the same person in my mind.

"Yeah," I say, almost to myself, "he was a good man."

CHAPTER 20
Going Back For Bill

"Absolutely not," my mother says.

"You have to let me go and try to find him."

"I said no, and that's that."

"But this is important to me, Mom."

"Calling me 'Mom' won't work this time, Son. There's no way I'm sending you off by yourself all the way back to the Yucatan. No way. Not now, not ever."

I get up from the table and pace the shelter.

"So you're just going to let him die there, then?"

"He's probably already dead," she says.

"We don't know that. You don't know that. If there's even a chance, then I have to go. It isn't right to abandon him there. It wasn't right when you abandoned me, and it isn't right now."

"I didn't abandon you, Son."

"Yes you did!" I turn to her and shout. "You left me down there. You left Dad down there. And you ran around up above watching your precious little drones slaughter humans, and now you're letting another good man die just like you let my dad die. It's as if you have no heart at all. At least Bill was there for me growing up, *Mom*. Unlike you, *Mom*. He watched over me on the beach. You were nothing but a fake memory given to me by my father, who you didn't even deserve, by the way. You didn't deserve him loving you. Not him, not me."

I'm breathless when I finish my rant.

My mother is looking at me through tears. She appears to want to say a thousand things at once but can't find the words for any of them. She stands, crosses the room, and hugs me. I resist at first, but then I sink into her arms and sob.

"I'm sorry, Son. I'm so, so sorry. I love you."

"Why do you love me?" I ask. "Why?"

"Because you're my son."

"But I'm also Radcliffe's son. And when . . . when I think about that, I want to jump of a cliff and just end my life."

"Don't say that, Son."

"But it's true. I don't want him in the world, Mom. Not in Hannah, not in me. I don't want him inside me."

She walks me over to the bed and sits me down. Then she kneels in front of me and looks into my eyes.

"You listen to me now. You are not defined by whoever happened to give you your DNA, Son. You're defined by your choices. And the choices you make are yours. All yours. And you even wanting to risk going back to rescue Bill tells me that you're so far from Radcliffe and that entire lot of lunatics he was in league with that you might as well be alien to them. Do you hear me. Son? Are you listening?"

I nod that I do, my throat too constricted to speak yet.

"Now, I've known Bill since he was younger than you are. And I'm the one who's responsible for him being where he is, whether he's out there alive or dead. So I'll leave tonight and go see if I can't find him, okay? I'll try, Son."

"No, Mom. It's too dangerous."

She smiles and wipes a tear from my cheek.

"Now you know how I feel about you leaving. But only one of us can go, or there'd be no way to bring him back here if he was alive. So I'm going and that's that."

Hours later, when Jimmy bounds in the door to show off the half-dozen rabbits he's killed, I can tell that he immediately senses something's wrong, because the smile drains off his face.

"What's goin' on?" he asks.

"Mom's going to go back and look for Bill."

"Oh," he says, nodding. "When's she leavin'?"

"Soon. She wanted to wait so she could say goodbye to you. She's down taking a soak in the hot spring now."

"Should we go down'n join her, then?"

I shake my head. "She said she wanted to be alone."

"Won't she be lone enough in the drone?" he asks.

Suddenly, I realize that she'll be alone out there for days, and an uncomfortable ache appears in my gut. I change the subject. "Where on Earth did you get all those rabbits?"

"You'd be surprised how easy it is to get 'em when there's snow on the ground."

"Yeah, but what are you doing with them?"

"I got an idea," he says. "Come and help me, will you?"

We take the only knife in the shelter, along with a pair of cutters from the hangar tool chest, and carry them out to the wall near the watchtower. Jimmy lays out the dead rabbits. They look like a family of bunnies sleeping side by side. Then he begins to gut them. But he doesn't throw away the entrails like we usually do. Instead, he carries all their parts and pieces into the watchtower and lays them out on the floor to dry. Skins cut and laid flat. Intestines stretched out on the stones. Tendons and ligaments carefully removed from the muscle.

"What's all this stuff for, anyway?" I ask.

"Jus' somethin' I'm workin' on," he says.

"At least tell me why we're putting it in here?"

"We can't leave it on the wall," he says. "It'll get carried off by scavengers. I figured this was better'n the shelter."

"It's going to stink, so you figured that part right."

When we're finished, we gather the edible pieces of meat up in our arms and carry them to the shelter and boil them.

"It's not as much as it looked like," I say.

"No," he agrees. "There's lots of extras on 'em."

We've got all the meat boiled, along with some dumplings I make from the leftover yams and breakfast barley, by the time my mother comes in, steaming from her bath. Her wet hair shines almost blue-black in the LED lights. It's slicked back against her head, making her appear more like a girl our own age than someone old enough to be my mother, and certainly not someone who's been around for over three hundred years.

"Smells good," she says.

We eat our supper around the table together, and none of us mentions my mother leaving. It's almost as if we've made a silent agreement that it won't be real until it's spoken of. But as our plates clear, I notice that we all begin to eat more slowly, picking at the last of our food.

"There's more if'n you want it," Jimmy says.

Mom smiles but shakes her head. "I'm so full already, I'm afraid I might pop," she says. "And besides, I had better get dressed now and get going."

She changes behind the curtain while Jimmy and I clean the dishes by taking them outside and rubbing them out with handfuls of snow. When she emerges again, she's wearing a crisp Foundation zipsuit. She's so small without all the furs and clothing that she looks like some young pilot just out of training and about to make her first flight. I have to remind myself that she's managed to survive for a long time already.

It's a depressing descent into the hangar for all three of us.

She triple checks the flight plan and makes sure she's got plenty of water and food loaded into the second cockpit from a store of rations she keeps in the hangar.

"What's that?" I ask, indicating the controller in her hand.

"This allows me to manually pilot the drone. The autopilot will take me to the temple; then I'll search for him on my own."

"Promise me you won't go in on foot," I say.

She nods. "I'll land just long enough to refresh myself and sleep. I'll give it a few days. That's all I have supplies for. Then I'll have to come back. I'll do my best, Son."

Then she starts to climb up into the cockpit, but she stops herself, backs down, and steps over and wraps her arms around me. I hug her back, and for the first time we feel like equals in that embrace: equal in our fear for the other's safety; equal in our commitment to doing right by Bill; and equal in our need for hope that no matter what happens, all will turn out well.

She pulls back and looks into my eyes.

"I love you, Son."

"I love you too, Mom."

When she turns to Jimmy, he sticks out his hand to shake, but she smacks it away and hugs him too. He's smiling hugely when she pulls away. Then she kisses me quickly on the cheek and climbs up into the drone.

"Remember the rules, boys," she says. "Take your shoes off inside. And don't you leave the door open, Jimmy. And stay away from those wild people too."

Then she grins at us and pulls the lid down, waving once

from behind the glass before turning to look down the runway. I'm vaguely aware of the tunnel door opening to reveal the blue twilight, even though I can't take my eyes off my mother in her cockpit. I expect her to look over at me for one last goodbye, but she just looks straight ahead, as if staring down her destiny. Then she's gone in a flash. Jimmy and I run toward the opening to see her off, but before we get there the door closes, sealing her out there somewhere in that big blue evening sky.

I never do get to wave my final farewell.

CHAPTER 21
Killing Time, Catching Eagles

I swear Jimmy kills every living thing on the mountain.

At least you'd think so by seeing all those curling pelts and shriveled entrails spread out on every inch of the watchtower floor. He even lays them out on the steps, and we have to descend the stairs on our knees to keep from slipping and cracking our skulls.

When he opens the door again to carry in yet another load, the reek of rotting flesh nearly knocks me over.

"Aren't you going to tell me what all this is for?" I ask.

"You'll see soon enough," he says.

Mountain hares, tiny deer, even a wild boar—there's so much meat from all these kills, Jimmy digs a hole in the frozen ground to store it all in, then covers the hole with heavy rocks.

"Is there anything you haven't shot?" I ask.

"Yeah. I seen a wild dog and froze. Couldn't let the arrow go. Looked too much like Junior. I sighted a big mountain cat too, but I jus' couldn't even raise the bow."

He covers his meat cache with his rocks again.

I just shake my head and say, "Well, whatever you're up to, if another ice age comes we'll be set to survive it. Assuming we don't die of scurvy or some stupid thing."

It's nearly impossible for me to sleep come night, because

all I do is worry about my mom. I know she brought supplies enough to search for as long as a week if she needs to, but I keep wondering when she'll be home. I feel sick with guilt over having encouraged her to go, but I think I would have felt just as bad if we had done nothing for Bill. And this new guilt is added to the ache already in my guts over Red. There has to be some way to free him, to free all of Holocene II. I know my mother must be working on something, and I even sit down at her computer to see if she left any clues about it, but I can't bring myself to betray her trust by turning it on.

The next morning, apparently satisfied with his collection, Jimmy skips hunting and locks himself away in the watchtower, working on whatever mad designs he's dreamed up for the dead beasts in there. I go for a walk alone along the wall.

It's still too cold yet for the snow to melt, but the wind has blown it away from the high places. It's now mostly stacked up in deep drifts that soften some of the harshness of the mountains. It's beautiful, really. I know this wall is ancient, and I can imagine the ghosts of tourists standing here before the War, marveling at the snowy landscape and snapping photos of one another to share with friends back home.

I walk a little farther, and the wall fades away into hardly noticeable heaps of old stone. Those early scientists with the Park Service must have maintained their section of wall for this outpost, before their numbers began to thin. I wonder why so many of them ended up committing suicide. But then I'm only fifteen, no, almost sixteen, years into my millennium.

I stand on the wall and gaze east, wondering about my mom. She's so far away, though, I might as well turn and look west for the same news. Nothing. Just blue winter skies and me here half a world away, wondering if she's alright.

Jimmy comes in from the watchtower long after dark and gives me a rawhide lanyard.

"What's this?" I ask.

"So you can wear your dad's pipe like you used to."

I admire its craftsmanship. It really is a thoughtful gesture, and I waste no time threading the pipe onto the lanyard and hanging it around my neck. Feels like old times.

"I appreciate the gift," I say. "I just hope it didn't take all those animals to make it or else I'll feel bad."

"Nah," Jimmy says, "I's jus' tryin' out my technique."

"Technique for what?"

"For braidin' my rope."

"What are you making a rope for?"

"You'll see," he says, "you'll see."

We eat a cold supper and turn in, lying in our hammocks in the dark and listening to the wind whistle faintly by outside.

Jimmy must hear my thoughts, because after a long time with no talking he says, "She'll be alright."

"Thanks, Jimmy. I really hope so."

I eventually drift off, and if I dream I can't recall it when some sound at the door wakes me. Could it be my mother? No, she'd come in through the hangar below. I get up and go to the door and open it. The mountains to the east stand black against just a hint of blue dawn. A basket and a clay pot of milk rest on the ground in front of the door. I step out and just catch sight of the fur-clad gift giver padding away down the path and into the shadows.

After breakfast, Jimmy leads me out to a plateau several minutes hard hiking from the shelter. Once there, he begins to dig a hole with the rock he used to dig his meat cache. It looks like slow and difficult progress in the frozen ground.

"I'll help you, but only if you tell me what you're doing."

"I'm diggin' a hole."

"Yeah, I can see that much. For more meat?"

"Nope."

Giving up on getting any answers, I pick up my own rock and kneel down to help him.

"How deep's it gotta be?"

"Jus' deep enough for me to lie down in," he says.

"Well, whatever you're doing, I sure hope you don't turn out to be digging your own grave."

With the hole dug we hike down past the hot springs until we find some trees with needles still on their branches. Jimmy breaks off a pile of heavy limbs, and we drag them back up to the bluff, the needles sweeping the trail behind us as we go. He covers the hole with the branches and stands back with his hands on his hips, admiring his accomplishment.

"It isn't deep enough for a trap," I say, "so what it is?"

"If I tell you what I'm doin', will you help me?"

"How can I answer that if I don't even know yet what I'd

be helping you with?"

"I'm gonna get me one of them eagles."

I know he's not kidding about it either, because the next morning he wakes me up early, dressed like some mad, fur-clad zombie risen from the dead. He's covered nearly head to toe in animal pelts, and he's wearing a rawhide glove to his shoulder. He has a small lasso of woven rope looped around his waist and a dead rabbit in his ungloved hand. I look him over from my hammock and yawn.

"You look ridiculous."

"Come on," he says, "they like to hunt in the mornin'."

"What about breakfast?"

"Grab some jerky. I already melted snow and filled us up some water bottles."

At least he's taking my mind off of worrying about my mother, I think, as I begrudgingly get up and dress. It's still gray out when we leave the shelter. The entire hike to the plateau I can't take my eyes off Jimmy's insane costume. He lumbers along the path, walking woodenly with the loose parts of his costume flapping in the light breeze.

"Who are you supposed to be?" I finally ask. "Some wildlife version of Frankenstein's monster?"

"Who's Frankenstein?"

"Oh, it doesn't matter," I say. "Just some character from an ancient book I read. The point is, you look ridiculous. Do you really think you're going to fool an eagle with that outfit?"

"I ain't tryin' to fool him," he says. "It's for protection."

"Protection?"

"Yeah, I wet the hides and dried 'em so they's almost like armor. Here, feel."

"Jimmy, I think you've finally lost your mind."

When we arrive at the plateau, Jimmy slides back the pine branches, uncovering his hole. Then he crawls in and lies down.

"Here," he says, handing me up the dead rabbit. "Put the branches back over me. Make sure I'm covered. Then lay the rabbit on top of 'em and make it look encitin'."

"How do I make a dead rabbit look enticing?"

"Jus' be sure it's on its side so the eagle can see its shape."

"Then what should I do?"

"You can watch if you wanna, but you gotta get far away and hide somewhere."

I look down at Jimmy, lying in his hole and covered in his mismatched pelts. If it weren't for the look of determination in his eyes, I'd think him totally insane.

"Okay, buddy. How long should I let you lie in here?"

"I guess 'till I come out," he says.

I drag the branches over him and lay the rabbit on top of them on its side. Jimmy reaches up through the needles and adjusts its pose from underneath.

"What?" I ask. "Didn't I make it enticing enough?"

"It's fine," he mumbles. "I's jus' checkin' to make sure I've got a clear reach."

I walk away, shaking my head.

He's either braver than I am or crazier than I am.

I hike several hundred meters out to a high point and hide behind a rock outcropping where I can look down on him. The rabbit stands out small and pale against the dark pine branches, but I see no hint of Jimmy hiding beneath them.

Maybe he's onto something after all.

Sitting with nothing to do is boring, and my thoughts drift eventually to my mother, of course. I keep looking toward the shelter, even though I can't see it from where I am, wondering if she's back yet. But the only thing I know for sure is that she didn't find him right away or they would have returned by now.

As the morning wears on, the sky lightens, although high clouds keep the sun from showing, and nothing marks itself out against the gray above. No eagle, no hawk, no sparrow. I sit for hours, watching the dead rabbit and listening to my stomach grumble until the ground grows too uncomfortable to sit even a minute longer. I decide to hike down to see if Jimmy's okay.

He must hear my approach, because his disembodied voice from beneath the branches says, "You're scarin' the birds."

"There are no birds to scare, Jimmy," I say, feeling funny talking to a dead rabbit. "I just came down to see if you were all right, which was silly of me since you're obviously all wrong. I'm gonna go eat. You want me to bring you something?"

"No thanks," he says. "I've got some jerky in my pocket."

"What about water?"

"I got that too."

"What about the bathroom?"

"I brought my pee bottle."

"Well, be sure you drink out of the right one, then. I'll be back down later."

"Okay, but stay out of sight."

"How will I know you're okay?"

"I'll be fine," he says. But as I turn to walk away, he calls to me from his hideaway underground. "Hey, Aubrey . . ."

"Yes, Jimmy?"

"If your mom comes back, it's okay to come and get me."

I nod and smile, even though he can't see it.

The shelter is cold and lonely without Jimmy or my mom around. The workstation where I've become accustomed to seeing her sits empty and unused, the screen blank, as if any evidence of her has already been erased. The cold meat and milk I eat for lunch does little to improve my mood, so I climb down into the hangar and sit awhile in the cold, watching the empty runway tunnel and the closed door. When the lights finally turn off, I sit still and stay in the dark.

Three times I hike back down to check on Jimmy, but he's always hidden in his hole just the same as the time before, the dead rabbit staring blankly into the sky from its bed of pine. Once, I see a bird circling high overhead, maybe even an eagle, but it passes on, riding the wind to the west and disappearing.

For no other reason than boredom, I hike down to the hot spring in the late afternoon to bathe. I lower myself into the warm water until just my eyes remain above the surface. I watch as thin snowflakes drift down and meet the rising steam and melt. I remember sitting in this pool with my mother and hearing her story, and I wish more than anything that she were here with me now so I could ask her all the things I didn't then. What are her favorite books? We must have read the same ones since we both grew up with Holocene II reading slates. What's her favorite season? Her favorite color? Her favorite food? I know it can't be algaecrisps. And I want to ask her about my father too. Not Radcliffe, but my real father. Anything she might tell me about what he was like before I was born.

After my bath, I check on Jimmy again, but the rabbit hasn't moved. I'm torn between going down to see if he's okay and not wanting to disturb him, but the temperature has already dropped. It's snowing and almost dark.

When I pull the branches back, the look of defeat on his face nearly breaks my heart.

"There's still light left," he says.

"Jimmy, your nose is blue."

"Okay," he says, "help me up."

He rises like some frozen and stiff-legged apparition from the grave, and leans on me for support as we trudge together back toward the shelter. Flurries of snow blow across our path.

"I'm goin' back in the mornin'," he says, having guessed correctly that I was going to try and talk him out of it.

It takes him a full half hour to disrobe from his costume—pulling off his long rawhide glove, unlacing leggings, removing the leather chest plating. When he finishes, the pile of frozen clothing looks like some slaughterhouse garbage heap in the corner of the shelter. How he gets it all on again is a mystery to me, but by first light he's standing at the door, ready to go. I'm still pulling on my coat when we step out into a wonderland of white. Every inch of ground is covered in snow.

Jimmy retrieves the rabbit from his meat cache where he stuffed it the night before. It's frozen so solid that when he picks it up, it maintains its shape as if carved out of stone.

"Maybe we should wait until this snow melts," I suggest.

Jimmy ignores me, tucks the rabbit under his armpit, and heads off down the trail toward the plateau. By the time we reach the snow-covered hole, the rabbit has thawed enough for him to be able to at least reposition the legs.

"I want it to look more appealin'," he says. "Like it's alive but distressed, you know?"

"Funny, but that's kind of how you look to me," I reply.

When Jimmy's lying back in the hole, I cover him again and lay the rabbit down like he showed me. Then I wish him luck and take one of the extra pine branches and back away from the bluff, sweeping our footprints from the snow as I go. I hide behind my outcropping with the pine branch on my lap for extra cover and settle in to watch, as just like the day before, nothing happens. For the first time since we've been here, there's no wind. It's remarkably quiet, as if the snow has sucked the sound out of everything. My thoughts drift to my mother and how different the weather must be in the jungle as she flies over it, looking for Bill. It's hard to believe two people can have such different experiences at the same time.

Movement catches my eye on the snow below, and I watch

as a small rodent, perhaps a ground squirrel, scurries up to Jimmy's hideaway and sniffs the dead rabbit before moving on again. If Jimmy notices, he doesn't move a muscle. I pull some jerky from my pocket and nearly break my tooth on it, as solid as it's frozen. I tuck it in my cheek to thaw.

"This is really crazy," I mutter to myself.

The eagle appears late in the afternoon.

I spot it gliding on a current high above us. It passes, then returns, descending in wide circles. Does it see Jimmy's rabbit? It must. The eagle drops lower and circles again. But then it turns to fly away, taking my excitement with it. No. Wait. It turns back, tucks its wings, and glides down toward the rabbit with its talons outstretched. I expect it to snatch it and fly off, but the eagle lands on the branches, bowing them beneath its weight, and perches there picking at the dead rabbit with its enormous yellow beak.

Jimmy must be asleep, I think, because as the eagle feasts, there is no movement from Jimmy to trap it. I'm tempted to yell something to wake him up, but I know the slightest sound from me will scare the eagle away. Besides, by the size of that thing, it might be better if Jimmy doesn't catch it. As if I had spoken my thoughts out loud, the eagle lifts its head, a purple tangle of entrails dangling from its beak, and looks up toward where I'm sitting. It's still as a statue, just staring at me.

Then it jumps, as if startled by something. It unfolds its impressive wings and labors up off the rabbit, bringing the pine branches and Jimmy up with it. The branches fall away, and

Jimmy stands there, reeling on the snow in his incredible suit with the eagle's talons caught in his hand as it flaps wildly above his head, trying to get away. He looks like some frozen Viking warrior who's climbed out of his grave to hitch a ride up to the Valhalla on a Valkyrie.

I rush down from my post to try and help.

The eagle pulls Jimmy left, then right, nearly sending him plunging off the plateau, and then it gives up on getting away and turns to peck out his eyes. As Jimmy fends off its beak with his glove, I grab a pine branch and swing it at the bird, trying to distract it. It works long enough for Jimmy to slip out his lasso and somehow manage to ensnare the eagle's talons. Then he falls to his knees, jerks it down to the ground, and presses his hand into its wide back. The eagle hisses and tries to raise its head, but Jimmy keeps it pinned.

"Grab the hood," Jimmy says.

"The what?"

"On my belt there. Grab it and put it on him."

I pull the makeshift hood free from Jimmy's belt and kneel down next to the eagle in the snow. It stares at me with furious yellow eyes. Keeping my hand clear of its powerful beak, I slip the hood over its head and tie it with the tethers. The moment its eyes are covered, the eagle gives up its fight and goes limp on the ground. Jimmy slumps down breathless in the snow and pulls the giant eagle into his lap. He tries to sooth it by cooing softly and petting its ruffled feathers.

"I can't believe you did it," I say.

Jimmy grins from ear to ear.

"Not me," he says. "We did it, buddy. I never could have caught him without your help."

"How do you know it isn't a she?"

Jimmy looks at the bird, as if suddenly uncertain of its sex himself. The eagle shivers in its feathers then settles again.

"Shoot," I say. "If it's a he or a she hardly matters. What I wanna know is what are you going to do with it now?"

Jimmy shrugs. "I ain't thought that far ahead," he says. "Guess I wasn't convinced I'd really catch one."

CHAPTER 22
Flying Eagle, Falling Drone

It's hard to sleep with an eagle perched in the corner.

I keep thinking it will somehow get free and decide to feast on my eyeballs as I sleep. But Jimmy assures me that he leashed it securely to the chair on the back of which it's perched, and that he weighted the chair with plenty of rocks.

"Besides," he says, "I fed it lots of raw rabbit meat."

"Oh, that's reassuring," I grumble.

"Shh . . ." he says, "my eagle's tryin' to sleep."

A little later, I say, "I can tell you this much, you're gonna have to find a new place for it when my mother gets home."

Jimmy doesn't respond to this comment. I begin to worry that maybe he thinks she isn't coming home.

"She'll be back any day now," I say. "Maybe tomorrow."

"I know she will," he replies. "She'll be fine."

We're awakened in the night by a wild clatter and the LED lights coming on. The eagle is flapping around the shelter, dragging the chair with it. Jimmy leaps out of his hammock and manages to seize the bird and hood it again. Then he returns it to its corner and reweights the chair, tying an exceptionally large rock to its base this time.

In the morning, the eagle's hood is off again. It waits for us to rise with its unblinking and patient yellow eyes, as if it hadn't slept at all. Jimmy lengthens its leash and feeds it by baiting the floor with chunks of rabbit meat and making it flap off its perch to retrieve them. I heat leftover porridge on the stove for Jimmy and myself. After breakfast, Jimmy hoods his eagle and coaxes it onto his gloved arm.

"Jimmy, that thing's nearly as large as you are."

"It ain't light neither," he responds. "I'm gonna have to build one of them braces that fella on the horse was usin'. You wanna come watch me train him?"

"Maybe later," I say. "You go ahead."

With Jimmy gone I head out to the tower to watch for my mother's return. The sky is gray, and dark clouds pile up on the horizon to the east, but it does not snow again. I stand all day at the window with no sun to mark the passage of time, and when the sky finally fades toward black, signaling that the short winter day has come to a close, I head into the shelter, defeated.

"Nothing?" Jimmy asks.

I shake my head.

"She'll be back, Aubrey. I'm tellin' you."

"How'd you do?" I ask, changing the subject.

"I got ol' Valor here to fly and return to my arm for some meat. Still on the leash, of course."

"Valor?"

"That's what I named him. I thought on it all day. My pa said eagles is fearless. I think that's what valor means, don't it?"

"It does and it's a good name."

"Maybe you could come out and help me tomorrow," he suggests. "Watchin' and waitin' won't hurry her back."

"Thanks, but I'm going to stay around here just in case."

She doesn't come home the next day.

Or the next day after that either.

I sit my vigil in the tower, watching the sky and trying not to think of all the things that might have happened to her and to Bill. Jimmy takes breaks from training Valor to deliver me hot soup, but he no longer tells me she'll be coming back; he mostly just sits quietly and watches the window with me.

On the afternoon of my third day watching, the ninth day since my mother left, I spot the drone. I rush to the window for a better view, uncertain if I can trust my eyes after all this time of waiting and hoping. But sure enough, the sun glints on its wings as it approaches from the east against a clear, blue winter sky. I'm leaving the window to run down to the hangar to meet her when something catches my eye and stops me. As the drone turns for its final approach, I see the Park Service crest on its nose. That can't be; my mother had sanded it off of hers. Then I notice that there are no cockpit covers on this drone either. Before I can react, the drone launches a missile.

At first, I think it's coming for me. But it passes by the watchtower and explodes against the mountain beneath the wall, just missing the concealed hangar door. The fireball fades, and dislodged rocks go tumbling down the mountainside.

As the drone flies by, no doubt intending to come around and try again, I race down the watchtower stairs and out onto the wall. I run full speed to the shelter and slam the door closed behind me. I'm down the ladder three rungs at a time and nearly on the hangar floor before the motion sensor lights even come on. I grab the rocket launcher.

As I head for the ladder again, a voice in my head says, "There's no time, Aubrey, and if the drone destroys our runway, there won't be any way for your mother to land."

Instead of climbing the ladder, I slap the emergency door open button on the wall. The door slides away from the end of the runway, and daylight washes the tunnel. Adrenalin takes over, and I bolt toward the opening, carrying the rocket cradled in my arms. I get to the edge and stand there, looking out from inside the mountain at nothing but blue sky. Then the drone rises into view, heading straight toward me, so close already that I can see the red tips of missiles inside their tubes.

I raise the rocket launcher to my shoulder, aim, and fire.

The rocket leaves the tube with enough force to blow me back a meter or two. I land on my rear and slide several more meters on the smooth runway. Just as I come to rest, a massive fireball appears in the sky outside the opening, and then a shockwave slams into my chest. I toss the empty launch tube aside, get up, and walk back to the door.

What's left of the drone lies in a twisted heap of smoking metal several hundred meters below me where the mountain levels off. I stand and stare down on it for a long time. The next thing I know, Jimmy is standing next to me.

After a while, he says, "That wasn't . . ."

"No," I say, "it wasn't her."

It takes us nearly an hour to hike down to the wreckage. When we get there it turns out to hardly have been worth the time. We search for weapons or anything salvageable, but very little remains other than scrap. Jimmy collects several pieces of metal that he thinks might be useful for one thing or another, and we carry them back up to the shelter.

Ours is a quiet supper. Even Jimmy's eagle seems to sense the depressed mood, sitting quietly on its perch, only moving to snatch the occasional piece of meat Jimmy tosses its way.

"It's not a good sign, Jimmy," I finally admit, since neither of us has talked about what's happened.

"Whaddya mean?" he asks.

"I mean for my mother coming back."

"Why would you say that?"

"Because Hannah and the professor obviously know we're here. And they must have been manually controlling that drone from the Foundation. They're programmed to target people, and that thing was trying to destroy our runway."

Jimmy sighs and pushes his bowl of stew away.

"Or," he says, "It could tell us your mom at least ain't been hurt by them yet."

"How so?"

"They was tryin' to destroy the runway, right?"

I nod and Jimmy continues.

"Well, if they knew that your mom was hurt or somethin' worse, then they wouldn't have bothered. So it's a good sign."

Jimmy's insight is small comfort, but I carry it to bed with me like my last hope on Earth. I lie in my hammock and imagine a thousand scenarios that might have held my mother up. Maybe trouble with the drone. Or maybe she found Bill, but he wasn't fit for travel, and she's nursing him. Or what if she had some other errand to run that she hadn't told me about? This last thought jolts me awake with the realization about just how little I know about my mother and her plans. I know she wanted to rescue me, but she must have had some longer term plan to take over the Foundation from Hannah. There's no way we could live forever on the run from the Park Service.

I quietly get up, but the lights snap on anyway and give me away. Jimmy rolls over in his hammock and covers his eyes with his forearm. The eagle cracks one yellow eye and follows me with it to my mother's workstation. I sit down and turn on the monitor. Her last sent message is open on the screen:

Leaving tonight to search for Bill. Should be back within one week. If you don't hear from me by day zero, go ahead with the mission on your own. May history be on our side. Signed, your affectionate Chief.

There's an unopened reply message beneath it, but when I try to scroll down to open it, the computer locks and calls up a password screen. Great. I'm locked out. Wanting to commit it to memory, I repeat the message I just read: "If you don't hear from me by day zero, go ahead with the mission on your own."

What mission? I wonder. And who was she writing to? She also said she should be back in one week, and tomorrow will be the tenth day since she's been gone. Now I'm even more confused and even more depressed than before. I'm tempted to wake Jimmy, just to have someone to talk to, but he's sound asleep in his hammock. I tiptoe up to his eagle and look at its solemn face. It stares back at me as if it understands everything in the world but has for some secret reason decided to care nothing about any of it. Perhaps it's wiser than we are, after all.

Fatigue hits me like an aftershock from the day's wild events. I return to my hammock and fall asleep before the lights can even turn themselves off.

CHAPTER 23
The Return

I dream she's home and then the dream is real.

Jumping from my hammock, I nearly trip and break my neck on my way down to the hangar. Sure enough, the door is just closing out the gray light of dawn, and the drone is parked on the runway beneath the LED tunnel lights, with ice crystals still sparkling on its wings. The cockpit glass is fogged so that I can't see inside. I impatiently lift it open.

"Oh, God, Mother."

She's slumped in the seat with her eyes closed. Her skin is pale, and her hair is soaked with sweat. Her breathing is labored and shallow.

I turn and scream, "Jimmy! Help me, Jimmy!"

Jimmy is by my side in a flash, and we lift her from the cockpit and lay her on the floor. As soon as she's out, I realize how bad it is. Her right leg is swollen to twice its normal size, hemmed in and horribly misshapen by the stitching of her zipsuit. Jimmy runs for a knife while I try to wake her up. But she won't speak to me or even open her eyes. Jimmy returns and carefully cuts the material away from her leg. He peels it back, revealing the blackened and swollen flesh. Her skin has cracked near the calf, and a gaping wound leaks yellow puss.

"What the hell happened?"

"Snakebite," Jimmy says. "I seen it before."

"Then you know what to do, right? You have to know, if you've seen this before. What do we do, Jimmy?"

He looks gravely at her leg and shakes his head. "I dunno. My mom always had snakeroot, but I wouldn't know how to find it or if there's even any around here."

"We have to try, Jimmy. We have to do something."

"Okay," he says. "I'll go. Make her comfortable. And get some liquids in her."

Her head is in my lap when I hear the door slam above.

"You're going to be okay, Mom," I tell her, even though she doesn't appear to hear me. "We plan to fix you up."

I climb the ladder and drag her bed over and toss it down into the hangar along with her blankets. When I have her on the bed, I hold her head up and squeeze drips of water into her mouth from a wet towel. Her eyelashes flicker as if she wants to open them, but soon she's gone again. I go back upstairs and search everywhere for a first aid kit but can't find one. Instead, I boil water and a cloth and then I carry the hot pot carefully down the ladder and spend a solid hour cleaning her wound. Dark tendrils spread out and run up her thigh from the bite, and the way her calf has split open and blackened reminds me of Jimmy's brush with death in the cove. I have to keep reminding myself that this is the result of venom, and that I can't be sure yet that it's even infected.

I hear the door above open, then close. Jimmy comes down the ladder followed by a woman bundled in furs. She kneels and takes my mother's wounded leg in her weathered hands and looks at it closely. Then she opens a bag and pulls out a plump, live bird, resembling pictures I've seen of doves. She produces a tiny knife from among her clothing and slits the dove's belly open and presses it to my mother's leg, wound to wound. The dove doesn't make a sound; it just rests in the woman's hand with a trickle of its own blood now running down my mother's swollen calf. It twists its small head on its rubbery neck to look at each of us in turn. A minute later it begins to convulse. Two minutes later, it's dead.

The woman turns and says something to Jimmy in a language I can't understand. When Jimmy holds up his hands, confused, she picks the towel up and motions as if tearing it into strips. Jimmy nods, climbs the ladder, and disappears. I want to ask her if my mother will be okay, but I know we don't speak one another's language, and the woman has hardly even acknowledged that I'm here.

Casting the dead dove aside, she opens a deerskin pouch, pulls out a gnarled root, bites off a chunk and chews it. She holds the root out to me, signaling that I should do the same. We sit together, chewing over my sick mother, our jaws frantically working the tough root. The texture is pulpy, and it swells in my mouth like dough. The woman spits the chewed root into her hand and then holds her hand beneath my mouth for me to spit mine. Then she mashes the chewed root into my mother's open wound. I wince, imagining her pain. Fortunately, she's so out of it she doesn't make a sound.

Jimmy comes down, carrying strips of cloth that he's torn from the clothes we discarded when we made our kilts. He hands them to the woman, and she wraps the leg and ties it off. Then she takes another small bite of root, chews it, and wraps it in one of the cloths, making a small ball. She dips this chewed root ball into the pot of water. Then she holds my mother's head upright with one strong hand and puts the dripping cloth into her mouth. She massages my mother's neck, coaxing her to swallow. Then she dips the root again and repeats the process.

When the woman is finished, she lays my mother's head back. Then she hands me the cloth and the leftover root and signals that we should continue to feed her the juice.

"How often?" I ask.

When she looks at me blankly, I point to the root in my hand and then to my mother's mouth. The woman points and arcs her finger, signaling the sun moving across the sky. Then she holds up four fingers. I take this to mean four times a day.

"Thank you," I say, bowing.

She lays a hand on my mother's forehead as if blessing her, then she gathers up her pouch and rises to leave. She picks up the dead dove, slips it back into her sack, and climbs the ladder. Jimmy follows her up, I presume to say goodbye. I stay by my mother's side.

It's three days before she's well enough to speak.

I'm sleeping beside her on the floor, or at least trying to sleep, when she mumbles my name. I sit up and trigger the lights. Her fever has broken, and for the first time since she returned there's no sweat on her brow.

"Mom, are you okay?"

She opens her eyes. They seem to look at nothing. Then her pupils slowly dilate, she focuses on me, and smiles.

"Oh, Aubrey."

I reach down and caress her cheek. "Mom, I love you."

"I love you too, Son," she says.

Then she closes her eyes again and sleeps.

In the morning she tells me she's hungry. Jimmy says it's a great sign, and he makes her a pot of broth. She drinks it all and asks for more. Later, after the calories have restored her energy, she wants to see her leg. I pull her bed against the wall and prop her up. Then I remove the bandage for her. She sees the blackened flesh and turns away.

"It's not as bad as it looks," I say. "It's not infected, and Jimmy says other than nasty scarring you should be okay."

"I never was much for shaving and showing off my legs anyway," she jokes. Then she caresses my cheek and adds, "Thanks for looking after me so well."

"We had help from the wild people."

"You did?"

"Yeah, Jimmy went and found them. He said he'd seen their camp when he was out hunting. It probably saved your life, but certainly your leg."

"That's twice now," she says. "We'll have to find a way to thank them. And Jimmy too."

"What happened out there, Mom?"

"I tried, Son. I really tried to find him."

"Did you see any sign of him at all?"

"It was stormy a lot, and it rained almost every night. I'd sleep under the drone's wing to stay dry and then fly again at first light. I was out of rations but I decided to give it one last day. That's when I saw the smoke."

"So you did see him?"

She shakes her head. "I thought so," she says, "but no. I saw the smoke and landed the drone and hiked in on foot. But when I got there, it was just a tree that had been struck by lightning and burned down to a stump." She grits her teeth and plants her hands on the bed to adjust her position before going on. "I was hiking back when the snake bit me. It hardly hurt, but before long I couldn't walk. I thought I was dead, Aubrey. I crawled the last kilometer to the drone and just managed to get inside and hit 'return home' before I passed out."

"Well, you're safe now," I say.

"But I didn't find Bill, Aubrey. I failed you."

"No you didn't fail, Mom. You tried and that's all anybody could do. I'm really, really, proud of you."

She closes her eyes and sighs.

When she opens them again she says, "Do you think we could get me out of this hangar and upstairs? I feel like an old drone mothballed for maintenance."

It takes a long time and lots of careful maneuvering, but I manage to help her up the ladder, using only her good leg and her hands. Then I sit her on a chair and go back down and carry up her bedding. She's lying down and in better spirits by the time Jimmy comes bounding in with his eagle on his arm.

Mother looks at him as if not quite believing her own eyes. I see her move a hand over to pinch the skin on her forearm.

"Hi, Miss Bradford."

"Jimmy, what in the name of science are you doing with that feathered dinosaur on your arm?"

"This is Valor, Miss Bradford. My eagle."

"Your eagle." She says it quietly as if repeating it to herself might help make some sense of what's she's seeing.

"You should have seen him trap it, Mom. It was wild."

"I'm sure it was. Don't you dare think that that thing is sleeping in here, Jimmy. If you want to keep it, you had better keep it in the watchtower."

"That's fine by me," he says.

After Jimmy makes his eagle comfortable in the tower, he joins us back in the shelter for dinner. In addition to spoils from Jimmy's hunting, the gifts have continued to appear at the door. We eat boiled potatoes and fried meat and chase it all down will long drinks of milk from the jug. Afterwards, we sit around and fill one another in on our adventures. Jimmy tells us about how Valor now flies and returns on command. My mother tells us about a flock of geese that decided her drone was their leader and how they formed up behind her in a V and followed her all over the jungle. She says she felt so bad leading them in circles that she finally sped up and maneuvered to shake them. Her story reminds me about my own adventure with a drone, and I tell her about the one we shot out of the sky while she was gone.

"You're right about them knowing we're here," she says. "Someone was manually controlling that drone. They'll likely be sending more. We're going to have to be on the lookout."

None of us mentions that I used the last rocket to take down that drone, but we're all thinking it.

A knock on the door startles us from our quiet reflection. Jimmy and I look at one another and rise from the table at the same time. Jimmy pulls out his knife and cups it in his hand and I grab the key and unlock the door, having locked it before we sat down to dinner. When I pull the door open, a bearded man is standing there in the late afternoon light. He looks like one of the men Jimmy and I saw that day on horseback. His face has no expression, but he hands me a piece of bark with strange characters written on it. I show it to Jimmy, but Jimmy just shakes his head. I hand it back to the man.

"We can't understand this," I say.

The man nods, as if he'd been expecting as much He tucks the bark away amongst his furs and mimes the act of eating by touching his hand to his mouth.

"Oh, you're hungry," I say, nodding. "Come in and eat."

I step aside and wave him in, but the man shakes his head. He points at each of us, including my mother where she sits in her chair, then points back down the path up which he came.

"I think he's askin' us to join 'em for dinner," Jimmy says.

Jimmy mimes eating and then points down the path. The

man nods. Jimmy points up to the sky, shrugging and holding out his hands to indicate that he's asking when. The man nods that he understands, points himself to the sky, and mimes the sun crossing it from east to west. Then he holds up two fingers.

"I think he wants us to join 'em for dinner at this time two days from now," Jimmy says. "I can take us there."

I turn to look in at my mother where she sits.

"Mom, what do you think about that? Are you up for it?"

"It would be awfully rude to say no, considering they've saved my life twice now. I'd tell you to ask him what we can bring, but I'm afraid you'd be there with the door open all night trying to scratch it out. And it's getting cold in here already."

I turn back to the man and hold up two fingers and nod. He bows slightly, turns, and walks away down the path.

When the door is closed again, my mother looks at Jimmy and says, "Jimmy, do you think you could stitch me up one of those kilts you boys wear? It seems like you all saved my leg but destroyed my zipsuit in the process. Besides, I doubt those folks want to see the Park Service emblem anyway."

"Of course, Miss Bradshaw. I'll start it tonight."

"And maybe tomorrow you could kill something fresh to bring. I'll bet those folks eat a lot of meat. And Aubrey, you'll have to help me down to the pools so I can wash my hair. I look much too horrid right now to dine at anyone's table, even if these wild people take their meals on the dirt, as I suspect."

CHAPTER 24
Dinner with Friends

My mom walks pretty well on her new crutch.

Jimmy wanted to bring his eagle along, but we convinced him it was rude to show up to dinner with a pet. Instead he's carrying three dead rabbits that he shot this morning to give to our hosts as gifts.

"How's your new kilt, Miss Bradford?" Jimmy asks.

"I'm loving it, Jimmy. Thank you. We should fit right in."

Jimmy beams when she says she loves the kilt. It's obvious that he respects her a great deal, and that makes me proud.

We each take a side and help my mother down the rocks to the river and discover that the strangers have placed flat-topped stumps in a shoal, creating a dry path for us to cross.

"Thoughtful for such a wild bunch," my mother says.

Safe and dry on the other side, we continue on to crest the hill where Jimmy and I saw the eagle kill the deer. Then Jimmy leads us directly toward a granite cliff that rises hundreds of meters into the sky; a cliff so steep and impassible that if he had not brought back that healer to our shelter for my mother, I'd seriously doubt that he even knows where he's taking us.

Then we hear the music: a beautiful song echoing off the cliff face, as if the rock itself were singing. We stop for a moment and listen. The sun has dropped behind the western peaks, and the soft afternoon light adds to the mystery of the music—strings beneath a melody of throaty notes that create an ethereal experience. I could stand here all day and listen.

"Come on," Jimmy says. "The entrance is right over here."

We walk straight toward the stone wall of music, and I try to puzzle out what illusion is making it possible. Then we crest an almost imperceptible rise in the landscape, and I see that Jimmy has brought us to a portion of the mountain that is actually made up of two cliffs meeting. From a distance the granite all blurs together, tricking the eye into believing it's a solid wall, but there's a hidden gap where the cliffs overlap. Standing in front of this secret entrance is the source of the song—a small man cradling a tall, stringed instrument in one arm and drawing a bow across it with the other. His face is uplifted, as if perhaps he's serenading the sky, and the sound that rises from his throat seems far too powerful to be coming from such a humbly-statured man.

"This is quite a welcome," my mother says to me.

The man keeps right on singing as Jimmy walks past him and around the corner and into the gap, as if he were walking into his own home. My mother and I follow. The narrow gap has a blind turn at the end. I notice that the dirt path is trampled as smooth as stone with nicks of horse hooves visible on its edges. When we round the corner, I can hardly believe my eyes. I'm looking at a hidden valley containing a kind of permanent camp. Steep cliffs rise up on three sides. A waterfall tumbles down into a pool and fills a dredged channel that runs through the center of the valley until it reaches the far end and drains out through a narrow gorge, showing just a crack of sky between the two cliffs that hem it in. Multiple wooden bridges crisscross the channel, beautifully constructed with gentle arches and decorated rails. A maze of pathways leads to an assortment of tent-like structures. The narrow slice of sky above washes everything in a sort of magical glow. Torches line the bridges and the walks and reflect back out of the water. Many of the tents glow with the promise of more fires within. I see a fenced corral of horses with their heads buried in feed bins. Another pen contains goats fattened for milking.

I take all of this in with hungry eyes in just a matter of seconds, because when I see the boy standing on the nearest bridge to greet us, I can't look at anything else. He's dressed in red robes embroidered with intricate gold patterns. Two men stand behind him, holding the train of his royal garments off the ground. He wears a quilted crown embedded with precious stones, and by the expressionless look of curiosity on his young face, I'd guess that he's just as comfortable in this gaudy get up as he was in the furs we saw him wearing while on horseback the other day. The old man with one eye stands beside him, overshadowed by the boy and his costume.

My mother nudges Jimmy, and he unstraps the dead rabbits from his waist. We each take one rabbit cradled in our open palms, just like Jimmy taught us to, and walk as a group toward our hosts with our gifts outstretched before us. The boy looks at each rabbit in turn. When he nods, the old man steps up and collects them from us. Then the boy unfolds his heavy robe and reaches up both arms as if to take my face in his hands and kiss me. But when I bend down to accommodate this gesture, he pulls my head to his nose and smells my hair. He repeats this strange custom with Jimmy and with my mom. Then he speaks a few words none of us understand, and he turns along with his procession and leads us over the bridge and into the camp.

He takes us into a large community tent with an enormous clay stove in its center. Several shirtless men work at the stove, their sweat-covered backs glistening in the firelight. They stir pots and turn meat and make small balls of dough into cakes that they fry on a flat, clay cooktop. The smells set my mouth to watering. The old man carries our rabbits to the stove and hands them over to the cook, who takes them one at a time and turns them each toward the firelight and inspects their faces as if perhaps he might recognize them. Satisfied, he carries them off somewhere.

"Looks like you shot good ones, Jimmy."

"Thanks," he says. "Those was the fattest I could find."

The two attendants gather up the boy's train and hold open his robe while he steps out of it. He's wearing a thinner, less extravagant robe underneath, and he emerges from the cocoon of the formal robe much smaller than he was while wearing it. I can't help but imagine how small he'd be if he kept on disrobing, robe after robe after robe. The boy crosses to where a royal red curtain hangs from one end of the tent and sits down cross-legged on a pillow in front of it. The old man strikes a gong, and suddenly several men appear from behind the curtain and line pillows on the floor in a semicircle around the boy. Then the men disappear behind the curtain again, as if by some magic. There must be a door back there. The two attendants, having now discarded the boy's formal robe somewhere, return and stand on either side of him. Then the old man sits on a pillow and motions for us to do the same. When we're all seated, the woman who came to treat my mother's snakebite appears and sits next to the old man. There are a dozen other unoccupied pillows, and one by one people of apparent importance appear from behind the curtain, bow to the boy, and sit. Only when all the pillows around the boy are occupied does some silent signal bring the rest of the village into the tent. They all come carrying their own pillows, and they form into family circles of various sizes until nearly the entire floor surrounding the stove is covered.

My mother watches this all unfold with a look of shocked appreciation.

I lean over and whisper to her, "They sure don't seem so wild now, do they?"

She smiles and shakes her head.

Someone brings the boy a large decorative cup. He dips his finger into it and then flicks his finger into the air. The old man takes the cup next and sips it with great ceremony, holding it by its base with both hands. When the cup reaches me, my mother stops my hand, leans over before I can drink it, and smells the contents. She shakes her head no. I try to hand the cup back to the attendant, but he indicates that I should do as the boy did, so I dip my finger and flick a drop into the air. Jimmy does the same. My mother drinks. I elbow her playfully.

As soon as the passing of the cup is finished, the food begins to arrive. We're each given beautiful bowls carved out of tree burls, and then the cooks come into the circle carrying clay platters of food that they present to each guest. We follow the lead of those next to us and hold our bowls in the palms of our left hands and take up food and eat only with our right. The cooks return to their oven and refill their platters. There are meats spiced like no meats I've ever tasted, barley cakes stuffed with delicious fat that melts in my mouth when I bite into them, cheese-filled dumplings, venison kabobs, and hunks of fried potato as big as my fist. An attendant seems to always be at my elbow with something to drink. My mother is vigilant at first, allowing us only tea and milk, but as the meal wears on she either tires of checking the cups or stops caring. Jimmy and I begin to get intermittent sips of some fermented beverage that burns my throat, warms my stomach, and makes my hands begin to float.

As the little bit of light coming in from the open tent door fades, and as the flames of the cook stove diminish to coals, lanterns are lit and covered with colored-paper shades that cast the entire scene in a royal rainbow of soft light. Laughter and talk comes from the other circles, but ours is entirely quiet. I get the feeling they are not speaking out of respect for us not being able to understand them. Two little sisters come by with a basket of sweet candy made from honey. When they get to Jimmy, they stand back and blush until the older sister pushes the younger one forward. Jimmy takes a candy, pops it in his mouth, and smiles. The little girl runs off giggling with her basket. I guess flirting is flirting in any language.

When the meal is finished, our bowls are taken away and removed from the tent. Then the cup is passed again. The man who was singing when we arrived appears again with his odd fiddle and stands beside the boy. He plays and sings with such power and beauty that when he finishes, you could hear a pebble drop. Then two men step from behind the curtain with eagles on their arms.

"See," Jimmy says, nudging my ribs, "I told ya I shoulda brought mine."

The men release their birds into the tent. Each swoops off in the opposite direction, hugging the interior walls to cross within inches of each other at the other end, then circling back to cross again. They keep circling, faster and faster, until they whip by and cross right above us in a flurry of golden-feathered gymnastics that manages to stir enough wind to move my hair, as short as it still is. The boy sits on his pillow, watching with an enormous smile. Each time the eagles crisscross in front of him, he claps his hands and giggles. It's the first time I've seen him act like a child. The birds make their fastest pass yet, and it's a miracle of aviation that they don't collide and fall to the floor. Then they slow and cross once more as they return to their masters' arms. The men bow their heads and carry their eagles out behind the curtain.

The boy rises abruptly, as if signaling that the dinner is over, but the woman healer—whom I have come to believe must be his mother—rises with him, takes his hand, and leads him around the circle to say goodnight. He stands in front of each of us where we sit and leans to smell our hair again. Then he turns once to the entire group and bows before taking his mother's hand and following her from the tent.

As soon as he's gone, the mood lightens. The musician, who had been eating a quick meal while the eagles flew, picks up his fiddle again and plays a more upbeat tune. The others drag their pillows over and circle up around us until we're all one large group. Most of them recline, with their fingers laced behind their heads to watch the lanterns play colors on the ceiling, or cross their legs and bob their feet and heads to the music. A larger cup comes around.

Then the old man calls out something to the group, and everyone backs several feet away from him with their pillows. An attendant sets a chest down in the open space now in front of the old man. I wonder if he plans to charm a snake like I've read about in books. But he opens the chest and removes a pointed stick and a brush, and then he tips the chest over and dumps a pile of sand onto the floor. He sets the empty chest aside and smooths the sand with a pass of his open hands. Then he picks up his stick again and begins to draw in the sand. We all kneel on our pillows and lean forward to watch.

He works the stick like a paint brush—drawing clear lines one moment, flicking his wrist for a shadow effect the next—and he composes an image of such realistic beauty that I forget entirely that I'm looking at a pile of sand. He draws a picture of a city, complete with skyscrapers and streets. He draws a pair of happy faces greeting one another in the foreground. Then, with a slight embellishment from his stick, he makes the people look up. And now in the line of their sight, he draws a missile descending toward the city from the sky. Then he grabs his brush and sweeps it across the sand, erasing the city and its people. There is an audible gasp from the villagers watching this slide show of sand.

Next he draws an image of ruin—smoke billowing above the city, buildings collapsed to rubble, people burning in the streets. This picture he also erases to begin yet another on the clean slate of sand. His art is so masterful that I find myself forgetting where I am, my mind filling in the details he so gracefully suggests. I sit and watch the story unfold like a film before my very eyes.

He tells of a devastated people rummaging through the wreckage and migrating to the clean and unblemished hills to start a new life. He tells of hardship and toil, celebrations and joy. And then he tells of drones appearing in the sky like great mechanical birds of prey, slaughtering entire villages. He tells harrowing tales of survivors and of fresh starts cut short by new slaughters. And as the people thin, he tells of their constant search for shelter from the drones and of their eventual migration to these cold mountains for the safety of their clouds and cliffs. Then he draws a woman standing on a wall, facing down a drone. Here he stops and points with his stick to my mother and smiles.

The room is silent, the music having long ago stopped as the fiddler came to stand and watch the story himself. But now the old man lays the chest on its side and pulls the sand into it, sweeping the remainder inside with his brush. Then he closes the chest up and signals for it to be taken away. He pinches a bit of sand between his thumb and finger from the remainder on the hard-packed dirt floor and throws it over his right shoulder. Then he claps his hands and calls to the musician. The musician picks up his instrument and begins to play again.

The old man scoots over to Jimmy and me and looks at us with his one eye. I do my best not to let my gaze drift to his empty socket. He reaches into his fur and produces his jade bottle and palms it to me with what I think is a wink, but it's hard to tell since he blinks with only one eye too. I look at the little bottle in my hand and remove the stopper carefully. A fine brown powder rests in the spoon that comes out attached to it. The old man signals that I should sniff it, as I'd seen him do that day on his horse. I hardly get the spoon to my nose when I feel my mother's strong grip on my wrist. She pulls the spoon toward her and inspects it, even leaning down to smell it. Then she nods and releases my wrist. The snuff stings my nose and sets me coughing. The old man pats me on the back and takes his bottle back. He hands it to Jimmy. Of course, he doesn't cough. Then the old man points to my neck. I look down and see my father's pipe on the lanyard that Jimmy made me. I take the pipe off and hand it to him. He inspects it in the low light as best he can, holding it close to his one good eye and running his rough fingers over the butterflies carved into the bowl. Then he heaves himself up from his pillow with much effort and walks off with my pipe. I rise to go after him, but Jimmy grabs my hand and pulls me back down.

"But he took my father's pipe," I say.

"He'll be back with it," Jimmy says. "I think they only consider it a gift if you hold it out to them with both hands."

Sure enough, the old man returns a few minutes later with his own pipe and a small wooden box of tobacco that must be a treasure in these high and hidden lands. He loads both pipes, hands me back mine, then reaches over and lights a small stick of wood from the flame of a lantern, and hands that to me as well. As I puff my pipe lit, my mother just smiles and shakes her head.

We sit in the dim-colored light and drink and smoke and listen to the music while just the tiniest patch of starlit sky is visible in the ceiling smoke hole. The old man puffs his pipe and strokes his beard, his one eye closing and opening, as if he's having a hard time staying awake but doesn't want to sleep either. Jimmy has found one of the eagle masters and is deep in conversation with him, their communication comprised entirely of gestures. I puff my pipe and look at my mother. She must have had her share from the cup, because she's lying back on her pillow with such a peaceful look of contentment on her face that I only wish I could find a way to paint it there forever.

If only my father could be here to see this. The moment is so perfect that it almost feels like this entire life has been one big dream and that I'm finally in the real Eden. I blow a smoke ring and watch it come slowly apart as it rises toward the ceiling until it disappears out the smoke hole and into the night.

"I'll always love you, Dad."

"What's that?"

"Oh, hi, Jimmy. I was just thinking out loud."

Jimmy flops down beside me on his pillow. I try to hand him my pipe, but he shakes his head. The music plays on, quieter now than before, and soon others around the room begin to chant softly along. The acoustics of the tent mix the voices together into a lofty harmony that tickles my scalp.

"I think your mom's sleepin'," Jimmy says.

I look over and see that her eyes are peacefully closed.

"Did you get some good pointers for Valor?" I ask.

"These guys are no joke, man. I'll bet I have him huntin' in less than a month."

Jimmy's comment sets my mind to wandering. Will we even be here in another month? Where would we go? What would we do? We couldn't possibly live on the run from drones in these mountains. Or could we? These people seem to have things figured out pretty well. And this valley sure seems like a safe place. Then I remember the serum. My mother and Jimmy and I will all live to be nearly a thousand years old, but none of these people will. The entire length of that history he wrote in the sand, nine hundred years plus since the War, forty-five generations of these people, that would only cover our lives. How could we ever grow close to anyone? Are we fated to live a nearly eternal life of sadness like Finn, burying our loved ones and our friends? I wish now I had thought things through a little more before taking that serum. Sometimes a gift too good to be true can turn out to be a gift too true to be good.

Jimmy and I are lying side by side with our heads propped on our pillows. A red lamp behind casts outsized shadows of our matching silhouettes against the canvas in front of us.

"Hey, Jimmy."

"Yeah."

"You ever think about how long we're going to live?"

"No," he says. "Not really."

"Well, why not?"

"I dunno. Guess I'm too busy livin' it to think about it."

I clamp my pipe in my teeth and nod. Sometimes he says the damnedest things that make me wish I were more like him. A little later, I have another thought.

"You ever think about Red?"

"Sometimes," he says.

"Do you feel bad about it?"

"There was no way to know we wasn't comin' back."

"So we just do nothing, then?"

I see Jimmy's shadow shrug.

"You gotta cook the bird you shoot," he says. "At least that's what my pa used to say."

I listen to the chanting and the music and watch our heads swell and shrink on the canvas with the flickering of the flame.

"Yeah, maybe you're right," I finally say. "Maybe there is nothing we can do."

I puff my pipe but it's gone out.

CHAPTER 25
A Message in the Sky

The short days of winter give way to longer days of spring, and the snow recedes into the shadowed folds of the mountain.

My mother spends most of her days in the shelter in front of that mindless screen, working on some boring project I don't even pretend to understand. I try to watch over her shoulder, but she always stops and tells me to go out and play.

"Play with what?" I ask.

"Whatever it is you and Jimmy do out there."

"He's busy with his eagle."

"I know what you can do," she says. "Hike up and adjust the antenna for the repeater dish."

"Again?"

"My connection is spotty after last night's wind."

I agree and go do it, grateful to at least feel needed.

Jimmy's eagle seems to always be on his arm. I joke with him that he's developing a lopsided physique because of it. He shrugs off my comment, but I notice that he's carrying Valor on his other arm the following week, having made a matching left-handed glove. They make quite the pair—Jimmy always talking to the bird as if it could somehow understand him and the bird just perched there ignoring him all the while.

It's a solid month beyond what he'd predicted, but Jimmy announces over dinner one night that he's ready to test Valor the next day. "You have to come," he says. "Both of you."

"I wouldn't miss it, buddy."

My mother shakes her head and says, "I have no interest in watching that tic-infested accipitridae kill a helpless deer."

"Please," Jimmy pleads. "This is my day. If Valor makes the kill, he's a worthy bird and I'm a worthy master."

"What happens if he doesn't?" she asks.

"Then I gotta set him free and find another."

"Who told you all this nonsense?"

"Our friends, the Motars."

"Motars. Worthy master. You speak their language now?"

"No. But there's other ways to talk, you know."

My mom smiles and rubs Jimmy's shaggy head. "I'll come and watch, but only if you let me give you a haircut."

"Aw, come on," he says. "It's just growing back in."

The entire trip there the next afternoon, Jimmy whispers encouragement into Valor's ear. My mom and I walk behind him and make silent jokes with each other about it. Every so often the eagle spins its head nearly all the way around to look at us, and I swear that bird understands more than it lets on.

The Motars meet us on the bluff above their hidden camp. They're all sitting horseback. They have three other horses with them, I'm guessing one for each of us. The boy looks more childlike and less kingly now that he's wearing his furs again. He trots his horse up to Jimmy, reaches down, touches the crown of Jimmy's head and then the eagle's head. Then the boy says something, and one of the men presents Jimmy with a horse. Jimmy mounts up one-handed, with Valor still on his arm. But when my mother is presented with her horse, she steps away and holds up her hands.

"It's not that bad, Mom. We rode them on the island."

"Sorry," she says. "But I'm not getting on that thing."

She doesn't appear to be open to negotiation, so I refuse my horse too. The riders then nudge their horses forward to the edge of the bluff. We join them on foot.

The bluff overlooks the valley and another small deer is staked on the hill below, looking like a toy as it grazes on the grass. The old man places a hand on Jimmy's shoulder and chants a song or maybe a prayer. He finishes and points to a high point several meters away. Jimmy starts his horse toward it. When he reaches the high point, Jimmy halts his horse so close to the edge that flakes of rock break free and tumble down the face of the cliff. I'm worried that the horse will lose its footing, sending them all down together—Jimmy, horse, and bird, all. My mom must worry too because I feel her hand grip my arm. But Jimmy doesn't seem afraid. He sits his horse like he was born on one. His proud posture is mirrored by Valor's, perched like a statue on his arm.

He points to the deer staked into the hill far below. Valor's head leans forward, its feathers ruffle. Then, with a flick of his forearm, Jimmy sends the eagle soaring off the cliff. The eagle's wingspan is enormous. Its golden feathers catch the sun for a moment, giving it the appearance of some flaming phoenix come to bless the entire valley. It swoops down, passes the little deer by, and rises again to climb out of the valley on the far side. I see Jimmy hang his head. But then I remember how the eagle circled and returned the day Jimmy caught it, and I turn my eyes back to the sky ahead. Sure enough, the eagle banks a right turn at the valley's farthest edge and swoops back toward the deer with amazing speed. At the last second it pushes its talons out before it and tucks its wings.

The only sound we hear is Jimmy's cheer.

He pumps his fist in the air and watches from his horse as Valor flaps and fights on the hill below, finally coming to rest perched on top of the dead deer. Jimmy turns his horse and joins the others. He high fives me as they pass us by on their way down to ride off the bluff and retrieve Valor and his kill.

My mother and I stay put and watch.

"I guess the verdict is 'good bird and good master'," I say.

"I'm so happy for him," she replies. "He worked hard."

"I'm really happy for him, too. After everything we've been through this crazy year, it's good to see him smile."

"He's a great friend, Aubrey. You two are fortunate to have found one another in this crazy world."

I nod without taking my eyes away from him as he enters the valley below with the other men. As they ride up toward the hill, I get an uneasy feeling in my gut. I hope it isn't jealousy after everything we've been through now. But when the hairs on the back of my neck stand up, I'm sure it isn't that.

Then a shadow passes over my mother and me and shrinks to the valley floor below us and continues on toward the riders. My mother's fingers dig into my arm as I look up and see the drone. She pulls me away from the edge, dragging me by the arm toward cover, but I jerk free and turn back and scream:

"Jiiiimmmmyyyy!"

Jimmy is almost to the hill. He must hear me because he turns back briefly on his horse and waves at me. But he doesn't even see the drone overhead. As the riders approach the hill, and as the drone approaches the riders, a replay of the slaughter in the cove flashes in my mind. I'm raising my hands to my mouth to yell again when the drone fires.

But it's no missile that comes out.

Instead, there's a puff of smoke from the launch tube, and a huge banner unfurls in the blue sky, spreading out behind the drone and attached to it by a cable. The drone circles the valley and the banner comes broadside. I read what it says:

AUBREY, WE NEED TO TALK

I don't know whether to laugh or cry.

My mother appears beside me, her mouth agape just like mine. The men on the hill below are busy inspecting the kill and congratulating Jimmy. They don't yet even see the drone circling the valley above their heads like some crazy sky-bound advertisement from the past.

"'Aubrey, we need to talk,'" my mother says, reading the banner aloud. "Isn't that the damnedest thing?"

We spend all evening in the shelter trying to figure out what Hannah could possibly want. My mother agrees to make an exception for one night about Jimmy's eagle, and he parks it in the corner and tosses it hunks of rabbit meat that it snatches from the air without leaving its perch. My mother watches and shakes her head. I finish my dinner and push my bowl away.

"Maybe she wants to talk about a truce," I suggest.

My mother laughs. "I do love your optimism, Son."

"We don't know," I say. "She might have changed."

"People don't change, Son. Not that much. She may have some deadly trick up her zipsuit sleeve is what she might have."

"What do you think, Jimmy?" I ask.

He tosses Valor another chunk of meat. "I dun' trust her. But then I never have, and you know that."

"And you're right not to, Jimmy," my mother says. "The acorn didn't fall far from the tree on that one."

"That's not fair, Mom. You can't judge her for her father

unless you intend to judge me just the same."

She reaches across the table and takes my hand. "I'm sorry, Son. You're right. That wasn't fair. But she has done plenty on her own to prove that she's not trustworthy."

"I know it better than anyone," I say. "But we have to try. We have to find out what she wants. If there's even a chance to just save Red, it would be worth the effort to try."

My mother leans back in her chair and sighs.

After a few quiet moments thinking, she says, "Even if we wanted to talk with her, how would we arrange it?"

"Send a message through our friends in Holocene II."

"Okay, but we can't risk giving away their identities. That might even be her whole plan. You know she knows by now that you had help escaping."

"Why can't you have them send up an anonymous note on the supply train? She won't know who sent it."

"That might work," she says. "What would it say?"

"The message? Ask her to meet me alone somewhere. Just the two of us. Nobody else."

"Alone?" my mother asks. "Are you crazy?"

"Yes, Mom. Alone."

"I'll go with you," Jimmy says.

"I know you would, Jimmy, but this is something I've got to do by myself. I need to negotiate with her."

My mother stands up from the table and paces the room, as she's wont to do. She's so deep in thought she doesn't even notice when Valor evacuates his bowels onto the floor.

"Fine," she says, stopping to turn to me. "Where do you want to meet her? Somewhere neutral."

"Tell her to meet me at the bungalow on the beach. Where

Radcliffe brought us together. There's a landing strip there, and it's a safe zone from drones."

"Okay then, when?"

"We should leave the date up to her since we have no idea when she'll get the message or how she might respond."

"That's the other question," she says. "How will she?"

"Just have her send another banner with the date, and we'll take that as our confirmation."

She absorbs this for a moment, then smiles with pride.

"You're brilliant, Aubrey. You really are. And I'll tell you what else: I'm proud that you're my son."

She doesn't see it because she's already turned to log onto her computer, but my face blushes, and I have to wipe a tear away from my cheek. Jimmy notices, but he just smiles at me and turns his attention back to cleaning up after his bird.

CHAPTER 26
A Birthday Surprise

The snow melts.

The days lengthen.

And the trees bud with new leaves.

Then, three weeks to the day after we send our message, the shelter door bursts open and Jimmy enters, out of breath after running home, and motions for us to hurry outside.

The three of us stand on the wall and watch as the drone turns to come around again. It's hard not to run when I see the Park Service crest come into view. What if this is a trick? What if it fires on us? But the drone comes alongside where we stand, and I look up and read the message on the banner it's trailing.

MARCH 22 – 1400 HOURS

"Oh, that's cute," my mother says.

Jimmy nudges me and whispers, "What's it say?"

"It says March twenty-two at two o'clock."

"What's that mean?"

"It means she wants to meet on my birthday."

I don't know where my mother gets the cake or the sixteen candles, but ten days later, she and Jimmy wake me up singing the traditional Holocene II birthday song.

Yet another year older you are
And we're here to help you ring it in
We're proud you've made it this far
Because we all remember you when

Someday we'll gaze up at actual stars
And once again see our long lost friends
For you're not really alive until you reach thirty-five
Then your new life will surely begin
For that's the day you get to retire
The day you move into Eden

I don't know whether to feel embarrassed or creeped out when they finish singing. I haven't heard that silly song since my father sang it to me last year, on my fifteenth birthday, just before I was called up to the Foundation. But Jimmy is smiling with pride over having learned the lyrics, and I just can't bring myself to say anything to break his happiness.

"Blow out all the candles," my mother says. "And don't forget to make a wish."

I remember hearing somewhere that wishes don't come true if they're made for selfish reasons, but I close my eyes and wish anyway for the thing I've really wanted for myself since this crazy adventure began. Then I blow the candles out. Jimmy goes to get the milk while my mother cuts the cake.

"Really, Mom?" I whisper when we're alone at the table. "You had to sing the Holocene II birthday song?"

"It's the only one I know, Son."

"Well, you could have changed it up. Maybe replace 'Eden' with something else."

"We tried," she says, "but nothing seemed to rhyme."

After we eat our cake and wash it down with goat's milk gifted from the Motars, Jimmy hands me a present wrapped in a piece of bark and tied closed with braided horsehair. I open it and find a beautifully crafted deerskin pouch. Inside the pouch is a strike-a-light, the flint shaped like a crescent moon and the steel striker handcrafted and honed to look like an eagle. He must have been working on this all those long afternoons he's spent with the Motars at their camp.

"Thank you, Jimmy."

"You like it?" he asks.

"Like it? I love it."

"It sparks real good, too," he says. "Now you can start a fire anywhere. Or light your pipe. I'm still workin' on a trade to get you some tobacco, but the old man keeps a tight grip on it."

I stand up and hug him. When I turn around, my mother hands me a larger box, also made of bark.

"I hope you two didn't cut down an entire tree just to wrap gifts for me."

"Of course, we didn't," she says. "Trees outgrow their skin sometimes too you know. Go ahead. Open it."

I open the box and find a reading slate tucked inside. I can't believe my eyes. After giving mine to Bree on the Isle of Man, and then after leaving Holocene II for China, I thought I'd never see one again. I pull it out and turn it on.

"It's got the entire Foundation library on there," she says. "So I know there are some you haven't read. Plus, the best part is that all you have to do to charge it is to read in the sun. I modified this one before I left the Foundation. The device shell is made from the same solar material that charges the drones."

I throw my arms around her. "Thank you, Mom. This has been the best birthday ever."

"Well," she says, hugging me back and kissing the top of my head, "technically you'll spend your birthday ten thousand meters over the Pacific Ocean since I didn't actually give birth to you until two-thirty-seven a.m., in a different time zone, sixteen years ago tomorrow."

I pull away and look at her. "Was it hard?"

"Giving birth? No. They had the doctor do a cesarean since the plan was to get me back up to the Foundation as soon as you were born."

"I meant leaving. Was leaving me hard?"

"It was the hardest thing I've ever done, Son," she says. "You were just a little angel those few minutes I got to hold you in my arms. You looked like a tiny old man, actually. But you were perfect. Absolutely perfect. And you still are."

I don't want to cry in front of her or Jimmy, so I suck it up and hold back my tears. The thought of leaving them both and not knowing for sure if I'll ever make it back rips me up inside. It feels as if my guts have been stirred with a spoon. I set my presents on the table and grab a towel.

"I'm going to head down and take a bath before I go."

"We can all go," my mother says.

"No, I want to be alone."

My mother and Jimmy look at one another, then back to me. Their expressions give away their worry, but before either can say anything, I step outside and close the door.

When I get down to the hot springs, I undress and wade into the steaming water. It occurs to me that these pools have likely been here for a very long time. I wonder how many people have sat just where I'm sitting and worried about their futures and how things would turn out for them. But I know how things turned out for them. They're all dead. Every story I've ever read, the same thing. I find myself hoping for a happy ending, but really it's only a happy pause, because if you let any story play out long enough, they all end. We're all gone. And even though the three of us each have the serum, there's still a lot that can go wrong between now and happily ever after.

I don't want my mother to die.

I don't want Jimmy to die.

I don't want to die.

The sky is getting lighter by the minute, the sun about to crest the western peaks, and I know it's only a matter of hours before I climb into the drone and say goodbye. I try to push these thoughts from my head and enjoy the fresh air.

After a while I hear footsteps coming down the path. The maples and bushes that surround the pool have already leafed in, and I can't see who it is. Then Jimmy steps out from behind the trees, strips off his clothes, and joins me in the water.

When we make eye contact, Jimmy shrugs as if apologizing for having interrupted my solitude.

"Your mom said I stink," he says.

"I'm glad she said it before I had to," I joke. "In fact, the real reason I'm flying halfway around the world today is to get away from your smell."

Jimmy's smirk disappears beneath the water and reappears moments later much closer to me. He spits water at me and laughs, saying, "Sometimes I miss it, you know."

"Miss what?"

"Swimming. Seems like I grew up in the water. Then ever since that day in the cove, it just ain't been the same. When I remember it now, all I see is blood."

I nod that I understand. "I'm sorry Jimmy."

"Do you ever miss it?" he asks.

"Do I miss the water?"

"No," he says. "Underground. Where you grew up."

"I miss my dad a lot. And now that I know he wasn't my biological father, I think I miss him even more. He was a good man to have raised me like he did. But miss underground? No way. I spent my entire childhood down there dreaming of being up here. Sometimes I wish I had something to miss, though. It's like I don't have a home. Not even in my memories."

"Well, maybe someday you will," he says.

"Would you be there?"

"Where?"

"Wherever my home is."

"I wouldn't wanna be nowhere else."

After a moment of silence, I ask, "Did you mean what you said back in Holocene II? In my old childhood apartment?"

"What did I say?"

"Nothing. Never mind."

We share an awkward silence.

A small clutch of birds veers down and alights in one of the trees, shaking its branches and giving Jimmy something to look at. I watch him as he watches the birds. No matter where he is, he looks like he was meant to be there, perhaps carved out of the very landscape. And he looks exactly like he did when I first saw him crouched over the water on the rock that day, except his hair is shorter, and he has a bit of stubble on his chin. I guess it won't be long now, and we'll both be shaving.

He turns and catches me staring at him. "What?"

"Nothing," I say. Then I add, "Your hair's growing in."

"Yours is too," he says. "So you better not let Hannah cut it this time. You know she would."

I sigh. "I'm not looking forward to seeing her."

"Are you gonna tell her?"

"Tell her what?"

"That she's your sister."

"Half-sister."

"Sure. Are you gonna tell her?"

"I don't know. My mom and I discussed it a lot. What I should say. What I shouldn't say. Stuff like that. I'm going to try and get her to release Red, I know that."

"My pa always said you can't trade unless both sides have somethin' the other wants. Whatcha gonna give her for Red?"

"I think she knows we have support down in Holocene II. And I think she's worried sick about it, too."

"You mean Mrs. Hightower and that lady that took the bracelet off my ankle?"

"That's right," I say, nodding.

"You ain't gonna give 'em up, are you?"

"Of course not," I say. "But if she'll agree to release them somehow without my naming them, then we both win. She gets back Holocene II, and we get them."

"Release 'em where?"

"Back here, I hope."

"I dun' think you should trust her for nothin'."

"I know you don't, Jimmy. But I have to try."

"But why?" he asks. "Why should you be the one to have to go off and do it? Haven't we been through enough?"

"Because I couldn't live with myself otherwise, Jimmy. I think we have to try to do right. That's what makes us human."

"Yeah," he says, looking down. "I guess you's right."

We soak in the silence for several minutes. As the morning air warms, the thick steam that had been drawing off the pool's surface fades to a faint mist.

"I guess we better get back," I say. "Otherwise my mom might eat the last of that cake. I'd sure like to have another piece before I go."

We climb from the pool, wrap towels around ourselves, and walk up the path barefoot, carrying our kilts, shirts, and shoes. As we near the shelter, Jimmy stops on the path. I turn back to see what's wrong.

"I meant it," he says.

"You meant what?"

"What I said in your apartment."

"You did?"

He nods.

We drop our cloths on the ground and hug each other. The path and the mountains and the entire world seem to slip away beneath us until only he and I remain. Then the sun rises over the peaks and warms my naked back. Of all the birthday gifts ever given in the history of the world, I can't imagine one better than an embrace like this from your best friend.

My mother is just logging off her computer when we enter the shelter. Jimmy must sense that she and I need some time alone together, because he heads out to feed Valor again.

"Are you nervous?" my mother asks once we're alone.

"I'd be lying if I said that I wasn't."

"Well, it takes courage to admit it," she says. "I was able to hack into the satellites. The weather appears fine for a flight. You're leaving here at about ten, and it's sixteen hours to get there with a twelve hour time difference. I think you should arrive right on time. I've programmed the drone to take you straight to the landing strip in the Keys and then bring you back again. I'll send the manual flight controller, but only use it in an emergency, the way I've shown you."

"I know, Mom, I know. We've only been over this like a hundred times already."

She sits down on her bed and pats the mattress, signaling for me to sit next to her. I flop down and look at my feet.

"Can I tell you something, Son?"

I nod and she continues.

"Mondays were my favorite days at the Foundation. You know why? Because I used to get reports on you. Beth would tell me all about your progress in class. How smart you were; how much you'd read that week. Bill would send messages about you at the electric beach. He'd tell me you were doing pushups and trying to gain weight. I know you felt alone a lot. I feel that way myself sometimes still. But I want you to know that you were never alone. I was always up there thinking about you. And I'm proud of the man you've become."

"You are?"

"Yes."

"But I don't feel like a man, Mom. I'm scared and I'm selfish, and I'm having second thoughts about even going."

"Are you going to listen to your fears and stay?" she asks.

"No," I reply. "I'm going, no matter what."

"And that, Son, is why you're a man now. When a child starts doing what's right even though they don't want to, that's when he or she becomes an adult."

I turn and look at her. When we'd first met, I'd recognized her as the mother my father had always described to me. But for the first time, I recognize her now as the mother I'd always wished I'd had.

"Mom, even though you say I'm a man now, do you think you could do something for me? Something I always dreamed about when I was a kid?"

"Sure, Son. What is it?"

"Could I lay my head on your chest and have you just hold me for a while?"

"Oh, Aubrey," she says. "I've dreamed of the same thing."

She reaches out and pulls me into her arms.

By ten o'clock I'm sitting in the drone's cockpit, watching my mother try not to cry. She stands beside the drone, faking a smile, and Jimmy stands next to her doing the same.

"I'll be fine, you two," I announce. "There aren't even any venomous snakes where I'm going."

"No, there aren't," my mother replies. "Except maybe the one you're going there to meet. Be careful."

She leans in and kisses me on the cheek. Then Jimmy steps forward and hands me his pee bottle.

"Here," he says, "you might need this."

"Jimmy, I'm not peeing in a bottle."

"Well, keep it anyway. Jus' in case."

They both step back and look at me. My mother crosses her arms and rubs her shoulders as if to keep warm.

She forces another smile and says, "I love you, Aubrey."

Jimmy nods toward her.

"Yeah. What she said."

"I love you both too," I say.

Then I reach up and pull the canopy closed.

The door opens and the runway fills with light. I look at Jimmy and my mother and place my hand against the glass.

And then they're gone.

CHAPTER 27
Face to Face with Hannah Again

Her drone is already parked on the runway when I land.

My drone taxis, turns, and parks next to hers.

I click off my slate and do my best to forget the Roman poem I had been reading about a beauty who became so ugly she could turn onlookers to stone. When the canopy opens, I step out and stretch my legs. Then I retrieve the bottle Jimmy lent me for the trip and empty the contents onto the ground.

The steps leading down to the beach are nearly buried now beneath sand, but the path to the bungalow is still visible. The porch has been swept clean. I knock but no one answers. I step over to look in the window, but all I see is the cramped and empty room where Radcliffe brought Hannah and me. It's hard to believe that was only seven months or so ago now.

A breeze tickles the hairs on my neck, and I turn and see her coming toward me along the beach. It can't be much after two, but dark clouds have passed in front of the sun. The filtered light casts Hannah's red hair, as it waves wildly in the ocean breeze, in stark contrast against the sand, giving her the appearance of being on fire. I stay on the porch and watch her approach. As she gets closer, it becomes clear to me that she's much older than sixteen—so much so that I can hardly believe I fell for her lies before.

She stops at the steps, her hand gripping the railing, and we lock eyes—the silence between us broken only by the waves slapping the sand, sliding up the beach, and then hissing as they retreat again.

When she finally speaks she says, "I suppose I should wish you a happy birthday."

"I wondered if you knew when you picked this day."

"Of course, I knew," she says, smiling flirtatiously as she climbs the steps onto the porch. She motions toward the deck chairs. "Shall we sit or would you rather go inside to talk?"

I answer by taking a seat.

She nods and lowers herself into the other chair and leans back as if she were on vacation, gazing out to sea.

"It's nice to get away from the Foundations for a while," she says. "I can see why my father liked to come here."

"Was it really your first time here when we came?" I ask.

"Of course, it was," she replies. "I told you that already."

"Like you told me you were sixteen?"

She smiles but doesn't look at me.

"I see someone's been filling you in on some things. The traitor who's harboring you, I assume."

I don't bother replying to her comment, and we both fall quiet for several minutes. The wind momentarily picks up, and I watch as a whirling dervish of dust appears, races along the beach, and then disappears as quickly as it had formed.

"My father always said she was a smart woman," Hannah says. "He liked her a lot. He told us she had died in a drone crash in China. Maybe he even believed that, but I think he knew she was alive and left her alone. He always was much too sentimental. Same as with Finn. Which is curious, because he always thought a woman wouldn't have what it takes to run the Park Service. But he was wrong. It was him who didn't have the guts. You know why I chose today to meet, Aubrey?"

"Because it's my birthday?"

"Yes. There's that. But also because this was the day that my father planned to turn everything over to you."

"Is that why you betrayed me, then?" I ask. "Because you were jealous your father was going to turn things over to me?"

"You can't betray a trust you never wanted in the first place, Aubrey. I did what I did because it was necessary. You have no idea what it was like for me: trapped at that house and waiting for my sixteenth birthday and my chance to contribute to the cause, only to be told that I wasn't ready, that a suitable mate wasn't ready, that I needed a man. Then the hormones and the shots began. Keeping me young. Young and waiting. Waiting for what? For you. For you to score well on some stupid test. A stupid, silly test and my father was willing to put more faith in you than he had in me, his own daughter."

"That's not why he called me up, Hannah."

"What do you know, Aubrey? He told me all about it. He said how we would make a great team and how I would learn to trust you to lead. Can you imagine?"

"That's not what I meant, Hannah. I said that he didn't call me up because of the stupid test."

"Then why did he?"

"Because the woman who you called a traitor is actually my mother, for one thing. She tried to rescue me. That's why the train crashed. That's why she had to disappear."

"Well, that makes sense then," she says. "My father would have valued you for her DNA and not just your test score."

"But that's still not the reason he called me up, Hannah."

"Well, aren't you just full of surprises," she says. "Since you think you know everything, why don't you go ahead and tell me why my own father called you up?"

"Because he's my father too."

She turns so quickly to look at me that her hair swings in front of her face and a strand catches in her mouth.

She spits it out and says, "You're lying. That's not true."

"It is true, Hannah. He got my mother pregnant with his frozen sperm, and he sent her down to Holocene II to have the baby. To have me. That's why he made you wait all that time. Because he finally had the son he'd always wanted."

She plants her hands on her knees and stands.

"I'm hungry," she says, "Are you hungry?"

"No."—I shake my head—"I ate in the drone."

She crosses to the railing and looks out over the water. A minute later, she pulls her hair back and ties it in a ponytail with a band she fishes from her zipsuit pocket. Then she turns, leans on the railing, and looks at me.

"How's Jimmy?"

"He's fine," I say. "How's Red?"

"As annoying as ever. I've kept my promise, though, and seen that he's been taken care of."

"What did you bring me here for, Hannah?"

"I want to make a deal with you."

"Okay, let's deal then."

"I know you have friends down in Holocene II, and I want to know who they are."

My mother was right about why Hannah wanted to meet with me. I hold my tongue and rerun my conversations with her about how I should handle this.

"What are you prepared to give up?" I ask.

"I'll give you your freedom."

"We already have that," I say.

"No, you do not, you silly boy. What you have is a daily reprieve based on my willingness to let you live. A reprieve that I can rescind at any time."

"Maybe you don't know this or remember," I say, "but I shot down your drone."

She laughs. "We wanted you to, stupid. The professor guessed that the traitor—your mother now, I guess—had a rocket left. That drone was a test to find out and to get you to waste it if you did have one. Now what I have is enough drones circling the area right now that I can scramble them in an hour and blow you all clean off that mountain."

"If that's true, then why am I here?"

"Because I'd rather not kill you, that's why. Believe it or not, Aubrey, I did have feelings for you. Jimmy I couldn't care less about, but you have potential. And if we really are half siblings like you say, and that's a big if, then you have even more potential than I thought. There's no reason for me to kill you unless you make me. So if you agree to tell me who the traitors are in Holocene II, I'll promise to steer clear of where you are and let you and your mother and Jimmy live in peace."

"I thought you planned to eradicate all of humanity," I say.

"Oh, I do. And if it comes down to a time when only you three and those other savages are left, I'll wipe you all out and then take my own life last of all. But even if that happens, it will take a long time. So this is your choice. Take the years I grant you or die now."

"I have a better idea that I think will satisfy us both."

"Oh, I'm excited to hear this," she says. "Lay it on me."

"Okay. I want Red. I'll wait here while you return to the

Foundation and get him. Then you let me take him back with me and leave us in peace."

"And if I do that, you'll tell me who the traitors are?"

"No, but I'll do something just as good."

"Maybe you forget that I'm not just some stupid kid."

"Just hear me out. You know there are people working against you in Holocene II, and you'll never sleep as long as they're there. At any moment they could tell people the truth, and then you'd have an uprising on your hands."

"And I could drown them all with the turn of a switch."

"Yes, but who would build your drones? And who would keep you fed? I think we both know you're not going to go trap animals and eat them, Hannah."

"So what's you're brilliant idea then, Aubrey?"

I get up from my chair and join her at the railing.

"I think I know a way where we both win. You reopen the hole in the Yucatan where we escaped from and let them sneak away. Just them. None of the others who don't know the truth. I'll send the drone to pick them up and bring them back to us. Then you close the hole again, and you'll have Holocene II back without anyone down there who knows. It's win-win."

She crosses her arms and looks at me.

"So there are only two of them then," she says.

"I didn't say that."

"You didn't have to. That's all that will fit in your drone."

"Whatever. One is too many for you to have down there. The truth spreads like a disease once it's out. You know that."

"What I know is that humanity spreads like a disease once it's out. And you're asking me to not only let you live, but to send Red and these two mystery traitors off to live with you."

"Come on, Hannah, you know it's a fair compromise."

"You might think so," she says, "but compromise and fairness are not high on my list of things to achieve. Let's go inside and eat, shall we? I'm hungry."

The shelter is quiet, and the air smells stale. She heats water and brews algae tea. The taste sends me right back to Holocene II, making it hard to drink. We sit at the small table and eat meal bars and watch out the window as the surf comes farther up the beach with the tide. We try to make small talk but eventually give up and just sit and eat in silence.

Then out of nowhere, Hannah says, "There is another option, you know."

"What's that?" I ask.

"You could come back to the Foundation and run things with me. We could be partners."

"Why would you even ask me that?"

"Because I could use the help. Because it would be better for you than scraping by out there in the wild. And honestly, because I get lonesome sometimes."

"I wouldn't have guessed you for the type to feel lonely."

"That's a fair thing to say, I guess," she replies. "But I do. The professor isn't the best company, as you know. And he's been crazier than usual lately. I had him in the chair twice just last week. And, of course, the tunnelrats are nothing much to talk to." Then she reaches out and takes my hand in hers and says, "If this project takes longer than I had hoped, we might need to have some children after all."

I pull my hand from hers. "Gross, Hannah. Even if you weren't twice my age, and even if you hadn't lied to me and then tried to kill me, we're brother and sister."

"No, we're half brother and sister. And so what?"

"So what? Are you absolutely insane?"

The smile fades from her face and she stares at me with calculating green eyes. "Do you want the deal or not?" she asks.

"What do you mean?"

"I mean, do you want to save your friends or not? I offered you your freedom in exchange for the names, but now you want Red and the traitors spared as well. But that's not how negotiating works, Aubrey. If you want me to give something up, you've got to give something back."

"I don't understand what you want from me," I say.

"I want what you already have. It isn't fair to leave me at the Foundation all alone. I have nobody to talk to. Nobody to love me. Nobody but me. I want some company."

"Oh, come on, Hannah. Get real."

"I am being real. I want those things. And I also want somebody who can carry on the cause after I'm gone."

"I'm not coming back with you, Hannah."

"You don't have to," she says.

"Then I don't understand what you're asking for."

"Come on, you're not a kid any longer, Aubrey. Can't you read between the lines? This being your birthday and my dad's handover date aren't the only reasons I picked today to meet."

"Why else did you pick today to meet, then?"

"Because I'm ovulating."

Her words hit me in the chest like a hammer, and I can hardly breathe. I spring up from my chair and bolt for the door. But I hesitate with my hand on the handle, not wanting to spoil any chance for a deal, not ready to say no.

"I'm going for a walk," I say. "I need some fresh air."

"Fine," she says. "Think about what I'm offering you, Aubrey. I'll stay here and turn down the bed."

I walk far enough away down the beach to be out of sight from the bungalow. I sit on the sand and watch the storm roll in. The sky fills with dark clouds, and the wind draws whitecaps upon the dusky water. The sand glows almost white against the surf pushing ever further up the sandy beach. Eventually, the tide comes so high up that I have to scoot back to keep from getting soaked. But the sound of the crashing waves is a welcome distraction from the insane argument taking place inside my head.

There's no way I can do what Hannah is asking of me. But then there's no way I can't do it either. I'm trapped again with an impossible choice. What is wrong with these people, anyway? Radcliffe wanted to exterminate all of humanity, but he loved himself so much he kept having kids with everyone. And here Hannah is doing the same thing. And to think that I'm related to them both, that these people are somehow family. Ugh. The thought makes me want to puke.

Could I even live with myself, knowing I might possibly have a son or a daughter growing up in that dungeon under the lake and being raised by Hannah to hate all of humankind? But then again could I live with myself knowing I was responsible for killing Red and possibly Mrs. Hightower and Jillian too? No matter what I do, my conscience will already be burdened with leaving the others down in Holocene II, letting them die one by one in Eden. I keep telling myself it's okay because they don't know any better, but that's just a lie and I know it.

Then I think about what Hannah said about the drones. She said she had enough of them on standby to kill us all on the mountain at any time. That not only means me; it means my mother and Jimmy. I really have no choice. I have to say yes. And Hannah knows it. That's why she pinned me into this decision like she did. How bad can it be anyway? I wonder. I was into her once, wasn't I? Maybe if I just close my eyes and pretend that I never knew we were related.

The first raindrop hits me as I'm walking back. By the time I reach the bungalow, it's a full on downpour and I'm soaked through. The rain pounding on the porch roof masks the sound at first, but as I reach the door I hear screaming inside. Then a chair bounces off the Plexiglas window. Confused and fearing the worst, I pound on the locked door. The door flies open, and Hannah is staring at me with murder in her eyes. I see the overturned table behind her and the chairs on the floor. Then I notice that the wall-mounted LCD screen is turned on and displaying a familiar head of wild hair above wild staring eyes— a video feed of the crazy professor from the Foundation.

"You little idiot," Hannah growls. "You just killed yourself and everyone you love."

"What are you talking about?"

"You know damn well what I'm talking about."

The rain slaps harder on the porch roof, and the wind whips at my back. Hannah's ponytail has come undone and her hair blows around her face as she stands in the open doorway, the professor leering at me from the screen behind her.

"What are you talking about, Hannah?"

She steps aside and turns to address the professor on the screen. "Show him," she orders.

The professor's hand fills the screen as he reaches to turn the camera and when he pulls his hand away again, I see Mrs.

Hightower hanging limply in the grip of two tunnelrats, her head bowed and her chin resting on her chest. One of the tunnelrats grips her hair and jerks her head upright. She hardly appears conscious. Her lip is bleeding; her eye is swollen.

The professor turns the camera back to his face.

"Good to see you again, Aubrey," he says. "I'm sorry that your little mutiny didn't come off exactly as you'd planned it. But I can assure you that your friend here will have a lot of time to think about it while she's in Eden."

I step into the room, closer to the screen.

"Don't you dare—"

"Say goodbye to your little buddy Jimmy for me too," the professor says, cutting me off. "If you get the chance, that is." He smiles his lunatic grin, all the more maniacal for his missing front teeth. Then he reaches up and turns the camera off.

"Hannah, will you tell me what's going on, please?"

"Don't play dumb, Aubrey. Do you expect me to believe it's a coincidence that our computer system is hacked so your friend and her tunnelrat pals can make a play to take over the Foundation just when I happen to be away and meeting with you? And I was going to agree to your terms, you fool. But now the deal's off."

She storms to the open door and waves me out.

"Hannah, let's talk about this," I plead. "Please."

"Get out now or I'll lock you in here and let you rot."

The rain thunders on the porch roof and pours off it in sheets. The wind is catching it and sending sprays of water onto Hannah's face and across the threshold where she stands.

"I said, GET OUT!" she screams.

The expression on her face sends me flying past her and

out into the rain while I still have a chance. She slams the door closed, punches in a code, and storms past me, heading toward the runway and her drone. I run after her on the path.

"Just stop and talk to me a minute, Hannah. Let's just talk. This is all a big misunderstanding."

She ignores me and continues marching through the rain, climbing the steps toward the runway. Then she struts across the wet tarmac toward her waiting drone.

"Hannah, stop! You don't want to do this."

I race after her and grab her shoulder.

She spins and jabs a Taser into my chest and electrocutes me. I fall to the tarmac and lie on my side, convulsing. Her Taser left behind some kind of electrode stuck in my chest. I clutch and claw to try and remove it as my muscles spasm. My vision fades. My head throbs. My legs kick involuntarily. I'm acutely aware of the rain drops splashing down around me, and I become terrified of them in my delusional agony, as if the drops themselves were shocking me.

I force myself to breath and I watch as Hannah climbs into her drone and closes the glass observation bubble. Her face looks somehow sad, and she reaches forward from her seat and lightly touches her fingers to the glass, as if some small part of her regrets how things have turned out between us.

Then her drone is gone in a flash. Her image lingers for a few moments in the falling rain before fading away as I close my eyes and pass out from the pain.

When I come to, the rain has stopped.

Mist rises off the runway, shimmering in the red sunset.

I peel myself off the pavement and stumble to my drone. My vision is still foggy as I watch the bungalow and the beach fade away beneath me. I know I have a lot to think about at the moment, but I hardly slept on the flight in, and now I can't keep my eyes from closing. When I open them again, my aching legs tell me many hours have passed, and I'm now far out over the Pacific. But even so, a red rim remains on the horizon, as if the sun had only just now set. I guess I'm racing it west.

The sky above the fading horizon is deep blue and already punctuated with stars. Later, when it's finally dark, I see a satellite go streaming by overhead. I wonder how long it's been in orbit. Certainly since before the war. Here a thousand years have gone by, and Earth has erased from its surface nearly all evidence of humankind's reign, save a few Mayan pyramids, a stretch of ancient Chinese wall, and our leftover satellites circling on the timeless edge of space. I wonder who will be here to see them when we're all gone.

Whatever happened back there at the bungalow, I have a feeling that the result of it is a death sentence for all of us. A sense of overwhelming dread haunts me the entire flight. The only thing I can think is that my mother took advantage of Hannah's absence from the Foundation and went behind my back to try and launch some kind of takeover operation. And here I had Hannah on the verge of agreeing to make a deal. My diplomacy was destroyed by my mother's betrayal. I'd be even more furious with her than I am if I weren't so worried.

I see the fires from a long ways off.

High clouds hover over our burning mountain hideaway, catching the firelight and reflecting it back so that a second fire seems to burn there upside down in the night sky. The horror of what I'm seeing takes several seconds to sink in, and then I'm pounding on the cockpit glass as the drone descends.

"Let me out!" I shout. "Let me out now! Oh, God, please let my mother and Jimmy be okay. Please."

As the drone approaches, I glimpse just how bad it is. The shelter walls are gone, and the exposed living space is engulfed in flames. The watchtower is burning too. Smaller fires dot the dark landscape on either side, and a few fires even dance like windblown torches on top of the wall. It looks as if some kind of burning accelerant were dropped from the sky. Then the view is wiped from my window as the drone sinks beneath the flames to enter the hidden runway underneath it. If the door even opens, I'm fully expecting to land in a furnace and cook to death where I sit in this stupid cockpit. I even brace for it.

But the door opens, and the drone comes to a halt in the untouched hangar. No flames, no destruction. The canopy lifts open, and I leap from the drone and race for the ladder. I'm halfway up it when I realize that the hatch leading to the shelter above is closed. There's a keypad on the ceiling next to it, but I have no idea what the code is. Then I hear crying coming from somewhere below. I look down from the ladder and see feet sticking out beneath a spare portion of drone wing that's leaned against the hangar wall. I drop to the floor and rush over and pull the wing away.

My mother sits with her back to the wall, her knees pulled up to her chest. Her head is down and she's sobbing. I drop to my knees in front of her and gently lift her head up. Her face is covered with black soot, and her eyes are red from crying. She looks surprised, as if she doesn't believe she's really seeing me, but then she throws her arms around my neck, pulls me to her, and clings to me as if her life depended on it.

"Where's Jimmy, Mom?"

Her muffled sobs continue. She doesn't answer.

"Mom, where's Jimmy? I need to know where Jimmy is."

When she still won't answer me, I pry her arms loose from my neck, pull away, and look her in the eyes.

"Damn it, Mom. I asked you where Jimmy is."

She cocks her head as if she didn't understand what I said. Then I see why. Blood trickles from each of her ears.

"Mom, are you okay?" I ask, mouthing the words clearly so she can read my lips. She nods that she is. "Where's Jimmy?" She shakes her head. "Mother, tell me where Jimmy is." When she still doesn't answer me, I scream at her. "Tell me, dammit!"

"He went to warn them," she says. "I tried to stop him."

"Warn who? The Motars? At their camp?" When she nods yes, I point up to the closed hatch. "What's the code?"

She reaches for my neck again, but I push her hands away.

"Tell me the code or I'll jump out the damn hangar door."

She drops her chin to her chest. Then she raises her hand in front of her bowed head and holds up three fingers, then two, then five, then three again. I let go of her shoulders and race up the ladder.

As I punch in the code, I hear her say, "Be careful."

The flames whip wildly in the wind, showing a path then covering it up again. I weave my way across the ruined shelter, dodging the fire, and emerge on the other side unscathed. I can smell burning flesh from our meat locker and my own singed hair. On the path now, running—down and up and over. Quiet your mind, Aubrey, focus on the task. The clouds reflect back the fire that I'm heading for and illuminate the mountains like a strange hellscape I might have run through in a nightmare. I hear distant explosions and faint screams. In the glow of this dreamy apocalypse, I see drones flitting across the red sky above the Motar's hidden valley, like enormous bats or sky-bound Manta rays, ejecting bombs from their bellies and then banking left or right to make way for more of their kind. For one brief moment those burning clouds twist in my frantic mind to become waves of red hair, and I see Hannah's face leering at me from the night sky like some she-devil risen from the depths of hell to claim as her dominion the mountains and the night and each of our sad souls.

We should have killed her when we could.

I ford the river at a dead run. I know the water must be cold, but I can't feel it. The drones have finished their work, and by the time I arrive only a few glide overhead, their silhouettes black against the burnt sky. I pay them no mind. The valley leading to the hidden camp is dotted with flaming carcasses of horses and of men. I zigzag between them, checking for Jimmy. I come on sights of horror where horse and rider have melted together into one pile of burning flesh. I see a man with a perfectly round hole blown in his chest and just the fatty edges of it rimmed with sizzling blue fire as he lies on his back, staring with frozen bewilderment at the burning sky as if to ask it why. I see another without his head. Two charred women are laid out arm in arm on the ground, as if they'd spontaneously combusted while embracing there. I wander through this scene of senseless slaughter, stopping at each new sight of gore just long enough to make sure it isn't Jimmy before moving on again. One man clutches my ankle as I try to walk away, but he's lying in soil drenched with his own blood. The last of his life is leaking out of him in weak spurts from his two severed legs. There's nothing I or anyone can do. I jerk my foot away and keep moving.

As I approach the cliff that leads to the hidden camp, my panic is replaced by a slowly building horror. I pass through the secret entrance and walk toward the blind bend, expecting the worst. The worst I can imagine turns out to not be bad enough though. The waterfall reflects back the fire and seems itself to be made of liquid flames. The channel of black water passes beneath the remnant embers of the bridges, and the framework of tents stand strangely intact and still burning. Nothing is left untouched by fire. It smells sweet and putrid and nauseatingly like charcoal. There are bodies here too, but mostly those of women and children. I wonder if the men had mounted their horses in an attempt to lead the drones away.

Then I see him standing in the middle of the burning camp, wide-eyed and naked as if he himself had just been born from the flames. If he sees me, it does not register on his face. I wade into the channel, swim across, climb out the other side, and run to him where he stands.

"Where's Jimmy?" I ask. "Where's my friend?"

The boy just looks at me queerly.

I strip off my wet shirt and cover him. Then I walk him toward the exit, but he plants his feet and pulls away from me.

"Come on, we've got to get you out of here," I say, my voice drowned out by the waterfall and the crackling flames.

The boy turns and runs farther into the camp. I chase after. He leads me across the hidden valley along the winding central path. He's surprisingly fast, and I follow by the glimpses of him I catch in the firelight as he passes the burning tents. I'm nearly out of breath by the time we reach the end of the camp, where the backside of the enclosed valley narrows to just a crack that the channel water spills out of, into the blackness of the gorge beyond. The boy stops at something on the path. When I catch up to him, I see his mother, the healer, lying heaped on the ground with a gaping hole in her side. The boy takes my hand and pulls me farther along the path to where the channel gives way to rapids that tumble down the gorge. There we find the old man. We're beyond the flames now and in the shadows in which he lies, I can't tell what wound might have killed him, but his one good eye has rolled back into his head. It stares up at us whitely from his blackened face.

When I look up I just catch sight of the boy slipping from my view onto a narrow ledge that leads out from the camp and into the gorge. I flatten myself against the cliff and follow him. Rough steps of wet stone lead down alongside the cascading falls, and in the dark and rumbling spray of shadowed mist I find the boy kneeling over Jimmy. I drop and gather my best friend in my arms. He's limp and cold and badly burnt.

But he's breathing, dammit, he's alive.

I look around instinctively for help, but other than the boy's shadow standing nearby, we're completely alone. I look to the crack of light above us where the camp still burns, and I begin to piece together what must have happened. The riders headed out the front to lead the drones away, while the others tried to sneak the boy out the back. I can see the relay now as he was handed off from his mother to the old man and finally to Jimmy who managed to see him safely out before collapsing.

I look back to Jimmy in my lap. As my eyes adjust to the dark, I see that the left side of his face is covered with pale patches of waxy and oozing burns. He trembles in my arms.

I stand and get behind him and gently hook my arms under his pits and begin dragging him back up the steps. I stop when the boy blocks me. He points down, away from the camp. I'm too wrecked by shock and grief to argue or ask why, so I turn Jimmy carefully around and ease him down instead, following the boy into the shadows of the gorge.

It's slow going. The wind picks up, and the clouds that had been reflecting the fire drift away and reveal the clear, cold sky above, the stars twinkling there as if nothing at all has changed.

The boy runs ahead, disappears, and comes out again with a lantern. He leads me the last several meters down the gorge to the entrance of a cave. The cave appears to have been carved by some undercurrent in a time when the water raged through here much higher than it does now. Although it's not deep, it's well-protected and dry. Several stuffed mattresses line the far wall, and the boy leads me to one of them with his lantern. I lay Jimmy down. The sight of his face in the lamplight makes me cringe. I can't imagine the pain he must be in.

I take up the lantern from the boy and inspect the cave. There are recesses in the walls filled with supplies. I hand the boy an empty clay jug and motion for him to go outside and fill it with water from the falls. Then I find some blankets and a clean bundle of cloths. I remove Jimmy's kilt and inspect his bruised and battered body, but other than a few bad blisters on his left hand and arm, the bulk of his burns are isolated to his neck and his face. He's shivering, either from cold or from shock, and I cover him up to his chest with the blankets. The boy returns with the water and I wet a cloth and gently begin to clean Jimmy's burns, scraping away the dirt and the charcoal and the seared pieces of outer skin. The worst is a portion of his cheek that was pierced by something hot. Although the wound is cauterized and not bleeding, I can see his lower teeth peeking through. When his wounds are clean I drape them with dry cloths. Then I sit on the edge of the bed and watch him, wondering what else I can possibly do except pray.

"You're gonna be okay, buddy. I'm here now."

He opens his eyes and looks at me, and then he shudders with a spasm of pain and closes them again.

I sit watching him for hours, not daring to take my eyes off of him lest he might suddenly stop breathing. I play a mental game with myself, willing him to inhale after every exhale and holding my own breath until he does. He sometimes stirs and moans, but other times he appears to be peacefully sleeping. As the night passes, I'm vaguely aware of the boy squatting nearby, getting up and leaving several times, but always coming back again. Then, just as the first light of dawn is spilling into the cave, he comes back from one of these outings with my mom, both of them wet from swimming the channel.

She kneels beside me where I sit my vigil and looks down on Jimmy. She winces when she pulls the cloth away from his face. She's on her feet again immediately and rummaging through the supplies, laying things out on the floor to inspect them in the dim light of dawn.

"Will he be okay, Mom?"

I take her lack of an answer at first as meaning that she doesn't think he will, but then I remember her bleeding ears and I turn and ask again louder. When she doesn't look up at me from sorting her supplies, I give up and turn back to Jimmy. A few moments later I feel her hand on my shoulder.

"Move aside, Son," she says.

I rise to let her work. I'm walking out of the cave to wash my face in the cold falls when I hear her say:

"Yes, he's going to be fine."

CHAPTER 29
Dust to Dust

The tent frames and bridges still smolder, but the bodies don't.

The smell is so overwhelming that I can taste it. I hold a cloth over my nose as I walk through the wreckage of the camp looking for survivors. The boy is now clothed in tattered furs he's collected from the rubble. He picks through the ashes ahead of me, poking at things with a tent stake he's pulled from the ground. He seems curiously detached and unaffected, as if this were just some random place he'd stumbled on and decided to explore before heading back to his home. But there is no home for him now. Or for any of us either.

I come upon the old man's story chest, lying on its side with the sand spilled out. I kneel and scoop a handful up and watch the breeze catch it as it falls out through my fingers. If each grain is an hour of our lives, where does it all go? The old man's stick and brush are protruding partway from the chest. I take them up and draw the face of God in the sand.

Then I ask of it, "Why?"

It does not answer, of course.

I remember the old man drawing the city, the bomb coming down, and the destruction that was left in its wake. I look around at the camp now, and I can't help but think that his scene has lifted off the sand and sprung to life.

My mother nurses Jimmy all day in the cave while the boy and I dig the graves. The shovel handle is short, half of it having burned in the fire, and it makes for difficult work in the hard soil. The boy drags over a pickaxe nearly as large as he is and begins to help. It isn't much of a burial, but by early afternoon we've got most of the villagers lined up in a shallow trench and are covering them with soil, sand, and ash. I reach inside the old man's bloodied furs, retrieve his jade snuff bottle, and hand it to the boy. He looks at it in his hand for a moment as if he'd never seen it before. Then he stuffs it away in some hidden pocket amongst his clothing. We toss our tools to the far bank, swim across the channel and collect them again, move to the outer valley, and begin to dig there.

The horses we leave, but where the riders and horses have been burned or blown to bits together, we try to sort out as best we can those parts which are human and drag or carry them back to our hole to be interred. I whisper an apology to the legless man who clutched at me for help the night before. As I drag him backwards over the bumpy ground to the grave, his head lolls and bobs this way and that, as if to say that it's no big deal. The sun has nearly set by the time we cover them.

We pass the night together in the cave, but we might as well each be alone. My mother's hearing is still fragile at best, and the boy speaks a language I don't understand, so there is little talking between any of us as we huddle beneath blankets to stay warm. When Jimmy sleeps his breathing is irregular and shallow. When he wakes he moans with terrible pain. We pile blankets on him, heat water and make tea and try to coax him to sip it when he's alert. So far he hasn't said a word.

In the morning, the first of the survivors arrives.

I wake to find a young warrior standing over me and the boy standing by his side. The boy points to Jimmy then to me and talks with a great sense of urgency. The warrior hears him out, then nods, turns, and runs from the cave. He's back by late morning with three elder sisters. They gather around Jimmy and inspect his wounds. One of them massages his limbs while the others mix up medicines from the cache of supplies. Less than an hour after they arrive, his burns are coated with a white paste and covered again with fresh cloths.

My mother and I leave him temporarily in their capable hands and hike back to our ruined shelter to retrieve what we can. It's a solemn march there, and I feel several times that my mother wants to say something but doesn't dare for fear that I blame her for Jimmy. I guess I do, a little.

When we arrive at the shelter, the fire is completely out. It must have rained the night before, because puddles of black water collect in the low parts of the floor. I put my hand out and stop my mom from going farther when I see the strange pod lying where our table used to be. It's a huge half cylinder made of carbon fiber and concave on one side.

"Do you think it's a bomb?"

"Come again, Son."

"A bomb, Mom. A bomb. Do you think it's a bomb?"

"I don't know what's inside this one," she says, "but it's a cargo carrier for a drone. We used them to deliver supplies."

"Well, I doubt she sent us algaecrisps," I say.

"I doubt that too, Son."

"Let's just leave it alone."

We walk as far around the cargo container as possible, punch in the hatch code, and descend into the hangar. With the shelter now destroyed, I can see how it serves as a bunker and why my mother retreated there. I retrieve my reading slate and my strike-a-light from the drone. My mother digs through her supplies and comes up with a small first aid kit.

"I wish we'd known that was there when you were snake bit," I say. "It would have helped."

"I'm glad you didn't," she replies. "There are painkillers in here, and now we have them for Jimmy."

"I had her agreed to a deal, Mom."

"What's that, Son?"

I'm not sure why I chose now to confront her, but I can't keep it in any longer.

"Hannah, Mom. She had agreed to release Red. And the others too. But then the professor told her what happened at the Foundation, and the deal was off."

My mother leans against the drone and hangs her head.

"I'm sorry, Son."

"Why did you betray me?"

"We had been planning this for a long time now. When Hannah picked your birthday to meet, it was just too perfect."

"So my birthday was day zero?" When she looks up at me, I repeat myself. "My birthday. It was day zero in your note?"

"Yes," she says, nodding. "I had programmed a virus into the Foundation's software system years before. It was supposed to shut down their warning systems so we could sneak into the control center, take over the drones, and prevent Holocene II from being flooded long enough for the others below to rally support. Then they'd planned to bring up a train filled with enough converts to physically take over. But I never should have let Beth and Jillian try it alone. And my hack failed. The warning systems worked."

"Mom, your hack probably failed because we reloaded the mastercode after the Foundation flood. That's why we went to the Isle of Man, remember?"

"I thought you went for the encryption code," she says.

"We did, but only because we had first gone down to the basements and retrieved the backup mastercode and reloaded it. I thought I had told you that part."

She sighs and says, "I'm afraid this is all my fault, Son. I blew it."

"Don't say that, Mom. This is Radcliffe's fault, and this is Hannah's fault, but this is not your fault. No way."

Her eyes well with tears, and her voice quivers when she says, "So you don't blame me for what happened to Jimmy?"

I shake my head no and hug her. We stand there in the hangar, wrapped in one another's arms, and we both cry gently for a long time. We cry for what's happened to the Motars, we cry for what's happened to Jimmy, and we cry for what's happened to us.

When we climb back up to the shelter, I find a single eagle feather floating in one of the sooty puddles. I almost pick it up for Jimmy, but then I think better of it.

We're several meters down the path when I stop.

"I have to know what's in it."

"What's that?" my mother asks.

"The cargo container. I have to know what's in it."

She seems to agree. We hike back up to the shelter and eye the container from every side.

"Maybe it fell off a drone by accident," I suggest.

She shakes her head. "What are the chances of it landing right here, if it did? No. This is meant for us."

"What if it's a trick? What if I open it and it explodes?"

"I have some cable down below in the hangar," she replies.

"Maybe we could use that."

Thirty minutes later, we're crouched on the wall twenty meters away with the end of the cable in my hand.

"Pull it hard," my mom says. "Even though we unlatched it, they're air tight and they sometimes like to stick."

I count to three. When I jerk the cable, the cargo container pops open but nothing happens. We wait a minute, then I creep forward to see what's inside. A few days ago my mother would have insisted on going first, but something has changed in her after the other night.

"Be careful," she whispers behind me, as if I were creeping up on some sleeping beast that might wake.

The container is as wide as a drone and nearly as long. It opens on its end rather than its side, likely designed that way to hold more weight in flight. But because it's so deep, I can't see anything inside other than shadows. I kneel down and reach in, but I don't feel anything either. So I lie down and reach in all the way to my shoulder and feel around. Still nothing. I crawl inside the container, waving one arm in front of me. My hand closes on something soft. I grip it and pull. Whatever I'm dragging is heavy and hardly gives, but then something breaks loose, and the thing I'm gripping gets light. I back out of the container into the daylight, sit down and look at Red's hair and the top of his sawed-off skull in my hand. Crude staples bend out from the fleshy edges of his scalp where the crown of his skull that I'm holding had been reattached.

I turn and vomit on the ground.

When I look up again, my mother has her back turned and her head hung. I want to fling the thing away from me just to get it out of my sight, but it somehow doesn't seem like a proper way to treat a dead friend's remains. I set Red's scalp of red hair carefully to the side and crawl back into the container. When I drag his body out, my mother is waiting there to help me. We pull him clear of the container and lay him out on the ground. We look at his naked body and his gaping skull.

"That monster Hannah must have put him in Eden while he was still awake," my mother says.

"How do you know that?" I ask.

"Because his eyes are open."

I bend to close his eyes but the lids won't shut.

My mother walks away and comes back a minute later with two small stones and covers them.

"I guess we should go and get the shovel," she says.

"There's another one."

"Another shovel?"

"No. Another body?"

She looks like she might faint. Then she steps over to the open container and kneels to crawl inside. I rush to her and hug her, preventing her from going in.

"Why don't you get that shovel," I say.

She nods, stands, and walks away without a word.

It takes her over an hour there and back. By the time she returns, I have Red and Mrs. Hightower lined up next to the softest piece of earth I could find at the base of the wall. The spot overlooks the peaks and valleys to the east. It makes me happy at least to know that they'll be silent witness to a million amazing sunrises. My mother and I dig without talking. I've now buried, burned, and fed more corpses to sharks than I care to recall. Every time it's a somber and serious business.

When we finish we lay them side by side in the shallow

grave. I replace the top of Red's skull where it belongs. One of Mrs. Hightower's arms is frozen at the elbow, ninety degrees and pointing out. The hole isn't deep enough to cover it. I force it down to her chest, but it springs up again, so I find a large flat rock and weight her arm to her chest with it. Before we cover them up, my mother kneels and places her open hand on Mrs. Hightower's forehead.

She says, "Forgive me, Beth."

I say the same thing silently to Red.

With the hard soil packed back on top of them, we stomp it down. I feel like some mad murderers celebrating on their victims' graves. When we finish I'm crying. My mother wraps her arm around me, and we stand and look down the mountain together—two filthy and tired travelers missing their friends.

"This has to be stopped," my mother says. "Hannah has to be stopped. Somehow, some way."

I agree with her, of course, but her attempt to take over the Foundation failed miserably. The proof of that is now beneath our feet. Every one of her allies is dead except possibly Jillian. Her communications equipment is destroyed. All we have is one two person drone and the three of us here in these wild mountains, along with a few Motar survivors, trying to get by somehow on our own.

The sun sets on our way back. The sky explodes with pink light that seems to make everything seem farther away and more beautiful. We wade across the river and walk across the valley. I feel guilty for the peaceful feeling I have, knowing that this had been the scene of such horror just a few nights before. My mother seems to feel it too, because she smiles at me and takes my hand in hers without a word.

The sun, on its way to light some new day, is dragging the pink down out of the sky as we enter the hidden valley. In the soft light of dusk, with the bodies gone and covered up, the destruction seems almost necessary somehow for the birth of a new beginning. Someone has laid salvaged timbers across the burned bridge. We cross it and walk the path through the ruined camp. When my foot lands in the old man's sand, I stop in my tracks. My mother halts and turns back.

"Is everything okay, Aubrey?" she asks.

"You said Hannah needs to be stopped."

"Yes," she says, "I did."

"To what lengths would you go to stop her?"

"What do you mean?"

"Would you stop her at any cost?" I ask.

"I don't understand your question, but the answer's yes. I would stop her at any cost. Wouldn't you, if there was a way?"

"Yes," I say, nodding. "And maybe there is a way."

"What are you thinking, Aubrey?"

"Dust to dust. What if the end is in the beginning?"

"I don't understand what you're getting at, Son."

"Mom," I say, looking up from the spilled sand, "exactly how much do you know about thermonuclear weapons?"

Her weary eyes widen, and she asks, "Do you mean like the hydrogen bombs that were used in the War?"

"Yes, exactly."

"I know a little. Why?"

"I have an idea, although it might kill us if this works."

"Show me again exactly where it is."

My mother holds the lamp up over my shoulder so she can see in the dim cave. The boy, the warrior, and the three sisters crowd around her, looking too. I brush the old man's sand clear and draw for them again the mountain crater that Jimmy and I crossed so long ago now, sketching the missile hanging from the ice ceiling above its hidden lake.

"I fell in here. And the missile is maybe five meters or so from the shore in the ceiling here. And most of it is in the ice, but the front part is exposed."

I look up. They're all nodding, even though my mother is the only one who can understand what I'm saying.

"And you're sure it looked intact?" she asks.

"Oh, yes. You could still see the strange characters written on it. But how would we fix it, since it was a dud?"

"It's not a dud, Son."

"Then why didn't it go off?"

"Because it never got low enough. The mountain stopped it before it reached its targeted elevation."

"Don't they explode when they hit something?" I ask.

She shakes her head. "Too much of the explosion would be absorbed by the ground and wasted. These hydrogen bombs were designed to detonate at a particular altitude above their target. My guess is that this one was aimed at the Foundation, which was then a secret military base. It must have missed its mark and buried itself in the ice on the mountain's summit."

"But would it still be any good?"

"I don't see why not," she says. "It's been frozen in there all this time. The warhead should be fine. These things weren't designed to expire, you know. I think plutonium has a half-life of over twenty thousand years."

The warrior nods, the sisters whisper to one another, and the boy presses his open palms together and bows for some strange reason. I wonder what it is they think we're discussing.

"How do you know so much about these things, Mom?"

She shrugs. "We were still dismantling some of the arsenal at the Foundation when I arrived. We even used a few nukes to help open the canal that you passed through in the submarine on your way to the Isle of Man."

"Well, even if it is still good," I say, reaching to brush the sand clear, "it's probably no use anyway. That thing is way too big to get on our drone."

"You're wrong," my mother says.

She takes the stick from my hand and draws a missile in the sand, dividing it into sections.

"Look, only this front part here is the warhead. The missile itself was just used to fly it. We don't need that now. If we can separate the warhead somehow, based on how you described it, it would only weigh several hundred pounds. The drone could carry that. And wouldn't it be poetic justice to deliver it to Hannah in the same carrier that she used to send Red and Beth's bodies to us? You're really onto something here, Aubrey. This could be it. This could be the way to finally end this."

"What if she floods Holocene II?" I ask.

"She won't even have a chance to. No way. And if she has

some doomsday backup in place to do it for her, then there's nothing we can do about that anyway. But this bomb would destroy the Foundation for sure, Son. No Foundation, no Park Service. No Park Service, no drones. No drones and we're all free. Don't you see?"

I kneel and scoop the sand back into the chest.

"We can think about it," I say. "But we can't go now. Not until Jimmy's okay."

"We have to do it now," she says. "We can't wait, Aubrey. We have no idea when Hannah will send drones again. Or what all she has planned for us."

"I said not now, Mom."

"Aubrey, you're being silly. We cannot wait."

I close the lid on the chest and pick it up.

"Let's just talk about it later, okay?"

She reaches out, places her hand on my shoulder, and says, "There may not be a later, Son. We have to try this now."

She's right and I know it. But I also know that there's only room for two in our drone and I'm not willing to leave Jimmy.

"I won't leave Jimmy behind," I say.

"What if I want you to go?"

We all turn to look at Jimmy when he speaks.

He's propped up on his elbow. His face is half-covered in yellowed-cloth bandages, giving him the appearance of a mummy having risen from its tomb. I set the chest down, cross to him, and kneel beside the bed.

"How you feeling, buddy?"

"I feel like hell," he says. "But I think them pills you gave me a while ago are kickin' in. I'm kinda floatin' a little."

"Good. Now you just let me know when the pain gets too

bad again, and we'll give you another one. Okay?"

"You have to go, Aubrey."

"Let's talk about that later."

"No. Your mom's right. There might not be a later."

"I don't want to leave you. Not now. Not like this."

"I know it," he replies. "But you have to go. You told me yourself that we got a duty to do what we can. That's what makes us human, remember?"

"I never said that."

"You did so."

"When?"

"In the pool that day before you left to meet Hannah."

"Well, I went, didn't I? I did my duty. I tried."

"You ain't tried this."

"Come on, Jimmy . . ."

"Come on nothin'. You gotta go do this, Aubrey."

"But it's risky."

"So what? Ever-thin's a risk. Do it for Junior and for Bree. Do it for what Hannah did to Finn—her own brother, your brother. Do it for the whole Isle of Man. Do it for these people here." He nods to the boy and the others. "And do it for your dad, Aubrey. And for my family too. And if for nothin' else, you gotta do it for me. Look at what she did to me."

When he finishes, his good eye wells up, and a tear slides down his cheek. I can't quite tell if he's crying from the pain of having spoken so much or because of the list he just rattled off.

"You're going to be fine," I say.

"I'll live," he replies. "But I seen the way you looked at me when you was bandaging me up. I was out of it, but I still seen the horror on your face. And I've seen burns before, Aubrey. I know how they heal. She mutilated me."

"You look fine," I say.

"No, I don't," he says, shaking his head.

"Maybe not now, but you will."

"Dun' lie to me, Aubrey. Please."

I drop my head. "Well, you'll always look just fine to me."

"Jus' go do what's gotta be done, Aubrey. Put a stop to all of this. I'm askin' you. Now, if you dun' mind maybe you could bring me my bottle if it's still around, 'cause I gotta pee."

I look at his bandaged face, knowing full well that he's right about what he'll look like once he's healed. The anger that rises in me is enough to make me kill Hannah with my hands.

"Okay," I say. "I'll do it. But then I'm coming back for you, and we're finally going to be able to live without these drones over our heads. It'll be perfect. You'll see."

He smiles, even though it obviously causes him pain.

My mother and I spend the next seven days preparing to leave. We pick through the burned camp and collect anything that might prove useful. We salvage lengths of rope, unburned animal hides, and metal tools. Then we recover what we can from the shelter too. The container that Hannah sent the bodies in is too large to fit down the hatch, so we rig ropes through pulleys, lower it down the mountainside, and pull it into the main entrance of the hangar. We raise the drone with the same ropes, tuck the landing gear, and set it down onto the container, which attaches magnetically to the body of the drone. But the container is meant for much larger drones, and there is no way to drop the landing gear with it attached.

"How are we going to take off and land without wheels?"

"Where we're going," she says, "We don't need wheels."

"We don't?"

"No. We need a ski."

My mother breaks out her tools and spends the afternoon using an electric plasma torch to craft a ski from the salvaged wing of the old drone she shot down. When we run the hangar battery dead, she uses the drone's battery to power the welder and attach the ski to the bottom of the carrier. She only has one shield, and I stand back and try not to look as she welds, but it's amazing to watch her work. When she's finished, the modified drone looks like a giant bumblebee sculpture that will never be able to get off of the ground.

"You sure this thing can even make it that far?" I ask.

"I hope so," she says. "But even if it does, it won't be able to fly fast, so we can plan on a long trip."

Then something else occurs to me as I'm looking at it.

"There's one thing I don't understand," I say. "If we plan to load the warhead into the carrier and drop the carrier over the Foundation at the Dam, won't our ski drop with it?"

"That's the beauty of it," she says. "We won't be going back to the mountain anyway. Without the carrier attached the landing gear will be free to come down."

I nod, admiring her engineering skills. "Smart."

She smiles. "Radcliffe didn't call me up for nothing."

Next we fill the carrier with anything we think we might need—ropes, cable, tools, spare drone parts, extra clothes— everything that will fit, we stuff inside. We load in the last of the ration bars, not knowing how long it will take us to dismantle and deliver the warhead. Since water's heavy, we decide not to bring extra beyond what we'll need on the flight, figuring instead that we can melt snow at the mountain.

With the drone buttoned up and ready to go, we close the hangar hatch and head back for our last night in the cave.

Jimmy is feeling much better, although he's still in a lot of pain. We sit around his bed and eat a meal of fresh venison and potato soup made from the cave's stash of supplies. We've learned that the boy's name is Ananda, and that the warrior is called Gazan. The three sisters are Naron, Saron, and Talmon, although they all look so alike I can't keep them straight.

Gazan points to Jimmy's uneaten venison and asks him something in his native language.

Jimmy makes a show of taking a big bite. "Good, yes," he says. "Very good. It jus' hurts still to chew."

The warrior nods as if he understands.

When we're finished eating, the boy stands in the middle of the cave and performs a song for us. His voice is so beautiful that I soon forget where we are. I see nothing but the boy in the soft lamplight, singing us his story. Even though I can't understand the words, his mimes, gestures, and melody lead me to believe that the song is one about the sunrise and new beginnings. It's a song I need to hear, a song we all need to hear. He finishes with a bow.

I make my bed of furs for the night on the cave floor next to Jimmy. I'm more aware now than ever that he's been by my side almost constantly since these crazy adventures began. I can't imagine leaving him in the morning. Long after the lamps have been blown out, I lie awake in the dark and listen to him breathe. Once he stirs and says my name, but when I answer and he doesn't reply, I realize that he must just be talking in his sleep. Later, I hear Gazan get up and leave the cave, probably to go pee. Then he comes back again, and by the sound of his breathing, falls almost immediately back asleep.

In the profound and absolute darkness, I lie awake and remember everything Jimmy and I have been through together. I remember those fun days in the cove and the horrible ones that followed. I remember crossing the mountain. I remember finding Junior. I remember the lake house and meeting Hannah, Gloria, and Mrs. Radcliffe. I remember the professor, the Isle of Man, and our adventures there. And I remember the escape from Holocene II and being in the jungle with Jimmy, Bill, and Roger. I remember first meeting my mother—the shock of it, the joy of it now. I remember getting to know her and coming to love her like I do. Then I laugh out loud when I remember Jimmy lying in that hole and trapping his eagle. I remember the dinner we had with the Motars and how lovely it was with my belly full, smoking my father's pipe. It's strange, because as horrible as everything has been at times, and as terrible as things have turned out, I already feel nostalgia for these days gone by.

I must fall asleep at some point, because the next thing I know the cave is washed in the gray light of dawn. Gazan and the boy are gone, probably out hunting. I get up and step quietly past the sleeping sisters and my mom and walk outside to relieve myself. When I turn around, Jimmy is standing in the entrance to the cave with a blanket over his shoulders.

"You shouldn't be up," I say.

"I'm fine," he says. "I had a dream last night."

"You did. What about?"

"About us."

"Was it good or bad?" I ask. "Because I don't know if I can stand to hear about it if it was bad."

"No," he says. "It was good."

"Well, what was it about?"

"It's hard to explain," he says. "Maybe 'cause it's a dream. But we was in this valley, and there was water. Like the waterfall out here, but maybe a river or maybe a stream. I dunno. But we was sittin' there watchin' the sunset, and all this wheat out in the valley jus' turned to gold. And the breeze was dancin' across it. And Junior was there with us."

"He was?"

"Yeah, he was leapin' through the grass, chasin' a moth or somthin'. But he'd stop ever once in a while and look back— you know, like he used to do, makin' sure we was still there. But that was the thing about it. We wasn't goin' nowhere no more, 'cause wherever it was, we was finally home."

He finishes recounting his dream. I look at him there, standing wrapped in his blanket, half his face bandaged and the other half fixed in a peaceful smile. Neither of us speaks for a while as we listen to the relaxing sound of water bubbling by.

I don't care anymore if it feels awkward or not, I cross to him and hug him, being careful not to pull at his bandages. He hugs me back, and it feels good. When I pull away, I hold him by the shoulders and look into his face.

"It's not just a dream, Jimmy. I know it's not. And it isn't a picture of heaven or some afterlife either. I'm coming back, I promise you. I'm coming back, and we'll find that valley and make our home there and settle down."

"No more runnin'?" he asks.

"No more running," I say.

He looks beyond me at the gray sky with a sort of wistful expression on his face. Then he sighs softly.

"I'd like that."

Despite both my mother and me protesting loudly, Jimmy insists on making the trip to see us off. The three sisters stay behind, but they redo Jimmy's bandages and generally fuss over him as they have been since arriving. Then they demand that he drink an entire pot of tea before they'll let him leave. After loading my mother and me up with supplies for the trip, they see us off from the cave entrance.

The boy and his guardian follow behind us, but they keep at a distance and speak only occasionally to one another in their native tongue, blending into the surroundings so that it seems like just the three of us together making the trek.

We cross the valley, the river, and the hills beyond. I watch the steam rise and disappear into the morning air as we pass by the hot springs. I remember bathing with my mom and with Jimmy, and I wish we weren't leaving and could instead all relax in the pools and talk until the end of days. But I know this may in fact be the end, and that I may never get that chance again.

Jimmy shakes his head when he sees the destroyed shelter, hardly recognizable now with most of the walls gone and piles of ashen debris on the exposed floor. I point out to him where we buried Red and Mrs. Hightower. He nods and says that we picked a perfect place.

The climb down into the hangar is even harder than I had imagined it might be. As I help Jimmy off the ladder, the look on his face tells me this is just as hard for him too. When Gazan and the boy come down and see the drone, they shy away and crouch against the wall like frightened horses. But we all reassure them, and they eventually step forward and walk around it in awe, touching the smooth metal with their fingers as if reading something there by braille. My mother loads the supplies given to us by the sisters into the carrier, seals it shut again, and gives the drone one last inspection.

"Did you program the flight? I ask her.

"We're flying manually," she says. "I don't have longitude and latitude for the mountain, but even if I did, the bombing destroyed my computer and my satellite link." Then she nods to Gazan and the boy. "You'd better say your goodbyes, Son; I want to seal the hangar entrance before we leave."

Gazan shakes my hand at the ladder, then pumps his fist in the air, making a warrior call that seems to me to say, "Go get the bastards." The boy reaches for my neck, pulls me down to him, and smells my hair. Then he kisses the top of my head. With our goodbyes now said, my mother leads them up the ladder to say goodbye herself, leaving me alone with Jimmy.

"Shoot," Jimmy says, looking away from me. "I forgot to bring you my pee bottle."

"My mom thought of everything," I reply. "She's got one for each of us in our cockpits, along with food and water."

"I'd be curious to see how she uses it," he says.

"Uses what?"

"Her pee bottle."

"Yeah," I say, laughing. "I hadn't thought about it, but I guess we've got it easier than she does when it comes to that."

Jimmy looks at me then, lays a hand on my shoulder, and says, "I'm real proud of you, Aubrey."

"You are?"

He nods. "I ain't real good at sayin' stuff sometimes, but I remember when I first seen you there passed out on the shore. You was so young. Like a little kid that I wanted to take care of.

But now you're a man, Aubrey. A good one. And I look up to you. I used to feel like I needed to protect you. Not no more, though. Now I feel like I need you to protect me."

I swallow the emotions that are coming up. "Me protect you? That's silly. You're the strong one between us."

He smiles a knowing grin and shakes his head. "There's sometin' else too," he says. "You remember when you come up on me again later? When I's huntin' them pigeons, and you wouldn't let me alone. You remember that?"

"Yeah, I remember. I followed you all the way back and you talked your dad into letting me stay that night."

"Well," he continues, "I lied to you about somethin' then. I wanna make it right now and tell you before you go."

"What did you lie to me about?"

"I lied about jus' runnin' into you there."

"You did?"

"Yeah. I came back jus' to find you."

"I knew it," I say.

"You did not."

"Well, I'd hoped you had, anyway."

We stand looking at one another, something important remaining yet to be said between us, but neither of us knowing exactly what or exactly how to say it. Then my mother climbs down the hatch, and the moment is gone.

"Aubrey," she says, "you had better go and relieve yourself once more before we leave. It's a long flight."

"I'm fine, Mom. Jimmy and I were actually just trying to figure out how you plan to use your bottle."

"I hope not to," she says, "but you'd be surprised what a lady can do in a pinch. Have you two said your goodbyes now?

It's time we got this bent-up bucket of bolts in the air so we can see if it even flies anymore."

"How's it gonna take off without no wheels?" Jimmy asks.

She shrugs and says, "With a prayer and a hope, I guess."

Then she climbs into the front cockpit and motions with her eyes to the open hatch, letting me know that it's time to see Jimmy out. I walk him to the ladder. I want to hug him, but I feel funny now with my mother watching, so I only shake his hand. He just smiles at me and nods. Then he climbs up the ladder and closes the hatch. It locks. I trudge back to the drone with my head hung and climb in.

My mother turns to address me before closing her cockpit. "You should go hug him goodbye, Son."

"You think so?"

She smiles and nods.

I leap out of the drone, climb the ladder, and punch in the code. Jimmy is already standing on the wall with Gazan and the boy, their backs to me as they look over the mountainside, waiting to see us take off. I run to Jimmy and tap him on the shoulder. He spins around and sees me. He smiles so hugely that the bandage partially pulls free from his burned cheek. I wrap my arms around him and hug him tight. By the time we finally pull away from one another, we're both crying. I strip my father's pipe over my head and press it into his hand.

"You hold onto this for me, okay? I'll come back for it."

Jimmy looks at the pipe in his palm and nods. Then he wipes a tear away with his other hand and waves me away.

"Go on," he says, "get out of here. These two jokers won't let me go back for lunch until we see you off, and I'm gettin' hungrier than a bear come spring."

I know he's full of crap and that he wouldn't miss watching me leave for the world. And I love him for it. I stop once at the hatch and look back. Jimmy smiles and holds up the pipe, as if to say he'll keep it safe until I return. Then I climb down the ladder and seal the hatch.

I know my mother sees my crying eyes, but she doesn't say anything. She just waits for me to climb into the drone, then she nods and pulls down her canopy. I take in one long breath of fresh, cool air and close mine, too. Then the big door opens, and with a wild screech, the drone skids and slides along the runway. It plunges out from the mountainside, almost falls down the slope nose first because we don't have enough speed, but catches itself just in time and powers up, lifting off into the clear blue afternoon.

My mother circles and does one flyby.

Gazan and the boy stand on the wall and wave goodbye.

Jimmy stands beside them with his head down, looking at my pipe in his hand. I know he doesn't want me to see that he's still crying. I crane my neck, hoping that he'll look up and make eye contact with me one final time. But the last image I see is the top of his bowed head shrinking away with the wall.

Part Three

CHAPTER 31
Engineering a New Beginning

We fly east as the planet spins.

Speeding sundown behind us, speeding sunup ahead.

When the great Pacific meets the shores of America, we're flying in the perfect pink light of a spectacular new dawn. I know we're passing over terrain that Jimmy and I once crossed on foot. From such a height it's strange to imagine us toiling away down there with no clue where we were going. But then I guess everything is clearer once you look at it from a distance.

The mountains are socked in beneath a ceiling of clouds, making it impossible for us to locate the crater and land. My mother turns to me through the glass and shakes her head—a silent apology before cutting north and continuing on. I know we can't risk setting down anywhere with our makeshift landing gear ski, but my entire body is screaming to get out of this cramped cockpit. I pass the time looking out the window at the scenery below us—mountains and valleys, rivers and lakes, and eventually, a never-ending vista of evergreen trees.

It's all so beautiful, I can't help but wonder just who Dr. Radcliffe thought would enjoy it once people were extinct. There must be a better way, I think—some solution to the over-consumption, some plan for humans to live within their means, some boundaries to preserve the natural environment. But then I wonder just how different my mother and I are, planning to drop yet another nuclear bomb. We have good reason to, of course. But doesn't everyone believe their reasons to be just as valid, just as true? Part of me thinks that what we're doing is wrong. But then I close my eyes and picture Jimmy's burnt face, his slaughtered family, Red's missing brain. And if those images weren't enough, I picture the Isle of Man erased from existence, and the Motars killed in their camp. Finally, I picture my father strapped in that killing-room chair. Then the last bit of doubt about using the bomb is smothered and gone.

It's late afternoon and our third pass around before the clouds clear from the mountains. As we circle the summit that Jimmy and I crossed, I can see from up here that, although it's the tallest mountain, its glacier really was the only way for us to traverse the range. My mother turns and points to the crater. I give her a thumbs up. She passes over the summit several times, eying the crater's oval bowl for the best landing angle. Seen from above, it looks much smaller than I remember it being. It occurs to me that our ski has no brake.

I'm still wondering what will stop us after landing when my mother banks left and descends toward the crater. The drone bounces once when we touch down, then goes sliding across the crater on its ski. Rather than slowing, though, it feels as though we're picking up speed. I expect my mother to full-throttle us in an attempt to abort the landing and take off again. But no— instead she reverses the engines. The drone bucks, vibrates, and finally goes into a spin that has me seeing nothing but the crater rim and blue sky swirling by outside my window again and again. I'm certain that we'll launch off the other side of the crater and tumble down the mountain to our deaths. But then the spinning slows, the drone comes to a stop, and I sit still in the cockpit and wait for the world itself to stop turning.

The cockpit canopies lift. Cold air rushes into the cabin and fills my lungs. My mother climbs down out of her seat and stands on the crater, holding onto the drone's wing for support, laughing hysterically. It occurs to me that she didn't expect to survive the landing herself.

I've been crammed in the cockpit so long that I have to hold onto the drone for a minute myself when I climb out. I look around at the crater and get my bearings.

"Sorry," I say. "It's smaller than I remember."

"Maybe you're just bigger," she says.

"Yeah, maybe so. I think I fell in over there. By the edge," I say, pointing. "And then that side is where I climbed out."

"Well," she says, her smoky breath rising into the cold air, "let's not waste any more daylight then."

We open the carrier, remove our ropes, and drape them over our shoulders. Then we walk across the crater to the edge.

"I think this is a *randkluft* you fell into," my mother says.

"A what?"

"It's a German name for the place where a glacier—or in this case the crater ice—pulls away from the rock."

"How do you know that?" I ask.

"I read it," she replies. When I look at her questioningly, she adds, "Hey, you might have everything in your reading slate memorized too by the time you're three hundred years old."

"Did you read anywhere why there might be a lake beneath the crater?"

"No," she says. "But that's not hard to guess."

"Then tell me," I say.

"Okay," she puts her hands on her hips and looks around.

"I would assume that the snow probably piles up pretty thick every winter and weighs itself down into new layers of ice on the crater here. At the same time some geothermal heat source melts the ice from underneath. So, new ice on top, melted ice beneath, there's your secret lake and the reason for this missile melting out from the roof of it."

"Why the gap then?" I ask. "Why not just ice on water?"

"Good question. But remember, water is denser than ice."

"I know that. Otherwise an iceberg wouldn't float."

"Exactly. Which means as the ice melts into the denser water below, it leaves behind a gap, which was fortunate for you when you fell in."

"And fortunate for us now," I add.

"That remains to be seen," she says, taking her rope off her shoulder. "Let's tie off to that horn-shaped outcropping there and lower down."

My mother descends into the crack first while I watch. It's not a straight drop; more of a steep slope. She can actually walk herself backwards into it while feeding the rope around her waist. I know she's at the bottom when the rope goes slack.

A few seconds later, I hear her shout, "Holy hell!"

I wrap the rope around my own waist and back down after her. When my feet touch down flat, I let loose the rope and turn around. My mother is standing on the shore of the lake with her eyes locked on the missile and her mouth agape. The mountain and the crater might be smaller, but the missile is just as large as I remember it being.

"It's big, isn't it?"

She nods yes. "It will certainly leave behind no trace of the Foundation if this works. The only question is, will we be able to get the warhead down?"

I look around. The lake shore is wider than it was before, probably because it's spring and not summer, but the missile still hovers several meters out from shore, its equally evil twin looking back from the mirror surface of the black water.

"Could we get a rope around the warhead?" I ask.

"We're going to need to get every rope we have and the cable around it too," she says. "The big problem is how to get it to the shore here so we can pulley it up to the crater surface and the drone."

"What do you mean?" I ask.

"I mean, even if we have that thing roped well, and even if we somehow manage to hoist it up there and dismantle it, the warhead will fall and sink, taking our ropes with it."

"What if the water's not that deep?"

"Oh, I bet it's deeper than our ropes. But that hardly matters, because I doubt we could raise it again anyway."

I walk the shore as far around as it goes, inspecting the situation from every angle. I look at the way we came down, knowing that we'll need to drag the warhead up the slope somehow. Then a plan begins to form in my mind.

"I've got an idea, Mom."

"What is it, Son?"

"What if we tied the warhead off with the cable and the ropes—everything we've got that will stretch that far? Then what if we secured the other ends to the rock up there at the top of the rankfluffle thing, or whatever you called it."

"Randkluft," she says.

"Mom, don't interrupt. I'll lose my train of thought."

"Okay, sorry," she says. "Go on, please."

"So, if we had the ropes and cable really taut, then when the warhead was freed from the missile body, wouldn't it swing down pendulum-like and land there on the shore, right where we need it at the base of the slope?"

She looks from the warhead to the opening above and then to the bottom of the slope, calculating the distances. Then she smiles.

"That might just work, Son. And the full load would never really hit the ropes, so we wouldn't have to worry about it breaking. But how will we get up there to secure the ropes on the warhead to begin with?"

"That's on you," I say. "I did my part."

She tousles my hair, which makes me feel small. But then again I'm glad to have some hair finally growing back.

"You're a smart boy, Aubrey."

I correct her quickly. "Smart man."

"Smart young man. How's that? Now, I don't know about you, but I'd rather sleep down here tonight than cramped up in that drone. Let's go up and start bringing our supplies down."

It takes the rest of our daylight to lug the supplies from the drone and lower them down to the shore of the lake. When everything is unpacked, we climb back out, sit on the crater rim, and watch the sunset. The sky is painted a thousand shades of orange. We sit side by side and watch as the last wedge of sun slips into the Pacific. Then we watch as the color drains away after it, replaced by a veil of blue sky already twinkling with stars. A cold wind rises up the slope at our feet, and we gather our furs tight and make for our rope to descend into the safety of our subterranean camp. It's pitch black and cold, and although we did pack lamps, we leave them unlit and lie next to one another in darkness, listening to the wind howl across the crater above.

My mother's already up working when I wake. She has the ropes and our cable stretched out on the lakeshore. She's pacing them off and making calculations on an ice wall, using a screwdriver as a pen.

"Good morning, sleepyhead," she says, once she notices that I'm awake. "Grab yourself a meal bar there. You're going to need your energy today."

I walk to the rope and start the climb up.

"Where you going?" she asks.

"To get a little privacy."

"Just go down here," she says. "I used the corner there."

"I'm not peeing in front of my mom."

She laughs and returns to her work. "Fine, but hurry back. We've got a lot to do today."

After I've freshened up and eaten my meager breakfast, my mother shows me what she's put together. We have enough rope and cable to tie off to the warhead and then to the upper rock, making about three passes, which should be enough to hold its weight. Once it's down, we'll use the pulleys to try and get enough leverage to bring it up the slope to the drone.

"Okay," I say, "this is basically what I said yesterday. But how do you plan to get up to the warhead to remove it?"

"Easy," she says. "There's enough rope left to make a harness. We'll use the pulley and slide from the upper rock along the cable to the warhead. We can lead the plasma torch out on one of the other ropes, and if we bring the drone to the edge of the randkluft, the power cable will just reach."

She's smart, but she's missing one important thing. I

almost hate to have to point it out to her.

"That's great, Mom," I say. "It really is smart. But there's a bigger problem."

"What's that, Son?"

"Well, getting on the cable from up there and sliding down to the warhead shouldn't be a problem. The angle would be just about right. But you're forgetting that we've got no way to get the cable secured to the warhead in the first place."

"Oh, don't be such a naysayer, Aubrey."

"I'm not being a naysayer, Mom. But the last time I looked, neither of us had wings."

"We don't need wings," she says. "We have neodymium."

"We've got what?"

She holds up a black metallic disc with a hole in its center.

"Magnets, Son. We sinter these out of neodymium powder down in Holocene II. They're what make up the basis for our drone engines. We'll need our engines, of course, so I cut this one out of the supply carrier this morning."

I step toward her to get a closer look, but she jerks the magnet back and steps away from me.

"Do you have your strike-a-light in your pocket?" she asks. I nod that I do, and she shakes her head. "If there's enough iron in that steel striker, this thing will rip it clean out of your pocket and maybe take my fingers off in the process."

"They're that strong?"

"They pull thirteen hundred times their own weight."

"And how much does that magnet weigh?"

"About a pound and a half."

"Well, holy hydrogen, if we get a few of those up there on that warhead, they'll hold then for sure."

"You see," she says, "we don't need wings after all."

We start with the longest and strongest rope. My mother loops it through the magnet disc and ties a two half hitch. Then she moves anything metal as far as possible down the shore. She coils the rope at her feet and hands me the end for safekeeping. She swings the magnet in wide arcs, slowly letting out slack as I imagine rodeo riders might have done as they prepared to lasso a calf. Then, when the momentum is right, she releases the magnet and its trailing rope toward the missile. It misses and lands in the water with a splash. When she draws it up again, the rope comes nearly straight out of the water at the bank, answering our question about how deep the lake is. She twirls the magnet again and lets it fly. This time it hits its mark and clamps onto the warhead with an audible clank.

"You did it!" I shout.

By late afternoon we've got two ropes and a cable strung between the warhead and the horn of rock at the edge of the randkluft, plus a harness and pulley system to carry us out to work. My mother goes first, sliding herself out along the cable with an ice screw she made from a steel spring.

"Why do we need that?" I ask.

"Because we need something to attach to when we're out here working," she says, as she twists it into the ceiling next to the warhead. "You have to remember that we're cutting the warhead free. We don't want to drop with it when it falls."

"But doesn't that create another problem, then? Once the warhead falls with its ropes, won't you just be hanging out there over the lake with no way to get back?"

"Actually," she says, looking down at me, "I was kind of hoping you'd make the final cut."

"Well, wouldn't I be hanging out there then?"

"Sure"—she shrugs—"but you can swim."

"You want me to drop into that cold, black water?"

"Unless maybe you've grown those wings you were talking about," she says.

When the day's work is finished, we sit on the shore in the dim blue light leaking in from the various openings above and eat cold jerky and drink cold tea. We marvel together at the crazy architecture of wires and rope we've managed to thread together between the missile and the crater edge. It looks like some circus performance in the making.

"Tomorrow we'll start cutting," my mother says.

"You think that little torch has what it takes?"

"It's going to have to," she answers. "That damn warhead is coming down if I have to hang up there for the next hundred years and chip away at it with my fingernails."

This night is the quietest night I've ever spent. So quiet I can hardly sleep. We lie wrapped in our furs on the shore. Not one draft of wind or even a drip of water is audible in all that darkness above. The silence is so complete that I find myself shifting in my bedding just to verify by the sound that I haven't, in fact, gone deaf. When we wake, I understand the source of the silence. A pile of fresh snow lies on the lakeshore beneath our opening in the crater ceiling above. When we climb out, the drift piled outside our randkluft is so deep that I have to scramble several feet up the rock face to even see above the snow. The sky is laden with gray clouds; the crater is laden with snow. Only the very top of our drone is visible.

For the next week we wait. My mother makes several trips out on the wire to inspect the missile, carrying with her a sharp stone and marking out with scrapes where she thinks we should cut. When it's not snowing, I lie at the base of the opening and read my slate in the cold, gray light. By the fourth day the lamps are out of fuel, and we can no longer melt snow, so we fill our bottles in the lake. Then, on the morning of day five, just when our spirits are on the verge of breaking, we wake to the sound of dripping water everywhere and an amazing light show of golden sun reflecting through blue ice. We're both anxious to get working again, but it's another two days before the drone is completely freed from its prison of snow.

I'm prepared to push it to the edge of the randkluft, but to my relief, my mother hops in, fires it up, and taxis it across the crater, using the engines instead. The power cord is not quite long enough after all, but my mother cuts the cord from the welder and splices the two together. Then she connects the plasma torch to the drone and secures it to another pulley on one of the ropes. She carefully guides herself and her precarious assembly out over the lake to the missile. I sit nervously on the shore with my arms wrapped around my knees and watch. The compressor kicks on with a stutter, and she draws the blue bead of plasma along her score marks, sending a shower of orange sparks down to meet their rising reflections on the black surface of the still water. I know the nuke shouldn't blow, but my guts still coil up with fear. Then again there's little to worry about, I guess, because if it did somehow explode, I doubt we'd even know. We'd just be here and then we wouldn't—which is a small comfort to me, knowing that the same goes for Hannah if this scheme of ours works. She'll be caught up in whatever she's doing, and then she'll be vaporized into a memory. And aren't memories what each of us is destined to become?

When my mother's arms are tired, we trade places.

It's a funny feeling hanging from an ice screw above an underground lake and cutting a nuclear warhead with an electric torch. We're cutting just beyond the last of the bolts that secure the warhead to the rocket with the plasma set at full amperage, just hoping that it cuts deep enough to free it.

On the morning of our third day working with the torch, just as my mother is beginning to worry over the drone's battery, I'm out cutting when there's a loud peel of metal, and the warhead pulls partly free from the rocket's casing. I freeze there on the ice screw, my feet dangling above the lake.

"You've got to keep cutting," my mother says. "You can't come back now on the line; it's too risky."

"You sure this thing won't explode when it drops?"

"It's set to go off with an interior altimeter, Son."

"What if that altitude is just another few meters?"

"Aubrey, trust me. It won't go off."

"Okay," I say. "I sure hope you're right."

Nothing more happens for the next several hours as I make the final cuts. The harness begins to synch into my legs. My shoulders ache, and my arms seem to be made of lead. Then there's a loud crack, followed by a snap as the cable goes taut and the warhead drops free and swings beneath me on its lines and slams into the shore just on the edge of the lake. Time seems to stop. I dangle from the ice screw with the torch hissing in my hand and stare with wonder at this thing we've set free. My mother looks at me, and we're momentarily connected in a strange federation of relief and fear. I turn the torch off, and the cavern goes silent.

"What do I do with this thing?" I ask, indicating the torch.

"Just let it hang there," she says. "We won't need it now."

I look down at the black water. For some reason I'm afraid to drop into it. It's not just because I know it's cold, but because I'm worried I might sink to the very heart of the mountain. I hoist myself up for slack and pull my legs free from the harness until I'm just hanging from the screw by my hands.

The shock of the cold water sends me paddling for the shore as if I'm being chased by something. My mother reaches me a hand, pulls me out, and wraps me in a dry fur. I sit there on the bank, shivering as she rubs warmth back into my limbs.

We both keep stealing glances at the warhead lying beside us and my mother keeps saying over and over again, "We did it, Son. We really did it."

The next day we haul it up. It's even heavier than I had thought, and it is no small feat of engineering for the two of us. Yet between the ropes, the pulleys, and the pulling power of the drone's engines, we hoist it out and over the edge until it's lying in the bright sunlight like some horrible, indigestible relic of war ejected from the bowels of the earth. It's no smaller task loading it into the carrier. Another centimeter or two larger and it would never even fit. But by late afternoon we have the warhead sealed safely inside and the drone parked at the far end of the glacier for the best possible shot at picking up enough speed to take off with the added weight.

Ready or not, neither of us suggests going right away.

Instead we sit in the afternoon sun on the eastern edge of the crater rim and look off past the river and the evergreens toward the distant blue sparkle of the lake. We both know it may never look the same again. My mother seems relaxed and content but also somewhat sad. I watch her face, trying my best to read the clouds of thought crossing her dark eyes.

"Hey, Mom, can I ask you something?"

"Sure," she says, as if waking from a dream. "What is it?"

"If this works, how do we go forward from here?"

"What do you mean?" she asks.

"I mean how do we start over again and make sure people don't end up making the same terrible mess of things? How do we make sure that this is the last bomb and not just the one that paves the way for future wars?"

"Those are good questions, Son. And the fact that you're even asking them tells me that you're ready."

"Ready for what?"

"Ready to lead the new state of nature."

"A state of nature?"

She turns and trains her eyes on me and says, "I've been asking myself those same questions for a long time, Aubrey. It seems to me that even the most atrocious horrors are born out of some truth. Radcliffe wasn't completely wrong."

"What do you mean, Radcliffe wasn't wrong?"

"Every other animal has external checks on its population. Humans need one too. But it needs to come from us."

"I don't understand how you'd do that, though."

"Well, even in the most primitive states of nature, humans give up certain freedoms in order to enjoy those same freedoms from others. If you murder someone you can expect their tribe to take revenge, and so on and so forth. Unspoken agreements are created. But now we need to make a collective agreement. Once a stable population is established, no one should have the right to more children than it takes to replace themselves. And no one should have the right to destroy the planet's resources for future people who haven't had a chance to enjoy them yet. Our knowledge and technology is advanced beyond that now."

"But who gets to decide that, Mom?"

She waves my comment away. "Someone has to."

"Isn't that the same thinking that got us here?" I ask.

"Oh, Son. I wish things were so simple. You're ready but you still have a lot to learn. Everything I know and believe is in that reading slate of yours under the title *State of Nature*."

"You wrote a book?"

She shrugs. "More of a long essay, really." When she sees the shocked look on my face, she adds, "What did you think I was working on at that silly computer all the time?"

"Mom, how come you didn't tell me any of this?"

"It wasn't time. And now isn't the time to talk about it either. Let's just sit here quietly and enjoy the view."

She puts her arm around me. We sit together and watch the sky turn red and the lake reflect it back like a molten pool of fire in the center of all those pink mountains and dark trees. There will be plenty of time tomorrow to think of bombs, and of new states of nature, but right now all I want to think about is how safe and warm it feels sitting here next to my mom.

"I'm really sorry that I wasn't there for you growing up," she eventually says.

"It's okay," I say. "You're here for me now."

She nods but doesn't respond.

"I love you, Mom."

At first I think she doesn't hear me, but a minute later she squeezes me tighter and says, "I love you too, Son."

CHAPTER 32
No, Mother, No

I dream that my mother kisses me goodbye.

I wake and the dream was real. My mother is gone.

I've never moved as quickly as I do now, casting off my bedding, racing for the randkluft, climbing the rope. I roll out into the dim-blue dawn just in time to see the drone skating across the crater, engines laboring loudly under the warhead's weight, skis kicking up chunks of ice. I run after it and watch with horror and disbelief as the drone hits the upward slope of the far crater edge, launches out, and falls down out of sight.

"No, Mother, no!"

Only my breathless cry chases the drone now.

I reach the edge and look over to see the drone fighting to pull out of its heavy downward glide. I know if it gets too low, the nuke will detonate. But the drone eventually levels out. The glacier falls away beneath it. I don't know whether to cheer, curse, or cry. I stand silently by and watch the drone shrink into the distance and disappear from my sight over the dark treetops. I shake my head.

"Why, Mother, why?"

Wind whistling in the crevasses is the only answer I hear.

Despite the cold, I don't dare go back for my fur. I just sit on the crater's edge and look out toward the lake and the paling blue sky and pray that she delivers the bomb and comes safely back for me. An intolerable fear keeps telling me otherwise, but I push it from my mind. The minutes tick past; the waiting becomes unbearable. I count to a hundred and back to zero, then start again. Why, I don't know—maybe just to mark out with some arbitrary number the last moment of this world as I've come to know it; this last bit of hope for my mother's safe return that I cling to with every breath.

The sun has yet to rise, but on my count of sixty-five, it is suddenly there in front of me, with such white-hot brilliance that I instinctively raise my hands to cover my eyes. I can see every bone of my fingers intricately set in the red-glowing flesh that surrounds them. Only when the light and the heat have faded do I remove my hands and look with terrific awe at the ball of orange fire above the lake. The fire fades, consumed by an enormous black and blue-glowing cloud, the edges stitched with a dazzling display of electricity. Then the top blows off, and a thick column of black smoke rises, mushrooms, and rises again until its three times as high as I now sit, and the top of it is dragged away east in the jet stream.

Thirty seconds later the shockwave hits.

I see it advancing across the treetops like a hurricane wind. When it reaches the slopes, it brings with it a continuous crash of thunder that rumbles, cracks, and echoes back from the surrounding peaks with such an awesome noise that I sit open-mouthed in awe and face down the hot breeze, just listening. I can hear the clack of falling ice and the soft resound of distant avalanches long after the wave has passed.

The black mushroom cloud seems fixed in place above the lake, as if it were now a permanent scar on that horizon. and I know in my head and in my heart that no one, and I mean no one, could have flown that drone low enough to drop that bomb and then have had enough time left to escape its terrible unleashing. Hannah, the professor, and my mother are all mixed together now with the same decaying particles of radioactive waste rising above the lake and into the blue morning sky. Here one moment; not a single distinguishable cell left the next.

I sit for a long time and watch the cloud form, rise, and change shape. I sit until the other sun rises and catches the floating particulate in a rainbow of light that would move me to tears for its beauty on any other morning than this. I sit until the sun is high in the sky and the radioactive cloud has been pulled away further east, leaving the site of its destruction almost visible through the haze—the blast radius, the scorched trees, the draining lake. I sit until the sun is at my back; the snow melts around me and soaks my clothing through. I sit until the sun finally sets and the scene that I still can't quite believe fades once again from my view, retreating into the blue out of which it had come like some apocalyptic vision visited on the world from humankind's collective nightmares.

When I sat with her here yesterday she knew, she knew. And now I know it too. She's never coming back.

When I finally rise from the crater edge, my legs walk themselves to the rope. I somehow descend into the dark cavern below without really even wanting to. I walk the shore blind and find my mother's bed by memory and curl up on it. I bury my nose in the damp and musty furs and smell them for any lingering scent of her that might remain. But even that seems too much to ask of this cruel world.

I know I sleep at some point because I wake in the pitch black of night. It takes me several moments searching my foggy mind to recall the horror of exactly where I am and why. My father and my mother gone. Jimmy far, far away. Even the thought of Hannah and the professor being dead leaves me more saddened than glad. Everyone and everything that I've ever loved is gone or at least unreachable to me now. I lie in the dark crater of the mountain and turn these thoughts over again and again in my mind as one might turn over an interesting stone. But there's no joy in this inspection. No, no joy at all. Only the cold hard reality of a pill too big and too jagged to swallow. It's just me left here all alone.

In the morning I lie to myself about what has happened— my mother is just up getting something out of the drone. But the decapitated missile hangs above the lake as a stark reminder otherwise. Our abandoned plasma torch hangs from the ice screw next to it, and I would give anything to see my mother up there working. And maybe she is and always will be. Maybe the crazy professor was at least right about that. Perhaps time is just some cosmic trick to prevent everything from happening all at once. But true or not, I guess I'll never know. And if my mother is still somehow beside me now, I sure can't feel her presence through all this heartache and sorrow.

I have no idea what to do or where to go.

But I know I can't stay here.

I pack up the remaining rations along with my reading slate and a few potentially useful tools. I tie them in my mother's fur, wrap it around my shoulders, and secure it with straps made of rope. Then I fill the canteens in the lake, coil the remaining rope, and climb onto the sunlit summit. I stand there deciding which way I should go. I know from crossing with Jimmy that the lake side is a much gentler slope, but I can't even bring myself to look in that direction now. Instead I head for the western edge to leave the summit and the sight of my final memories of my mother behind.

I'm vaguely aware of coming down the glacier. Then again, maybe I've fallen into a crevasse and this is all just a dying dream. I almost wish it were. I stumble and climb, descending in wide switchbacks from one end of the glacier to the other. The crevasses are less open now in spring than they were when we had come up last summer. The recent snow provides some traction. One wide crevasse proves impassable, and I have to drive my mother's long screwdriver into the ice, tie the rope to it, lower myself past it, and leave the rope behind.

By late afternoon I'm nearly down. I sit on a wide ledge of glacier ice, chew tasteless jerky, and drink water from my canteen, watching clouds pass in front of the sun. I remember sitting here with Jimmy and marveling together at the moon, neither of us sure we would survive to see the summit. I'd give anything to go back there now—to have Jimmy here with me, to have my mother still alive in China, to have my father still alive underground. It's hard to imagine that since that night when we sat here, just clueless kids, not even knowing yet who was behind the Park Service, everyone we had met since then was gone. Mr. and Mrs. Radcliffe—Gloria and her brother Tom—my father—Finn, Bree, Junior—all the people on the Isle of Man—Roger and Bill—Seth and Mrs. Hightower and Red—the Motars—the professor—Hannah—and now my own mother—every one of them dead.

I'd cry but there seems little point anymore.

Evening finds me on the lower mountain at the top of the trail where we met that wild man and his mutant boy all those months ago now. I keep on moving down, crossing the river in the dark with my clothes and my makeshift pack held over my head. It occurs to me how silly I must appear to the eyes of watching animals, a pale and steaming refugee climbing from the water shivering and naked, ill-suited to this unforgiving life. I'd give anything to change myself into the lowest squirrel and be able to scamper away without a thought or care beyond my burrow. Instead I torture myself with an endless loop of what-might-have-been and if-only.

In the morning I follow the river north, not wanting to see the trestle again, and not wanting to go near the cove. I do the only thing left for me to do. I walk. I walk sunup to sundown, in fine weather and in rain. Each night I unpack, sort my meager rations, wrap myself in my furs, and try to sleep. Mostly I sit awake and listen to the night sounds. Days pass into weeks, how many I can't possibly know. My pack lightens, and the soles of my shoes wear themselves through. I tie tree bark to them and keep walking. I'm sleeping more and eating less. When my rations run out I begin to scavenge, eating frogs, salamanders, and worms from overturned stones.

A hailstorm catches me one morning in the middle of an open meadow with nowhere at all to go. I sit down where I am, hold my fur pack over my head, and watch the huge balls of ice pound the ground around me. When it passes, the meadow is so thick with hail I can hardly keep from slipping. I cross it with my arms outstretched for balance like a crazed lunatic on roller skates. I corner a small trout trapped in a riverbank shallow, snatch it up and bite into it raw, the fish still flexing as I eat. When I finally cast the fish aside, I look back and see a lone wolf dodge out from the shadows where it had been following me to finish off what I left behind. Come night I make a fire. The strike-a-light that Jimmy made me for my birthday works perfectly. I sit long after I have the fire going and look at it in the glow of the flames.

In the morning the wolf is still on my trail.

And it's there the next day too.

Every day it gets braver and closer. I can make out its mangy, patchwork fur and its hip bones articulating beneath its thin flesh as it jogs along behind me with its long tongue lolling from its slavering jaws.

Then one morning the smell of smoke from my burned-out fire wakes me just in time to see the wolf flattened to the ground and crawling toward me. I rise, slower than I'd like, and chase it away with stones. It snarls and backs off into the brush, but when I set out walking again, it follows. At first I'm worried. But then a strange sense of acceptance settles on my journey. Perhaps this is how things are meant to end for me. Earth knows I've eaten my share of creatures in my short time here. And isn't providing energy to a starving wolf a worthy way to go? I know Jimmy would have it roasting over coals as he wore its fur, or perhaps he'd train it and have it fetching him small birds that he'd drop from trees with arrows. I wish Jimmy were here with me now, but he might as well be on Mars.

It eventually becomes comforting to look back and see the wolf stalking along behind me, to wonder when it might make another move on me, to guess if I'll have energy or willpower enough even to resist it. Together we follow the river up to higher country where the trees thin and the water runs clear. I carve a crude spear and hunt quick trout in pools of ice cold glacier melt, making sure to always leave enough behind for my new friend. But not too much. I've got to keep him hungry for me when my time comes.

Several days into the mountains, we're passing a strand of evergreens in the twilight when I look back and see the wolf not five meters behind me, trotting along as if we were partners on this strange journey to nowhere. Then there's a flash of yellow. A cougar leaps from the trees and seizes the wolf's neck in its jaws and drags it into the shadows without as much as a single whimper or growl. I stand for a long time and watch the trail where the wolf had been.

"Take me, you coward!" I yell. "Come back and take me!"

That night I sleep again in the dark without a fire.

A week later the people begin to come.

I'm in a gulch descending the high country when Red steps from behind a boulder and falls in beside me. It's a long time before he says anything, and even then he only says, "Isn't this some kind of afternoon." He says it as if he expects no reply. I'm not sure I'd even know what to say to him if he did, so we just walk together quietly. When I notice he's no longer beside me, I turn and see him standing on the trail with his hand raised to say farewell. I raise mine, then turn and keep walking. When I look back again, he's gone.

The next day I walk without stopping and continue on into a forest. By nightfall I come upon a fire at the edge of a dark glade. Jimmy is sitting there with Junior on his lap, stroking his fur. I sit down across from them but neither appears to have noticed me. Jimmy's face is unmarked by fire, and I wonder if they aren't perhaps ghosts, or conjured visions of my own imagining. But I can feel the warmth of the fire and smell its smoke. The big dipper eventually rises over the glade, and so much time passes that I'm not quite sure what to say. When I do finally speak, all I can think of is to repeat Red's words.

"Isn't this some kind of afternoon."

But Junior and Jimmy are already asleep.

No trace of the fire remains when I wake. I leave the glade behind and wander into the woods. Without the river to guide me, I choose my course by whim and change it as often as new paths appear to my crazed mind out of the maze of trees. It occurs to me that I haven't eaten in a long time, but for some reason I'm no longer hungry. I come upon a fallen log covered with butterflies. When they lift away in a blue cloud, I see that it's no log at all but a skinned bear, all wrinkled, gray, and rotting, its long claws tucked against its chest as if in some strange gesture of shyness over being seen there naked on the forest floor. I step over it, and the butterflies settle again, adorning the carcass in a beautiful death-coat of blue.

The butterflies make me think of my father's pipe. I reach to my neck to feel for it before I remember giving it to Jimmy the day I left with my mother—my mother, my mother, my mother. No sooner does my mind turn to my mother and I'm sure I see her ahead of me on the trail, but she dodges out of sight behind a tree. I run and look, but she isn't there. Then I spot her again farther on. I spend the day walking in circles and looking behind trees. When it's too dark to continue, I sit where I am and whistle in the cold night, trying to remember childhood tunes. Soon others are whistling with me. When I stop they stop too. Then I laugh and they laugh with me. I find the whole thing so funny that I roll on the ground in a riot of laughter and clutch at my belly because it hurts so good. Eventually, we all fall quiet and sleep, but I know they're there just the same.

After days of walking I come across a stream, drop to my knees and drink until I can drink no more. Then I stand with all that cold water swinging in my gut and follow the stream out of the forest. I'm accompanied now by a small army of silent friends. When I come out onto the promontory that overlooks the valley, I know then that this is where my journey ends. Here in the valley of Jimmy's dreams.

Hemmed in by mountains, the valley is wide, lush, and green. The stream I've been following cuts down in a tiny waterfall and crosses to join a silver river that winds through rolling hills of grass, wildflowers, and groves of oak and evergreen trees. It's about as beautiful a place as ever I've seen. I would be happy to post up here and rest for eternity.

By sunset I'm sitting on a hill next to a sprawling oak with my feet stretched out before me. A perfect picture of the river and the sun is framed in the western edge of the valley beyond a distant field of wheat waving in the breeze. I sleep there for a day, maybe two. I wake in the afternoon, surprised to still be alive. I see Hannah down bathing in the river, and it startles me. But when she turns I see that it's not Hannah at all, but her mother, Mrs. Radcliffe. I remember her warning me about the drawbacks of the serum and a long life of boredom, loneliness, and pain. Here I am at just sixteen, and I already know what she meant.

I get up and walk down to the river, but I seem to move in slow motion. By the time I get there, she's gone. I kneel at the bank and drink. After only a sip, I'm full. I pry a large, flat-edged stone from the riverbank and take it back to the hill and use it to dig my own grave. It's shallow but it will do.

When the grave is finished, I gather wood and build up a

fire at the base of the hill. Then I sort through my belongings, setting aside my mother's reading slate and Jimmy's strike-a-light. Everything else I pile onto the fire and watch burn. Next, I strip naked and pile on my own threadbare and filthy furs. A black and acrid smoke rises from the fire, as if the hell I've been through had somehow clung to my clothes and is now finally being released. I look down at my naked and wasted frame—my ribs, my hips, my scar. I remember my former self, ages ago now it seems, living underground in Holocene II and desperate to become a man. I laugh at the boy for his naiveté, but I love him now just the same. I think he'd be glad to know that he made a difference, that he had friends, that he loved and was loved, and that he finally got to rest beneath the stars he so desperately dreamed to see.

I walk back up the hill, each new step a struggle, each one past a relief, and lie down naked in the shallow grave and claw as much of the dirt over me as I can. The soil is cool, fresh, and rich. Then I clutch my mother's reading slate and Jimmy's strike-a-light to my half-buried chest. I close my eyes and dream. I dream, and I dream, and I dream.

CHAPTER 33
The Other Side

"Aubrey, wake up!"

Bill looks down on me, his face framed by blue sky. I know I've gone wherever souls go when the body dies.

As he works to unbury me, he talks.

"Why am I always digging you out of something?" he asks. "If it isn't sand, it's dirt."

"But I don't want rec time to be over," I say, my voice sounding faraway.

He props my head up in his hand and holds a canteen to my lips. My tongue is swollen, and the cold water runs from the corners of my mouth and chills my neck.

"Did Red bury me again?" I ask, coughing.

He shakes his head. "Red isn't here."

"But Red's dead, isn't he?"

"Yes," he replies, looking sad, "he is."

"Then why isn't he here on the other side?"

"Because you're not dead."

"Then why are you here?"

"Because I'm not dead either."

"I don't understand," I say.

He smiles. "That's alright. You don't have to understand anything right now. Just relax. You're okay. Do you think you can get up, or do I need to carry you?"

"I'm comfortable right here."

"Well, that's too bad," he says, "because Jimmy would love

to see you."

"Did you say Jimmy?" I ask, rising on my elbows.

Everything suddenly comes into sharp focus—the valley, the river—but I look around and see no trace of Jimmy.

I lie back. "You're just another trick. Leave me alone."

"Okay, then," Bill says. "I guess I get to carry you."

The next thing I know, his strong arms are lifting me from the ground, and I'm slung like a sack over his shoulder. My teeth clack as my chin bounces against his back. I watch his heels rise and fall as he walks me down the hill. Then he slumps me in a seat, covers me with a thermal blanket, and buckles me in. Now I'm looking out past the landing gear of a drone. I reach and grab his arm to stop him as he climbs in beside me.

"My reading slate and my strike-a-light."

"I've got them right here," he says, setting them in my lap. "Now hold on to them tight; the ride's going to be a bit bumpy getting out of here."

I jostle and bounce in the seat as the drone runs along the lumpy ground, following the river west, and finally picking up speed and lifting off just in time to keep from plunging into the water where the river banks a hard left. The ride goes smooth and easy now, and the drone climbs into the sky. I turn and look back on the shrinking valley—the golden wheat, the green hills, the wildflowers. The sunlight reflects off the river, giving it the appearance of liquid gold pouring out from the clean mountains and winding its way through God's country toward the sea.

I know I can't trust my mind right now, but I swear I see Mrs. Radcliffe, Red, my father, and my mother and all the others standing beside the river, waving goodbye to me.

"Where's Jimmy?" I ask.

"He's out looking for you," Bill says. "We've all been out looking for you."

"Are you taking me to him now? I want to see Jimmy."

"Of course, you do," he says. "And he wants to see you." He hands me a meal bar. "Here, you better try to eat a little."

My fingers won't seem to work. I struggle with the wrapper until Bill takes it away and opens it for me. I manage to choke down half of it before I start to feel sick and give up. Then Bill passes me a canteen. My senses begin to return. I see that we're in a drone like the one Radcliffe took Hannah and me in to tour the park. I look out the glass bubble at the coastline passing below, and I realize we're heading south.

"Where are we going?" I ask.

"I'm taking you back," he says. "We've got a camp set up at the temple. You remember the temple, don't you?"

"Yeah," I say, "we left you there to die."

"I made you leave," he replies. "And besides, you sent the Chief back to look for me. I'll never forget that. I told you that you were a good man, Aubrey."

"But my mother said she didn't find you."

"She didn't," he says. "Jimmy told me all about it."

"Will you please fill me in on what's going on?" I ask.

"Do you want to hear this now, or would you rather rest?"

"No, tell me. Please."

As the mountains, the Pacific, and the golden coastline slide by beneath my window, Bill pilots the drone and tells me all about his adventures.

"It nearly killed me, but I eventually found the spot where Gridboy dropped us off. I was too late though, of course. They had already filled it in. I knew my only hope was if Jillian could somehow open it again, so I stayed nearby and made camp. Turns out I had learned a lot from watching you and Jimmy."

"Did you finally eat meat then?" I ask.

He nods. "And a lot of other things I thought I'd never eat too. But you were right; the meat wasn't half bad."

"I ate worms," I say. "Did you eat worms?"

"Oh, I've got you beat there. I chased vultures away from a big dead cat and lived for two days on the maggots I picked out of its rotting flesh. But let me get back to my story. Months went by. The weather got hotter and wetter. I got pretty good at living there alone in the jungle, but I began to think I'd die there. I spent a lot of time talking with Roger."

"He survived too?"

"No," Bill says, with a sad shake of his head. "But I talked to him anyway."

"I know what you mean," I say.

"Well," he continues, "then one day I heard my name being called. I thought I'd lost my mind for real. But it was Jillian. Gridboy had brought her and few others in a subterrene. They were out in the jungle searching for me."

"How'd she know to go looking?"

"Your mother had been in contact with Jillian up until that failed attempt on the Foundation. Beth got caught, of course, but she never did give up Jillian. So when the Foundation just disappeared from the grid sometime later, Jillian guessed that you all had managed something, but she wasn't sure what. She brought a few others into her confidence and led a small group to come south to look for me and some answers."

"What did you do once they found you?"

326

"I hugged Jillian and then ate everything in her pack. Then we went back to Holocene II. Engineering was working on a few drones for the Foundation, and Jillian had them modified to carry passengers. Then she had the tunnelrats deliver one to the jungle. They laid us out a runway with the subterrene, and we went to China looking for you."

"But I wasn't there."

"No, but Jimmy was. And he told us what you and your mother had gone to do. He told us about the bomb. Then we knew for sure what had happened to the Foundation. You did it, Aubrey. You and your mother set us all free."

"Maybe," I say, "but my mother left me in the end."

"I knew she would," he says. "That's why we've all been out looking for you."

"How did you know she'd leave me behind?"

"Because of the E-M-P."

"The what?"

"Electromagnetic pulse. Nuclear explosions like that send out powerful magnetic fields that destroy, or at least interrupt, electrical systems. That drone would have fallen out of the sky as soon as the blast occurred. There was no way to outrun it. Your mother knew that, so I knew she'd leave you behind to deliver it herself. And I was right, because here you are."

Any lingering anger I had for my mother abandoning me that morning vanishes. My heart opens and my eyes well up with tears. I try to hold them back, but it's no use. They just come and come and come. Bill pretends to be interested in something out his window, looking away to let me cry.

When I can speak again, I ask, "How did you find me?"

"I decided to look farther north today. And I'm glad I did.

I noticed smoke from your fire. You can probably imagine my surprise when I touched down and found you half buried. I thought the worst at first. But other than looking thin enough to be a cadaver, you don't seem at all dead to me."

"Well, I feel dead," I say. "I think I'll rest for a bit now."

Bill just smiles and looks ahead.

I pull the blanket tight around me, lean back in my seat, and close my eyes. A lot has happened. I'm sure it will be a long time before I'm really able to process it all. I only know a few things for sure. My father and my mother might be gone, but they loved me. I know this because they each told me. But more importantly, I know this because they each showed me. And that's a pretty lucky place for a boy to be.

"Will Jimmy be there when we land?"

"I thought you were sleeping," Bill says. "He'll be along a little later. Don't worry. We've each been out searching sunup to sundown and sometimes after, flying back just to refuel and rest. But he'll be there. And, boy, will he be happy to see you."

"Probably not half as happy as I'll be to see him."

It's dark outside when the drone's landing wakes me. I rub my eyes and look out the viewing bubble, past the runway to the camp. It's not like one of our camps, or even the Motars', because the tents are all perfectly symmetrical and made from synthetic fabric that glistens in the dim wash of LED lights. It's clear they're making these things down in Holocene II. Farther out, I see the glowing nosecones of several subterrenes working on some kind highway through the black jungle.

"How come they're working out there in the dark?" I ask.

"Tunnelrats," Bill says. "They refuse to be above ground any other time. Come on, wrap that blanket around yourself, and let's go. I've got a nice bed for you to rest in."

I nearly collapse when I step down from the drone, but Bill grabs my arm, holds me up, and leads me to the tents.

"Is Jimmy here yet?" I ask.

"Not yet. I'll tell him you're here as soon as he arrives."

"I need a bath," I say.

"How about some sleep first?"

"No, I want to look clean when Jimmy gets back."

"Okay, then," he says, veering me toward a different tent. "But I have to warn you, we don't have hot water yet."

The cold shower actually feels energizing. I scrub myself with several pumps of soap while Bill stands outside the shower tent, whistling a tune that I had been whistling myself when I was lost in the woods. I wonder if he had done the same thing.

After I'm done and dried, Bill leads me to a tent and gives me one of his clean zipsuits to put on. Then he takes me to a bed, pulls back the covers, and tucks me in. It makes me feel like a child, but I don't complain. He sets my reading slate and my strike-a-light on the small table. Then he leaves, returning a minute later with a bottle of soymilk and some meal bars. He sets them beside the bed and tells me to eat if I'm hungry and rest as much as I can. He turns down the LED lamp, stops at the tent entrance, and looks back.

"We're all very proud of you, Aubrey."

"You shouldn't be proud," I say, shaking my head on the pillow. "Not if you knew how afraid I was all the time, or even half of the stupid and selfish things I've thought about."

"Oh, yes, we should," he replies. "We should probably be even prouder. You see, the world doesn't judge people on their thoughts and fears, kid. It judges them on their actions. And yours will go down in history as having saved humankind. Now get rest. The sooner you sleep, the sooner you see Jimmy."

That's all he has to say, and my eyes are closed.

I wake sometime later when I hear voices outside the tent, but they drift off. The only sound remaining is my growling stomach. I reach in the dark for the soymilk, prop myself on an elbow, and drain it. Then I lie back and fall asleep again.

Rain pummels the tent roof, pulling me out of a dream. I look around in the dim gray light that penetrates the tent's skin and slowly piece together the events of the day before and where it is that I am. I'm debating whether or not to try and get up when I see a flash of brighter gray as the tent flap opens. Then Jimmy steps inside. He stands there with his face cast in shadow and his furs dripping on the floor. He looks at me for a long time. When he moves, he brings over a folding chair from the small table and sits sideways alongside the bed. He looks at me with his right eye, and I see that he's crying.

"I knew you were alive," he says. "I jus' knew it."

I reach to wipe away a tear from his cheek but he grabs my hand, brings it to his lips, and kisses my fingers. Then he clasps my hand in both of his and smiles sidelong at me, his tears coming even faster. When I realize that his tears are tears of joy, I'm suddenly crying them too.

"I found it," I finally say.

"What did you find?" he asks.

"Your valley. The one you dreamed about."

"Was it beautiful?"

"It was more than beautiful."

"Well, you'll have plenty of time to show it to me when you're better."

"Jimmy, why won't you look at me?"

"I am looking at you," he says.

"I mean straight on. Why won't you face me all the way?"

He pinches his lips together, closes his eyes, and sighs. Then he turns in his chair to face me. I'm too late to stop myself from flinching. I know he notices me do it because he frowns. His burns have mostly healed, but the whole left side of his face and neck is disfigured, as if the skin had turned to wax and dripped before solidifying again. His left eye seems okay, but the lid droops and only half closes when he blinks. His hair has grown back, as has mine, but he's pulled his bangs forward and swooped them to cover the worst of his forehead. It's strange, because the right side of his face is the same Jimmy, but I'd never recognize him by just his left side now.

"I've scared myself already with my reflection, Aubrey, so dun' even try and tell me it ain't no big deal."

"Does it hurt still?" I ask.

"Sometimes," he says. "Mostly when I'm tryin' to sleep."

"Will it hurt if I touch it?"

"I dunno why you'd wanna, but go ahead."

I reach up and caress his scarred cheek with the back of my hand. It occurs to me that he got his scars doing something very selfless and very brave. When I remind myself that it is that bravery that they represent, the scars become beautiful in a way. I sit up, wrap my arms around his neck, and hug him.

"I missed you, Jimmy. I missed you so much."

He rests his head on my neck.

"I missed you too," he says.

CHAPTER 34
All I Ever Wanted

Three days after my arrival, Bill brings me to see Jillian.

Her tent is set up like a general's forward command post, with maps spread out on makeshift tables and couriers rushing in and out, carrying messages.

"Have a seat, Aubrey," Jillian says, indicating a stool.

After I'm seated, she and Bill take stools across from me, looking at me and smiling until I feel uncomfortable.

"How are you feeling?" Jillian finally asks.

"I feel fine," I reply. "I've gained some weight."

"Good," she says. "You look much better already."

Another courier rushes in with a note. Jillian takes her glasses from her zipsuit pocket, puts them on, and reads it. The courier stands at attention with his arms stiff at his sides and steals shy glances at me. He's about my age, but he must be from another level because I don't recognize him. Jillian hands the note back, nods, and he runs out. Then she takes her glasses off, tucks them away, and looks back to me.

"The reason I wanted to meet with you today, Aubrey, is we need your help. You've probably noticed that there's a lot going on around here. What you don't see is that there's even more going on below in Holocene II. A large percentage of people don't want to come up. None of the tunnelrats do, of course, but many of the others, especially the older ones, seem perfectly content staying below. And that's just fine since all of our manufacturing capabilities are down there right now."

"So let them stay," I say. "Just give them the choice."

"Exactly my thoughts," she replies. "I'm glad to see we're on the same screen here."

"Was that all you wanted to talk with me about, then?"

"Not exactly," she says.

"Well, how else can I help?"

She pauses and looks at Bill.

"It's about the longevity serum," Bill says.

"Okay. What about the serum?"

"The thing is," Jillian says, "rumors have spread about it, and some of the residents are beginning to demand answers."

"Yes," Bill adds. "Without Eden to look forward to now, people are considering death for the first time."

"That's understandable," I say, not liking at all where this is going, "but I don't get what it has to do with me."

Jillian clasps her hands together and leans forward on her stool. In a quiet, conspiratorial tone she asks, "Are you sure the last of the serum was at the Foundation when the bomb went off? Could there be any left somewhere else?"

"Hannah had the last of it in her lab, as far as I know."

"And you don't have it, right?" she asks. "In you. I mean you weren't injected?"

"Would it matter if I had been?"

She shrugs. "Maybe. There might be some way to reverse

engineer it by looking at your blood. It could be worth a try."

The hungry look in her eyes reminds me of our first time meeting in Holocene II and how eager she was to learn about the serum even then. It reminds me a little of Hannah too.

"No," I say, deciding some lies might be okay. "I never had it. None of us did. Only Hannah. And she's gone."

Bill looks relieved to hear it. Jillian looks disappointed, but she appears to believe me.

"Would you be willing to go down and tell people that for us?" she asks. "It would really help."

"Go down to Holocene II?"

"Yes. You've become a sort of hero, in case you haven't noticed. I think they'd listen to you."

"No way," I say, "I'm never going back down there again."

"That seems awfully selfish, doesn't it?" she says.

"Selfish?" I ask. "Really? How dare you even say that."

Jillian narrows her eyes at me, but Bill jumps in before she can say anything else.

"He doesn't need to go," he says. "I'll tell them myself what he said. That will have to be good enough. Come on, Aubrey, you look like you could use some more rest." He gets up from his stool and waves me to the door.

Before we exit the tent, Jillian says, "Make sure he's ready for the matchmaking. He needs to lead by example now."

I look back, but her head is already bent over her maps.

Once we're outside the tent, I turn to Bill and ask, "What did she mean by matchmaking?"

"Oh, it's tomorrow," he says. "Most of the Holocene II residents adventurous enough to make their new home here on the surface are young, so we're pairing up the single ones with mates. You'll be fine. Everyone wants to be with the hero."

That night I sit in bed with the lamp on and my mother's reading slate in my lap. It takes me nearly an hour to build up the courage to even turn it on. Then I scroll though the library and click on the title she told me about.

State of Nature

By

Aubrey Bradford

A treatise on humankind's failure to find a long term, sustainable means of peaceful existence on the planet; and a proposal for a new state of nature that will allow our species to remain extant and do just that.

The screen goes blank when I turn the reading slate off. I'm not sure why, but I just can't read it. Maybe because I remember sitting with my mother on the crater edge when she told me about having written it, and I remember something she said that bothered me. She said that Dr. Radcliffe wasn't all wrong. I guess I'm worried that this new state of nature she's proposing might include things that will change the way I feel about her. And maybe I don't want to read it because I also remember her saying that I was ready now to lead. I don't want to lead—not this new state of nature, not anything.

Bur what do I want?

I set the slate aside and reach for the lamp.

Before I switch it off, I look across the tent at Jimmy, sound asleep with a peaceful look on his face.

The matchmaking ceremony takes place the next morning in front of the temple. It's the first time I've seen everyone in one place. All these people milling about a two thousand year old temple wearing Holocene II zipsuits makes for a strange sight. It looks like some invasion by an alien race. It's obvious that some of them have just arrived as new recruits—brought up on the subterrenes that cruise the highway through the jungle, ferrying supplies and people between the opening and the camp—because they're still looking around with wide-eyed wonder at the blue sky and green jungle that surrounds them.

Jimmy stands next to me with a scarf around his neck and his hair combed over his forehead. He's wearing a zipsuit too. He looks about as nervous as I feel.

"I dun' really understand what we're doin'," he says.

"I'm not entirely sure either," I reply, "but I think they want us to find partners so we can start a new society up here."

"I dun' remember anyone askin' if that's what I wanted."

"Well, let's just see what happens."

When Bill and Jillian arrive, they have those of us who are single and participating form into lines in front of the temple—boys on one side, facing the girls; and girls on the other side, facing the boys. There are about thirty of each of us. Genetic tests have been run from the databases in Holocene II, and all the boys get either a blue or a red ribbon pinned on their chest. I'm red. Jimmy gets one of each, since he's compatible with anyone. The girls are each given three ribbons, either red or blue, depending on the results of their genetic tests.

Jillian paces between the lines and explains all of this to us as we look past her, girls looking up and down the line of boys, boys looking up and down the line of girls. The older couples watch from the temple steps with great interest, as if some kind of sporting event were about to take place.

"Now," Jillian says. "Here's how this works. The girls get to choose first. As I call your name, ladies, step forward and give a ribbon to your first choice partner. Red for red, blue for blue. Boys, if she gives you a ribbon and you accept her as your mate, take her hand and leave the line. If not, keep the ribbon, and the girl will move on to her second choice, and so on. When a girl is out of ribbons, and if no boy has accepted, she returns to her line alone. The boys who end up without mates will pick from them later, going in order of who has the most ribbons. We'll do this until everyone is paired. Here we go"— she pauses to look at her clipboard—"the first to choose, based on her tests scores, of course, is Laylani."

Laylani steps forward with her three red ribbons, walks straight to me, and hands me one. I look at the ribbon in my hand and then at her. I shake my head. She frowns and moves down the line to another young man. He smiles, takes her hand, and they leave the line together. Then Jillian calls another girl, this one with a blue ribbon, and she brings it to a young man she had been making mutual eyes with all morning. He immediately accepts, and they too leave hand in hand. This goes on for some time. Every girl called out with red ribbons offers her first one to me. It quickly becomes obvious that they all think of me as some kind of hero, just like Jillian had said. But I turn each of them down with a silent shake of my head.

Even though Jimmy can be asked by any girl, red or blue, not one offers him a ribbon. Instead they stop to look him over and then turn away at the sight of his burns and move on down the line. By the time we're half finished, Jimmy's head is bowed, and he's looking at the ground.

Jillian keeps calling names, I keep turning down mates, and then only two red girls remain across from Jimmy and me. I look at my fistful of red ribbons. Then I look at Jimmy and he has none. The sad look of rejection on his face breaks my heart.

"Okay, Aubrey," Jillian says, an edge of frustration in her voice. "We need you to be a team player here. It's your turn to pick from the two remaining girls." Both girls perk up when she says this, then frown when she adds, "Jimmy will pair with the other by default. So, Aubrey, who do you choose?"

I look at the two remaining girls, both fine-looking with ordinary features and hopeful, expectant expressions etched on their young faces. The sun has risen above the temple, and they both squint into it, their virgin Holocene II skin shining pale in its golden glow. Jillian stands tapping her foot impatiently and looking down at her clipboard as if she were reading something extremely important there. She strips her glasses off and looks up when she hears the crowd murmuring loudly. Her mouth is half opened to say something to me, but when she sees that my ribbons lay on the ground and that I'm holding Jimmy's hand, she closes it so suddenly, I hear her teeth clack together. Then she looks around, as if someone might appear who can tell her what to do. Bill steps forward and claps his hands together.

"Well, folks," he announces, "looks like this matchmaking ceremony is over. That means back to work for everyone."

Jimmy and I stand hand in hand as the crowd grumbles and slowly descends from the temple steps. As soon as Bill has us alone in our tent, he motions for us to sit on the bed. Then he ties the door shut, pulls a chair over, and sits in front of us. He runs his hands through his hair and sighs.

"Is there something I need to know?" he asks.

Jimmy just looks at me, so I speak up first.

"As far as I'm concerned, you don't have a right to know anything unless we want to tell you. The last time I checked, we don't work for you or for Jillian. And if my mother were here, I have a feeling you'd both be working for us."

"Listen," he says, holding his hands up as if surrendering, "you don't have to tell me that Jillian can be a bit overbearing. But she has good intentions."

"Yeah, so did Radcliffe."

"Hey," he says, "that's not fair."

"Maybe not. But I don't trust her, Bill."

"Do you trust me?" he asks.

"Yes, I trust you."

"How about you, Jimmy?" he asks. "Do you trust me?"

"You ain't never given me no reason not to," Jimmy says.

"Good. Then the two of you need to tell me right now what's going on."

"What's going on with what?"

"You know," he says.

"No, I really don't," I say, getting frustrated.

"With the serum. You both have it inside you, don't you?"

Jimmy and I look at one another. Then I turn back to Bill and nod. He gets up from his chair and paces the room.

"This will never do," he mumbles. "Never, never, never. She'll have them down in Holocene II being tested straight away." Then he stops and turns to us. "Is it just you two?"

"Yes," I say. "Hannah was the only other, and she's dead."

He sits back down in his chair and looks at both of us with a worried expression.

"Here's the thing, fellas," he finally says. "The rumors are already circulating about the serum. If you two stick around, you won't age, and they'll think for sure we still have it. That means rebellion and chaos just when we're trying to settle things down. Even if they do believe that the last of it was destroyed along with the Foundation, they'll have you taken below for testing in the labs."

"You mean Jillian will have us taken for testing," I say.

He nods. "She has good intentions, I told you, but she also has ambitions."

"So what do we do?" Jimmy asks.

"I don't know," Bill says, "I don't know."

Jimmy looks away; Bill looks down at his feet. I look over and see my mother's reading slate beside the bed. I have an idea. I reach and pick it up.

"I'll tell you what we'll do, Bill. We'll make you a deal."

"I'm up for anything. You know I'm on your side here."

"Good," I say, "because it sounds to me like you could use a little leverage with Jillian. And I've got just the thing that will do it right here in this slate."

"What is it?" he asks.

"Everyone called my mother Chief, right? Even Jillian?"

Bill nods. "She was like a mother to us."

"Well, she wrote a plan for a new society on the surface. It's called *State of Nature*, and it's in here."

"What does it say?" he asks, reaching for it.

I pull it away. "I don't know. I haven't read it."

"Why not?" he asks.

"It doesn't matter why I haven't."

"Okay, but what's the deal then?"

"I want the valley."

"What valley?"

"The one you found me in," I say. "I want the valley and thirty kilometers in every direction set aside for Jimmy and me to live in forever."

"That shouldn't be hard," he says. "It's a big continent, and there aren't very many of us out here. Plus, Jillian's worried about you having too much power because of your fame, so

I'm sure she'd be okay with you leaving."

"That all good," I say, "but you have to do something more permanent."

"Permanent how?" he asks.

"Your promise isn't good enough."

"Why not? You said you trusted me."

"And I do. But you have to understand that . . . that you'll die, and Jillian will die, and we'll still be alive for nine hundred, maybe a thousand years. That's a lot of generations gone by. So you need to set us up some kind of constitution or something. Create us a nature preserve in the valley, a reservation that no one can enter. No drones and no people allowed. Ever."

"I think I can manage that," he says. "Although I'm not quite sure how to explain it to Jillian without her knowing."

"Just tell her that we want to live there and die there and know that our bodies will never be disturbed. She's got the rest of the world; she shouldn't care."

"When would you want to leave?" he asks.

I turn to Jimmy and notice that he's smiling, a real genuine smile, maybe for the first time since he was burned.

"Jimmy, is this all okay with you?" I ask.

He nods that it is and says, "This is all I ever wanted."

"Then when should we leave?"

"I dunno," he says. "Why can't we leave right now?"

I turn back to Bill. "We'll leave as soon as you can round us up supplies. We'll need rations and tools to get us started."

"What kind of tools?" he asks.

"Hatchets and saws. Maybe some hammers and a shovel or two. Anything metal that we can't make on our own."

"That's no problem," he says. "Jillian's already got that stuff cranking out of the sintering plants on Level 4 for use up here. Most of it she designed herself."

"Great," I say, holding out my hand. "We have a deal."

"When do I get the slate?" he asks, hesitating.

"As soon as you drop us off in the valley."

He shakes my hand. Then he shakes Jimmy's too.

"I'll miss you both," he says. "But I think this is the right thing for you. I really do."

When he stands to leave, I say, "There's one other thing."

He stops at the tent flap and looks back.

"Sure," he says, "you name it."

"I want a supply of tobacco from Level 5."

CHAPTER 35
A River of Love

It takes Bill longer than he thought it would.

But by the morning of the fifth day after making our agreement, we're standing on the runway getting ready to board the drone that will take us away forever.

After inventorying the supplies, Bill and Jimmy climb into the drone. I hesitate and turn to look back. Everyone in the camp has gathered around the runway to see us off. Even Jillian is there, looking somewhat sad about us leaving. Despite the sentimental sendoff, it seems strange to me that these are my people, because I hardly recognize a face in the crowd at all. Maybe a few, but it feels as if I knew them in some other life.

Before I can even climb aboard the drone, someone begins clapping. Then another joins them, and soon the entire group is clapping, even Jillian. I feel my face blush. Then I tell myself that this honor is not for me, that this is for the real heroes— this is for my mother, and for my father, and for Jimmy. I stand up straight and accept the praise on their behalf. Then I take a final bow, board the drone, and buckle into my seat.

Before I can even collect my thoughts, the runway is run out beneath us, and the drone has lifted off. Bill circles once, and we wave goodbye to the crowd below and watch them and the temple pyramid shrink away into the jungle. It's a fitting place to make a new beginning, I think, and I sure do wish them all the best with it too.

I turn to look at Jimmy. He smiles at me with a silent thank you in his eyes. I pat his knee and turn my attention to the horizon ahead and our new life together, far away from all this heartache and death we've been through.

When we reach the Pacific, Bill follows the coastline north; retracing the path that he and I took after he rescued me in the valley. I look out on all that blue water stretching west to the horizon. I think about our adventures in the submarine with the professor. It's hard to believe how little I knew then, that I had no idea yet that my mother was alive, or that my genetic father was Dr. Radcliffe. And I had no clue how evil and deceptive Hannah and the professor would turn out to be. Even so, I can almost forgive them now that they're gone.

Spring is quickly giving way to summer. I've never seen the world look as beautiful as it does now—puffs of billowy clouds, snowy mountains, green forests, and silver rivers pouring down. Bill takes us low, and we see stretches of golden beach littered with napping sea lions; then the beaches give way to wild cliffs with waves crashing against them. When towering redwoods appear ahead, I know we're nearing the cove. I look over at Jimmy, but as we pass it by, he just leans forward and places his open hand against the viewing bubble glass. I can't tell if he's saying hello or goodbye.

An hour later we approach the valley. I don't know what's more beautiful to look at, the green valley cupped between the surrounding peaks with its winding river, bright wildflowers, and lush trees, or Jimmy's growing smile as he practically falls out of his seat, leaning forward to drink in the view.

"It's perfect," he says.

"As good as you dreamed it?" I ask.

"Even better than that."

"Bill, would you mind taking us around once so we can get the lay of the land before touching down?"

Bill nods and flies the drone over the valley. It must be a full five kilometers wide and another twenty long with high, snowcapped mountains rising up on the southeast and feeding the river that runs through it. Lower peaks of alpine forests border the other edges. I can't imagine a better place to hide away from the rest of the world and live in peace.

"You sure about this?" Bill asks, looking at the wilderness.

"I've never been so sure about anything," I reply. "You can go ahead and set us down."

After circling back, Bill glides in low and follows the river northwest until we come to the stretch of relatively level bank where he landed before. He touches down. We buck and bounce, slow, and then skid to a halt. The door is hardly open and I'm out. As soon as my foot touches the soil, I know I'll never ride in another drone again. And that's fine with me.

Jimmy steps out and looks around. I can see him already calculating where he'll hunt and fish and build our shelter.

Bill joins us. He looks around and sighs. Then he nods, seeming to accept that this is where we'll be saying goodbye.

"Well," he says, "I guess we should unload the supplies. Where do you want them?"

"Jimmy, where should we make our camp?" I ask.

He points to the hill with the oak tree. "That's where we build." Then he quickly adds, "I mean, only if you agree."

"I was hoping you'd pick that spot," I say.

After unloading and double checking everything, we stand at the drone, not quite knowing how to say goodbye. I hand my mother's reading slate to Bill. He takes it and nods.

"You sure you don't want to know what she wrote?"

"I'm sure," I say. "Just promise me you'll do your best to do the right thing by her. And by me."

He swallows and nods that he will.

"What about the rest of the books?" he asks. "I mean, what will you read?"

I shrug. "I've read most everything in there twice anyway. I think I'll be happy to just read the river and the leaves."

"You sure you won't get bored?"

"Bored? I don't know. If I do, maybe I'll write something of my own. I've always liked poetry."

He turns to set the reading slate inside the drone. Then he reaches under his seat and hands me my father's tobacco tin.

"That's as much as I could get," he says, "but it's full."

"Thanks, Bill. I appreciate it. I want you to know that I'll always remember the way you looked after me growing up. My mother told me you used to give her progress reports on me."

Bill smiles and looks for a moment like he might cry.

"You were a good kid, Aubrey. And I'm just glad that your mother lived long enough to see you grow into a really great man." Then he looks down and says, "I'll miss you."

I hand the tobacco tin to Jimmy, step up, and hug Bill goodbye. When he pulls away to look at me, his eyes are wet.

"Sure you don't want me to check on you?" he asks.

"No,"—I shake my head—"we're going to be just fine."

"I believe you will," he says, nodding. "I believe you will."

I take my tobacco tin back from Jimmy and step aside so he can say his goodbye. He steps up and hugs Bill too.

"You look after this guy," Bill tells him, nodding to me.

"And make sure he looks after you."

Jimmy smiles. "That's the way it's always been with us," he says. "Ain't no reason to change it up now."

Bill bites his lower lip and bows his head. It appears for a moment like he might want to say something else, but then he turns and climbs into the drone, closes the door, and prepares the controls for takeoff. We step back to watch him leave. He looks out at us and salutes, but before I can even salute him back, he throttles forward and the drone races away in a flash. It lifts off just before the bend in the river and climbs into the late afternoon sky. I look up and watch him go, anticipating that he might circle around for one final farewell, but he flies straight up out of the valley and shrinks into all that blue sky until the drone is just a speck on the horizon. Then even that too is gone from our view.

We stand for a long time after, just looking up at nothing and thinking our own thoughts. Then Jimmy unzips his zipsuit, strips out of it, runs, and dives into the river. I laugh to myself and shake my head. You can take the boy out of the wilderness, I guess, but you can't take the wilderness out of the boy. I carry my father's tobacco tin to our oak tree on the hill.

In the evening we sit around our fire and watch the sparks rise into the darkening sky and eat fresh roasted trout with our fingers. We've got plenty enough meal bars to last for a long time, but I don't think either of us has any taste left for them. When our fish are gone and our fingers licked clean, we lie back and look up as the stars come out one by one over the valley.

"You know what I's thinkin' today," Jimmy says.

"No, what were you thinking?" I ask.

"I was thinkin' that it's almost my birthday."

"Really? What day is it?"

"Hell, I dunno what day it is now," he says. "But it's the next full moon."

I wonder how long it will be before I no longer have any idea what day or month or year it is. I won't miss knowing.

"Well, what do you want for your birthday?" I ask.

"I already got ever-thin' I could ever want for."

"You must want something."

"Well . . . there is jus' maybe one thing," he says.

"You name it, and if it's within my power to give it to you, you know it's yours."

There's a long silence between us. The fire crackles, the river hisses as it slides by out there in the dark.

"You can say no if you dun' wanna do it," he finally says, "but I was thinkin' maybe you could teach me to read."

"Shit, Jimmy, I just gave away my reading slate to Bill."

"I know it," he says, "but I didn't wanna read none of that stuff anyhow."

"Then what did you want to read?"

"I wanna read those poems you said you might write."

I can't help but smile so wide my cheeks hurt.

"Okay, Jimmy. I'm going to write you a poem for your birthday, and then I'm going to teach you how to read it."

"Now I really got ever-thin' there is to want," he says.

By the time the leaves turn, we have our little cabin on the hill roughed out, roofed in, and ready for the fall. We'll need stronger shutters, and maybe more firewood, but our food shed that Jimmy built up between a pair of high branches in the oak tree is already filled with enough smoked fish and cured meat to see us through whatever winter the valley throws at us.

Late one afternoon sometime in October, I step out onto our porch and light my father's pipe. I sit with it in the chair I carved myself, lean back, and enjoy the sweet taste of the tobacco and the good feeling that comes from another day's hard work. A gentle breeze sweeps up the valley, and the first leaves fall from our oak tree. I watch them glide down and land in the river, twist and turn, and ride the rapids like golden fish tumbling toward the sea. My pipe smoke rises into the cool air. Almost everything in the world is as it should be.

After a while, the last of the sun dips out of sight and everything loses its shadow. The pines on the bluff across the valley stand stark and clear against the pink autumn sky. I watch as Jimmy appears from a distant grove of trees and walks across the wheat toward our cabin. It's a long field, and he's a long time coming. I can see his smile even before I see his eyes.

He stops at the field's edge and stakes something into the ground. Then he comes on up, and I see his catch off rabbits.

"There's some stew on the coals still."

"Thanks," he says. "I'll put these in the smoker and join you in a minute."

When he comes out again, it's nearly dark. He sits in his chair where he keeps it set up next to mine so that his good side faces me. He props the wooden bowl in his lap and goes straight to eating his stew. I puff my pipe and watch him.

"Trout were jumping today."

"You catch any?" he asks, between bites.

"No, I didn't even throw a line."

He just nods and keeps eating.

As dusk drops like a curtain on the valley, I see a familiar shadow slink across the edge of the field. It stops at Jimmy's stake, grabs the dead rabbit he left there, and turns to run away. But the string catches, and the rabbit jerks from the fox's mouth. It turns back and sets to eating it where it lays, with one eye on the hill, watching us.

"You really think you're going to tame that fox?" I ask.

"I can tame anythin' that's got a stomach," he says. "It jus' takes time, is all."

"You mean like I've been taming you with my stew?"

"Exactly like that," he says, laughing. Then he shows me his empty bowl. "'Cept you're doin' a better job of it so far."

"Speaking of better jobs," I say, "I wrote another poem."

"You did? Where is it?"

"Beside your chair there."

"Well, hold on. Let me go in and get the lamp."

He goes inside with his empty bowl and comes out again with the lamp. He sits and takes up the piece of bark that has the poem scrawled on it, angles it toward the light, and reads.

Leaves will fall, cold will creep in
A circle of life that ends where it begins
It may take a thousand years and a thousand poems penned
But my hair will someday gray and my back will bend—
Then my shadow will join my body in the earth once again.

I know not the way, or even the when
Or who chooses that day we're called away to ascend
But you bathed me in your bravery and forgave me my sins
You made a home in your heart for mine to live in—
And in return, my friend, this poem is my oath that a river of love
will run through it until the very end.

After he finishes, I see him read it again to himself. Then he sets the bark in his lap, leans his head back, and closes his eyes. Several minutes pass. I sit with my pipe half-raised to my mouth, waiting to hear what he thinks.

When he finally opens his eyes, he says,

"I love it."

"You do?"

"Yes," he replies. "I love it, and I love you."

I lean back, puff my father's pipe, and smile like I never knew I could. Now everything in the world is as it should be.

Epilogue

He came up out of the fog sometime in September of the year the State of Nature celebrated its diamond jubilee.

He was leading a horse. The horse's hooves clacked on the rocky ground, and the wagon that the horse pulled squeaked on its axels. An old fox trotted along behind the wagon. The entire sad and solemn procession heaved, moaned, and tottered up the hill, appearing piece by piece from the fog as the two park rangers sat their hoverbikes watching.

"Should we call in a drone?" the ranger asked his partner.

"Let's maybe see what they're about first," she replied.

When the wagon came up level to them, they eased their bikes forward and blocked the path.

"Where are you heading to, kid?"

The kid looked at the rangers, their bikes, and the crests on their bikes.

"Who are you?" he asked.

"We're park rangers," the male one replied. "And I asked you where you're headed to, kid?"

The kid looked away and spit on the ground.

"I'm not a kid, and I'm heading wherever I please."

The rangers looked at one another, dismounted their bikes, and approached him from either side with their hands on their weapons. The old fox came to the kid's feet and sat there, looking from one ranger to the other, unsure what to do.

The kid reached down to pet him.

"Easy there, old boy."

"What's in the wagon?" the ranger asked.

"I don't understand what's going on here," the kid said. "I've lived around these parts a long time. I'm just minding my own business and trying to get somewhere."

"I asked you what's in the wagon."

When the kid didn't answer him, the ranger removed his weapon from its holster, stepped past the kid and the horse to the wagon, pulled the blankets back, and looked down at the old man lying there on his furs. Then he came back around to join them again.

"Is that your grandfather back there, kid?

"No, he's not my grandfather."

The female ranger looked at him. She saw the goodness in his grieving eyes. She said, "You do know where you are, don't you, young man? This is park property. Why don't you let us escort you to one of the reservations?"

"No, thanks," the kid said. "I'm on my way somewhere."

"Did you cross that valley back there?" she asked, nodding the way they'd come up. "Because that's a preserve, and you're not supposed to be there either. I'm thinking maybe you don't understand the trouble you're in."

The kid stood looking at her, but he didn't say anything. Eventually, she shook her head and walked back to see the old man for herself. No sooner had she peeked into the wagon that she came back looking as if she'd seen a ghost.

"Did you see his face?" she asked her partner. "The burns? That's Jimmy back there."

"Jimmy who?" he asked.

"Didn't you learn anything in school? Jimmy, as in Aubrey and Jimmy from the Revolution." Then she turned her attention back to the kid. "You need to tell us where you're bringing him, young man. And you better tell the truth or we'll take you in."

The kid sighed. "I'm honoring his last wishes."

"And who were you to him?" she asked.

The kid glanced back.

"He was everything to me. I think he'd have said the same about me if you'd have asked him."

"And how'd you come to be in the valley, then?"

"I'm sorry, but I don't see how any of this is your business, ma'am. Now if you don't mind, I've got to get on."

The kid took up the horse's lead and started forward with it to go around the bikes. He'd only taken a few steps when the male ranger got ahead of him and trained his weapon on the kid's chest. The kid stopped, but the fox kept going and sank its teeth into the ranger's calf. The ranger screamed and kicked it away from him, swung his weapon, and shot it dead.

The ranger stood with his weapon still pointed at the dead fox and looked down at the blood soaking through his zipsuit where he'd been bitten. Then he looked at his partner and said, "That's an authorized use of force. You saw it."

The kid looked at the fox and the smoking hole in its side. He walked over, knelt, and petted its face. Then he lifted it up and kissed it. He carried it to the wagon and laid it in next to the old man. He lifted the old man's stiff arm around it, and then he covered them both with the blanket again.

The female ranger stepped up beside him.

"You're Aubrey VanHouten, aren't you?"

"That's impossible," her partner said.

She ignored him, saying to the kid, "I knew it was true."

"Knew what was true?" her partner called out.

"You had the serum, didn't you?" she asked, still ignoring her partner and addressing the kid. "The lessons said that you didn't, but my father said that you did."

"If I tell you, will you let us go on?"

"We're not authorized—"

She silenced her partner by holding up her hand. She nodded to say that she would let them pass.

"This is Jimmy in the wagon. And that fox your partner just killed was his favorite and the last of its line."

"And you're Aubrey?" she asked.

"And I'm Aubrey," he said.

She immediately looked embarrassed. She holstered her weapon and reached out her hand, saying, "I'm really sorry, sir. I hope you'll forgive us."

Aubrey nodded but ignored her offered hand. He left her standing there, walked up, and led the horse and the wagon around their hovering bikes without another word to them.

"Hey, sir," she called after him. "One last question. If you had the serum, how come Jimmy didn't?"

He didn't answer, but had she been able to see the pained look on his face, she might have regretted having even asked.

They arrived at the cove two days later.

The sun was shining through high clouds. He stood on the bluff and looked down at the beach, remembering. He saw them swimming together there as kids, and it ripped at his heart that he couldn't go back and do it all over again. Time seemed an evil and unrelenting mechanism to him.

He unhitched the horse from the wagon, smacked its hindquarter, and shooed it away. It ran a few meters, then turned to come back. He chased after it with his hand raised.

"Get out of here!" he shouted. "You're free now."

The horsed shied, neighed, and stepped back. Then it turned away and began to graze.

The rigor had passed. When he picked Jimmy up from the wagon, he draped him limply over his shoulder and carried him down off the bluff and into the cove. Jimmy's frame had been wasted by age and by disease, and he hardly weighed anything at all. Aubrey brought him to their cave and sat him against the wall. Then he returned to the wagon for the fox, brought it down, and laid it out across Jimmy's lap.

It took him most of the afternoon to break the wagon apart and haul its wood down into the cove. Then he walked the beach, collected driftwood, and added it to the pile. He slept that night with Jimmy in his arms. The fact that Jimmy had now been dead several days did not bother him at all. The fact that he himself was still living did.

When the sun rose, he rose. He was not hungry, so he set right to work on constructing the raft. He tied together the wagon timbers, lashed the wagon basket onto them, and then piled it high with driftwood. After ensuring it would float, he carried Jimmy from the cave and laid him out on the raft. Then he laid the fox in his arm and tucked the fox's head in the nook of his neck. He bent and kissed them both.

He paused before lighting the pyre with the strike-a-light in his hands, remembering that birthday party long ago and half way around the globe. He had never wanted to cry so much as he did now, but he was numb with grief, and no tears would come. So he struck a spark. After starting several small fires around the base of the pyre, he fanned them with his hands to coax them up. Then he pushed the raft out into the cove and sat down on the sand to watch it burn.

"Say hello to your mom for me," he said.

The raft rolled gently on the waves. The fire rose up and engulfed his dead friend. It burned and burned and burned. Eventually the pyre caved in on itself and sank, hissing and smoking, beneath the waves. Three hours later the tide washed Jimmy's charred corpse up onto the beach at his feet. He sat looking at it with disbelief—the blackened flesh, the scorched grin. He went to his friend on his hands and knees. He sat in the shallow water and took him in his arms. He cried and kissed his head, cried and cried some more.

"I love you," he said. "I love you so much, and I miss you. I know you told me to forgive her, and I know I said I would, but I hate her, Jimmy—I hate her, I hate her, I hate her. I'm not as good as you. I never could be. Oh, God, I miss you. Please, let me break my promise and come with you. Please."

The tide was coming in as he spoke. Soon the waves were lifting them. Water was entering his mouth. He was coughing and talking incoherently and crying. He pulled his friend to his chest, laid back, and kicked off past the waves and away from the shore. As they floated together out of the cove and into deep water, the sun was setting on them. He looked up, and he could see Jimmy there in the molten sky, lean and bronzed and forever young, a wide smile stretched across his proud and perfect face. He hugged his friend close and closed his eyes. As his head dropped into the silence beneath the waves, he could hear the children laughing in the camp and Jimmy's mother calling them in to supper just one last time.

Some three hundred years later, their legend was still alive. Families on vacation could rent bungalows on the edge of the valley and look down from their glass decks at the fields and the river and what was left of the rotting cabin on the hill. Some said that if the wind was gentle and just right, you could hear poems being read. Yet others said that on still winter nights, you could sometimes glimpse a lone campfire burning across the way at the valley's edge, high in the cold and lonely mountains where no living soul, night or day, dared tread.

At least that's what they said.

THE END

About the Author

Ryan Winfield is the *New York Times* best-selling author of *Jane's Melody*, *South of Bixby Bridge*, and *The Park Service* trilogy.

For more information go to:
www.RyanWinfield.com

CPSIA information can be obtained at www.ICGtesting.com
Printed in the USA
LVOW06s1723120314

377128LV00013B/492/P